Praise for *Displ...*

"The immigrants hide truths from e... ...
of lying one of Schwarz's best subje... ...
functions as a means of mercy as well as harm, a symbol of what
both binds and threatens the Jewish community, whose imperfec-
tions Schwarz astutely illuminates. . . . Schwarz's smooth prose
expertly, often amusingly, adopts her characters' tics of thought
and speech. . . . *Displaced Persons*—like the émigrés themselves—
gains strength in its later moments, concluding on a masterfully
unresolved chord."   —*San Francisco Chronicle*

"Schwarz . . . captures perfectly, and with elegance, the highs and
lows, the grief and anger, and the paranoia of these refugees. In a
word, this is a 'humane' novel."   —*USA Today*

"A deft rendering of the emotional architecture of an ad hoc family
of Holocaust survivors."   —*Vogue*

"Ghita Schwarz poignantly reminds us that history chases us even
if we run from it, and that memory ensnares us wherever we turn.
Displaced Persons is a big, ambitious novel, yet what's most strik-
ing is its humanity. Schwarz's characters span continents and
generations, but she draws them all with a startling deftness of
touch. *Displaced Persons* is a terrific novel."
—Joshua Henkin, author of the *New York Times* Notable Book *Matrimony*

"Ghita Schwarz makes her mark with this remarkable debut. *Displaced Persons* is a brave, brilliant, and haunting work of art."
—Colson Whitehead, author of *John Henry Days* and *Sag Harbor*

"This is an amazing novel. The writing is piercing and clear, and the
humanity of the author and her characters will inhabit my thoughts
for years to come."
—Anne Roiphe, author of the National Book Award–winner *Fruitful*

"In her warm portrayal of the postwar highs and lows experienced by Pavel and his family, Schwarz aptly evokes the emotions of those who survived."   —*Publishers Weekly*

"Poignant and sharp, this engrossing first novel takes a . . . look at a time and a people defined by deep inner strength. Recommended for a wide range of readers, and a perfect book club choice."
   —*Library Journal* (starred review)

"Deceptively simple in style, Schwarz's narrative discloses depths of tragedy, of suffering, and occasionally of hope. . . . Stark, un-adorned fiction, well worth reading."   —*Kirkus Reviews*

"In this powerful debut novel, author Ghita Schwarz, a child of Holocaust survivors, hypnotically spins the tale of a Polish Jew named Pavel, who bravely rebuilds his shattered life in the after-math of World War II. . . . Schwarz brilliantly gives us the long view of what postwar survival really meant."   —Associated Press

"An exquisite rendering of the internal lives of survivors."
   —*Jewish Daily Forward*

"A haunting and memorable debut. . . . Fascinating."
   —*St. Louis Jewish News*

"An epic tale."   —*Brooklyn Paper*

DISPLACED
PERSONS

DISPLACED PERSONS

Ghita Schwarz

HARPER ● PERENNIAL

NEW YORK • LONDON • TORONTO • SYDNEY • NEW DELHI • AUCKLAND

HARPER ● PERENNIAL

A portion of this novel, "Oral Histories," appeared in a slightly different form in the Spring 2006 issue of *Ploughshares*.

A hardcover edition of this book was published in 2010 by William Morrow, an imprint of HarperCollins Publishers.

FIRST HARPER PERENNIAL EDITION PUBLISHED 2011.

Designed by Jamie Lynn Kerner

The Library of Congress has catalogued the hardcover edition as follows:
  Schwarz, Ghita.
     Displaced persons : a novel / Ghita Schwarz. — 1st ed.
        p. cm.
     ISBN 978-0-06-188190-9
     1. Holocaust survivors—Fiction. 2. Psychological fiction. I. Title.
  PS3619.C4879D57 2010
  813'.6—dc22

                                                                    2010020365

ISBN 978-0-06-188177-0 (pbk.)

11 12 13 14 15 OV/RRD 10 9 8 7 6 5 4 3 2 1

For my mother and father

I hear that the axe has flowered,
I hear that the place can't be named,
I hear that the bread which looks at him
heals the hanged man,
the bread baked for him by his wife,
I hear that they call life
our only refuge.

—PAUL CELAN

CONTENTS

STONES

Identity Papers

1945–1950

The Widow's House

May 1945

A JEEP OF BRITISH SOLDIERS dropped him and Fishl at the edge of a large town, with a map, tins of food, half a loaf of bread, and a number of little amenities. Cigarettes. Almost better, a toothbrush for each of them. Identity papers, protected by a brown envelope. Pens. He could feel the shape of the good one in his breast pocket. He felt wary and afraid but almost relieved to be away from the soldiers, at least until they arrived at the refugee assembly center. It would have been better to be among the Americans, who had liberated him. He was not sure about the British, who shouted at him as if he were deaf, or a donkey. He could not yet speak the language, but he was not a donkey. He was not a donkey, although at times he still felt himself to be a zebra, what they called the men who had nothing but their striped prisoners' uniforms. He wore clean clothes on his narrow shoulders, having organized for himself a used suit from an acquaintance who worked in the storehouse of clothing in the abandoned camp. He no longer looked like an animal. He no longer looked, but he felt: he was a zebra.

They shuffled through the gravel near a large villa, empty and quiet, perhaps belonging to a former *Kommandant*. Late spring rains had settled the dust from the rubble, making the roads easier to walk past the long gardens and toward the forest. It seemed to him they were walking quickly, but the sound of his footsteps came at a labored pace. His shoes were hard, their bottoms thick. He had hammered scraps of stolen rubber onto the wooden soles, for himself and for Fishl too. Still he could feel the sharp outlines of stone under his feet.

But the shoes were to him better than bread. At the thought of bread he felt his right knee tremble a little, then steady itself. These shoes could bring him to bread, could bring him to any provisions he could organize, could bring him to a resting place in the assembly center for the stateless, a day's walk away. To clear his mind from bread he pressed his hand into his breast pocket and pulled out a cigarette. He let it hang from his mouth. He could wait before using one of his matches. Saliva welled around the corners of the cigarette, his stomach began to burn again with the sharp tang of hunger, but still it felt good to have something in his mouth, the almost-taste of the tobacco making him walk faster. In a moment Fishl too would take out a cigarette, and they would share a match.

They walked along the town outskirts, along the border between trees and road, ready to flee into the woods if anyone came after them. Newly liberated, this town, the British expanding their authority, the townspeople quiet in their houses, afraid. He liked the idea of Germans waiting inside, not knowing who would knock at the door, drag the man of the house, or the mother or the child, into army headquarters for questioning or punishment. He liked the idea. Still the quietness bothered him. He and Fishl saw a young boy with a large dog playing in the road ahead of them. Without speaking to each other, they began moving deeper into the woods, walking slowly among the trees, seeing the road but not visible from it.

Under a wide plum tree they stopped and leaned against the bark. Now came time to strike the match, and the two of them inhaled the tobacco almost in unison. He looked at his fingers, holding the cigarette away from his mouth. His hands, always slender, looked not brittle but merely thin. Yes, he was stronger now. His hair grew back thick and dark, still short but beginning to curl. He felt the roughness around his chin and cheeks, and felt a shiver of relief: the British had let him use their basin for a shave only yesterday, and already he needed another. It was a healthy man who needed a shave every day.

He looked at Fishl pushing the last bit of the cigarette between his teeth. Perhaps another hour, and they would start to eat a portion of the provisions they had collected from the British. It was important to save. A man knew how to save, how to organize, how to maneuver. He knew Fishl thought the same way. Before the war, he and Fishl had lived in neighboring cities, and their girlfriends had been close; they knew each other only slightly then, trading pleasantries in the same dialect of Yiddish. But now it was as if they had had the same parents, the same home. They were like brothers, a new kind of brother.

JUST THREE WEEKS BEFORE the liberation, convinced they were all to be shot, the two of them had cut through the electrical wire near their work barracks during a blackout and escaped to hide in a deserted farmhouse, one sleeping while the other kept watch. In the beginning, still weak, they had hidden in the barn of a farmhouse until the house was requisitioned by the soldiers, Americans with their shocked faces, equipped with a soldier or two who could translate from German. It was rumored that soon the Russians would come, hunting for women. He and Fishl knew to leave. They had refused to return to the camp, converted from a prison into a refuge. Instead the two of them had moved to the floor of an empty schoolhouse, sleeping, with dozens of others, men and women together, in disinfected military blankets. The soldiers fed them. Not too much, but more than the liberated prisoners received in the camp. People there still died every day, hungry, sick, encircled by wire and guarded by the conquering armies afraid to let the prisoners out into the world, afraid the hunger and sickness would spread and infect. But from the moment the liberators arrived he made sure they understood what he was made of. He would work and learn. He made chess pieces from discarded bits of metal found in the former camp factory, and sold them in sets to the young soldiers, who drew out the grids of a chess game on a bread board or lumber scrap taken from a German family. Yes, a human could make something out of anything, could make the ugliest of objects into a source of pleasure. He still ate the bread they gave him too quickly, he still made a rattle when he scraped the bottom of his bowl with his army-issued spoon, he still craved what the soldiers themselves ate, their meat and their eggs and their milk, but he knew he was coming alive.

WALKING AMONG THE DARK trees, they heard a steady rhythm behind them, footsteps, the slow turn of wheels. They turned. Two men in wool coats, seeming even from a distance to sweat, each dragging behind him a loaded wagon. The wheels of the wagons caught on the tree roots, and the men pulled with their necks bent forward, their shoulders straining ahead of their legs, bodies at a diagonal. They looked like children, small boys playing at a race. But they were men. Not strong, but men. Middle-aged, perhaps office workers, functionaries, Germans.

The Germans stopped moving. He could feel Fishl's breath turn warmer next to him. An idea with no words ran through his head and pushed his legs forward. He saw Fishl move his hand into his pocket, the pocket with the knife. They went slowly toward the Germans, and he could feel the same rage pulsing between him and Fishl, and without even opening their mouths to speak they knew they were right: the wagons were filled with valuables, money, bagfuls of reichsmarks, gold and silver finery. The men trembled and begged as they gave up their watches, their rings, and their stolen jewels, they looked at the two thin Jews as if it were they, he and Fishl, who were killers. Even as he concentrated his mind on keeping the fury inside his body, he could understand how funny it was, these men in their uniforms, fat men, afraid of former prisoners who perhaps could denounce them, prisoners with one knife between them, liberated prisoners still in their cage of hunger.

In one of the men's coats—he and Fishl let them depart with only their jackets—was a velvet pouch. They leaned against a birch and opened the soft bag. Two dozen tiny stones.

Is it something? Fishl said. Can you see?

It is something, he answered. In the first work camp a cutter, an older man whose labor he had done on occasion, had taught him to recognize cracks and facets in a diamond. They had been able to keep some of their possessions then, and the man had taken out his loupe and his dead wife's ring and made him understand how to see. Now in the forest, he and Fishl could only guess. But would men wear wool coats in spring for a velvet pouch of glass?

He took twelve of the diamonds and replaced them in the little bag. Fishl wrapped the other twelve in a scrap of paper, wrapped the paper in a handkerchief, pushed the handkerchief into the bottom of his rucksack. They rolled money into their rucksacks, into their new coats, into their shoes. Now it was he and Fishl spilling over with dirty gold, possessions stripped from the living as they were pushed through the gate of the dead. Spilling over with dead men's money, dead women's jewels. He and Fishl might be thin, they might think every hour of the bread they kept in their rucksacks, but already the hunger felt less like a stabbing and more like an itch, for here was the promise of food and more food, for weeks, perhaps even months. They were heavy, solid. Not so heavy that they could not walk—how ignorant these Germans were, how unschooled in the methods of carrying the world on their bodies—but enough so they could not run. The functionaries had run. But he and Fishl would stroll, coats over their arms, walking along the inner perimeter of the woods like two university students observing nature, breathing the green air. They had money. They had money, and they were together. Money could sometimes take the place of force and strength. The fleeing Germans had been right to try and hold on to their bloodstained gold; it could help them. But look how quickly they had given it up!

IN THE REMAINS OF a bombed-out train station at dusk they found an old woman begging for food. Papers and gold safely tucked into their clothes, they showed her their tins of fish and meat from the British and followed her to her house. She showed them to a large empty room upstairs. There was room for both of them in the bed, and they lay down, each covered with a blanket.

All day and all evening the excitement of ownership had made his skin tingle. But now the tingling had become an itch, an uncomfortable dryness on his back and arms. A small chill came over him, and he folded his knees close to his chest.

Fishl, he said.

But Fishl was already breathing in short gasps and snores. Fishl could sleep through fear and thirst. It was a gift, a great piece of luck, a talent, to stop oneself from reflecting and thinking, to conquer the dread with a command to the body: sleep, sleep. His back pressed into the thin mattress, and he breathed in and out. It was good to have a bed again, after the few days in the British military headquarters, where each of them had been given a cot for a few nights, then sent on their way.

He turned on his side, curled his spine. His eyes had adjusted to the darkness, and he looked at the dull wall. A framed drawing of a tulip hung above the chest of drawers, the only decoration. The petals of the tulip were open, one petal almost falling away from the flower. The old woman had a garden. She was afraid to have men in the house. She had walked behind them after opening the door to the house, waited until they climbed the stairs before she herself came up. They had arrived just before nightfall, and at the corner of the road they had seen three houses crushed inward, the skeletons of rooms only half-standing. But this part of the street was untouched. Yet it seemed no one else came to give her food. He shook his head in anger at himself—should he feel sorry for this woman, alone but safe? The walls of her home were still intact and her blankets had not yet been sold for food—this was not a suffering to pity. His grandmother should have had such a decision to make, his father should have suffered so! No, he was not sorry. He thought of the food the old woman would cook them in the morning, perhaps coffee and the fish warmed from the tin. They would trade for her, they would keep their part of the bargain.

Sleep, sleep. In camp he had not been able to fall asleep quickly, the constant fear of the next day troubling him into the night. But now, even with an empty day before him, he felt the same inability to translate his fatigue into rest. Fishl's snores had faded into strong breaths. He tucked his hand underneath his trousers, pushed his fingers into the hidden pocket, felt for the cotton bag he had sewn to the inside. The cotton was still there, its slim contents pressing against his thigh. He rubbed his thumb and forefinger together, the cloth warming his hand. A cotton strip of handkerchief, that was all, but it held his most precious possessions. Photographs, one of his mother and one of his father. He liked to touch the handkerchief that protected them, but he did not want to squint in the dark. And they would be spoiled by their exposure to the damp air. He had taken them out so often that when he remembered his mother and father now, he saw them as they were in the pictures, their bodies creased and wrinkled, their skin the color of brown stone, their mouths steady and grave. No, he would not take them out. One had to be careful, not greedy, even with a photograph. One survived a prison if one kept his secrets hidden, as Joseph had survived his prison in Egypt, emerging to bring his family out of hunger, to see his father, who wept that the favored son was alive. There was no seeing his father now, he knew. But he had had contact with his sister in 1943, and with his second brother a short time earlier. Even a cousin—his aunt's boys, they were strong ones—perhaps they had come out.

He tapped his pocket again. He would give away any of his gold and stones and money, to hold on to those photographs. Still the papers and the money gave him the means to sell and to travel. The photographs might help him sleep, but the money would help him find. He dropped his arms along his sides, feeling the bones of his legs through his trousers.

STRIPES OF LIGHT CAME through the window, and he opened his eyes to a prison cell, cement walls, a damp and tattered blanket around his chest. He did not know how he had come there, but when he turned he could see Fishl lying next to him. He breathed out with relief. Then he tapped at his trouser leg, felt nothing, tapped at his breast pocket, felt no lump from a makeshift pocket, and he sat up in fear. They were gone, how could they be gone? He remembered a word he had learned from the soldiers in English: *jail!* Had he been searched by the British, the Americans, whoever had given this punishment?

But to the new soldiers the contents of his pockets were not valuable. Just to him. Fishl, he cried, Fishl, but Fishl was silent. The air was cool, but when he felt his own neck, it was coated with sweat, and he could sense the stench of bodies—where? outside?—seeping into him, staining his skin. They could be here for weeks, rotting from hunger, shitting and eating out of the same bowl. He heard the step of the guards. Perhaps these wardens would give them other clothes, new prisoners' clothes, take away from them the stolen wool trousers and jackets meant to make them look like ordinary citizens, humans. Yes, perhaps even these weak disguises would be taken, and they would be left with nothing but their battered faces and worn bodies as identification. He turned over on his side and watched a brown beetle make its way through the damp mud in the corner. The beetle moved slowly, with an even, careful rhythm. It buried itself inside a pile of dark sand, emerged again, then disappeared behind a crevice in the stone wall. The beetle would escape. The beetle would be free. He stretched out his hand toward the beetle and saw his arm was still covered by his own stolen jacket. This was something. Still he knew they would tear the clothes from him, tear them into strips for the hanging, and he pushed the blanket away from his body—let them take it! Let them take it already!

But he was awake, it was sunrise, and he was cramped and hot. He looked next to him, Fishl stirring. There was a toilet downstairs, and when he heard the old woman busy in the kitchen he padded down the steps in his socks. Upstairs again, he saw Fishl already dressed.

I can't go anywhere, he whispered.

All right, said Fishl. I will go to Belsen, see what is what.

He slept again, then awakened, then moved downstairs to the toilet and returned to the bed, sweating and cold. But it was all right. He did not feel the sickness of typhus upon him. It was only a fever, a small delirium, a reminder that his body was still unfamiliar with its strength. No more typhus. No more—he would be occupied now only with little illnesses, flashes of heat, the obstacles of an ordinary life. If he could live through typhus in war, he could live through a mild fever in peace. He went to his rucksack and pushed down a corner of hard bread. He would rest one day, then venture out in the morning to look for the living with Fishl.

He lay down, curled himself toward the wall of the room, then tucked his hand underneath his trousers, pushed his fingers into the hidden pocket, felt for the cotton bag he had sewn in the lining. He was alone. The wariness he felt at night had dissipated. He could let himself look.

Still there, still there: the two tiny photographs, creased and dirty, the worn paper giving off a sour smell, images he had miraculously saved, hiding them when he had to in his fist, under his tongue. Fishl and all the others he had known would be jealous, pained with envy, if they knew what he kept with him at all times, in his used, free-man's clothes, clothes with hidden pockets that could protect his images of the human world. The photographs, crumbling and dampened—he must have been a young child when they were taken—were to him like identity cards, identity papers, wordless evidence. He looked at his father's narrow eyes, his mother's solemn face. It was a serious thing to make a portrait. His father looked angry when he tried to be serious, but his mother, more calm perhaps, had a softness. Whatever fierceness she had inside her she disguised from the local photographer. More gentle than his father. He could not remember so much as a shout from her. His father, that was a different story. And yet they had made a family.

Yes, he knew who he was. He had not betrayed himself. He may have been desperate for food, he may have been filthy, but he had tried to wash when he found water. He may have stolen, but almost never from someone weaker than himself. He had not hurt or beat, even in the one barracks where he had been in charge of the others,

even when beaten himself by a fellow Jew for not beating the others—
a fellow Jew!—that man whose memory he would never block out, he
was the enemy, he was worse than the enemy! Suddenly a wave of
anguish rose up in his throat, and he coughed to muffle it, to prevent
it from becoming a cry. He would not, he had not, become what they
wanted them to become, animals desperate to live, no, something ug-
lier than animals, for animals did not kill except for food. He had not
fallen in war, and he would not fall now. He still had his photographs,
and now he had money. It was peace.

He heard a footstep, the old woman padding about. He stood and
leaned against the windowpane, his eye on the doorway. The room
was clean, but the paint looked years old, and there was a smudge
on the doorframe, a few centimeters below the top of the door. His
heart started beating fast, for no reason, and he shook his head to
calm down. It slowed to normal, and he sat down, no thoughts in his
head.

From the mattress he could see outside. The bedroom window
looked out upon the garden blooming with white summer flowers:
lily, gardenia, sweet pea. The old woman came out to the garden in
the afternoon to tend it. He watched her. It was a modest house but
large for one woman. There were men's clothes in the wardrobe of his
room, but not too many. A widow, he imagined. Perhaps with grown
children. He watched her bend in the dirt, go into the house with
flushed cheeks, breathing hard.

He turned again at the doorframe. That smudge. Then he got up
to look closely, his heart steady now. No, it was not dirt but a little set
of holes at a diagonal, as if—but there was no other explanation. A
mezuzah had been ripped out. This had been a Jewish house.

When he came down to the kitchen an hour later the old woman
was gone, a cup of tea prepared for him, no longer hot.

⌒⌒

FISHL RETURNED IN THE evening, face gray. I'm going, he said.

What!

It's something—it's something terrible there. Nowhere even to—
they've burned down the barracks to kill the rats.

They'll come back, he muttered.

Yes, said Fishl. Here at least it is clean.

What did you eat? he said.

Soup, a thick soup. And I have flour and sugar. I gave her the
flour. She should not know what we have.

The reichsmarks we can give her.

Maybe.

They were both silent for a moment.

There was an office to give a list of names, Fishl said. To give and
to see. But there were none for me.

He could find no answer to Fishl and stayed silent.

Fishl continued. In Zdanow perhaps I will find.

First we could go to the American zone. We have money. We have
stones. We can go anywhere. There they will have more lists.

I am losing time, said Fishl. Some might have returned already.
And perhaps my father's property still stands.

He looked at Fishl. Here we are together. Yours will come here,
looking.

Fishl shook his head. They could go anywhere.

They had money. Money made one free and not a prisoner. With
money, one purchased food and ate it slowly. With money, one moved
about the country, not trapped in a transit center as if one still were
a slave, awaiting death. He had saved Fishl's life more than once,
and Fishl had saved his too. Now money could pay to save a life in
danger. They had money and stones. With money and stones, Fishl
was willing to leave him, travel alone, despite knowing little remained
at home. With money, Fishl was willing to go, and he was willing to
stay.

◇

WHEN THE FEVER PASSED the next day he washed his American army undershirt and hung it from the window. It looked alone there, white and thin. The blue shirt he had from the camp storehouse was not too dirty. He thought of taking some of the widow's husband's clothes— what, should he buy from her?—but he did not.

After washing he dressed, his blue shirt against his skin, wandered out into the warm air, venturing to the end of the road, near a house with three walls. He stood apart from the house, clutching his rucksack in his hand, watching the road. There were orders that any driver should pick up a refugee and take him as far as he was driving. A farmer stopped to load him onto the back of his truck, where three men pushed aside the empty potato sacks. The men came from a region of Romania that bordered with Poland, and within the first moments on the truckbed, exchanging information in Yiddish, they knew they would not find a name in common. He took in the smell of the raw potato skin, mixed with the odor of dirty burlap and the men's unwashed bodies. But it was only a few kilometers to the refugee camp, and the cool air that bit into his skin wafted the smell away. He could see them looking at him with curiosity, envy, his voice steadier than theirs, his clothes mended. He thought to open his rucksack and offer them a tin of something, then thought better of it. They were on their way to fuller rations at the camp. He would let them go ahead of him in the lines.

Half a kilometer from the entrance of the camp the driver stopped to let them down. He tried to walk a bit behind the trio, but they were so slow that at last he moved ahead of them, his eyes fixed on the wire fence surrounding the camp. He turned his head once to see them growing smaller behind him, the tall one leaning on the other two, bodies linked together, each gray costume blurring into another.

◇

A WOMAN WAS MAKING a commotion at the registry for ration cards. The British soldier at the metal desk was shouting, every word enunciated in terrible German, incomprehensible. The woman was speaking in three languages at once, a stuttering German scrambled with Yiddish phrases and Polish words.

He stepped to the side of the line and called out. Let me translate for you, he said in Yiddish. They can't understand you.

No, she called back, they can't.

I can help, he offered in German. The British soldier motioned toward him. He pushed himself forward to the front.

She's making trouble over a thief, said the soldier. Tell her the ration card is for her, not for him. Only one for each refugee!

Only one—he began—

But the woman had understood. What, you want to help them in this? What will you get from them? My brother's ration card, no doubt. Have you no shame, stealing from your own?

All right, he said. She was a sharp one. He wanted only to help, perhaps find himself in a position to help the soldiers. All right.

She saw his offended look. Her face softened. It's the boy, she said. They have falsely accused that he—

The British soldier interrupted. Enough, he said in German. One for each of you, now go. He was already stamping the green cards, not even asking for identity papers. It has nothing to do with us! The soldier glared at the woman. Your brother should have known better than to steal like a little animal.

They moved away from the metal desk and into the barracks corridor. But now, out of the hearing of the soldier, the woman turned her speech to him, the words tumbling out, pressured, in Polish. He's only a boy, she said. Only a child, who had not learned to recognize any law, but a clever one, a good one, they had found each other in a marketplace in their home province, how would he know that the mere act of trading cigarettes, it was not even stealing, only trading, and then of course his false passport, that was what called them to drag the child off like a dog, like a criminal—

All right, he said in Yiddish. You don't have to explain it to me like I'm a soldier. I know what a hungry child might do.

But she could not stop. The soldiers had taken all the passengers off the wagon. It was like the beginning, all over again! Her brother had fallen in with the smugglers' brigade, smugglers of food, gold, cigarettes, smugglers of refugees into the western zones, those Jews desperate to go anywhere near a port, a port that would lead them to Palestine or America. She herself, she wanted only to be near the others. What port she was in while she waited, that did not matter, only to be away from the Poles and—

How lucky you are, to have found a brother, he interrupted.

I, she said, her voice suddenly scratching. I—please.

Don't be scared, he said, the words coming out of him suddenly in Yiddish. Don't be scared, he repeated. I won't.

It's that he isn't. Her face was flat, but her voice was animated, defiant. I don't know him. He's just a young boy who helped me. I said it for them to listen. My brother—I have heard nothing from my brothers, my real brothers—but he—he helped me.

Her blank face and sharp voice pulled at him. He said, The problem is—among the British—it's difficult to bribe. If it were Russians, we could pay—

She looked at him.

I have money, he said.

She shifted her weight. How do you have money?

Now that she spoke softly, he could hear from her voice that she was at least twenty, a woman. I have money, he repeated.

They stood in silence a moment. Then she spoke. But what—she began—then paused—what is your name?

The question startled him. It was an intimate thing to be asked one's name. Already he was used to writing his name again in solid lettering, but to say it aloud still made him cautious. One did not say one's name—those who knew it used it, those who didn't received a false answer—even on the truckbed with the refugees he had used a borrowed name. He had been name after name, Mendl Abramsky, Abrasha Pavlovich, names that mimicked his own should he be surprised by someone he knew, names that belonged to the missing. He had a friend, a dear friend from the war, who knew him only as Miloch, the name of a dead man he had never met. Miloch: whose root was king. He had liked that name, had pulled it around his mouth before saying it, in a way he never had with his own name, the name he had used in childhood, the name his grandfather called him, the name his teachers uttered in praise.

The young woman was waiting for his response. And he should give it. There in the moldy corner of the registry barracks, he had nothing to hide.

I, he replied in Yiddish, I am Pavel Mandl. Pavel. Abram. Mandl.

And then, the next question, as if they were meeting at an outing for young people: And what is your name, miss?

Her name was Fela Berlinka. And the boy, she tried to add, Chaim—

Don't cry, Fela, said Pavel, although there was not a tear on her face. Don't cry. We will find your little friend and we will take him out.

They walked out into the courtyard and leaned on the side of the building, their backs against the splintering wood of the barracks. A group of three women, one covered in nothing but a blanket, moved slowly toward the corner where Pavel and Fela stood, then hurried past the open door.

Let us think, Pavel said, facing the road, his eyes on the backs of the British soldiers who guarded the wire fence. It was nice to speak to a young girl, even if her belly swelled from her bones like an empty pocket, even if her dust-blond hair parted to reveal spots of scalp. He could see, not from her skin, not from her body, but from her manner, that she must be pretty, used to attention from men. That was why she pushed him off a little. Aloof. A woman with dignity.

He rolled his shoulder to shake off his rucksack. He carried with him the valuables, hidden by several tins of meat and a quarter-loaf of bread. She was hungry. But when he pushed his hand into his rucksack, he did not take out the bread: instead he withdrew a slim scarf. Look what I have, he said. Red, with white. If we have blue we have the Americans.

She paused. Also the British.

I prefer the Americans.

To me they're all the same. But she fingered the scarf in his hands, then took it from him and tied it at her neck.

I have an idea, Pavel said.

THE BRITISH KEPT CHAIM among a group of boys in a locked barracks a kilometer away from the main camp. A handsome child, light-haired, with a surprised look on his face as a soldier brought him out into the sunlight. Fela whispered to him while Pavel stood from afar, watching them. He could see how they might pass for brother and sister, and their resemblance gave Pavel a feeling of relief and confidence. The lie he had persuaded Fela to tell—that the widow with whom he boarded lived in the house of Fela's own relatives, that it was only right that they take back what had been taken from them—the lie seemed closer to true.

A night passed, another day, but for a watch and only one of the gold chains a man sold Pavel a bicycle and agreed that the house in Celle, only ten kilometers from the camp, had belonged to Jews, and yes, Fela looked terribly familiar, just like the family who had lived there before the war. By the time Chaim had memorized the look of the long tile kitchen, the bathroom with hot-water plumbing, Pavel too was almost convinced that the widow's house was the home where Chaim and Fela had spent holidays as very young children, children visiting their cousins who still lived in Germany, family who had not fled to Poland in the years before the war.

THE WIDOW WAS IN the front yard, tending the garden. Two British soldiers, accompanied for translation by a German Jew from the refugee camp, swung open the garden gate.

What is this? Pavel heard the widow say. This is not a boarding-house.

He waited a few meters away, with Fela and Chaim beside him. The soldiers spoke in low voices, but Pavel could make out a few words in English.

"House," murmured the younger one. "You must—"

"Jews," the other soldier said firmly.

The German Jew was more talkative. You see, he said to the widow, nodding at the same time to the soldiers. They have proof. It is all down on paper, authenticated. He flashed the sworn testimony of the man Pavel had bribed.

They are lying! cried the widow in German. That man, he boarded here in my house! Those two, who knows who they are!

The German Jew smiled at the British soldiers, shrugged his shoulders. After a brief conference in English he turned to the road, where the three still stood.

Stay here, he said. Wait.

The soldiers and their translator disappeared into the house with the widow. Pavel and Fela and Chaim waited, it seemed for almost an hour, finally entering the gate to cross the garden and sit on the stoop at the threshold. When the translator pushed at the door again, it was to hold it open for the widow, who held a suitcase, and for the younger soldier, who carried a trunk. Pavel did not dare look at Fela and Chaim, who sat next to him, their breathing almost synchronized. Chaim kept his face blank, innocent. Perhaps it was wrong to show a young boy how to take a home. But what should they do instead— scavenge for a roof, fight for space with the rats in the camp? No. This was not stealing. This was living.

He watched the old woman's face as she walked past him—he could accept whatever empty curse she put on him, just as she had accepted the curses of the family that had been expelled for her. But she kept her eyes straight ahead, refusing to look at him. Her skin sagged a little from her chin, and he thought to grab another tin from his rucksack to give it to her, a pale trade for the house. But he did not move.

The older soldier, who appeared to have more authority, approached Pavel with something in his fist: the widow's key. Then the soldiers loaded themselves into their jeep and started the motor.

The three of them stood in the garden, Pavel grasping the seat of his new bicycle, watching the soldiers' jeep putter down the street and turn out of sight.

So, said Pavel.

He looked at Chaim and Fela, who did not respond. They seemed to wait for him to do something.

We will live as one family, Pavel announced. Then, with his new key, he opened the door.

Provisions

May–September 1945

COFFEE HE KNEW HOW to say in every language. *Cigarettes* too. *Bread. Shoes.* German was almost as natural to him as his native Yiddish and Polish, but now, only a short time after the liberation, he could speak in complex measurements to the Czechs and Romanians and Hungarians with whom he traded. A meter of nylon. Two kilos of potatoes. Three dozen shirts without buttons, four cartons of eggs, words for large quantities that had not occurred to him to learn in camp. As Pavel grew stronger, as he learned again to taste a spoonful of soup before swallowing, words and sentences began to form in his mouth and expel themselves without so much struggle.

Now, if asked, he had something to say to the British: "I live in a house." Pavel was proud of the English sentence, the phrase that made him more than an ordinary refugee stumbling over single words. The house might be modest, but it appeared to the world to be his, and he

soon felt a lightness about sending the widow off. If he had trouble
falling asleep at night, it was more often from the memory of taking a
dying man's spoon in camp. No, taking possession of the house might
have been an ugly act, but it was one that enabled him—and two
others!—to live. He had a warm drawer to hold his parents' photographs and all the scraps of brown paper on which he had written the
names of places where family members had last been seen. He had a
home, or if not a home, a resting place, with a woman to care for his
needs and a young boy to look after. He was a man.

THAT FIRST MORNING FELA came downstairs at sunrise, shoulders
wrapped in the blanket she had slept in. Her shoes, uncomfortably
wide, flapped from her heels.

Good morning! Pavel emerged from the washroom.

Ah! she cried. Then she collected herself. I'm—good morning.

His clean-shaven face sparkled with a few drops of water his towel
had missed, and he reached for his cap. Did I scare you? he said. But
there is nothing to fear. The old woman—already she is a few towns
away. She has a daughter. No one will come to disturb us.

No, she said. Of course not. Where do you go?

He pushed out his bicycle from behind the door. Now that we
have a household, we need more than she stored here. He cleared his
voice. I don't go far, he said. Just for sugar and eggs. There's a bit of a
loaf I left for you in the kitchen.

At the word *sugar* Fela felt a flinch inside her belly.

Sugar and eggs, Pavel repeated. And I still have a coupon for
bread. Don't worry. He averted his eyes from her bare arms. Then
the door shut gently behind him, and Fela heard his bicycle creaking
down the street.

She opened the washroom door. Clean toilet. A round mirror

hung above the white basin. She kept her face to the side of the mirror, not yet ready to see herself, ugly and swollen, the face of an old woman on a young woman's hungry body. Instead she splashed herself with cool water, wiped the night's sweat from her chest and neck. She could bathe now, with Pavel out of the house, or she could wait until Chaim awoke to keep watch should strangers seek to enter. She peered out from the bathroom window. The garden, sprouting with the summer vegetables the old woman had cultivated, seemed frightening, an open space in which a human being was a target. Perhaps they would have felt safer in the refugee camp, surrounded by British soldiers.

She shuffled to the sofa to peer at Chaim, sleeping with his mouth open, covered with a coat. With his eyes closed he looked helpless, pale, not a trace of the sophistication and cunning he had displayed when they had met, finding her in a corner of the market at the provincial center, a city neither of them knew well, a small distance from her hometown, only a day after she had seen her family's house for herself. She had been in the first trains from Siberia for the repatriated Poles, and she had expected—but she did not remember what she had expected. Now that she had seen the reality—once-familiar neighbors looking at her with curiosity, even hostility, a man she did not know installed in her father's dry goods shop—she could not remember what she had thought she would recognize.

But Chaim had recognized her. He had known—from what? from her fear?—that she was a Jew, even as he, in his Polish army uniform, tapping her on the shoulder, had fooled her.

"*Buongiorno,*" he had said. "*Buongiorno, signorina.*"

She had felt something cold etching down her chest. It wasn't any language she had known. She was silent.

He switched to Polish. You look like you want to go to Italy.

Why do you say that? she managed. I have no desire to cross any borders. I am here looking for—

Or perhaps you are Greek.

Greek? No, no.

Are you sure? His eyes were sharp blue but friendly, and for a moment he looked almost childlike. I know a Greek song. That is why I ask. He began to sing: One, one, who knows one? One, one. I know one.

His voice was soft but clear. Against the music of the buying and the selling of eggs and milk, no one else could hear, but she could: Hebrew. A little Passover song.

He went on. Two, two, who knows two? Two, two. I know two.

She opened her lips. That is not Greek, she murmured in Polish.

No? The young man had smiled. How strange, he said. Because I have a Greek passport. He took it out of his pocket and showed it to her. You see? Greek.

A passport could get her into the western zones, where the British and American soldiers would protect them from the locals. A woman alone was not safe in the Russian zone, with the Red Army soldiers going after any woman they saw. Accompanied by a boy in a uniform, she was perhaps more protected. I have a ring, she said. As she said it, she touched the small blue stone in its tight setting. The one possession she had kept, but to give it up now seemed easy.

Ah, no, said the boy—she could see, suddenly, that he was a boy, no more than thirteen or fourteen, disguised in his uniform—no. Keep it until we board the truck. That ring can pay for both of us.

Was it generosity that he did not take it from her? He could have taken the ring and abandoned her to cross into Germany alone, but he had not. They rode with several others, Romanians, four men and a woman, whose dark clothes and mouths emitted a muddy odor. They murmured small greetings in Yiddish, nothing more. If they were to communicate it was to be in Hebrew, which sounded like Greek, the boy said. Fela knew very little Hebrew. Only the boys had religious lessons in her family, modern though her father had tried to be. Chaim—he had given only his first name—had some difficulty himself. His hometown was not so far from her own, Mlawa, but if he had had a religious education at all, it must have stopped with the war. But he had the phrases, could rearrange words from prayers to make a sentence. He could make a sentence in any language, he said, with a seriousness that made her decide not to call him a braggart, not to joke with him. Even sitting in the back of the truck he was careful and alert. He stretched and brushed the dust off his uniform every hour until they crossed into the British zone in Germany. She grew fond of him on their journey, as she would a brother with whom she had lived all her life but only just now started to know.

YES, SHE WOULD WAIT to bathe until Chaim awoke to keep watch. She moved into the kitchen. The widow had kept the sink clean, but dust from the bombings had gathered on all the shelves, a thick layer of white and gray. She would have to clean the house from top to bottom. There was little furniture—two beds, one sofa, one chest of drawers—and only a bit of crockery. Yet the rooms were wide and the wallpaper in good condition. Perhaps the possessions had been sold.

Chaim came in as the coffee boiled, dressed in a shirt left for him by Pavel and the pair of trousers he had worn to sleep, his feet in a pair of torn socks.

He sat in a chair as she put a plate before him. Has he gone for more food?

She nodded. The coffee burned her tongue a little. She put the cup down again and blew at the steam. Chaim had a slow way of speaking, rolling his words around his tongue. He spoke slowly, but he ate fast. In the smugglers' truck he had murmured words to himself, Polish and German and Russian, talking himself to sleep. Meat, soup, spoon, fork, knife. Once she had looked at him directly as he moved his lips, and he had seen her, but he had not stopped. Milk. Chicken. Chocolate. Porridge. Potato. Still a child.

Careful with the bread, Fela said. You lose crumbs when you rush.

Her own place at the table was clean, and she smoothed out the paper she had found in the widow's drawer and looked down at her letter. *Bluma*, it said. *Dearest Bluma*.

What do you write there? His mouth was full with bread and coffee.

I write to my sister. I know she—I think she—but the others. Fela looked at the neat Polish letters on the page. *I am alive.*

That was all she had written. She wanted to think out her words before she scratched them onto a valuable scrap of paper. Chaim was looking at her. She is in Palestine, Fela added. That's why I know she—I believe she—of course maybe she has heard something—her address I always remember. I remembered it everywhere.

So write to her, said Chaim. Don't let me disturb you.

If you don't want to disturb me, eat.

I have heard nothing. Who else has written to you?

Are you reading my letter?

No, no.

You look like you are reading it.

She got up to pour him more coffee. Pavel said he would try to find sugar from someone. Do you know where he will get it?

I can guess, said Chaim. He leaves this area, that's certain. Did you see at the end of the street? There's a row of rubble, then half a house, just open, no roof, no upper floor. Yet in our row of houses it looks as if nothing has happened.

Fela pushed her letter to the side of the table. I don't want anything to stain it.

What do you tell her?

Nothing. I tell her nothing. There is nothing to tell her. Just like you. Nothing to tell.

Chaim got up from his plate. I told Pavel my name last night. Traum. We don't have to be brother and sister now.

All right, said Fela.

I'm going to wash, he said.

Fela shook her pen. Still a little ink. She wanted to write: Do you remember Sieresz, who bought leather on credit from Father every Christmas? I saw his brother. He asked me: For what did you come back? That to me was worse almost than—

But instead she would be brief. *I lost Moshe*, she wrote. *I am alone.*

IN JUNE PAVEL ORGANIZED a second bicycle. The German girl who sold it to him had tied a wooden crate onto a piece of metal above the back wheel. She used the crate as a basket to carry food back from the market. He could see on the girl's face her regret at giving up the bicycle; but hunger was bigger than regret. So she would walk! He had the girl ride alongside him until half a kilometer away from the house. He gave her an extra tin of pork for her trouble, and in the look on her face he saw not just gratitude for the food, but relief. Yes, they were still a little afraid, these Germans who had lived near the large camp during the war. Now that the armies were here, ready to condemn and to hang, these Germans were afraid of the Jews.

Pavel presented the gift to Fela in the garden. He called out to her from the front of the house, near the kitchen window. He stood in between the two bicycles, his face somber. He did not want to look too arrogant to her. Still, look what he had done in an hour at dawn! A good piece of craft, this little thing.

But she looked skeptical when she saw him.

He felt offended. For you, he said. I didn't steal it.

No, no. Her neck flushed; a red spot appeared on each cheek. I do not know how, she said.

No? Pavel smiled.

My father never permitted us, she said. But I always loved the way it looked, a group of young people, especially the girls, with their skirts floating over the wheels. It was always the very sophisticated ones in the town who went off on outings. They knew how to ride so as not to entangle their clothing.

I will teach you, said Pavel. It is very easy.

She unbuttoned the lowest button of her dress, so as not to rip the cloth over the metal frame. He could see she was unsure about letting him touch her. He let her lift herself onto the seat of the bicycle. One foot, on tiptoe, still touched the ground.

Don't worry, he said, walking behind her. I have you. He held the basket at the back of the seat steady. His arm did not even brush her dress, which fluttered a bit at the waist. Look, even if you lift your foot, you won't fall.

She pedaled hesitantly, one meter, two meters, the bicycle shaking under her weight. Pavel stepped quickly after her, right hand gripping the crate. He could see his forearm tensing. Yes, his arms and hands grew thicker and stronger every day.

Oop! she cried. And dropped her foot down to brake herself.

Good! said Pavel. Very good.

No, no, said Fela. I'm afraid. Too afraid for it. But she started again, slower than before, the bicycle leaning from side to side.

If you go a little bit faster, said Pavel, just a little bit, it won't shake so much.

She stopped again, unbuttoned another button near the hem of her skirt.

Pavel trotted behind her as she moved her pale legs. Many times he had perched girls on the frame in front of him, grasping them by the waist, cycling in the forest behind his grandfather's town so as not to create a scandal. But here he was, so many years later, no community to scandalize, no one left to be shocked, and he was careful, more careful than he ever had been.

◡◠

IN THE EVENINGS THE three of them smoked in the garden, playing card games on a folding table they had found in the pantry. A few times Chaim brought home a friend he had met at his job in the camp print shop. The friend brought camp newspapers and bulletins in exchange for the food Fela made. Pavel approved. He liked that his house should welcome refugees as a camp could not. And it was good Chaim had a friend. Everyone needed a companion, Pavel thought. A young boy especially. A wheel on its own would not go anywhere, but attached to a frame and another wheel it could be a bicycle, and a bicycle could travel, move, carry, and work. God gave Moses the commandments in two stone tablets. Two was a stronger number than one.

They played rummy, and a version of poker Fela would not reveal how she had learned. Before the war, Pavel didn't play cards. But early on, after he had fled to a town not yet clean of Jews, he had stayed with a family he knew only slightly, and the father and daughter had taught him to play in the evenings, when no one was allowed out. They knew him only by a false name, Miloch, but he became close with them, especially the daughter and her husband, and he learned the game fast. He could make his face a mask and trick the others into thinking his prospects were bad. It was a good skill.

The war had ended, but still he played with deep concentration, breaking his thoughts only to watch as Fela cast out a card, or mocked a mistake of Chaim's, or laughed as she laid out her winning hand. Fela made fun of his gloomy expressions.

So serious! she would say. We're still alive, even if you lose the game!

He would want to answer, Who says I will lose? But he kept quiet, instead letting out a mournful sigh as he shifted in his seat.

He saw that Fela was the most cheerful when she played cards.

The rest of the day, her chores and her cooking, her letters to Palestine and to Poland, her squinted reading of the camp newsletters, she approached with grim drive. He liked to keep her playing cards as late as possible, so he could hear her shouts of victory and affectionate jokes before he went to sleep.

PAVEL AWOKE IN THE middle of the night. He got up and went to the drawer where he had placed his wallet and a little envelope of his pictures. He caressed the brown packet. He did not need to take the pictures out. If he stopped moving altogether, he thought he could hear Fela rustling in the bedroom across the corridor, Chaim's hard breaths in the living room. They seemed at peace. In the day it was easier for him than for them—Fela afraid to go into the garden, Chaim lying on the sofa and humming—but at night they were free. Perhaps their thoughts exhausted them during the day, and their bodies had no choice after the sun went down. Meanwhile Pavel was alone, trying to explain things to himself without the help of a night companion or a fellow traveler. When Fishl had been with him there had been an understanding. He had been a guide, recognizing Pavel in the entry room of the death camp, advising him how to keep alive. The skills he and Fishl had taught each other kept him alive even now. Yet now Pavel was confused, more confused than he had been in years. He could speak more languages than a military interpreter, but still he did not know what to call this house and these companions. He needed an instruction manual to tell him how to wait calmly for food, how to talk with confidence to a soldier, how to sleep.

He returned to the bed. When they were children, his mother had given each of them a piece of chocolate in bed each night, in the dark. After her death, when he was sent east to live with his grandparents, his grandmother did the same. Now, the memory of the taste made him close his eyes, trying to fool himself into sleep. Had his brothers and sisters been given chocolate in the homes of the aunts and cousins where they had been sent? He had not thought to wonder before this moment. After his father remarried and he was returned to his home in Katowice, he did not remember chocolate. Well, he was already an adult then, almost fifteen, and his grandfather was ailing, his grandmother preparing to live with one of her surviving daughters. His mother's family knew how to take in the grieving and the abandoned without making them feel as guests or burdens.

Pavel let his eyes close, tried to push into his mind pleasant images, half-conscious dreams. He saw his grandmother, standing and smiling, blind to the men loading wagons with her precious possessions. Silver, china, his grandfather's leather-bound Talmud, everything in piles like so many old rags. No, his grandmother did not see. Instead she called out to him, her voice more aged than he remembered. Eat, eat, you rascal, she said in Polish. Her croaked words caused him to give a nervous laugh, and his mouth began to itch. Her hand held out a bit of almond cake, and he knew that the almonds had come from the tree that had burst into blossom behind the house. His grandmother's voice turned softer, to Yiddish: Eat. Skinny boy. Do you understand?

Yes, he answered. But her words seemed to bounce against his ears and skull without falling inside him.

Eat, eat. Do you understand?

Yes, he repeated. And he almost did. But now it was she who did not seem to hear him. Her face was removed, yellow, as in a picture or film. Yes, Grandmother, yes. He said it in every language he thought that she knew, Yiddish, Polish, Hebrew, German. Yes, yes.

Eat, she continued, her voice in a singsong. Eat, eat. My *yingele*, my little one, my lamb, eat.

AFTER A MONTH OR two Fela was stronger, her legs no longer swollen, and she agreed to set out with Pavel on her new bicycle to the camp. They filled their satchels with cheese and bread, as well as a bit of gold, on a warm September day. There was no reason to be afraid; already she could move the bicycle in the side roads, and they would walk part of the way if she became tired.

Look how well you have learned, said Pavel, riding behind her. Very steady.

I had a good teacher, she called out.

They stopped to eat in a clearing near a half-repaired train station, a quiet area not far from a bustling one. Fela looked past the line of birches and smoothed their blanket on the grass.

I'm sorry I'm so slow. Really, I am very afraid. She laughed with a little hiccup, looked behind the row of trees again.

It is safe with me, said Pavel. Two is a stronger number than one.

She said nothing.

Pavel said, We are together. He took her hand.

She moved her hand from his. Pavel felt something move inside his ribs, a wind of fear. But he pushed it down. They sat silently. He waited a moment, then took her hand again.

Again she pulled her hand away. He looked at it as she drew it into her lap: white, small, the knuckles slightly chapped.

Pavel, she said. I am looking for someone.

Ah, said Pavel. She was looking at him straight in the eyes.

He managed a soft expression. But really he was surprised. With her resting in the house, her fear to go outside—how could she look without looking? He had thought—but he turned away from her, faced the bicycles, the frames flat on the grass, the spokes turning slowly in the breeze.

Finally Fela spoke. And you? You are such a good-looking man. So kind, decent.

He said nothing.

She waited, then said it directly. You too, perhaps, are looking?

No, said Pavel. Not—there was—but I already know what happened. I look only for my brothers and sisters.

He did not look at her face, busying himself instead with his bread. They finished their meal in silence and mounted their bicycles again, Fela in front so he could watch as she rode. Why should anything change? She would look, perhaps she would find. He still could protect her while things remained this way.

He pushed his legs forward on the pedals and watched her hips on the frame ahead of him. He still could protect her. Already he had found a use for another gold chain. A little woman in the British camp knew how to counterfeit American identity cards. He could expand his business, give Fela what she needed to make a nice home, and then they would see what they would see. Already the zones were tightening, the paperwork to cross each border and enter each new town growing thicker and more complicated. Today he would pick up the American papers to add on to the British ones. He could go back and forth, do business in all zones, American, British, even Russian. He was making new connections. Only last week he had brought a truckful of provisions into the camp and left half with the refugee camp hospital, then sold what remained to the Germans for clothes, hats, jackets, and a wallet. A citizen of the world! He laughed to himself, but Fela did not turn around. Liberated, but not free. That was what they said in the camp, the slogan the refugees used to build organization, to argue for visas, for Palestine, for graves. A young woman, but she too was not yet free.

A few meters ahead of him, Fela's light hair blew slightly, restrained by the scarf she had tied around her head. Yes, she was a lady.

The Bremen Zone

September–October 1945

PAVEL WANTED TO THROW himself into something that would make him full. The trading was not enough. He tried to busy himself by attending the committee meetings of the Jews in the camp. The men had noticed that the younger refugees, the boys of fifteen or sixteen, were terribly ignorant. Could not they begin classes of some kind, something to make up for the time these children had lost? Were there no teachers among the survivors? Someone had volunteered to make a search some days before, and Pavel had not paid so much attention. But as he cycled with Fela home from the camp, he had an image of himself sitting with Chaim in their garden, teaching him all that he knew. Three days later, Pavel presented the boy with a stack of papers fastened with a clip.

Chaim, he said, blowing on a cigarette after his coffee. How old are you?

Ah, said Chaim. Fourteen or fifteen, I believe.

You believe? said Pavel. You look younger. Don't you remember when you were born? Let us see—in 1939, were you—

Pan Pavel, said Chaim, no. You are right. I am fourteen, and my birthday will be next May.

And what of your father? He put you in _kheyder_, of course? How long was it before you were—

No, said Chaim, suddenly flustered. We—I went for some time, but—we—my father—he believed in the Bund—

But Pavel had already made his decision. Whether Chaim was a good student or no before, now things would be different!

Chaim was stammering. It's that our family was not so—

All right, Pavel interrupted—everyone had secrets to keep, and who was Pavel to interfere with a child's desire to hold his past to himself? All right. Well, in any case, it is the time, a little late, of course, but around the time, that you begin to prepare to become a bar mitzvah. It's time to learn. I suppose you learned something in your family of Hebrew, even without—

Something, said Chaim, softly. A little, I could recognize, of course, but not—

Not enough, no. Never enough. I'll teach you, my friend. Nothing to be ashamed of. In fact, Pavel lied, I was very slow with Hebrew myself.

CHAIM SAT DOWN TO Fela's dark bread and soup of boiled meat. He would not look at Pavel. He would eat slowly, in silence. Still his body began to feel heat, as if it knew a discomfort and pain were coming. Why should Chaim obey? He bent to his soup, taking each sip like a medicine. He felt a needle begin to move inside, ready to become a knife, thrusting inside him, carving names into his guts. He would not look at Pavel, but when he glanced at Fela he saw her eyes turn down to her plate, afraid to meet his gaze. A twinge of shame pushed through him, then an ugly gratitude that made him angry. Who were these people to him, making a false family, false home? Who were they? He had a sudden image of the raincoat that Pavel had brought home for Chaim, a proud trade he had made, and Chaim wanted to leap up from the table and slash the coat into tiny pieces, until nothing remained but a pile of collar, pocket, useless squares of cloth. There was only so long he could contain his fury.

The soup trickled into his stomach. He took an English class each week, but it was not enough to give him a purpose or an escape. Perhaps a routine would help him leave the house, make his own life. He had inquired, without real interest, into work or training, among the aid workers. Perhaps that was his way out.

AFTER A MONTH IN the camp print shop Chaim accustomed himself to the operation of the large and ancient ink machine that rolled out the camp newsletter, little stories reviewed by the soldiers to ensure they carried no news of riots, protests, arrests. Death notices of the refugees were permitted. Also lists of names of the living, announcements of departures. Bundles of young people had already been let out to temporary homes in Britain and France, to be rehabilitated until—but until what no one yet knew.

His hands turned a dark blue-black every evening as he read through the lists before the ink on the pages was dry, the names rubbing off on his clothing and skin. Each week young men and an occasional young woman or two gathered in the early evenings outside the shop to pick up the new pages, skipping over the drawings on the front page, the poems on the second page, fingers running up and down the lists, eyes squinting, hands folding the short pages and then reopening, rereading. He watched them searching for a last name that meant something to them, a town in which someone had a cousin, a patronymic that sounded like a past neighbor's, borrowing pens from one another as they circled clues.

He continued to attend his English class in the children's school barracks, and Chaim left his post early on Tuesdays to make sure he found a seat close to the front of the room. One evening a man from the print shop came trotting after him as Chaim crossed the threshold. A young woman named Rayzl Traum had submitted an advertisement to the camp paper. The printman had written the advertisement and stopped at the last name, questioned her. She had a young cousin Chaim before the war.

The children were finishing their lessons, the teacher outside the room, waiting as they wrote the last sums of the day. From the doorway Chaim saw the small ones copying the scrawls from the blackboard into their slim notebooks. Then he turned his face to the printman's feet, his heavy brown shoes.

I had a cousin Rayzl before the war, Chaim answered.

HE REMEMBERED HER. RAYZELE. Now she was plump, filled with a rageful kind of cheer, another one who wanted to blot out the past, march forward. Their fathers were brothers. She held him close to her chest and breathed into his hair when she saw him.

They sat on a bench near the print shop, and he waited for her to tell him what she knew. But she did not say a word, instead looked at him directly in the eyes, as if to send out her message without speaking. Perhaps she waited for him to ask. But he did not want to know. Perhaps it was a family trait, to know and not to say, to write quietly in notebooks, as his father had done in his job as a translator—was that his job?—yes, of course, he had tutored Chaim in the Yiddish letters before Chaim could understand the words he read, of course that was his work, was Chaim forgetting these things already?

After a moment, he said, Where do you sleep?

Not here, she said. I live on a Zionist kibbutz, a new one they started a few kilometers south, on good farmland. So we don't have to depend on ration cards, like little prisoners again. We prepare for these British—her mouth turned fierce—to let us out of here, to let us into our homeland. Come with me there. You can smuggle yourself out of the camp. It's an hour's drive from here.

I—said Chaim—I have a place, not in the camp—I thought you could stay with us—

But she hesitated. They expect me back this evening, she said. And you—already you have missed convoys they let into Palestine. You are young enough to be an orphan—why did you not go on the list?

I don't know, he said. I am here, I live with—I have a warm place in a home until—I take English lessons—

English! cried Rayzl. To be a stranger in a strange land again! A Bundist, just like your father, refusing Palestine for class politics! Look how it helped him! And since when do the English let you into their country, or the Americans either? English!

CHAIM CAME TO THE house in Celle and lay down on the sofa. He bent his arm over his eyes to block out the remaining afternoon light, and he saw an image of his mother, her own elbow bent at her brow to cover her eyes, yes, once he had seen his own mother lie down like this, perhaps after the first action or perhaps at a different time, at some terrible news or another, he did not remember, saw only her thin body outstretched on the cot in the ghetto apartment, no, it must have been after, long after his brother had been taken—and the image itself made Chaim tear his own arm from his forehead, curl his body into a ball, sob.

After some time he opened his eyes and stared at the wall, covered with floral paper. He did not want to touch it, the false decoration of a home in which he lived as a strange guest. Sometimes he brought one of the young men he had met from outside the print shop to stay in the house, just to feel himself not so alone. But Lazar had not liked to sleep there more than one night at a time, even with the use of a clean sink and the promise of Fela's pastries. And suddenly Chaim too wanted to escape the little house, the little town, the questions that would surely come tearing at him in the evening as Fela laid out the food on the garden table. He did not want to see them. He wanted to escape every familiar face he saw, every reminder of something he knew. He wanted to be a stranger, completely alone, a newborn, learning new images and new faces.

He pushed his legs out of the house and took Fela's bicycle toward the camp. On the main road he saw a group of British driving to the Bremen zone, a small island of American soldiers.

"Work," he said, smiling, flashing his identity card. "I have work in the harbor." They let him into their truck.

The rubble still covered wide areas near the port, but a few businesses and houses had been rebuilt, and in a small café near one of the piers he sat alone and watched the Americans in civilian clothes flirt and drink with the German women. Two black soldiers walked past him, talking in soft voices too low for him to hear. They were always together, in groups, and it was understood they had their own brigades, separate from the others. He followed their faces as they walked, stared openly at them. They did not seem to notice. In the American zone in Austria he and Fela had passed a camp, but their driver, a Jew, had warned them not to enter, for the Americans forced the Jews to live and work with the Ukrainians and Poles and Latvians. Americans do not separate, the truck driver had said. They say that was what Hitler did! The driver had laughed. Everyone saw the Americans too made divisions. The British did not permit the camp newspaper to publish any stories about the military, but on the radio could be heard the stories of the skirmishes among the Americans, the Negro soldier left beaten on the street, the white soldiers protesting shared meal tables. When Lazar had been liberated, a brigade of Japanese from America had marched into his camp, frightening some inmates who thought the war had been lost to the Axis. Lazar laughed about it now, he confided to Chaim, but even he had been confused. But one could not be confused when one saw a black soldier. A black man was American, immediately recognizable for who he was, a symbol of freedom. When Chaim had first come to Germany, his heart had still jumped at the sight of a uniform, any uniform—but after the momentary shudder he knew to feel relief at the glimpse of a dark face, for he could see at once that these men were Americans, liberators.

Now in Bremen, Chaim sipped his coffee, feeling it spread through his chest. Townspeople bustled away from him. Even with his clean clothes and straight hair, he felt himself recognized. What was it? Perhaps his face gave out the light of accusation when a German hurried down a street of the American zone, carrying bread or holding a child's hand. Or perhaps—yes, he knew it—they could see the fear, a look he no longer had the confidence to hide. Townspeople could see who he was, could see through the calm mask of a young man idling, their quick glances registering German from refugee. For a long time he had forced himself to forget the faces of his family, the names of the companions with whom he had fled the ghetto. His talent for disguise had erased the fear from his face. But now it seemed that fear revealed itself like a caption below a photograph. Now it seemed he could be named.

MY DARLING SISTER. A letter came from Fela's sister in Palestine, the diminutives and nicknames falling off the page in Yiddish, mixed with the Hebrew that Bluma, so smart, so clever, now spoke every day. Bluma had heard nothing. She too had been writing to the synagogue in their hometown, to HIAS and the American Jewish Joint Distribution Committee for word of sisters, brothers, nephews, nieces, cousins. Bluma had heard nothing until the short letter from Fela, her dear one, her beautiful sister.

Fela wept as she read her older sister's letter. What chain was more strong than the chain to a sister, even one whom she had not seen since childhood, when Bluma had defied their father and left? Flesh of the same flesh. Bluma had gone to gymnasium when no Jewish girl in their town could dream of it—the eldest, Pnina, had gone to work to support Bluma's schooling, expensive even when the family store had prospered. And what had Bluma learned among the other students? She had picked up ideas, become a socialist, and at last joined a group of young Zionists and sailed off. It had been terrible at the time, the horror of her father and mother at the rebellion of their most gifted child, but now it seemed wise, prophetic.

Two sisters, one chain. And yet the relief that Fela felt when she opened Bluma's letter, the gratitude for a word from her blood, *my darling sister*, did not fill her. It was as if she were still starving and given just a morsel of bread to eat. She longed to see a family face in the refugee camp, longed to read even a distant cousin's name on a list of survivors. She longed for Moshe, the touch of him covering her, his breath like a blanket to warm her. Fela too had defied her father when she ran away, in the first weeks of the bombing, when it was still possible to flee to White Russia. But it was not for politics that she had disobeyed.

Thanks to Pavel's trading, Fela now had clean clothes and an adequate amount of food; the bloating in her legs and belly had subsided; she looked almost as she once did, and she had begun to menstruate again. But the ache hadn't left her. Now that her body could do more than subsist it began to remember other pains, not just hunger or fear. Once, cycling down the street with Pavel, she thought she saw Moshe, and as the small man with his brown curls and calm eyes had come closer, her neck had tensed, as if they were together, at night, he about to touch her. It wasn't him, of course; she saw that a moment after the constriction in her abdomen stopped. But now the face of the man in the street, the man who was not Moshe, became something she longed for, a reminder of the face she had loved and was beginning to forget. But she didn't see him, the false Moshe, again.

When she gave away her ring to the smuggler who took them across the border into Germany, she gave away her last clear picture of her love, the image she had of him twirling it on his finger, round and round, as she became too thin to wear it securely. Before then, she had sold a watch stolen from her father when she and Moshe had run away, she had traded the leather finery hidden in the house by her mother, but she had not let the ring leave her body. She had kept it close to her chest, under her clothing, after the news had come from a neighbor's wife that Moshe, kidnapped into the Russian army, had disappeared, after the baby, born prematurely with the shock of her grief, had withered from dysentery, dying from the sickness in her milk, after her flesh had vanished from a hunger so strong it crushed the grief. Now that her grief was back, the ring was no longer with her. She did not need it. It was the last thing she had from Moshe, yet when the time came she had not hesitated to rid herself of it. Some part of her thought that if she gave it up, she would find him alive. Some part of her wanted to blot out any piece of him that remained in the physical world in order to keep him to herself, inside her, whole.

They were all in her now. She got up from her cooking twice, leaving a pot simmering as she went to her room to read Bluma's letter again. Already she knew it by heart, and still it said the same thing, over and over again. *I have heard nothing.* Fela's letter had been posted by the British soldiers, thanks to Pavel's dealings. Bluma had received it, and she had received no other.

That night Fela could not play cards. Chaim was away, on an outing to the mountains for the refugee boys. Fela sat silently with Pavel in the garden, tapping her coffee cup. Then she got up, went into the kitchen. In the early weeks in the house she had found a lightweight cigar box. The box held eighteen loose cigarettes, not so stale that they could not be enjoyed. She returned to the garden with the box.

Let us try them, she said to Pavel.

They passed the first one back and forth, touching each other lightly as their arms stretched across the little table. They were used to American cigarettes now, bought on the black market, but these had a softer taste, unfiltered but still not as strong. They lingered over the one between them, taking care not to let any tobacco fall out from the crumbling paper.

After a few moments she let her knuckles graze his palm and then his forearm, bare but for the blue mark above the wrist. He moved his hand to her hair, as if to smooth it. But then he moved it away and instead touched her face, his fingertips at her cheekbones and lips. She felt a familiar chill inside her ribs but said nothing, looked down, then got up to clear the coffee cups from the garden table. At the door to the kitchen, saucers in hand, she turned.

Come with me, she said.

He followed her into the kitchen, stood away from her as she washed the cups. Then they went into his bedroom and slipped under the blankets fully clothed, undressing each other lying down, without looking.

FELA AND PAVEL WALKED arm in arm near the port. They had taken the train to the Bremen zone, where American soldiers stood on the docks to monitor shipments of coffee, flour, sugar, canned meats, used clothing, new wool, tin appliances, metal pans, medical bandages, syringes, pills, and serums. From Bremen a first wave of refugees had already sailed for Australia.

Australia! Pavel had said. These people, no patience! We, my friend—he squeezed Fela's arm—we will wait for America.

She did not answer. The Americans did not give visas. But Pavel was convinced. Americans have know-how, he would say. They respect it in others.

But she saw differently. In the Bremen zone the young American soldiers walked with German women, the widows or their daughters, desperate for a bite to eat from a man with power. On a corner near the piers she saw a redhead in a green uniform laughing and loud, poking at a plump German girl who gave a forced laugh herself. The Americans looked cold and large to her. They called and they joked, the young boys lumbering and wide, with open faces that in a moment might turn on the small fearful people who crossed their path.

She looked carefully as she stepped into the street. A man and a woman were bicycling along the curb, coming toward them, wobbling on the cobblestones. A flash of black hair waved out from beneath the woman's gray scarf. The man rode a little ahead of her, turning his head to the right and the left, vigilant. Fela stared at the man's face as it came closer, the pointed chin and broad cheekbones, and felt her breath pull down into her abdomen and her heart knock inside her as she stared, blinked, squinted, to make sure she saw what she saw. It was Moshe, it was her love, on a bicycle alongside another woman, and his face stared back at her with a look of shock and something else—joy? an emotion she could not name in that moment—he leapt off his bicycle, letting it clatter to the street, his mouth opened, and she felt her arms move to her sides, her body small and terrified as he cried:

Pavel!

Already Pavel had stopped, his hand covering his mouth, the other outstretched as his friend came to grab it and embrace him. At last Pavel murmured, Fishl, Fishl. I thought—I had heard such things from there—I thought never—

Fela stood still, her hands cold, blood rushing back to her face. She breathed in and out, looking at the two men. And now she saw— the sloped eyes of Pavel's friend were brown, not green, his compact body was broader, his hips less narrow. How could she have thought? The men were embracing and pulling away, looking at each other's faces, embracing again.

So—are you not to speak to your wives anymore? It was the woman speaking. She had leaned her own bicycle against a brick wall, then picked up Fishl's and nestled it against hers.

My wife—said Fishl—Dincja—Pavel—

Pavel stepped back, gave a grave smile. And this is Fela.

She stretched out her hand to the woman's.

Fela was in Russia, Pavel continued. Siberia, then—

Fela interrupted. Siberia.

The other three began speaking at once. Towns, camps, post-liberation hospitals. Pavel stopped for a moment at the name of one camp. My sister, he said to Dincja. I heard she had gone there after we lost contact—Hinda—Hinda Mandl.

I knew a Hinda, said Dincja. Small, with brown eyes, not so large as yours, yes? Broad forehead. We were in the same barracks there.

Fela watched Pavel's hand cover his mouth again.

They went east, most of the women there. Sent east after—I saw a friend from there a month ago—my friend was liberated in Lands-berg by the Americans. You should write to her.

God in heaven, whispered Pavel. God in heaven.

They stood silent for a moment. Then Fishl said, How happy I am to see you, my friend. We thought of going to Australia. But now we are on the list for America—

You got on the list?

I got on the list. Fishl threw a look at his wife. Dincja has an uncle in New York—it is the only way, my friend, everything else is closed.

New York, repeated Pavel. There was an uncle.

She has an uncle, nodded Fishl. And I had stones to help the paperwork along. It was a match.

I have not—Pavel glanced quickly at Fela, then looked away—I have not yet—

Ah, said Fishl, nodding. They embraced again.

Fela watched the men, a veil of sweat cooling on her brow. Pavel did not look at her.

WHAT STONES? SHE SAID later, on the journey back to Celle. Pavel was looking out the window as the train rattled past the German towns.

He meant money, answered Pavel. Fishl was always a good trader. He found someone to help him with the papers. We should do the same.

Fela did not respond.

But first, Feluchna, I write to Landsberg. I feel, I have a feeling. He took Fela's hand into his lap without looking. Perhaps Hinda is alive.

Pavel, said Fela. But then she kept quiet.

I had six brothers and sisters, said Pavel. Now I am one. But perhaps we are two. He was stroking her palm with his fingers. Two is a stronger number than one.

Two is a stronger number than one. It was true. Still she did not speak. Who was to say that Moshe, even if he was alive, did not think the same thought, did not find his own new woman to make a wife, to sail to Australia or Sweden or, God in heaven, South America? She was stupid, stupid, refusing to accept, wanting to interrupt Pavel's thoughts and say, I still look too. I still look too. But she was sure he knew what she thought. She was sure he knew she still waited.

She leaned her head against his shoulder, feeling the gesture itself was a lie to Pavel, a theft from Moshe. A chill of anger at both of them, at everything each wanted to take from her, rose in her face. She and Pavel now slept every night in the same bed, and she wanted her solitude back, the loneliness no one watched, the privacy of grieving.

Go, she said. Go yourself to Landsberg.

Will you not come with me?

No, she answered. We will be two in the house, myself with Chaim. We are two. The poor boy should not be alone. Go. Take your bicycle.

He looked at her, eyes almost begging, scanning her face for an explanation. His hand went to his breast pocket, tapped at his chest, touching, Fela knew, the cloth that protected his photographs.

Go, she repeated. Pretend I am with you, a bit ahead of you. Pretend. But go.

PAVEL FOUND HIMSELF AWAKE in the night, no dream to remember. Fela slept next to him, breathing quietly, and Chaim, his things in a neat pile in Fela's old room, would not return from his trip for at least another day. He got up to open his drawer and look inside. He did not dare take the stones out of the pouch. If she knew what he had, if she knew how he had it! But was it such a crime? Perhaps if he had come across the men now he would have stopped himself, he would have felt sickened at what he had, jewels taken from the murdered— but then he had been in a different world—and even then there were certain things—terrible things—that he had not permitted himself to do, not even in the most desperate of moments. And if he and Fishl had not taken, who would have had the stones instead? No, dirty gold and stolen gems had helped him take her into a home, make a warm place for Chaim. Now it could help him find his own. He still had a number of silver bracelets to leave with her, along with the money he had saved from trading.

He fingered his parents' pictures in their brown envelope. If he should find Hinda—he dared not think it even—if he should find her, he would show her what he had preserved—no, he would not think it.

He should tell Fela about the stones. He should give them to her for safekeeping. But even as the thought moved through his head, he wrapped his parents' pictures in a paper and slipped them inside the velvet pouch of diamonds.

I will carry them both, he thought.

Quarantine

IN THE LITTLE MOUNTAIN cabin a child began to cry. After some minutes another child began to shout at him, and then another. Be quiet, stop this sniffling and weeping, let us sleep, let us sleep. Chaim got up from his cot. He really was too old to be with this group, but the counselors had taken him on the youth trip, thinking he could help keep watch.

Yosl, he said. Yossele.

The boy turned away from him, coughing through his tears.

Yosl, come with me outside. You will feel better.

Yosl continued his weeping, trying to muffle the sound with a blanket.

Go! Go! shouted another child. Just go out and let us be! Give us peace for a moment! Another boy laughed.

At last Yosl got up and followed Chaim out. The night was not too cool. Chaim stood straight, took in a breath, and exhaled.

This is mountain air, he said. I never had it before. Did you?

Yosl said nothing, then wiped his nose with his hands. The crying had stopped.

Do you need to take a piss? Chaim said. Go. I'll make sure no one comes along.

Yosl trotted a few steps, then turned around and looked back, tears welling up again.

I'm right here, said Chaim. I won't let anything happen. Then he hated himself for saying it. But they were safe here, the two married counselors asleep with the three girls in a cabin a few feet away, the American soldiers' base a few kilometers distant in the Bremen zone. They would hike back in the morning after eating bread and cheese, return to Belsen by early evening, in time for a meal.

I'm right here, repeated Chaim. If I hear something I'll come to you right away. If you hear something, just cough, don't shout. I'll come.

Yosl returned calmer.

See? said Chaim. Sometimes that's all you need.

The child was quiet after they returned to their cots. But now Chaim could not sleep. His belly had stiffened in the moments outside, and he felt a needle at his abdomen, poking and sewing, bunching his insides together. On his back, he took in a deep breath, then let it out. A little better. But still the sewing continued. He was no longer hungry at every moment, but the sight of food, sometimes even the memory of it, aroused in him something painful, a stabbing he felt in his abdomen when he passed by a line of refugees waiting for soup, or at night when he awoke from a dream of bread. He renewed his food coupons every week and watched the soldiers mark off his name on lists for sugar, flour, salt. Watching them made him feel relieved. If he had not yet eaten his share, the marks let him know that he would receive. It was after eating, just before sleeping, that the fear, worse than hunger, began to thrash at him, a small animal scratching at his insides, struggling to get out.

He moved his knees to his belly, stretched his legs again. A little better. He thought of the face of the woman counselor, her skin brown and healthy from her life in Palestine, her walk confident and poised. Her legs, bare underneath a narrow skirt or lightly covered in blue trousers, were slim, not skinny, but athletic and lean. The couple had come from their kibbutz to volunteer among the refugees—the displaced persons, as the soldiers now called them—to prepare the lot of them for a life in the promised land, their true home, the place to transform themselves from diaspora victims, shamed and hungry, into masters of their own destiny. It was the woman counselor who said those words. Her husband spoke Yiddish only haltingly and no Polish at all. He had some fluency in Hungarian but addressed the children in Hebrew and depended on his wife and Chaim to translate the pains and fears of the little ones into simple language he could understand.

WHEN CHAIM RETURNED FROM the trip the counselors recommended him to work as an aide in the school the camp was building. Not like the others, the woman counselor said. A boy who looked to the future. The Polish boys did not like the sound of children crying, they could not tolerate it—but Chaim was very calm. Perhaps in two weeks he could begin, when they were ready for him. He could take his classes in the evening, play with the children in the morning.

Like a night watch, but in the day, Chaim said.

The woman counselor stared at him. He had said something odd and shameful, and wished he could take back his words and swallow them. He wanted to say, I was only joking, but already she was answering him.

Yes, I suppose you could say that.

The British authorities gave him a new identity card when he changed jobs. Chaim Traum. He looked at his name in its clean typed letters and thought: new, new. He rolled the English words around his tongue. "Displaced Person," he said. "Di Pi. D P."

The camp had changed since he and Pavel had first received their documents and food cards. The barracks were new, rebuilt, each with a clean entrance, and some had gardens in the back where refugees tended vegetables and trimmed mint weeds. Inside, Chaim knew, the bodies were still crowded in and stifled, the latrine buildings spilling with overuse. But some of the more settled refugees had their own apartments inside the camp, their own new families. When they stamped his new card, a man and a woman stood behind him with a newborn. He had turned to look at it, and reached out to touch it in its gray blanket, but the mother had pulled her arms back and drawn the child in closer to her chest, then murmured something softly at Chaim.

He did not hear her words. More than once a man in the print shop had shouted at him, What is wrong with you? You hear like an old man! It was true. Often he got up to leave his workstation because the thickness in his hearing so distracted him; he felt his head to be muffled, wrapped in a blanket that blocked out the noise but also warmed him. It was true; he heard like an old man, in fits, the result, he feared, of a long-ago blow to the side of the head that even now on occasion made him sense a ribbon of pain, the ghost of a bruise, moving through his skull just before he fell asleep. He should be brave and go to the camp doctor. He should be brave.

Eventually he did make his way into the line of sick people and new arrivals at the clinic. The nurses and doctors themselves were clean and quick. He whispered his complaint in his rehearsed English to a broad redheaded woman.

"I do not hear," he whispered. The words seemed loud inside his mouth, but he knew he spoke softly. "Hitted in head."

The nurse narrowed her eyes, then pulled him toward her and looked inside one ear, then the other. Then she laughed.

"Nothing a good cleaning won't fix, my dear!" She grabbed a bright metal instrument and tilted his head toward her breast, the better to scoop out the wax and dirt.

He walked out of the clinic with a soreness at his ears and temples, but within a day he heard more clearly. The world did more than become louder; it changed. Fine noises were easier to pick up, and ordinary speech seemed suddenly sharp and blared, as if the background buzzing had been cleared from a wartime radio broadcast. In the house he could hear the soft rasping under Fela's words; he could make out the clucks Pavel made under his breath as he played cards. In the last week of his work at the print shop the noises of the ink machines chugged in an even rhythm, a low drumbeat to the tune his workmate hummed to himself.

He came to the school with a songbook of freshly printed Yiddish tunes.

HE WATCHED HIMSELF AND his reactions around the children when they played roughly or became upset. A child's cry could scratch at him, a table knife scraping a half-closed wound. But he pushed his discomfort down. It was possible, he thought, that the infirmary had taken too much out of him. Had they removed a barrier that had helped him to walk around in some sort of peace? But nothing showed. Sala, the classroom teacher, patted his shoulder. You have a way, she said.

It was true, the children liked him. They spoke to him in Polish when they did not want the teachers from Germany and Palestine to understand and in Yiddish when they did not want the soldiers from Britain and America to understand. Others in the camp looked at the little ones as foreigners, to be feared. He could see in the camp streets a refugee take in his breath as the orphan beside him stumbled and cried out in pain. He accompanied a child who had fallen to the infirmary; a bone from her elbow pushing up, almost ready, Chaim thought, to poke through the skin. She had whimpered as he carried her there, but broke into full wails as she saw the lines of gray adults lifting their arms to be sprayed with disinfectant. Even in the weeks since he had had his ears cleaned the clinic had become cleaner, whiter. He looked at the floor, its new bright tile.

Tell her to stop! Chaim heard from the line. A man's voice, high, increasingly desperate. Tell her to stop! Stop! Tell her to stop!

Ssh, he said to the little girl. Ssh.

It was a warm day, and the clinic was full. He could hear shouting in English, not angry, just the nurses trying to make the refugees understand by speaking louder. Usually there were more Jews at the clinic; it was said the lead doctor was a refugee herself. But there was a protest in the camp center today, and perhaps the translators and aides had disappeared for the afternoon to attend it, or just to rest, just as Chaim liked to disappear and rest.

La la la, he whispered to the child in his arms.

She tried to become more soft. Still the tears and coughing and sniffling continued. The man behind them muttered and cursed. But Chaim pulled his belly in, breathed out. He concentrated his hearing on the specific tones of the crying. Yes, one could hear the difference between a child weeping over a twisted arm and the screaming from before. These cries were everyday cries, temporary griefs, the kind of casual suffering that occurred in a houseful of family.

He could protect her, even for an afternoon, while waiting in the line at the clinic. He could watch over her. He hummed a short tune in the little girl's ear.

IN THE LINE WITH her father, Sima did not cry. She heard the whimpering and the sniffling, but she herself was silent. She stood still, waiting, hearing the crying child, staring at the uniforms of the men at the sides of the clinic, the men who kept order in their green and brown clothing. They did not shout or push; she could not even see guns. These men were different, they help us, her father said, they were different from the Germans and Russians, different from the' Poles in their stone-colored uniforms who caused her father to draw in his breath. No, these men were different, British. It seemed they did not quite command the clinic; they puttered about, got up and sat down when the nurses called them, not when they themselves desired to move. Still, you could not let a soldier see you afraid, her mother always said. It brought out something ugly. What was the ugly thing? Sima had wondered, imagining mud and blood. She held herself upright, one hand in her father's, who did not seem to notice the noise.

A child is crying, she whispered.

Her father did not answer. Perhaps he was afraid. He was frequently afraid, he said. She looked over at her mother. Her mother was not afraid. Her mother was sick. She leaned on Sima's father, her face alternately flushed and pale, her breath warm and labored. She looked as if she were concentrating, perhaps trying to understand the shouts of the soldiers, perhaps just trying to remain cool in the crowded waiting area. Sima's father was perspiring and craning his neck around the line, trying to see where they led the families ahead of them, whether they were separated for the examinations required of every new arrival to the camp.

The child's crying became more distant; it had been led away. And then a soldier's hand pointed toward them and drew back: their turn. They moved behind a curtained area. But the soldier's arms kept moving, and he spoke, gesturing, pointing at her and her mother. He was telling Sima to go with her mother.

Sima's mother began answering in Polish. No, no, she should stay with her father. Just for now. I'm not feeling so well. Then she repeated it in Yiddish.

The soldier did not understand. He gave a gentle push to Sima's shoulders, trying to move her toward her mother. But Sima stood still, made herself heavy, kept her hand in the fast grip of her father.

The soldier threw up his arms. "Henrietta!" he called. But no one came.

He began talking in long streams, his voice strained and insistent, a false calm. He was working hard to be kind, Sima could see that. Her parents could see that too, she observed, both nodding with nervous smiles. Again the soldier made a movement, gesturing with a smile that she move away from her father. But Sima did not move. She was not to breathe her mother's air. She was to be healthy and strong, at least enough to enroll in the camp school as soon as all this with the medical exams and the food coupons was sorted out, the school which Sima's mother had heard was led by Jewish teachers and Hebrew tutors. Sima was almost seven; she had to be strong.

"Jesus," the soldier said. A familiar word! It made Sima want to laugh in recognition, but she stopped herself. The soldier tapped his knuckles to his temples and his face turned a bit pink. She would be quiet.

Finally he seemed to give up. A second soldier, who had been glancing over at them as they stood still, refusing to separate, rolled his eyes at his companion. He said something low, and the first one chuckled, shaking his head. Sima's mother threw her father a wink: they had triumphed. All together, a threesome, they shuffled to a corner of the room, behind a gray curtain that hung from hooks in the ceiling. A short redheaded woman stood by a table behind the curtain, writing something in a notebook. She raised her eyebrows at the soldier as he brought the three of them in, then sighed.

Sima's mother sat down on the cot without waiting to be asked. The nurse approached Sima's face, peering into her eyes and mouth with a tiny light, unbuttoning the top three buttons of her blouse, pressing on her chest with a metal instrument that hung round her neck and felt cold to the skin. Then a thin glass tube, painted with tiny numbers, to place under her tongue. Sima looked at her father. Perhaps she looked like him, a cigarette sticking out of his mouth, warding off hunger.

The nurse slid instruments in and out of a metal case, talking, motioning. It seemed she was explaining: Sima had met the requirements, and her father too. Sima's mother, resting on the cot, had been left for last, almost invisible as the nurse spoke in her incomprehensible patter.

Finally the nurse pulled the metal necklace onto her ears again, placed one shining end on Sima's mother's pale, blue-veined chest.

The nurse frowned. She took out the glass tube and pushed it between Sima's mother's lips, waited, then shook it out. She motioned for Sima and her father to wait outside the curtained area: this time they stepped out without protest. She called out something in English—a name, it seemed, for a man with his own metal necklace appeared, and together they began to speak in a low murmur behind the curtain while Sima and her father waited outside. Sima touched her hand to her chest. Her skin still felt cool from the touch of the metal.

At last they poked their heads out. Then they stepped out fully and drew the curtain behind them, Sima's mother still inside.

"Quarantine," said the man.

"Quarantine," agreed the nurse. Sima's father looked at them, puzzled, shaking his head gently. They repeated it again and again, motioning with their hands, other words blurring into the main one until it became a singsong. "Quarantine, quarantine."

The man jerked open the curtain. Sima's mother was lying down, her face smooth and glistening. The man stomped over to the wooden table where he had the glass tube. He pointed at a number on the tube to Sima's father. He made harsh, exaggerated gasps, then pointed to Sima's mother, who smiled encouragingly at her daughter.

"Kann ist gutt," he said. No good. German words spoken by someone new to the tongue. They came out thick, halting. Then he went

back to the other word. "Quarantine," he said. "Quarantine, *mutter,* quarantine."

"Karutina," Sima's father tried to repeat after the soldiers. He said it slowly, breaking the word up into small parts. Ka. Ruh. Ti. Na.

He said it again. And then Sima felt her father's hand grip hers tightly and suddenly loosen. "Ah," he said, almost pleased, Sima thought, with the clarity that suddenly presented itself. But then he pulled out a handkerchief from his pocket, wiped his forehead and neck. He looked at Sima's mother, who struggled to sit up, still not understanding.

"*Kwarantanna,*" he announced. They want to keep you here. Not for long, he continued, though beyond the one word that had miraculously translated itself into Polish, Sima knew he had no sense of what they were saying. Not for long.

Quarantine, thought Sima. My mother has quarantine.

She knew quarantine. There had been quarantine in Russia, in Siberia, the first place to which they had been deported. Typhoid. The deportees had spread it among themselves in the work camps, in the fields, in the factories. Sima's father had worked as a night watchman in the hospital, and after his arrest for theft Sima's mother had taken his place. There was a quarantine ward for the people who did not die first in their huts, who were kept in a spacious, rotting hallway of the hospital, where even the local doctor was afraid to stay for long. Quarantine was like prison: no one watching, just the hard labor of staying alive. You were left to die or to escape. From prison, Sima's father had escaped. Sima's mother had too, later, when it had been her turn to be arrested.

Now, with the nurse chattering on to her father, Sima looked at her mother, waiting for her to explain her way out, charm the man with the white coat, or fall to the floor begging, or show them they had made a mistake, she had no fever at all. But her mother said nothing.

Sima's father spoke. Dvora, do not worry. Simale will be in school tomorrow. When you get out, she'll already be teaching you, you'll see.

Sima moved her hand from side to side. A wave. No words, no sounds. Quiet, stay quiet. It would upset her mother to see her cry. You could not let them see you afraid.

BEREL MAKOWER WRAPPED HIS hand around his daughter's as they walked into daylight. He was tired. The sheet he had hung to protect his and Sima's corner had not blocked out the noise and mutterings of the others, who dreamed loudly and shook the wooden bed frames in their sleep. It was mostly a barracks for families, though it appeared there were some women alone as well, their hair painfully neat, freshly combed even at night, their faces smooth but gray.

Near the main office swollen refugees bustled to and fro. After one night, Berel knew the bustling ones were like him, recently returned, only beginning to understand that the rumors they had heard in Russia, the propaganda, had been true. It was the men and women inside the barracks, who slept or stared in the day and who hardly spoke, so listless they could not even be angry, waiting, waiting for nothing. After months in the DP camp, their bodies had recovered from the torments they had lived through. They were the reverse of spirits, Berel thought, just bodies, clothed, more or less clean, not so hungry, but empty.

He would have to keep the atmosphere from invading him. Register for school, register for work, register for visas. There were lists for all kinds of things here: for food, for clothing, for a better dwelling, for orchestra tickets. Orchestra tickets! Someone had told him in the barracks at night—the Jews had built a theater for plays and concerts, for music to keep the grief out—no, not the grief, but the heaviness, the dark blanket that kept even healthy ones in bed, at windows, alone on benches watching the slow entry of new arrivals.

Berel had a momentum, one that started on the train from Poland to Germany, that moved even when the tracks stopped, that kept going inside him. Himself, his wife, and his daughter, all traveling—by choice! what a joke—to the country of the enemy, now transformed into a sanctuary from Poland, where Jews who returned to their hometowns were being murdered by their old neighbors. He had a momentum, one that had sprung up after the rainy week they had spent in Przemysl, venturing into the tiny storefront that served now as the Jewish center, a center that was only temporary, a committee that existed only to tell the repatriated to leave again. For safety, the small, clean-shaven man at the center had urged. For family. He himself was getting ready to flee. There was no use in staying to look. And trying to take back family property or business now occupied by Poles was to invite an assault. In Germany, the man at the center said, they might still find someone. They might still find.

Berel had a momentum. He had a wife and a daughter to care for and protect. He had an obligation to make good on a promise—put Sima in school!—to Dvora, who, for all those years in Russian exile, had kept the three of them alive with her rage and efficiency, her insistence on sweeping the dirt floors of the huts they had slept in, her desperate and frequently victorious battle against her own hunger and fear. She could steal as if she were the eldest daughter of a skilled criminal, not a modest store owner.

His own record as a thief was unaccomplished. It was a joke to his wife and daughter, his fear. He would come back to their hut from a day in the mill in Osh and take off his shoes, empty them into a metal cup, slowly, so as not to lose a grain in the cloud puffing up from the table. It would take a week of stealing to make even a small loaf. Sometimes his fear made him laugh too.

But there would be no more theft. Or less theft—already he had heard that a black market thrived here too, just outside the confines of the camp, where starving German townspeople traded their family china, elegant clothing, for a pound of the refugees' Red Cross coffee.

But Berel was not ready to start with the trading. He needed work, real work, in order to give his daughter the sense that she lived with a father, a man, that all three of them were full, flesh-and-blood bodies, not just shadows who stole and traded and lied for their food.

In the main office Berel showed the identity cards he and Sima had been issued on their entry to the camp. There was a blank square for photographs of himself and his daughter, photographs that had been taken the day before and were ready to be glued in today, their first day as displaced persons.

Now it's official, Berel said, looking at his daughter. We have no-where to go.

But you do, said the man stamping their papers, mounting the cards into a dark holder. You have the kitchen—he pointed—and em-ployment. You must have work. Even when you first arrive. Believe me, I didn't rest from the moment I came, and it helps, you see? I have a good position. You can't let yourself rest here, if you rest, you think. You'll find a job easily, you will, my friend. There's plenty. You must have work.

And school. Sima's voice broke through the sound of men, a bird sound.

The man looked at her as if he hadn't seen her before, as if he had not been busy slipping her photograph onto a white page that held her name, Sima Makower, as if her voice was what made her real. His eyes, Berel saw, were suddenly glassy. A young lady speaking Yiddish, the man said. What a pleasure. Berel thought he heard a shake in the voice, a small tremble.

But the man went on. You must have been east, yes?

Yes, said Berel. From Poland to Bialystok, of course just at the beginning, and Siberia, and then Uz—

Yes, yes, said the man. It's only the people from the East who came back with children. And not so many of them, and of those, not so young, like this little one. Yes, *maidele*?

Sima's hand was a fist in Berel's palm. My wife insisted there is a school here, Berel intervened, almost apologizing. That's why my daughter asks.

Ah, said the man, but there is!

Sima giggled.

Another beautiful sound, said the man. The *maidele* laughing. But listen, my friend, not yet. He gave Berel a pointed look. If you bring her with you to look for jobs—poor motherless one—they will try not to give you manual labor.

It was true. Everywhere they went—the food line, the clothing room, the newspaper office with its lists of the living—workers of the camp looked at Sima as if she were a still photograph from a movie, a movie whose name was now forgotten but whose faces were familiar, adored. There were other children, to be sure—Berel had seen one or two young teenagers doling out food packages—but the sight of a small one, attached to her father—in fact the man who had issued their identity cards was right about the manual labor. Berel had been prepared to talk about his carpentry skills, his facility with lumber, but there was no need. Sima kept herself quiet—no mention of her sick mother—and Berel was given an assignment to do bookkeeping.

Report on time! said the managing clerk. Believe me, if you are late, twelve others will be ready to relieve you.

I would like to enroll Simale in the school, said Berel. Will I have time in the morning, early?

Come here at eight in the morning, said the man. You can take a break in the afternoon, and enroll her then. You have a daughter to support, a little lamb to protect, but I simply cannot hold the job for a newcomer if you are late.

Berel walked out of the clerk's office elated. Office work!

Let's go tell your mama, let's leave her a message, said Berel. She'll be happy to hear from us. Even if all we do is tell her by note that we are all right.

She's moving tomorrow, said a nurse at the entrance of the infirmary. You will be able to visit. You, but not the child, understand?

Berel nodded. By tomorrow he would be working at a desk, moving his pencil across dark ledgers, perhaps even feeling the need for a pair of glasses—he hoped not, of course—reporting the influx and distribution of shoes, skirts, hats, underthings. Sima herself would be at a desk, socializing with other young ones, writing in her own notebooks, making drawings, learning to sew. He would be able to tell Dvora: Today we made a start on a new life.

But tomorrow came and again they waited at the accounting office, Sima at his hip, until finally the man in charge of showing him to his place informed him the director was absent, on a trip to the American zone, something very important, Berel must understand, he would have to come back tomorrow. Yes, of course the job would be waiting, just be sure to be here in the morning, early. The managing accountant hated tardiness. And what a lovely daughter Berel had, little lamb. Berel should be sure to enroll her in the school, even if now it was perhaps too late, the children away on their afternoon games.

Berel decided they would visit Dvora after eating, so as not to look hungry when they arrived in the hospital. He wanted to appear before her with a look of energy and life.

Sima, Berel said as they entered the infirmary building, can you stay here and wait for me?

No, said Sima. I'll come with you. How will you find her without me?

I'll find her, said Berel. It's not so hard.

I'll come with you, she said.

If it was me in the hospital, you'd let your mother go, said Berel. You would know she could find me.

That's different, said Sima.

It's not for children, said a woman at the table for visitors. A woman who spoke Yiddish. Believe me, there is no use in trying to convince me.

You see? Berel said to Sima. There's nothing I can do.

He was given a mask to put over his mouth, and led by a nurse through a door and up a narrow staircase. He could see Dvora waiting for him on her cot, in a broad room surrounded by perhaps a dozen feverish women. Some of the cots were empty.

She had been much sicker when she entered the camp. But in the daylight pushing in from the window, she looked different. Her skin was bruised and spotted from malnutrition. He had seen the marks, he had seen her discolored body, but he had not noticed as he did now, when she was surrounded by other women, pale women, perhaps sicker women, but none with the same scattering of bluish stains. He himself was drawn, thin, continually hungry, he knew, his skin pale, but Dvora—had she looked so weak only two days before?

He sat by her bed, in a thin metal chair. She did not allow him to touch her.

Where is Sima? she asked.

Berel began. He smiled. School has started, he said. He felt his voice filling, projecting news of Sima like a radio giving out propaganda. Sima loves it. The games, the books. There's even a little garden for them to play in—Berel's image of it grew more lush—where they learn how to plant, and water, and dig. And listen, Dvora—he paused for a bit of drama—she's not so behind after all. Maybe in arithmetic, but she reads just as well as the others.

Through her fever Dvora beamed.

There's a music class! Berel exclaimed. I almost forgot.

Look! she said, voice tingling with pride. Look! She stretched her arm underneath her cot. Her hand emerged with a long bar of chocolate, a piece of bread, a half stick of butter. Look, Berel. They give us so much here. Take it. Sima is so thin and small. She must catch up.

She needs food for the mind, now, not just the body. Dvora laughed.

She was giving it to him as well as to her daughter, Berel thought. She let him keep his pride.

Dvora, he said, they give us enough—this is for—

She made a face. I hear what they give you, she said. The women say. Porridge, and bread, and coffee that looks like dirty water.

Berel shook his head.

We get eggs here! They cook us eggs. So here. Until you have better.

For a moment Berel thought he should not tell Dvora about his job; he didn't have it yet, it was not yet sure, and perhaps it was bad luck to announce something he might have to recant later. But it was too tempting. While she fed him from her little prison, her little rest from the struggle of the world, he was getting on with life. He was learning to live: work, school, sleep. She was still expending her strength to survive. When he told her she looked relieved, glad at his competence, happy for him, happy that he was again becoming a man.

He came downstairs to the same chair in which he had dropped his daughter. She was sleepy, but too heavy to carry, and he wanted her to walk outside with him, to see. Here was the land that Jews made. An ugly land, to be sure, ugly and deformed, filled with military props, watched over by British, but something they had made. Not the promised land, where, as he used to say to Sima, oranges were more plentiful than potatoes, and Sima's eyes would widen in temptation, but still a land Jews had made. Work, school, orchestra, news, even a little government.

He was not a pious man, but he wanted to go to a service, to sing a little. He still knew how to sing.

Sima, he said. Your mother gave us a bit of chocolate.

Should we save it? said Sima.

I suppose. Berel sighed.

THE BREAKFAST LINE TOOK longer than he had expected—some kind of argument several families ahead of them—and Berel and Sima found themselves trotting to the school building to make it in time.

The schoolroom startled him. Only a day before, he had not believed that there could be a school for the refugees on German soil. But once he knew it existed, the dream of it expanded to something luxurious, something even he had not had as a child growing up in his town of one-room schoolhouses. He had thought: a garden, and a music room, and perhaps even an area for reading, where children could stay quietly. But instead he saw one room carved out of office space in a barracks, where perhaps forty bony-faced children of all ages sat in metal chairs, writing on tables spread between them, sharing books. One or two faces turned to look at them. They had entered the classroom a few minutes late, and the teacher, writing Hebrew letters on a blackboard, was calling out words for the children to repeat.

An aide to a teacher, a young man, perhaps fourteen, came over to introduce himself.

Chaim, he said.

Sima said nothing.

This is Sima, said Berel. Sima Makower. Now, Simale, go.

Sima didn't move. Berel crouched down. Go, Sima.

Come, Sima, said Chaim. He held out his arms.

Sima shrank into Berel's chest.

Please, said Berel. But he could feel her shaking, and through his shirt the first drippings of tears soaked through to his skin.

Chaim said, When she's ready. He moved to a table where another child was writing.

Sima's silent tears gave way to muffled sobs. No, *Tatteh*, no. Don't leave me.

He put on his stern face. Sima. Behave. School is for ladies, not babies.

But she was sobbing fully now. Don't leave me, don't leave me.

The young man trotted back to them. You must not cry, he said in Yiddish, a look of anxiety on his face. It upsets the children to hear crying. It scares them.

Indeed, a child near them had her hand in her ear, and another glared at the back of Sima's head. What was Berel to do? If he was late, even twenty minutes late, someone else would step in to take his job, and he would be directed away again, back to the central office for other work, manual work. The process would begin again, the search, the fatigue, the lines for soup that barely filled him, the cramped cots behind the family sheet. They would remain in the barracks, unable to afford or even make connections for a private dwelling, a washroom and toilet, a little table to read and play cards. This was how people gave up their future. This was how people became the stopped bodies in the barracks. To stay here until she stopped crying—it was impossible. Dvora would know how to tell her to stop. Dvora would know how to feel the harshness, express the desperation. Now, all of a sudden, he just knew how to act it.

Sima, he said, whispering in her ear as he pulled her outside the classroom door. Think of your mother. How disappointed she would be.

Sima bawled harder. Quarantine! she wept. My mama has quarantine!

At one time it had shocked him, Sima's ability to keep silent at moments of danger. One night five years ago they had crept across an icy river into Bialystok, along with dozens of other families, and the memory of the quiet, even the smallest child perfectly silent, still haunted him. What a knowledge for a two-year-old to have! He and Dvora had done their best to protect her, but now, in the face of Sima's wails, he thought perhaps they had protected too much, keeping her locked inside their crumbling dwellings while they did their night work, blanketing her with their bodies as she slept, watching her every move if she wandered out to meet other exiles in the villages. She had been kept in a bright isolation, like a sickly child he had known as a boy.

Just for a moment, I'll wait, said Berel. But only a moment. You must study.

Sima looked at him, the tears streaming.

All right? But only a moment!

She quieted herself and moved into a small chair. Every few minutes she would look over at him to see that he remained. But by noontime he could see her attention was on the teacher, who drew letters on the board in Hebrew for the children to copy. Sima would be all right. Berel could leave without a fuss.

But he did not. He watched Sima etching letters, slowly, much more slowly than the others, and he watched her imitate the older boy at the desk next to her as he rubbed an eraser across his page and blew the dust from the eraser away. He watched her tap her thumb against her finger as she listened to the other students sing a song in Yiddish, a song he himself did not know. All morning and all afternoon Berel sat in his rickety chair, not getting up to eat or to drink, watching his daughter, her first day of school.

The Concert

CHAIM LEARNED HEBREW JUST as Pavel would have wished
him to: without struggle. He showed off his facility to Pavel
every Sunday evening. The letters he already had from Yiddish, and the grammar was so simple, so clear, that it seemed to
Chaim he had always almost spoken it, like a precise version of the
speech babies made. He was preparing to read for the Sabbath service
of his bar mitzvah, and he studied the whole portion, even beyond the
verses he would sing, the story of Lot's wife, the mother transformed
to a pillar of salt from looking back at her city, her home, her neighbors on fire.

He had heard the story in his childhood, but as an adult—already
fourteen, he had lied to make himself younger to Pavel, bewildering
himself even as the lie fell out of his mouth; he had no reason to lie
now, and yet any truth, no matter how innocent, still seemed dangerous to reveal—as an adult he read parts he had not remembered

from before, the panic of Lot to save himself, the family's sins after the destruction, the unnamed wife, mourned not at all. If there was someone to be punished, it should be Lot, who offered his daughters in sacrifice to the savage townsmen. It was unjust that he was to be saved, along with the daughters he would not protect. Abraham had spoken out for Lot. Why could not Lot speak out for his wife?

Because that's the story, explained Pavel, fingers tapping the kitchen table. The story is she looked, and became salt.

It is not right. Chaim looked at Pavel's puzzled eyes.

She disobeyed! said Pavel. God said not to look back!

Chaim turned his gaze to his reading, the worn gray pages. The books the charities sent from America were in poor condition, the bindings unraveled, the paper thick, sometimes crumbling. Pavel, returned from his travel to the American zone without having found his sister, had brought back to Celle a satchel of books.

It's not for us to argue with the story! It is a portion, it is important, a lesson.

I don't understand the lesson.

She wasn't lucky, but also she disobeyed. She risked and she lost. But the important thing is that she looked and became salt. The others, the husband and the daughters, they obeyed and they escaped.

Chaim rubbed his fingers on the sides of his face, feeling his skin. Smooth, mostly hairless, soft. There was a darkness inside him, a well of mud and dirt, but he kept himself clean with the milled white soap Pavel brought for Fela.

Enough for today, Pan Pavel?

Yes, said Pavel, suddenly absent. Yes, all right. And stop this Pan, Pan. I'm not old enough for Pan.

You're the elder of the house.

I am thirty, said Pavel.

⁓

Perhaps she had turned and looked back with a purpose. Like a suicide. Chaim had known cases himself. In the ghetto, a man had jumped from a window in a nearby apartment. Such things were reported more than a few times. There had been talk of poisonings, here and there. People who could not bear to look into a future without the home they had always known, the neighbors and the families, school, work, gardens. People who could not bear to look only forward and so looked back. To look back was to turn into a tall mound of nothing but grief, dry grief. Not a punishment but a natural consequence. She turned into salt because those who looked back turned into salt. Not a punishment. A fact.

He continued to attend an English class. Useful to know, even if America was not a possibility for him. Adults as well as the younger ones sat nodding and repeating after the teacher, a well-educated, large-eyed girl from the south of Germany, a tall one with soft, chocolate-colored hair and a crippled hand. She wanted to go to America too, Chaim had heard, but would not be let in because of the hand, rumored to have been mutilated in camp experiments. Chaim loved the way her words sounded, long and flowing, slow, not clipped and fast like the words of the English soldiers.

Her friend came into the class every few days. Her lover? The students, young and old both, wondered aloud. He was a bit older than she, and also very cultured, a music teacher from Vienna. He would listen to her from the back until she ended the class. She would fold her papers into her satchel and walk slowly, elegantly, to greet him at the doorway. On days the friend came in, Chaim would put his notebooks in his own satchel with care, to prolong the time he could watch Tina and Leo greeting each other. Leo would take Tina's crippled hand in his every time, and she would pull her hand away from him every time. Then he would place his hands in his pockets, and she would slip her arm through his elbow, her withered fingers hanging downward.

One day Leo came in earlier, in the middle of class. Tina looked up. He was accompanied by a child, a plump and surly little girl, perhaps ten years old.

"My friends," said Leo, in English, "we have a performance to give." The students looked up at him, uncomprehending.

They haven't learned those words in English, Leo. Tina addressed the group in German. A little concert, she said. Almost. An English song?

American, said Leo.

The girl moved in front of Tina's desk. She peered out from a hood of dark eyebrows at the gray teenagers and thin adults sitting at the long tables and began to sing.

"Heaven, I'm in heaven." Her voice was clear and confident, her sound oddly deep, almost a woman's. She took a breath, "And my ha-ht beats so that I can ha-ha speak."

Leo! said Tina.

Sssh! Don't distract her! whispered Leo in German.

But the girl had lost track of the words. Still she continued to sing the melody: "Dee dee dee dee da da da da dee dee da da"—her voice climbing, but steady, then another quick breath, during which Chaim thought he could hear someone giggling—"Dee dee da together da da cheek to cheek."

The words came back, or at least they were sounds divisible like words, Chaim couldn't be sure. She went through another verse, steadier, unsmiling, her voice controlled, a strange confidence for so small a child, a confidence no doubt instilled by the approval, the genuine seriousness, with which her teacher Leo treated her. Even Tina, her embarrassment somewhat quelled, looked at her with interest.

The child finished.

Bravo, said an adult in the back of the room.

Bravo, agreed Chaim. A few of the students began to clap. The little girl's mouth moved upward for a moment, a grimace of acknowledgment, not quite a smile. Then she turned away to stand by the door.

You are terrible, Leo, muttered Tina. Terrible! Silly! In front of my students!

But she was laughing a little. Leo thrust his chin forward and bowed to the class.

"Thank you, my friends," he said, "for your attention."

Someone clapped again.

He continued in German, Basia and I will take our leave and let you continue with your very serious teacher.

But Leo too was serious. He may have been playing, flirting with Tina, but also he wanted the class to be impressed with a talented child. And Chaim was impressed, not just by the little girl's nerve but also by the admiration she elicited. Chaim observed Tina's pale lips as she tried to bring the class back to its regular lesson, the past tenses of *come* and *go*, *have* and *be*. He didn't have all the words of the song divided out in his head, but he thought he understood the main theme of it, a man who felt himself in paradise with his lover. It was a lovely idea, that touching another person, another human, was what it felt to be in the presence of God. He liked the thought, and as he watched Tina, her face straight and calm, a mask, he thought that she too must like it. They had something in common.

TINA, TINA, TINA, SAID PAVEL.

Chaim felt his face grow hot.

Why don't you ask this Tina? continued Pavel. Let your teachers come, let them see what we have taught you.

TINA BROUGHT LEO. IN the Roundhouse, the domed building of the
camp where the committee of Jews met, the room used as a chapel
held a real crowd, linked, uneven, jagged. People binding themselves
to one another, humming to themselves, groaning through the memorial prayer. Chaim looked out at Pavel. Pavel looked solemn, a hard line
on his face to mark the seriousness of the occasion. And on the other
side of the aisle, there was Fela in a dress of dark red, and Rayzele,
who had helped carry the food to the Roundhouse that morning. A
wind of bitterness swept though Chaim—these were strangers, all of
them, even Rayzele, with her newly fierce gaze, strangers performing
rituals his father had neglected and his grandparents had wept over.
He wanted to paint over the images in the crowd with pictures of his
loved ones, but his imagination was stubborn, refused to do its work,
took in only the haggard young faces of the living congregants, the
pale smile of Fela, barley waves of hair framing her slim eyebrows, the
long chin of Pavel, jutting with ownership and pride.

He began his portion.

BUT WHAT BURNED MOST brightly in Chaim was after, when Leo
spoke about him to Pavel.

Such a lovely voice your Chaim has, said Leo. Very musical.

Only one mistake! said Pavel, sending Chaim a wink: there had
been at least two.

I mean what I say, said Leo. At another time, he really could have
made something of it.

His rib cage tight with pride, Chaim managed to say: Like the
singer Basia, no?

Not exactly like her, answered Leo, no, that's something different, and she is young enough, of course, but still, you are a very fine boy, one who can appreciate, who should be exposed—

Later Leo took him aside. My friend, I have been planning a little journey.

Chaim breathed in, expectant, lips pressed together, keeping in the air.

We—myself and Tina, you know—we had a plan to go to a concert in Hamburg. We were to take a couple of children. Basia, of course, will join us. And I thought you too would be interested.

A nervous laugh burst out of Chaim's mouth. His face felt unnaturally warm, feverish.

Yes, I thought you would like it. Here—Leo handed Chaim a scrap of paper, an advertisement from the newspaper of the town, not the camp. It is the Mozart *Requiem*, next Saturday evening. We'll take a car in the morning to Hamburg and stay overnight.

The rest of the morning passed in a wine haze, Chaim sipping freely from a silver cup Pavel had given him as a gift, chewing happily on berry strudels and apple cake, rushing up to kiss Fela, who stood quietly behind the little table of pastries, carefully unloading.

You are pink! laughed Fela.

Pink, yes! answered Chaim. Pink and red! Gold and silver! He was giddy, he felt himself spilling out of his skin, the tune to his haftorah portion, Isaiah's portion, spinning around and around in his brain. He wanted to keep his news to himself, hold it in, his reward, the small thing that would begin to compensate him for what he had lost. A concert.

THERE HAD BEEN OPPORTUNITY in the ghetto for him to hear a concert—the ghetto orchestra had performed once or twice for free— and when it came time to applaud he had dropped his hands so as better to hear the clapping of the crowd. He loved the sound of it, a huge number of hands improvising together to make their collective percussion. When the rain came through the trees in the forest, he had sometimes thought he could hear applause, the slow building of leaves against one another, a sudden crescendo for the little bow of the soloist, a dying down again until the listeners remembered their hunger and returned to their quarters.

He looked at his hands. A child such as the little singer Basia would clap her hands together, flat. It made more noise, but it would tire the hand out. He had seen someone make the shape of an S with their two hands, bending one hand at the knuckles, pushing the fingers of the other against the first palm. It was a sophisticated clap, softer but less tiring, one that belonged to adults. One, surely, that Tina and Leo would use when the conductor finished and turned to face the German audience.

They would be the only Jews there, no doubt. Well, let this audience see how a refugee appreciated the music of dead Germans.

LEO OBTAINED A SCORE and copied out the lyrics of the requiem in Latin, with a brief German translation to the side. He gave the lyrics to Chaim and little Basia to share. Basia had no patience for reading and seemed not to know written German with any fluency; she looked out the window when Leo left the two of them to study. But Chaim was fascinated. In preparation he scrutinized the Latin words with the hope of memorizing at least some of the sections. He looked for the familiar phrases: Jerusalem was the same for Christians. For Abraham, the Latin was *Abrahae*. This was what Mozart did when thinking of death. If one looked at it straight one became salt—or died, as Mozart did, in the throes of composing. But look, his wife, his companion, had worked to find men to finish it, to make a little memorial to her own love, her own grief, a vision not of the man she shared her life with but of the things he had made.

Chaim could not translate the Latin words on the page into sounds in his head, and even if Leo had been able to use the phonograph in the Roundhouse, he could not have found recordings of the pieces to be performed. Chaim would have to wait, counting every hour ticking by in the classroom or the house, feeling more and more enclosed in the house, longing to leave and visit the port city where the reconstituted orchestra of the vanquished would give its first performance.

HE HAD PLANNED TO let it out casually, as they ate on Friday evening, so that they would not see it was important to him, but Pavel forced it out sooner, in the morning.

I told Itzik Rakover you would tutor his nephew, Pavel called out from his room. He wants to talk to you on Shabbos.

Ah, said Chaim. I wanted to tell you—

Rakover can't stop talking about the boy. You know, they took him out from the priests, it's terrible, the child still crosses himself—

Pavel, said Chaim. Let's talk with him next week. I'm traveling a little this Saturday.

Hmm? said Pavel, emerging from his bedroom, wrapping his tie around his neck. Chaim was in the corridor.

I will be taking a trip, said Chaim.

A trip? said Pavel. On the Sabbath?

We travel to the camp every week for the service, said Chaim. You have traveled on the Sabbath. So yes, this Saturday I am going to Hamburg instead.

It is different to travel to pray, said Pavel, stiffening. And what, may I ask, calls you to Hamburg?

Ah, repeated Chaim, calm, authoritative, his voice firm and

deep—he could make his voice steady, he was a man—I am attending a concert in Hamburg.

Pavel looked at him.

The symphony, repeated Chaim. With Leo Meisel. He has made arrangements for his best students to go.

Pavel paused another moment. Then he said: Out of the question.

Pavel's voice was not loud, but in the kitchen, where Fela prepared breakfast, the clinking of the plates and silverware suddenly stopped. Chaim turned down the corridor. He would take his coffee, he would have a piece of bread.

Pan Pavel, he called as he walked, it is arranged already. Only for one night.

One night! Pavel's voice rose. And this you announce with your back to me!

Chaim moved toward Fela, who stood at the stove, and poured himself coffee into a cup. Pavel followed him.

Excuse me, young man, Pavel managed, his voice quieter now, quieter but tense, tight. Where will you stay for one night? In the concert hall? Or will Leo Meisel take you begging at a church?

You stayed in churches in your time, ventured Fela, with a smile, nervous. Come, Pavel, have your coffee.

And for what reason did you keep this from us until now?

I did not keep anything. What did I keep? Chaim swallowed, the coffee burning his mouth. No, he would not become angry. The more furious Pavel grew, the more Chaim wanted to be solid, calm, in control.

You knew, you had these plans! The man did not simply obtain tickets the way he picks up women!

Pavel, Pavel. Fela was humming his name, half afraid, half amused. What? Don't you have things you do not reveal? Don't you have things you keep quiet?

Not like this!

Yes like this! Of course like this. Fela touched Pavel's shoulder.

But Pavel seemed not to notice. Chaim, he said. It is impossible. I need you here.

For one night, Pavel, you do not.

And how do we know this fine scholar will bring you back, all in one piece? Hamburg! There, no soldiers will protect you if something goes wrong.

Pavel, interjected Fela. Let the boy enjoy himself.

You! cried Pavel, turning to her, looking straight at her eyes, his jaw jutting forward, his teeth clenched. And how do you have the authority?

But the teacher, Pavel, it is he who wants to give—

Leo Meisel! Leo Meisel does not run this household!

But already Pavel's voice was distant as Chaim fled the kitchen, grabbed his jacket, pushed himself out the door and onto Fela's bicycle, pedaling furiously, sweating, toward the camp, toward school, letting the cool air cleanse his eyes from his vision of Pavel shouting. Why shouldn't Chaim see a world? See and hear what he never had had in his life thus far, march forward? Did he have to go through life as Pavel did, looking back?

THEY BOTH RETURNED TO the house late in the evening and did not speak to each other before retiring. But at dawn, the door to his room opened, awaking Chaim with a start. He sat up straight, his feet touching the wood floor, then saw Pavel and stopped. Slowly Chaim lay back down in his bed.

Pavel sat on the bed, his face sagged with fatigue. Chaml, he said.

The diminutive, the sound of which Chaim had not heard since childhood, another lifetime, awakened in him the need to sob, to scream. He stopped himself.

I will go, Chaim answered, and turned his face to the wall.

THE OPENING PIECE—MUSIC without voices, Smetana, all bright violins—ended. Chaim had held his breath through the last portion, then let it out slowly. He had not breathed steadily since their first moments in the concert hall, the usher's downturned mouth as they walked in, the downcast eyes of the concertgoers in the seats around them. He could feel the audience around him recognizing them, if not by Tina's crippled hand and Basia's Gypsy-dark hair, if not by Leo's pointed, studious face, then by Chaim's nerves and discomfort. They could smell it on him. But how had he survived those periods of disguise as an itinerant farmhand in the Polish countryside, or those nights in the forest, pretending to be Catholic among the partisans? How had he survived all those months of the war, if this fear could so torture him now, in peace?

Night birds moaning. The orchestra had begun their second piece, and two men and two women had turned toward the conductor, their lips half-parted, ready to twist out the Latin words Chaim had so carefully memorized. Behind them, a dozen men and women—too few, Leo whispered to him as they pushed out their first notes—

Chaim could make out only snatches, syllables of the words he had seen on the page, as the roaring chorus grew more fierce, blocking him—then a pause and a man's voice, the soloist, and then the higher one, the woman's deep blood voice, and then the sound of the lightest bird, and the four of them together, with only a few of the strings behind them, so quiet, then again the calling—*abrahae, abrahae, kam olim abrahae promisisti*, the words taking him away from the sound for a moment, the words he had caught and remembered, studying in the barracks schoolroom.

He looked over at the orphan girl Basia. She was silent, open-mouthed, lost. Her face glistened in the reflected light of the orchestra pit. Could she be crying? Her breathing was barely perceptible—children did not cry silently. But Basia did weep. Tears rolled down her face and neck. And as he stared at her wet face, Chaim felt tears dart into his eyes too.

They ran down his face and touched his lips. Yes, this was how to mourn, with the roaring all around, with the ritual noise blocking out one's own grief. What did she remember, this little orphan girl, of her losses? Less than he did himself. But something moved her. In the schoolroom there was a child with parents, a child with no cause to look back. And he—he could recall, here in the concert, a reserved woman's hum, an aunt perhaps, not his mother, a girl's cry in the morning—yes, here his losses, the ones he could name and the ones he could not name, became sharper, pressed into his skin, more than they had at any religious service. This music was closer to him than the tales of harvests and rams, begetting and sacrifice. Or perhaps not as close. Perhaps the distance was what made everything so clear. He could understand and remember better when the roaring was not so loud, when it came to him in low tones, near whispers, when it came accompanied by violins, not human lamentation.

THEY STAYED THE NIGHT in a boardinghouse in Hamburg, so as not to drive back in darkness. He stayed in a room shared with Leo while Tina led Basia into one next door.

Was it beautiful? said Leo, shutting the door.

Yes, said Chaim. Yes, it was beautiful.

In the night he awoke, Leo wheezing next to him, the white curtain flat against the closed window. He thought of sitting up, then decided not to move. His skin was cool, his belly calm. He touched his hand to his forehead and remembered a flash from his dream, just the images, no sounds: an empty concert hall, the walls to one side blasted open, the remnants of a battle, a place he had never seen himself, a place out of pictures, a film. It once had been a beautiful building. Chaim closed his eyes and tried to remember more. He saw himself wandering around the orchestra pit, staring up at the remains of the art-covered ceiling, the fat blond angels and naked Greek gods. Some of the velvet seats for the audience still were intact. He climbed out of the pit and sat himself down in a soft red chair, to wait for the musicians to enter.

The Wedding

Y ES, SAID THE AMERICAN clerk in her stuttering German. We
have a Hinda Mandl. Shall I send someone for her?

But Pavel could not answer.

The clerk's hands fluttered through her papers. You are not permitted
in the women's barracks. Herr Mandl? I shall send someone for her.

Let her be warm, Pavel thought, sitting in the registry room of
the Foehrenwald assembly center in the American zone near Munich.
It was August and already the days seemed shorter; winter would be
upon them, and his little sister would have to be prepared. Let her be
warm, he repeated to himself. Let Hinda eat and be warm.

He had come back to the American zone with a small valise filled
with silk and wool, pounds of coffee for trading, even a set of ladies'
combs that Fela had insisted he bring with him, should he find his
sister. Pavel had come with these things, and coming with them made
him feel more secure. Pavel had a better system for searching than a
newspaper or a Jewish chaplain from the army. He had a desperation.

And with Hinda, even after the first failed expedition, he felt that something was right. His other sister and his youngest brother had perished with the rest of the children in the town when the ghetto was liquidated, and of his two remaining brothers, he still knew nothing. And yet Hinda—Fishl's Dincja had seen her alive, and no one knew of her being dead.

She had not been in Landsberg, and months had passed with few clues. But he had not allowed himself disappointment; a chaplain at Feldafing had responded after some time to his inquiry; her name had appeared on a list in a camp newspaper, with a contact address at Foehrenwald. He had sent a letter telling her he would arrive, he would arrive and wait for her, and with the letter he posted a box of cigarettes and scarves with an American army truck to the camp. He had bicycled in the heat for the next two days, his American papers secure inside his shirt, and now in the little office where a clerk at a metal desk ran through her list of recent arrivals, the papers seemed to press against his chest, making his breathing thin and slow.

He heard voices outside, more American attempts at German, and Pavel stood to wait in the doorway. Two figures approached, walking slowly. Was she weak? Was she sick? There had been a tuberculosis epidemic in the camp. Could she—the women came closer, and Pavel felt his heart hurtling against his ribs, as if to push his body toward the pair. But his body did not move. The woman's face became clear, sharp jaw, dark eyes, the same high forehead that marked the whole family, her tiny body a shadow in front of him, blocking his view of the dirt path, the row of barracks, the watchtower, the soldiers and inmates moving between the buildings. In his head Pavel knew that she came accompanied by a young messenger, but his eyes saw only Hinda.

SHE LOOKED SOMETHING LIKE her own self, older, of course, thinner than the last time he had seen her, in the spring of 1942. She had

come to Foehrenwald with a bundle of typhus-ridden women liberated from a barn crowded with remnants of a death march, hospitalized in one camp, then transferred to another. She was a small girl—
no longer a girl, Pavel supposed, she had grown to womanhood in
camps—but still sharp. Her chestnut hair, still short, had returned to
its wavy beauty. He touched it as they embraced, and as they walked
from the camp office he let his hands roam through it and embraced
her again. He stopped every few steps to look at her. It was hard to
breathe: a body created from the same bodies that created him, a living being from the same mother and father.

Hinda, he said, again and again. Hinda, Hinda.

Pavel, she said, Pavel.

They walked together to a small area near the camp school. They
would have some privacy. As they moved behind the building, toward
a small garden, Pavel heard his sister coughing. He looked at her. So
reserved a moment before, Hinda now had tears streaming down her
face, and as he watched her, he realized he himself was weeping.
They wept the same way: in silence. They sat on a bench, and Pavel
felt his skin chapping where the salt water had dried on his cheeks. It
was a humid and cloudy day.

After some time Hinda spoke: I want to get married.

Hmm? he said, surprised. To whom?

She had a friend, it seemed, someone who had gotten through the
war on Aryan papers—he fought on the Polish side in the Warsaw
uprising! Hinda said, with an uncharacteristic excitement—and who
cared for her, who had a great future in front of him, who wanted
to marry her and take her out, to England or to America, whichever
came first, to escape this new prison, to take her away and make her
life something calm and peaceful.

Pavel frowned. I should meet him before you decide anything, he
said.

No, Hinda said. I have decided. You should meet him, of course.

But I have decided, Pavel. You are not my father. You are my brother.

He said nothing.

My only living brother, she said. Her tears again flowed.

She seemed to think he had no say in the matter. After a moment, he said, I have a house. I live in a house. After I meet him, there we will make your wedding.

It would be something beautiful. Nothing like what the other refugees had, more and more marrying after one meeting, two meetings, a walk with the intended, a dozen onlookers crowded to watch the two say their marriage prayers under a canopy made from an army-issued sheet. Hinda's wedding would be different, not the impoverished little gatherings around a barracks of hungry people, but a party, something elegant and full, with pastries and delicacies and even, he thought, a little music. Yes, a little music. He would give to his sister what she might have experienced had she grown to be a bride under the watch of their father.

FELA AND HINDA DID not make a good impression on each other. Fela put out her hand when they met, and Hinda seemed not to notice it. Pavel saw, and a protest welled up in his throat: Hinda! he wanted to cry. But he said nothing, watching Fela start back in surprise.

The rest of their hour together was stiff, labored. Kuba, Hinda's intended, at the last minute had been obliged to attend to some business. Hinda entered the little house alone, delivered by a car that had been dispatched by Pavel. Now it was up to Pavel to move the conversation.

All right, Pavel thought. At least Kuba did business, unlike those refugees who slept all day in the barracks of the DP camp, moving about in a state of apathy, refusing to get up and work or even talk. But the meeting, which had been arranged so Pavel could assess Kuba, instead became a chance for Hinda to judge Fela. And here was Hinda, sullen and haughty, just as she had been years ago when their father married their stepmother, just as she had been when she had seen, by chance, Pavel in the street with a girl. Years ago.

You smoke too much, said Hinda, watching Fela strike another match.

Who did not smoke? It kept down the hunger. It gave the body the illusion of warmth. Few of the refugees had given it up. In fact Hinda smoked also; she had brought her own cigarettes.

Kuba has a good contact, Hinda said. He is so blond, it is easy for him to move around. He gets French ones, sometimes. I try to be careful; it is not so ladylike to smoke so much.

Fela blew out a puff from her mouth. The smoke came out in two little circles. Often when she did that, even as a joke, Pavel thought she looked like a film actress. But now he didn't. He was worried. He said, We all smoke.

He knew it was not an adequate answer. He could feel Fela's anger in the caress she gave his hand, which rested on the table, holding his own cigarette. She did not touch him in front of others, but now, in front of Hinda, she wanted to throw off her restraint. Her gesture had an effect: Hinda looked coldly at the two of them and said, Not all of us smoke so much.

Pavel and Fela retained a modesty in public, acting as friends, perhaps cousins. For what would others think of him, not marrying a beautiful Jewish girl with whom he shared a bed? Yet the explanation was even worse—that Fela still looked for her husband. So they were discreet, and they depended on Chaim—who had moved into Fela's room—to keep quiet himself. What did others need to know about their living arrangements? They had their own dwellings to worry about.

Yet here was Fela, openly touching, her pale fingers rubbing his knuckles. Was she taunting his sister, or perhaps him? He did not know. Pavel was relieved—no, not relieved, he thought, just tired, just

ready to rest—when Chaim hopped off Fela's bicycle and bounded
into the garden, giving Hinda a tip of the cap as she stood up to
leave.

PAVEL BROUGHT CHAIM WITH him to meet this Kuba near Munich.
It was better that way, men among men. Kuba stayed with a friend
from his childhood in a bare apartment only moderately clean. Pavel
sniffed a bit when he came in. Even without a woman living in the
home, one had to make attempts! His sister's intended did not seem
to waste money on luxuries. But Kuba was friendly, a round pink face
atop a small body, neatly dressed in gray trousers and a dark jacket,
and he shook Pavel's and Chaim's hands with vigor.

Kuba too had thought to have an observer. His friend Marek
brought glasses from the kitchen, and they sat down in the front room
with a bottle of schnapps, a gift from Pavel. Chaim unpacked from
his satchel a bundle of American cigarettes.

Marek took a cigarette first. He lit it with a match, then passed
the light on his cigarette to Pavel's. All this travel just to take a look at
the sister's groom, yes? That is a loyal brother.

Was he making fun? No, Pavel decided. He breathed out. She is
all I have, he said.

Kuba interjected. She talks of you like a hero. Smuggling letters
between work camps. Sending her packages in Foehrenwald, even
before you knew for sure she was alive. Then travel through the Russian zone to get to the American!

Pavel coughed, suddenly nervous. She is all I have, he repeated.

More than many of us, nodded Marek.

A silence.

Chaim said, We make the wedding in our house. Fela already
plans for the meal.

Pavel threw him a look—should it be given away so quickly that

Kuba had passed Pavel's scrutiny?—then looked back at Kuba with a grave face.

I see you must make good business, if you live outside a camp.

Marek and Kuba exchanged glances. We get along all right, said Kuba. We have our own connections. No doubt different from yours—

Marek interrupted. We don't have a car, that is for sure!

The two of them laughed, and Pavel joined in.

Coffee, said Pavel, is better than diamonds.

Chaim took a short sip from his glass. The car was borrowed, but it was true, Pavel had plans to make a purchase of something used; it would give them more freedom than bicycles.

And we do not have British papers, continued Kuba. It makes a difference to have them. Hinda says you have both.

Pavel smiled. Should you believe everything Hinda says? The three men laughed again.

Young to be a partner in such a business, eh? said Marek, looking at Chaim. His broad cheeks had reddened with the schnapps.

Not so young, said Chaim.

Smart, said Pavel. He already teaches in the Belsen school. Everyone talks about him.

It's not exactly teaching, Chaim interjected. I help with—

In any case, said Kuba, I want to marry your sister. I want to make something more than we make here. There is nothing for us here, business or no business. Nothing.

Pavel nodded. This Kuba thought ahead. There is nothing here, he agreed.

We went back to Kielce together, said Marek. We thought—I wanted to see my parents' bakery, I wanted some message—I thought in the Jewish community center—

You can imagine, said Kuba. You can imagine.

You cannot imagine, said Marek, his voice suddenly louder. You cannot imagine! After everything—Kuba does not know—I can see where you were, and he was not where we were, my friend—he does not know, but after everything, to come back and to have them massacring us again! We ran to the American zone so fast we left what little we had in our houses. Worse than before! I hate Poles more than Germans. I hate them more! Marek was shouting, his thin brown hair flapping over his forehead. I hate them more! At least here we have the chance to see the Germans hungry and defeated! There they live on our property and grow fat and they are delighted, overjoyed that we are gone! It is heaven for them. A little heaven.

Another silence. Kuba patted his friend's shoulder. I just wanted Pavel to know that I will leave here at the first opportunity, the first chance.

But until then, sighed Marek.

Until then, continued Kuba, we would like to invite you into our business. You have connections, we have connections. We have crossed borders without papers before.

Pavel looked at them, thin Marek with his eyes almost running with tears, small Kuba with his blond, sunny face. They did not have papers for the British zone. But Pavel did. He had everything. Perhaps he could help them. He had money, he had stones. Not as good as identity papers, but almost as good.

I participate in the Jewish Committee of the British zone, Pavel said. I will see what can be done.

IN THE ROUNDHOUSE, THE speeches of the leaders and the mutterings of their followers became more and more desperate and furious. Yidl Sheinbaum, accepting his reelection to the head of the committee, cried out about the cruelties of the British foreign minister and the hopelessness of the American Congress. We have crossed the Red

Sea! he shouted. But still we are in the desert! Should we wait forty years?

It was true, Pavel thought, clapping angrily with the rest. They had been slaves in Egypt and still had not found their freedom. The outside world busied itself with more important things than the suffering of the Jewish remnants. They were all on the lists to emigrate with the Joint and the International Red Cross and HIAS; they all hoped for America, of course, and they all came to the demonstrations for the British to open Palestine, though the life when they got there! They had heard the hunger was worse than in Germany. A few refugees managed to have relatives sponsor them to emigrate outside the quotas, and they left at the first chance of sea passage. No, not even the most powerful people in the world wanted to give them a place to live in peace, to seek home, not just refuge.

Still, Pavel had wanted an American for the wedding ceremony of his sister. He had faith in the Americans. He brought in his future brother-in-law and his friend to stay in his house a few days, and organized for them papers—legitimate ones!—and new ration cards. In gratitude, Marek offered to make arrangements—he had contacts. A lady friend knew some of the chaplains in the American zone in Bremen. Pavel did not want to ask too many questions. What a surprise for his sister it would be, a symbol of the new world to bring her into marriage. And as for entertainment, Chaim seemed to know a teacher connected with a group of musicians, hungry people who would be happy to travel out to the house for a reasonable fee.

FELA DID NOT LOVE to cook. She loved to bake. Three sponge cakes and a platterful of cookies had been ready since early in the morning, and there was nothing for her to do but boil the cabbage for the chopped meat. Pavel had expressed a wish for stuffed cabbage, but she was doubtful about the quality of the meats he had managed to find. The strong heat interrupted her concentration. Truth be told, she thought it a waste to cook a meat dish for the guests. She did not want to postpone any longer, but she thought that instead of beginning the cabbage she could perhaps work on to a small rack of turnovers with the basket of apples Chaim had brought home the night before. To keep the meal kosher, she could substitute a bit of oil for the butter in the pastry. Or should she just forgo the meat altogether? There was not so much that one could be sure every guest would have enough. Would it not be better to avoid the awkwardness and shame, to present the guests instead with the products of the flour of which they had plenty? No meat at all! It would be easy to sell it again before it went bad. Turnovers, cheese puffs, even another sponge cake, these would be plentiful, and would keep if for some reason the guests did not finish.

Sweating a bit as she sliced the apples, Fela heard the door open and close, Pavel's nervous chatter, Chaim's laugh, the voice that quavered between boyhood and adulthood. A stream of humid summer air pushed through the kitchen, mixing with the odor of warm cake. Kuba was not to arrive for another two hours, and the guests would be even later. There was time.

She had prepared for Hinda a little area in Chaim's bedroom to arrange her hair and to wash, with a little soap and cream and tweezers, all from the cosmetology class she took in the camp. Fela would dress in her own room. They did not feel a warmth toward each other. Hinda was still a girl. A bitter girl, but a girl. She had never been with a man at all, Fela surmised, not even Kuba. No doubt Hinda disapproved of the morals in the house, but Fela thought she could detect in Hinda's manner not just disdain but awe. Hinda's body had suffered. Hinda had experienced what all of them had experienced and more, the emptying of the mind of any thought unrelated to physical survival, the obsession, the mania of hunger and cold—and no doubt beatings, perhaps even tortures. But Hinda did not have what Fela had, a memory inside the body, a hidden cabinet of womanhood. And there was no one for Hinda to ask, to consult, no one with whom she could worry and laugh, as she might have with a sister, or a mother, even a girlfriend from school. Yes, thought Fela. Inside that coldness, Hinda felt awe. She resented Fela the way a child would resent an adored brother's blooming new wife, and Fela was acting, after all, the part of Pavel's wife.

More than acting. Fela felt that she was not performing a lie but living another life, a life next to her old one, the life of a twin. Sometimes she thought Pavel could see the twin next to her—in the evenings, when they smoked, or at night, when he touched the belly roughened by childbirth. But if he saw, he chose to ignore the twin. She did not ask him questions, and he did not ask her. She knew he assumed she had been married legitimately, by a rabbi, and she did not discourage his assumption. It seemed to her she had not been his first love, either. He too had a twin. And the twins watched them, each night, each morning, as they drew aside the curtains in their wallpapered bedroom or as they wrapped their heads in scarves before riding to their English class in the camp. Her mouth and face and hands felt new to her. She occasionally felt a flash of unsureness, as if the body working at eating and lovemaking was not completely hers.

But now it was she, Fela, cooking, baking, moving her hands through a busy but clean kitchen. She had crossed the border into this new body, after a time of being stateless, after a time of being no one, alone with only a memory of who she was, daughter, sister, lover, mother. She would pass into this new life. It was all right. She had crossed the border.

THE MUSICIANS ARRIVED ALL at once, in a line, almost marching. A man with a black-market violin—he once had played cello; a woman flutist, whose cheeks seemed puffed for a trumpet; and two men with identical wide guitars. Guitars, of all things! Pavel was not sure he had seen one outside of pictures. Rayzele had mentioned some kind of horn, a quiet horn, she said, but no one appeared with one. Still, this was more than satisfactory.

Pavel was wearing a plain dark jacket and trousers, made from thin Swiss wool. The others would arrive in their charity suits from America, used and mismatched. Pavel's shirt was pressed stiff, and his hair had been clipped in the barbershop of the DP camp. The red-and-brown skullcap he wore had been knitted by Rayzele, a gift.

Waiting for the rabbi and guests as the women prepared the table and the musicians took a bite to eat, Pavel and Chaim played cards. Chaim was good, but not so good. Pavel took pity occasionally, dropping a card he could see the boy wanted.

The men with guitars chatted with Kuba. The flutist held back, nervously cutting bits of dark bread into her hand and hopping them into her mouth, like a bird.

The rabbi arrived in a soldier's uniform, with three other men from the American zone in Bremen. Pavel jumped up when Rayzele came to tell him. It was starting! He felt a chill of excitement. Not warmth in his heart, not quite, but movement, a flutter of leaves at his ribs. A marriage. It seemed like a folktale, a story from outside his lifetime. But no! It was a normal event, part of the everyday.

The men withdrew to the sitting room downstairs to prepare the contract. The rabbi sat himself down at the center of the narrow table, Pavel standing behind him. Had he ever been witness to a signing? Perhaps as a child he had seen something like this, with the door ajar, the thin curtains flapping from the autumn garden, the smell of chicken boiling in the kitchen, the taste of apple cake stuck to the roof of his mouth, he had taken a piece without asking and no one had seen. His grandfather—

He called to Chaim. The boy should see.

But something was happening. A mutter, a flurry. From his place behind the table, Pavel floated back from his grandfather's house to the room in Celle, to the half-frowning faces staring at the rabbi, whose words Pavel could not quite make out.

He concentrated. The rabbi was saying: Yes, yes, but how do I know? What do I know about them?

Pavel forced his mind on the figure of Marek, who observed the rabbi and Pavel with a weary sneer.

The rabbi went on, in stilted Yiddish, with a few Russian words thrown in: They say we are in the family's house, but there are no documents. How should I know that her mother was Jewish? And we have nothing on the man, who looks as Jewish as the Pope. Now how can I perform—

Excuse me—Pavel interrupted—excuse me—

You understand—

Excuse me! Pavel turned to face the front of the man. He peered at the rabbi's mouth, as if to change the words coming out. What are you saying? You are saying you don't think we are Jewish? After all we've been through?

It's not what I think, it's the issue of documents—

Documents! We—documents—

Calm, calm, whispered Chaim.

But Pavel could not breathe. The words in Yiddish came out in chipped pebbles. My sister—how—brother—musicians—so much food! Around him the men were still, watching him.

And then, from the silence, soft tones of that odd sound, English. It was Chaim's voice, the voice of a growing boy, and his words seemed to Pavel to flow easily: "Perhaps, Rabbi, you do not understand. Our documents are ashes. In smoke. In the sky."

The rabbi's face turned stiff. "Yes, yes. Of course."

Pavel breathed again.

But the rabbi continued, returning to Yiddish. It's a question of my—you know, I must prove that I know, and how can I know? There is no proof. No certificates. I understand, but how can I show it? I have certain obligations, not just to the rabbinate, to the army—

Come, Mr. Chaplain, said Pavel, forcing a smile. Sit with me for a glass of schnapps. I have a fresh bottle for you to take back to your family in America—

No thank you.

Or to your friends in the barracks—

I said no.

Pavel looked down and saw his fingers folding and unfolding. The muscles in his arms had extended. He knew that his chin was out and his lips were trembling over his teeth. This was impossible! The musicians were here. He had paid a small fortune, for travel, for food for what was it?—thirty guests! God in heaven would laugh if he still had the nerve. A rabbi, an American, but an idiot.

This is impossible! Pavel croaked aloud. What you are saying is impossible!

Pavel, Pavel. Fela had trotted into the sitting room, pulled him away from the rabbi, pulled him into the front hall. His right arm was raised in an L, his fist was a stone. His voice was a whirring river trapped in his mouth. Pavel.

She is getting married today. He shook the words out of his mouth. The musicians are here. All this food!

Yes, yes, said Fela. Something will work out.

He won't take a gift! Nothing! Americans! So rich and so stupid, stupid!

Pavel, we can have the party today and the wedding tomorrow. Or someone else—we don't need a rabbi—

Absolutely not! Who ever heard of the party first? Hinda is getting married today, and by this rabbi, if I have to kill him.

You will not kill anyone. Fela's voice rolled flat, exhausted. Now is not for killing, Pavele. She pulled him down to the sofa, smoothing her dark blue skirt. Please, Pavel. Now is for thinking.

They sat in silence. Pavel was shaking. Fela's hand was rubbing his arm while she whispered at him: Shh. Shh. Now is for thinking. So? Let us think.

SIMA THOUGHT HER MOUTH would make steam when she exhaled, but she was wrong. It was strange: in the hardest winter of her childhood, her breath had come out of her mouth like smoke from a chimney, white clouds that took more than a moment to vanish. But here, where everything was heat, the perspiration on her skin, the tears in her eyes, even her burning hair, her mouth could not make steam. She told her mother of her discovery—but her mother lay still, her face toward the corner of the sheet that separated them from the others, the coolest part of the oven. It had been three months in the barracks already, and in that time the health Sima's mother had regained in the camp hospital had faded. She spent the painful August afternoons half-undressed, a wet cloth across her head and another on her neck. She was weak, her father said to Sima, very weak, and Sima was to be quiet around her, not to move so much, not to generate more heat in their small space.

Sima rinsed her mouth and swallowed from the container of potable water her father had brought for them at dawn. She stepped outside the sheet that sheltered their possessions and climbed down the barracks steps. She knew where to find her father. He had a card game that began in the late afternoons, when the men would emerge from the shade of their dwellings. Some of them had been in the refugee camp six months, nine months, a year, trapped behind the barbed wire that surrounded the low buildings.

It's Berele's daughter, someone said. Coming to help her father win.

I need the help, said Berel. Believe me.

Sima believed him. His worn blue shirt was unbuttoned to his navel, and his undershirt was yellow with dirt and sweat. But he concentrated on the damp cards in his hand. A red queen, a seven of spades. Sima was seven. She smiled.

Don't give me away, said Berel. Under the metal table he crossed his feet: a good hand.

Our mother is resting, Sima said, to no one in particular. She is weak.

Sshh! Sima! said Berel.

Our mother, chuckled a man at the table. There it is, Berele. Still tied to your *mammele*. She loves you to play cards, mm?

A man does not let his wife stop his leisure, said Berel. He put down his hand: three queens, a row of spades, three kings. Aha! You see?

Sima watched him grinning, happy.

Now have your mother tell me our luck hasn't changed, Berel chuckled. Hmm, Simale? If this doesn't tell her, what does?

It's the boy teacher, a man said. Sima turned around. Chaim walked with a quick thin step in spite of the heat, dressed in a slim blue suit. He looked different outside of the classroom, bigger and more sure. She backed into her father's arms, flushed with sudden shyness. He came toward them.

Pan Makower, he said. I would like to ask you a favor.

BEREL HAD NOT FOUND another opportunity for office work, but now that he had an assignment in the camp kitchens, he could convince Dvora that he had the luxury to sing on the Sabbath. She did not give too great an argument. Perhaps she was relieved that he had accepted a bit of religion, this late in life. He sang at the large Sabbath services at the Roundhouse and once performed Yiddish folk tunes at the close of a short concert in the camp.

He came into his family space in the barracks to tell Dvora of Chaim's offer. A Jewish wedding outside the camp confines. A man who wanted a traditional service, a cantor's voice, of course Berel was not officially a cantor, but who worried about such things now? He would first discuss it with them at the Roundhouse, and of course all three of them would go. Unless Dvora felt too ill, and he would just take Sima—

Dvora interrupted, sitting up, her forehead damp. Who gets married? she asked. The man and woman who live there?

No, said Berel. I believe it is the man's sister.

Ah, so this Mandl is already married to the woman.

Perhaps, nodded Berel. But he had asked Chaim the same question, and the boy had continued talking about the sister. Yes, I believe so.

Dvora blinked. He knew what the blink meant: some kind of scandal there. But she would measure in one hand a bit of scandal and in the other the opportunity to see a real home. Berel knew which hand would come out the winner.

I must change my shirt, said Berel. We will go now, I suppose. It's a long way.

A long way? We will have someone drive us! Dvora looked offended. We won't walk there, like peasants. If we are a cantor's family, we are a cantor's family.

I should go with the boy to the Roundhouse first. They brought the contract with them.

Can I come? Sima grasped at Berel's sleeve. I want to go to the Roundhouse again.

Berel frowned. No, you stay here with your mother.

Bring her, said Dvora. It will make an impression. And I need time to get dressed.

Sima wiped her mother's face with a towel.

Good girl, said Dvora. But don't let your father leave without me.

A SAD ARMY THEY were, Pavel Mandl and the pink-faced man who wished to be his brother-in-law, his thin friend Marek, and Chaim, the boy teacher's assistant from Sima's class. Dressed neatly, hair slick, eyes haggard. Impressive, Berel thought, only in their desperation. In the enormous chairs of Yidl Sheinbaum's office at the DP camp, their bodies appeared small, creased, and hidden.

Berel had been here before. Next to the offices Yidl and his new wife, Tsipora, had a grand apartment, filled with luxurious items captured from the local Germans. Berel had brought Dvora and Sima there the first time he was invited to sing at a wedding—so many of the refugees married under Yidl's canopy, no rabbi present—he had been overwhelmed by his first visit, the grandness of the place when compared with the little area of the barracks he lived in, thinly separated by a sheet from the other tiny families. He had been overwhelmed but somewhat distanced too. Yidl did not seem to Berel to be of so high a background, and the elegant silvers and carpets, the large rooms, a separate spot for dining, aroused in him both envy and disdain. Dvora had disagreed. At least there are some Jews, she said, who live as well as the Germans who murdered us and still have comfort!

But today the fine offices did not seem so full as they had before. Yidl Sheinbaum had received Berel and Simale with formality and calm. In public he was emotional, forceful, but here in his own territory his triangular face took on the aspect of a quiet bird, a sharp face atop a short, stocky body.

You have been asked to perform a good deed, Sheinbaum said.

Berel felt his mouth stiffen, suppressing a laugh.

Just a little singing, he said.

Ah no, Reb Makower. Much more than a little singing. Perhaps our friend—Sheinbaum gestured at Chaim—did not explain fully.

You are to perform what perhaps you have not performed since before the war, a wedding.

Since before the—

I know, Sheinbaum interrupted. How careful you have wanted to be about the ritual, Rebbe. I know! And such is the problem we face today. An American rabbi in the same position, yes, but without, shall we say, the authority you have to believe your fellow remnants.

I don't think I can perf—

Listen, said Sheinbaum. I know it has been far too long since you recited the prayers. A prayer book we have for you. And, of course, we have a British captain on his way to sign the necessary paperwork, attesting to your status.

Chaim spoke. That way we think we can convince the American to sign at least as a witness. In part it will be an American wedding.

Berel looked at the men.

My sister, said Pavel Mandl, his voice rasping and quiet. My sister. It is all I want in the world, to have her married to a Jewish man in a Jewish ceremony, by a rabbi, with a contract. It is not war, when anyone can do a ceremony. I want a rabbi. To have her have a Jewish child, just like your little one, Rebbe.

Berel did not dare look at Sima. But he knew she would keep quiet. He could feel her standing still next to him, her head a hand's breadth from his thigh.

I will do anything. I have stones, Pavel whispered. I will sell anything.

Berel saw the thin man, Marek, look quickly at Pavel, then turn away. But Sheinbaum interrupted again. Don't be silly. You want your sister to have a Jewish wedding, she will have a Jewish wedding. And an American one too. Isn't it so, Reb Makower?

Berel nodded.

Now, a little coffee? We will set out in a few moments.

Sheinbaum's broad new wife, Tsipora, came in to serve them, and he retreated into the recesses of his apartment to speak on the telephone. After some time he returned with a man in a high-level British uniform.

My friends, Sheinbaum announced in Yiddish, his voice low and serious, this is Captain Davies. He is here to solve our problem.

Please, said the captain, in German. How can I help you?

The group looked at Yidl. But Yidl looked right back. He spoke to everyone, even the military attachés, even the diplomats from America, in Yiddish. And German! He made it a point not to speak German. Tsipora said something in a language Berel did not know. French? It was said she had studied medicine in Paris before the war. She leaned over to Pavel and patted him on the shoulder and whispered in his ear, as if she had known him for years, a sister.

Pavel seemed to shrink under her touch. For a moment Berel wondered if he should say something, for suddenly he and his daughter were part of this group, this little gray mass that five minutes before had been strangers to him. But the captain broke the silence.

All this just to show one of you is a rabbi? Here, we'll put your seal along with mine—these Americans, he shook his head at Yidl. All I need from you, Herr Sheinbaum, is a word. I have seen it for myself. What you tell me is true.

The men looked at the captain, silent.

"What this man says is true!" the captain suddenly cried in English. "True!" And he slapped Sheinbaum on the back.

So! said Sheinbaum, passing the letter to Pavel with a slim smile on his face. Let us travel. For, of course, now I am invited, yes?

LYING ABOUT SUCH A thing—but what was a sin now? It had no meaning to Berel anymore. With everyone hugging one another, a few people crying, he wandered back to Dvora, a little piece of cake in his hand. He held it out to her. She looked up at him from her chair and blinked. Immediately he felt his mouth tremble, but he did not want the others to see his face lose its seriousness and shock. He bent down to Dvora's chair. Face muscles trapped, he felt his words come out half-strangled.

You always wanted a rabbi for a husband, hmm?

Dvora blinked again. Berel lost the battle: an unstoppable laugh began to move up his ribs. He coughed with his neck bent, hoping to make the noise sound like a sneeze.

Sima trotted over with a broad grin. What is funny? Her voice pierced through the angry mutterings of the adults.

Sh! warned Berel. He sucked in his cheeks, pursed his mouth as if to whistle. Nothing is funny. A very serious thing has happened.

But you are laughing!

Sh! He took her upper arm and pressed it, hard. Sima, you must behave.

The three of them huddled, Berel trembling with the last waves of his laughter, crumbs from the cake stuck to his palm, Dvora with her legs crossed, ladylike, calm.

This is what happens, Berel finally whispered. This is what happens when you try to do everything the rabbis say. They have no sense!

He is not like every rabbi, said Dvora. This one is an American, no?

Same books, said Berel. Same rigid ideas. Wanting a piece of paper that is burned into the sky long ago. He is a very pure man! No departures from the Talmud for this one! Young, why should he jeopardize his career with something like this?

So, said Dvora. You showed him better. Congratulations. But she was smiling. On their way to the car Sheinbaum had pulled him aside, demanded he be addressed as Yidl, and asked where in the camp he lived. Berel had told him. Terrible, Sheinbaum had answered. Just terrible. You should have talked to me before. It will be fixed.

Berel looked at his wife. Already, three months in the DP camp, things had changed between them. She had been the master of scheming and lying and stealing in the steppe, the ruler of the family, the protector. Now that they had what to eat and where to sleep, however uncomfortable, he saw frailties in her he had not seen before: how difficult it was for her to learn German, how slow she was to pick up the cloth-cutting skills in her training program, how short of breath she became after an hour of walking. He had felt himself growing taller and plumper even as she remained thin and pale. Now they had a crisis upon them, a small crisis, but a crisis, and he had risen to meet it. She was alive with pride at his trickery, a bit of heat surging into her cheeks.

It is lovely here, Berele.

Sima laughed out loud. I'm going to take more cake!

Take, take, said Berel. But he had stopped laughing. The humidity had broken a bit. Still he felt a sudden fatigue, a desire not to sleep but to lie down and cover his eyes. It was a lovely home, sunny and overflowing with people. But he did not know how Pavel and the others could bear it, the smallness and modesty, the normality of it, the living between two worlds in a house that had been built for families who stayed put.

DELAYED BY HALF A day, the ceremony had been beautiful after all, from Berel Makower's trembling melodies to the crushed goblet. But Pavel's rage had worn him out. Kuba had remained poised, even cheerful, smiling and nodding the whole day. Kuba wasn't too bright, thought Pavel. But what did that matter? Perhaps he was better off, nodding like a beast.

And watching his sister under the chuppah, her face solid and still in front of the man Yidl promised was a rabbi, had made Pavel cry. After all they had gone through, was this what a real life was, still so much struggle and pain?

Fela found him after, silently resting in a soft armchair. She kissed him, then stood again.

Ours will be less complicated, she said, looking at the room filled with guests. We will have it inside Belsen to avoid the paperwork. The British chaplain, or another rabbi, whoever you want. No little orchestra. Just a man's voice.

He looked at her. So she had given up. He was surprised, but only faintly. He waited for the air to spill out of him, the breeze of his relief cooling his skin, but nothing moved inside him.

She stepped behind his chair. Pavel felt her presence and smell around him as he continued to sit. He watched the soldiers and Rayzele dancing with fever and urgency, and he watched the musicians, legs no longer swollen with recovering hunger, clinking the love songs that once had seemed cheerful. Marek's lady friend drank and sang with some of the men. The American rabbi was roaming the table for rye bread and cheese, crumbs on his unshadowed chin.

So, muttered Pavel. So, let him eat.

The flutist, hair in her face, was tweetering out a little French ballad.

Pavel's tongue tasted bitter in his mouth. He rubbed at his wrist. Yes, he thought. Yes, let him eat.

Prisoner

September 1949–February 1950

Someone called out from a barracks, a woman's voice, louder and louder. Miloch! Miloch!

Pavel didn't turn. A woman finding a relative or friend. He was walking quickly to the Joint office, where his and Fela's visa applications lay in a pile of hundreds. This was the bad luck of the British zone: the refugees in the American zone had been processed much more quickly, helped by the Jewish soldiers. He needed a connection. Simply participating in the council meetings—that was not enough. He needed something more.

Miloch! The woman was upon him, and Pavel saw her face, paler, older, but hers.

Perla, he said. Perla.

There were tears in her eyes, and her cheeks were pink from running after him.

My name is Pavel, said Pavel, trying to order his thoughts, to explain. The name I was born with—I didn't hear—so long since anyone has called me—I didn't know anyone from that time, that time when I was—was still—

But he was overcome. Perla's face, round and dignified, two tears running evenly down her cheeks and neck, her thin, flowered dress— she was an old woman inside a young mother's body. There was a number on her wrist—so! Surely her baby son had not survived. And her father, an elderly man when Pavel knew him, elderly but wealthy, influential, who had saved Pavel's life with a bribe, merely because he had known Pavel's grandfather—

Your father, said Pavel.

No, said Perla. He did not survive. Myself and my sister, only us—and—I am married again.

They arranged to meet as two couples, for a coffee in the main street of the camp. Perla's new husband was from their province. It happened that Pavel had shared a barracks with him in one of the work camps. Tulek.

They sat outside, in a café modeled on the style they had in Berlin, where the Polish Jews could feel more of the West, sophisticated. Perla had once come from a very high family. In the fall breeze, Fela hugging a dark sweater around her slim shoulders, they found an empty round table. Pavel watched Tulek take in Fela's figure as she sat down, smoothing her skirt under her thighs. Yes, thought Pavel, I have a beautiful wife.

Miloch, said Perla. The girls who knew him in my town all thought of him as—

No more Miloch! interrupted Fela, only half-joking. Who is Miloch? My husband is Pavel.

Miloch, said Pavel, smiling. The name of a hanged man. I was afraid to use my own name at that time. I was on a list—

Pavel, please, said Fela. Let us not—

Perla reached across the table, patted Fela's hand. Pavel, of course

Pavel. I must accustom myself. But sometimes you have a picture burned in your brain.

It was true, thought Pavel. Sometimes a picture burned in the brain, a brand. He had one of Perla—coming home to her father's house in winter, wearing only a slip and an undershirt, almost naked, shivering, her white skin pink from the cold, her elbows bent at her sides.

You gave your clothes away, said Pavel.

What? said Perla.

Yes, that time—you saw a family without coats being sent—

Pavel, said Tulek. You must have heard who they have in the jail.

I hid in her father's house, said Pavel. He saved my life, that time.

You must have heard, repeated Tulek. Kresser.

Kresser? said Pavel. The name came out of him like a casual question. That name! A name he spat at. He felt his heart gallop a moment, then he stilled it. His voice came out quiet, serene. Kresser. Hmm. Still alive.

Oh yes, said Tulek. No one has killed him yet.

What, now? His old activities, I suppose? He was a thief before the war too. So I heard.

Tulek said, No, no. Listen: someone denounced him. They have him not for stealing but for crimes. You know, against his own prisoners.

Oh, said Pavel. Oh.

Fela was looking at him, worried. She wanted the conversation to change.

Perla said to her husband, Pavel knew him too?

Ha! Tulek gave a short laugh. Who knew him once would not forget him. Great creativity, that one. Great creativity. An artist, one might say. Original, inventive. Who says Jews cannot produce great works? That one could compete with some of the Ukrainians.

Pavel didn't laugh. A Jew in the jail for crimes. Probably they had caught him while up to some certain illegal activity, and someone else, a fellow smuggler even, had recognized and named him—many people went through that labor camp before it was liquidated. No doubt Kresser had managed to take another position of power when he moved on to the next one. Or perhaps not. Perhaps that little unit in eastern Germany, where they crafted helmets with machinery once meant for pots and pans, had been Kresser's only experiment with cruelty. Perhaps Kresser, once the typhus epidemic had wiped out half the unit's population, had seen Pavel and his comrades, those whose fevers were subsiding, carry the dead beyond the barracks, into an abandoned field designated by the camp commanders. Perhaps Kresser had seen the prisoners take the blankets of the dead, the blankets stained from shit and blood, scattered with lice, and search for a clean corner, a small strip of uninfested wool, to wipe the bodies for burial. Perhaps Kresser had seen.

SHE WAS A GRACIOUS woman, said Fela when they were alone again, strolling to the apartment. Really. You could see she was very fine. From a fine family. A lady.

Pavel saw that Fela meant it. She had a sweet little son, ventured Pavel.

Fela said nothing.

I didn't dare ask.

It is right not to ask, said Fela. Too painful to speak of it.

But what of this man? said Pavel. What do you think?

What man? Kresser? said Fela. It has nothing to do with you.

He paused a moment. The image of Kresser in a cell did not please him. It should please him, he thought. But there were Germans roaming free, Ukrainians obtaining visas. What did Kresser think now?

I want to go see him, Pavel blurted.

What? said Fela. Her voice still quiet, but alarmed. What? Why do you need the trouble? We have things to do here! Our applications, we need to earn—I have only six months left, and I want the child born on American soil. American.

I want to see if he's sorry.

Sorry! Fela gasped.

He was upsetting her. No, no, Felinka. No, not to say anything, just to confront him—so he knows—

He is not sorry! People like that—criminals like that—they never change, even if they are Jews! Especially if they are Jews. To do what that kind of person did! He will not change, Pavel, not for you, not for me, not for anyone. Please! What can it prove, what can it show?

But for him to be in an American jail—for them to—

Ah! Fela had caught him. You want him out!

He felt his face darken with shame. No, no.

You want him out.

I just want to ask him. For them to judge—

It is not you they judge, Pavel.

No, said Pavel. It is not. But this is something—this is something to keep inside, to keep among people who know what it means. These Americans! He stopped. Then started again, anger leaking out of his mouth. These Americans! They marry German women who sent their husbands off to war, and now look! Now it is all a court, a court to make a spectacle, a scandal, out of us!

It is not your scandal! It is not our scandal!

But it is!

No. Our scandal is that we are here. We are here! Pavel, how long have we been waiting? Four years since the end of the war. Four years in Germany, living with the Germans! That is the scandal, that is the scandal. Let these others make their little history. Let this criminal pay, Pavel, let him pay. A thousand payments like his would not be enough. Fela's voice shook, uneven, as if there were a bubble of air in her chest. Worry for your family, Pavel! You worry for your family, first! Then go to the others.

Pavel wanted to shout: Did I not take Chaim out of jail? But he knew that Fela would respond sharply and that he would not be able to find a retort. He looked at her face straight on: almost a challenge. Perhaps she might cry. Really, he wanted her to cry. If she did he would reach over to her, smooth her hair to her cheeks, rub her back, comfort her. If she did he would say, of course, *mammele*, my loved one, whatever you like, whatever you want, I will do.

HE THOUGHT IT WORTHWHILE to try his small access with Yidl Sheinbaum, again reelected as head of the Jewish Committee. Now everyone called him Yidl, soldiers, children, everyone. Since Hinda's wedding they had nodded at each other in passing on the street. Yidl had shaken his hand once or twice at the committee meetings that Pavel attended. An air of royalty about him, benevolent dictator of the refugees. It was rumored that the visas were slower because Yidl worried about the end of his reign, the kingdom he had made, its city of rebuilt humans. But this was too terrible to consider seriously. The British hated Jews; that was plain from the struggle they had made over the Palestine question, and from the stinginess they still had with immigration papers to England. Hinda and Kuba had received permission to go to England for only two years, and now waited for a visa to New York to come before time ran out. Even the young orphans they took in came back twelve months, eighteen months later, preparing for a life elsewhere, New Zealand, South America, all kinds of places. As for the Americans, Yidl did not have the same connections with the American authorities as he might have if he had allied with the Jewish Committees in the American DP camps. People had spoken about the possibilities, but plans had fallen through, who knew why; all those German Jews in the American zone committees, one of the Belsener leaders had said, they do not respect the Eastern Jews, what do we need this for, we've built enough by ourselves. Whatever the reason, Yidl had not made the alliance. And as a result, with the Americans—so careful with their visas, so willing to take in these others, gentiles, anyone fleeing the Russians, victims of the Germans already forgotten, already an annoyance, a problem, a trouble—Yidl did not have the influence he deserved.

But surely Yidl's friends had some way of maneuvering with the immigration authorities, for their own friends. Many had left already, only some through family connections already in the United States. Pavel himself tried to work through his second cousin, a man in New York from his mother's side, but of course Hinda would be first, as she already had a baby. Yidl must have some way. He was a good person to know. For this reason Pavel left word through his friend on the committee that he might have something to say, an opinion. Pavel was not yet sure what it was, but he had an idea about Kresser.

The office was plain, as he remembered it from Hinda's wedding three years ago. A large desk, of course, a secretary sitting outside, typing on a typewriter that made little squeaks as her fingers hit the keys, a broad window, room for some dozen people to sit, but only two or three plain, wooden chairs. Pavel was glad that the office of the leader of the Jews was spare, like an old synagogue, where one came to inscribe one's name in the books, even if here the books were the lists of those going to America, Australia, Canada. To Palestine, Israel, it was now easier to go, of course. But the scarcity there—it made Pavel shudder to think of Chaim alone there, laboring in the fields—Pavel wanted to wait for something good, for a good life for his child, his children, he would have children, like the plump ones born every week in the camp, born of marriages made quickly, the noise of infants and even older ones crowding out the quiet.

Yidl extended his hand. Then sat down in the chair in front of his desk, next to Pavel's, and said, leaning into Pavel's face, I know why you are here.

Yes, said Pavel. I told your assistant to let you know—

You know the man in the American jail. The Jewish man.

Pavel shifted his eyes. Yes.

Do you know anything good? Anything that might help us?

Pavel looked at Yidl: truthfully, no.

Truthfully?

Pavel pulled himself up, a little offended. I do not bear false witness.

There was silence. Then Pavel said, Still, as I said, I could talk to him—I could see if he—if he felt remorse—and then, if that were the case—

Tomorrow, Yidl said, I have a meeting with some of our representatives at the immigration committee. So! I cannot go tomorrow. But a delegation is to go down on Sunday. Myself, and Norbert, of course, perhaps two others. Come with us.

BUSINESS, PAVEL HAD SAID to Fela. Business. And it was true that he was to meet Marek to arrange a contract afterward. But he could see she knew it was something else. Germans did not do so much business on Sundays. Better this way, he had insisted, though she had said nothing. No one notices what we are doing, not on Sundays.

Yet Pavel thought the American soldiers could not help noticing the committee members disembarking from the long car hired by Yidl. They were small men—but for Norbert, Yidl's second in command— small in comparison to the soldiers, but dignified, their bodies stiff, their faces calm and accusatory. Pavel's cap remained firm over his curled black hair, his jacket was smooth, his shirt pressed. As they entered the jail of the Bremen zone—just a barracks office with a small row of locked rooms—Pavel felt himself to be a soldier, a peace soldier, perhaps, unarmed, but part of a large, disciplined whole.

In the bare room to which the group was led, Yidl announced: This is good.

Norbert nodded.

Yes, repeated Yidl, pulling a chair from the wooden table and motioning for the others to sit as well. This is good.

The door opened: Kresser entered.

Pavel stood. It was him. Fatter, of course, and perhaps more stooped. Still, it was the same man, with large green eyes and dark hair, olive skin, the wide mouth that spat. Pavel felt his blood knocking in his ears. Fear? But how could it be? It was not Pavel who was the prisoner. Still, his body felt tight, filled with a desperate attention.

The rest of them betrayed nothing; perhaps they felt nothing. They did not know him, this Kresser. Yidl too remained sitting. Do you know who I am?

Ah, yes, said Kresser, his voice clear, unwavering. The King of the Jews.

If you like, responded Yidl. We are here to speak with you.

Kresser lifted his brows, looked from one to the other.

Who we have here, declared Yidl, who we have here is a witness.

They all looked at Pavel: Pavel knew he was to speak. But what could he say? The man's dark skin seemed loose on his cheek, on his neck. Yet he could not be old. Perhaps five years older than Pavel. Kresser, he managed at last. Do you remember me?

Kresser looked at him in the face, then turned again to Yidl and shrugged.

No? cried Pavel. For how well Pavel remembered Kresser, the pound of his boot on his back, his head. But then he thought: What to me was a boot, to him was a shoe. Something to keep his foot warm. Pavel repeated, more quietly: No?

I did not say no, I did not say yes.

Yidl gave a look to Norbert and the two others. Let us leave Pan Mandl with the prisoner.

KRESSER, PAVEL FINALLY SAID. He had sat down again, with Kresser across. You may not remember us, but there are many who remember you. He spoke in Yiddish.

Me? said Kresser. Am I something to remember? His eyes were on his hands, wide hands. But he too spoke in Yiddish: the American soldier would not understand.

Yes, said Pavel. You are something to remember—you— He paused. To me, you—what you did—

Kresser waited.

The image in Pavel's head, the tight feeling in his arm and back, the memory of a terrible smell—it was the smell that he still could not wipe out from his body—all rose up in him and crowded his mouth. Pavel swallowed and felt the sourness recede back into his belly.

At last Pavel continued: Very many. There are very many who re- member you. Already I have met two men, three men, who are ready, more than ready, to testify.

I suppose I must be important, Kresser muttered. As important as the others, yes?

Yes, to us, yes, Pavel said, a sudden hope pushing at his voice.

So, said Kresser.

So! answered Pavel. Tell me.

Then Pavel paused. Tell what? he suddenly wondered. Kresser waited also, a thin smile on his lips.

Tell me, repeated Pavel. Are you not sorry? Are you not—Pavel searched for another word, but could not find one—are you not sorry?

What I am, said Kresser, is finished.

Pavel thought to himself: I do not bear false witness. But he said: Kresser, Kresser, think. Think. If you tell me, just a phrase, just a word of the remorse you feel, I will say something for you.

There is nothing anyone can do for me, said Kresser. I told you what I told you. I am finished.

Consider it, said Pavel. Consider what a trial will do to all of us. Not just to you. After all the pain you have caused, can you not find a way to stop the scandal now? How much easier if we avoided it. I would help you. Pavel paused, gave him a significant look. I would help you! Consider it.

Kresser looked at him, opened his mouth as if to laugh. But he did not laugh. Yes, he said. His voice was different: cheerful and inflected. Yes. I will consider it.

Kresser stood up. He was ending the visit. The muscles in Pavel's neck tightened. There was something he should say, one more thing that could escape his lips, to convince Kresser, to make him understand, but the words would not come. At last Pavel stood up himself, and the American boy accompanied him out of the room, leaving Kresser alone.

HE HAD DONE WHAT he could, Pavel thought while waiting for Marek to answer the door. He had done what he could. But the worry inside him did not subside. Only three years ago he would have testified with enthusiasm and vigor in a public court against Kresser. Now everything was different. It was important for the record to be clear. It was important for those who were left not to be stained. But sometimes there was nothing one could do.

He should push it aside. Worry for yourself! Fela had said. But he had. Already this morning Yidl had mentioned a new list he was forwarding to the Joint for their assistance, and Pavel had understood from the look Yidl had given him—a quick glance, but serious—that Pavel and Fela would be on it. So! Hinda would not be alone there with her husband and child. If this turned out. Yes, he had worried for himself, and his wife, and his child-to-be. It did not mean he would not try to contribute.

Marek opened the door. You are later than I thought.

I had something to take care of, said Pavel. Business with the committee.

Ah, said Marek. Pavel regretted even his small explanation. Marek had a habit of thinking everyone cheated him. No doubt he thought even Pavel made money on the side with Yidl and his friends.

Political business, Pavel corrected.

Of course, Marek answered.

They climbed the two flights to Marek's apartment. Now with Kuba gone, Marek lived with a new woman friend, but the home he had once shared with Kuba was unchanged. Empty. Pavel had met her only a few times; his business partnership with Marek was distant. Better that way. With Kuba, there had been a forced joviality, a wish to act like family. It had been awkward to disagree. But since Kuba and Hinda had left, Pavel and Marek had settled into a formality that was almost easier than what Pavel had with his brother-in-law. And besides, who was Kuba to complain now, with Pavel making enough even to send Kuba and Hinda a bit of money as they struggled in their new home? It felt good to have someone to take care of, now that Chaim had left too.

Pavel missed Chaim. He didn't blame him, but he missed him. The young cousin Rayzl had gone to Palestine before the war there had really finished, and she wrote to Chaim every week, begging him to hurry. She sewed shoes on a kibbutz, she could find him a space on her collective, she spoke for the new refugees on the council, she learned Hebrew at night, she had met a lovely man on the evening patrols, yes, women did it too, they were as equals, almost—there was no end to her pleading. And Pavel couldn't blame her either. Business or no business, Pavel craved to be near his sister again, he craved to be near his blood, if she had gone to the Holy Land he might have followed her there too. Still Pavel had had a thought, an idea, that young Chaim could come with them to America, even if it were difficult, even if Pavel were difficult to live with, Fela told him so herself. But did not Chaim adore Fela? No, blood mattered, at least to the stingy immigration authorities, and with no one to sponsor him to America, Chaim could not wait anymore. And so: just as quickly as they had absorbed themselves into one life, they separated: a family after all, a family that wept to be rent.

And perhaps it had been hard for Chaim when Hinda appeared, for the more Pavel had worked hard to connect himself with Kuba, and to bring Hinda into their little house life, the more Chaim and Fela returned to the strange togetherness they had with each other, as if they were conversing in silence, as if they were pretending to be brother and sister again. Chaim had not liked Marek. He rubs at me, he had said.

It had made Pavel smile. This skinny man? He only senses how intelligent you are. For this reason he is not so friendly.

But Fela had believed Chaim. You think you know everything, Pavel, but really you are naive, an innocent.

I, an innocent? He had laughed out loud at the sentence. The man is a childhood friend of my brother-in-law. What is there not to trust?

But now again in Marek's apartment Pavel thought, It will be good to return to my sister, even in a new place, even in America. Even if there is a new language to learn and use. It was significant, real blood.

Aloud to Marek he said, I have had word today. I have a feeling we will be going soon.

Marek glanced at him. You paid?

No! Not in money, legitimate. But—and I tell you this in confidence—

Of course—

I have something of value.

Stones, Marek said.

Pavel started. How could Marek know? Even Fela did not know, even Hinda—he might have mentioned to Hinda that he had valuables, but specifics, never—no one knew. Still he kept himself calm. Yes, Pavel said, I have stones. Who told you?

I heard you mention it once—you have forgotten, no matter.

I want to make a deal with them, and I want you to help me. Pavel opened his jacket, reached down into the inside pocket, and took the velvet pouch into his hand. For a brief moment he felt embarrassed, ashamed, almost idolatrous. But he shook away the thought. What had Fishl done with his share of the stones? He had taken advantage early. Now the opportunity was upon Pavel, and he would use it to arrive in the new country with resources, with a way to care for his wife and new child without depending on anyone. He shook the pouch over his spread palm and stretched his hand—glittering—out toward his partner.

Once, said Marek, you said coffee is better than diamonds.

It still is, said Pavel.

Maybe, said Marek, maybe not.

I do not need luxuries. I need to make a safe journey for my family. If I sell here, I can have a little more safety.

So?

So. So I ask you—I don't want it around that I have this—I worry for interference from the authorities, so close now to the departure. You can take ten percent from me, but I need for you to make the transaction.

Marek was silent.

I entrust them to you. Even my wife doesn't know I—

Of course! Marek burst in. Why should she know?

My man is in Hamburg. Not the buyer, but the intermediary. I have an appointment with Yidl Sheinbaum to discuss our papers. You do it, you meet this Hollander, then if you are still here when we go—

Ah, said Marek. Probably.

You have him as your connection. And that is that!

Marek paused. How will he know if they are real?

Pavel sighed. Marek. He already knows. That is why he wants to buy them. Call to him today, then we will travel tomorrow together to Hamburg. I'll hold them until then.

They brought out their ledgers.

On Monday, Pavel awoke to the sound of light rain. Soft wind hit the windows from the west, and Pavel pulled on his robe to look out. It was unusually dark, although the storm was not heavy. Yes, it would get worse.

He leaned at the windowpane, staring. Soon—but how long had he been standing there? ten minutes? an hour?—the sky began to brighten. Fela was not yet up. She slept longer now, deeper. She had not even moved when he got up from the bed; she remained on her side, spine curled away from him, body forming a semicircle, as if to protect the baby. This one had gone farther than all the ones before; the camp doctor assured them that this time, this time, things looked different. Fela even looked different, her amber hair lighter and thicker, her fine skin more easily flushed. She was past one of the danger points.

The first time she had lost a pregnancy, Chaim had discovered her, kneeling by her bed, dress dark with blood. Chaim had had the good sense to leave her there and bicycle for a military doctor; when he returned he had vomited the whole night through, Pavel pacing, witnessing the two of them in their sickness. Blood scared him also, especially the blood of a woman. His own mother had died within a day of giving birth to his youngest brother, so long ago. But the sight of both Fela and Chaim, their insides spilling, made him contain himself. He could remain composed, the eldest keeping watch. Chaim had been a nightwatch himself in the forest, he had told them—but now look: just a child, made ill and frightened by a terrible sight.

She would be a mother, Fela. She had a mother's instincts: leave this place. She had wanted to go to Palestine when Chaml had left—they had clung to each other when Chaim departed, and Pavel himself had wept. But Pavel had wanted to wait for the chance at America. And now he felt he had been right.

HAVE YOU HEARD? SAID Yidl. It was the next afternoon, and Yidl's face was bright, excited but not upset.

No, said Pavel, cigarette loose in the corner of his mouth.

Kresser, said Yidl. He hanged himself.

Pavel looked at him. He felt his hand move toward his mouth, take out the cigarette, feel the heat come closer to the tips of his fingers.

He managed a word: No. But as Pavel said it he realized he had already known, known on his way out of the kitchen this morning, belly warmed with sweet coffee, knew on his way up the stairs, as he'd looked at the calm face of Yidl's secretary, as he'd sat down in Yidl's wooden chair. He had already known when he left the jail yesterday, when Kresser had smiled, so lightly, as Pavel turned on his way out the door. Still Pavel said, No. Impossible.

Yes, said Yidl. He did. In the end we were spared. Now there will be no trial after all.

The committee would arrange for the burial. Would Pavel come?

Of course, Pavel said, of course. But he wanted to go in his own car. He could not, he would not engage in the politics, the committee talk that would scatter in and out on the hour-long drive to Bremen.

I will join you, he said. But I first—I had an appointment, I did not expect—

Marek waited for him in the entryway of the Roundhouse office. He shrugged as Pavel changed the directions; they would go to Bremen, make their plans on the road there.

Pavel, you are upset, said Marek. Let me drive. You have the money?

Of course I have the money. Pavel frowned. Sewn inside. I'll show you when we get there.

It was true, Pavel was too agitated to drive. He slipped into the passenger seat and gave Marek the key. The noise of the motor soothed him. Perhaps Marek would not expect Pavel to speak right away. He had surprised himself the day before with his ability to speak even a few words to Kresser. Speak, speak, Yidl had urged him as they had walked into the American jail. But Yidl was completely without inhibition about speaking. He could recite the most painful events, horrors about which no one wanted to hear, not the victorious armies, certainly not the vanquished. He could speak with great eloquence if not detail. Yidl would transform this terrible thing, this Kresser death, into a fable, a morality tale, or better, into a tiny, invisible item in the camp news, to be read only in Yiddish by refugees.

He hanged himself. Pavel heard and reheard Yidl's rushed words: He hanged himself.

Once Kresser had almost killed Pavel. And now Pavel had had a hand, perhaps not a hand, but a push, a light push, in Kresser's end. One more death. Did it matter? And what a one! A criminal, a piece of human dirt, refuse.

But also a man, a criminal man. He was surprised at his own shock and horror: that a man could die like this, and that Pavel could think on it and think on it. His own wife's miscarriages had been less strange—more painful, more grievous, but less strange. It was odd, unfamiliar: the death of one man, alone in a cell, meant something. One death meant something important.

Yes, it was a new time he was in, a new time, if he could think on one death. Death would continue, but it would be individual and strange, mourned. Kresser would have his own grave, and men would cover his coffin with dirt.

Funny. Pavel would know where Kresser was buried, but not the site of the body of his own father. His father had always said he would not allow himself to be gassed, he would be shot first, he would force them to shoot him, and Pavel hoped he had had his wish. But many had pledged this to themselves and then held on to the last shreds of hope that what they knew would happen could not happen. But his father, so stubborn, so rigid, surely he had gotten his wish—

Very difficult, said Marek.

Hmm? said Pavel.

The rain makes it difficult to see.

Pavel looked over at the steering wheel, the hands of Marek, thick and dry. He thought suddenly of a young boy he had recently hired to act as a messenger for him, a German boy, with pale, delicate fingers. Not a rural one. And young—too young to have been in the army. Clean hands, perhaps. A quick rage flew through Pavel, rage at this boy, who surely would know where his parents were buried. Pavel had asked—for no reason, it had just fallen out of his mouth—where the boy's parents were, and the young man had answered. He felt his forehead steaming, and he leaned against the car window. What had the boy answered? Father is wounded, he sits at home. Mother, she—

The boy had continued talking, but Pavel did not remember what he had said. He had not wanted to know what this German boy's mother did to help them scrape for food. Where was Pavel's mother? Buried, thank God, buried, for this they were lucky, but the grave-yards—he had heard that the Jewish cemetery in Krakow was a great rubble, the wall and stones crushed. He had a sudden vision of his mother's grave as it had been when he last saw it, steady and whole. The urge seized him, coursed through him like water—he would go before leaving for America. He had been to Berlin, to the Russian zone, when he heard that his aunt, his mother's youngest sister, had survived, come back from Russia to take a job with the Communists, he had surprised her and she almost fainted—why had he not gone to Poland to see the grave?

Kresser would have a grave. Perhaps not a completely right burial—it would be hard to find a rabbi to bury a suicide, not to say a criminal, an accomplice to murderers—but a grave, his own dark space. And a group of men saying Kaddish, a tainted Kaddish, to be sure, but a Kaddish.

This man would have a grave. How strange, how strange, that a man with a hand in others' deaths would survive to die, to take his own life and rest alone, with a private coffin and a private grave. This man, of all men, would have a grave.

The car made a quick swerve. Pavel's side of the car almost collided with a barrier. Marek! he said.

Ay, said Marek. This road hasn't been the same since the bridge was rebuilt—

So drive more slowly, answered Pavel.

Early on in the war Perla's father had stopped Pavel from certain suicide. Pavel had met him only once, having been pulled into a minyan against his will, he was hiding—when the police had broken in and taken several of the men. Pavel had jumped out a window. Then they threatened to kill all of them—this was at the start of it, when they still threatened first—unless Pavel turned himself in, and Perla's father had stopped him. Miloch, the father had begged. Miloch, you have everything to live for. An enormous bribe had been paid, and all but one of the men had been freed, although what happened to them later—and of course the one man, Weil—how by chance it all was—

and no doubt Perla's father himself was long since ash—but Pavel's choice, Miloch's choice, had been different, Kresser's soul had been sick—

Marek made a quick turn, swinging the car on Pavel's side centimeters from a lamppost.

Marek! Pavel said again, suddenly present. You are always a good driver! What is it now?

Perhaps something is wrong with the car, said Marek, not looking at him. I don't feel I have control over the steering.

It was in order this morning when I drove it. Pavel peered through the fog of the window at the hammering rain. It was still morning, but the sky was a night sky, gray as charcoal, striped with flashing light.

It really is hard to see, protested Marek.

Something in his voice scratched at Pavel. A tickle of doubt. But there were lights coming up, coming closer.

A train station, said Pavel. We'll stop there and I'll drive. I do not know what is wrong with you.

Another swerve, a shouted curse from someone—was it his own voice?—and his body twisting and spinning.

IN CAMP, TIME HAD passed in anguished routine, the morning roll call, the distribution of bread, the march to work, the evening roll call, repeated and repeated, the routine interrupted only by violent incidents of the day, by waves of sickness in the barracks, by the arrival of a new transport, by selections, by the liquidation of one camp and the miserable journey to the next. Now, again, he was in another place where time passed but did not pass, he saw things in a fog of pain, not the fever pain of typhus, not the pain of a beating, but a pain so long, so deep in his bones that it became his body, the soul of his body, radiating from his shattered leg to his jaw, carving through his abdomen and back when they lifted him to feed him juice through a straw, a pain interrupted only by the injections of morphine he received every few hours, the doctors speaking quietly to the nurses, never to him, the tiny young nun turning him over and emptying his bedpan. Once he thought he saw Chaim, standing at the doorway, but awaking knew he was gone, the light-haired man must have been— who could it have been? The way Pavel knew to mark time passing was by the appearances of Fela, who, the first day he was conscious of seeing her, looked large, swollen, like the woman he had met almost five years before, malnourished, bloated, in mourning and beautiful.

Had he gone back in time? He tried to say something—to ask her if she had enough to eat—but he could hear it as a groan, and a nun hurried over with a syringe.

Sometime later he saw Fela again, her belly even more round against her slim frame, and he understood, his mind was clear, he could not move the muscles at his jaw, but he tried to signal her with his eyes. He could see she sensed him awake and lucid, he was there with her, she knew, because she began to talk to him more slowly, the words moving through his pounding head in soft drops of water, soft drops of milk, the baby would be healthy, one did not want to say too much of course, bad luck, but it was a healthy pregnancy, and soon it was only three more months, only two more months, only one more month.

Emigration was out of the question now. Hinda, having left England for New York with Kuba and their infant, told him in a letter read to him by Yidl that he would not be able to come, that there had been a change, that their cousin Mayer, waiting in the American zone, would be next. Yidl had read it lightly, and Hinda's words did not go into detail, but Pavel had heard about it enough times that he understood. Americans did not want the injured, did not want those who would become what they called a charge to the public, dependent, unable to provide for their families, poor. It had been hard enough as Jews—the visas seemed to go only to the gentiles fleeing the Russians, it was Russia who was now the world's enemy—it had been hard enough, and now—well, now, where would he go with his family? Palestine would take them, would take anyone now that the borders were open, but how would Pavel make a living there, so broken, when all there would be for him was manual labor, physical work?

He lay there shaking, pushing out a question to Yidl, a name he would not let himself utter in front of Fela: Where is Marek Rembishevski? Where is Marek Rembishevski?

Yidl kept his face blank. Your wife wanted to find him, but we heard he went to America.

After Yidl left with the letter, Pavel turned his neck to the wall. There was no window here. When they came in to feed him his liquid food, he pushed it away. No.

He could not open his lips to whisper to Fela when she came to talk to him that evening, nor the next morning. She took his hand and stroked it, as she had in the early days of their marriage, and said, Pavel, Pavel, what has happened?

He wanted to answer her, comfort her. But when he opened his lips slowly, slowly so as not to injure his jaw further, he felt his mouth aching with shame. She hurried out to find a doctor, to insist that someone take a look, give her some answer, perhaps the food they were giving him had turned in his belly—

But when she had left, after the examinations, after the nurse gave him another pill ground up in his water, he heard the doctor speaking, not softly, not carefully, but casually, to the nurse: He will not survive this.

Pavel strained his hearing, but the doctor was speaking in a pleasant, clear voice. Pavel had heard correctly. He will not survive this.

Pavel forced himself upright, his lower back throbbing, his neck pulling—I will not survive this? Pavel cried—he was shouting, or perhaps it was only amplified in his head—I will survive you, Herr Doctor! Another German telling me to die? I will survive you!

After that, after the doctor stared at him, still shaking his head, and called the nurse to bring another syringe full of painkiller, after Pavel shuddered with rage through his heavy sleep that night, he awoke at the sound of a motor outside. It was still dark, and a nurse was nodding off in a chair next to his bed. Something felt different. His head was clouded but no longer pounding, no longer a hammer. He lay in his bed until breakfast, feeling the fog roll around in his head, moving, shifting, at moments letting in clear shafts of water and light.

Fela did not come at her usual time. Instead, Yidl, in a dark jacket and pale shirt—even from afar, Pavel could see the fine quality of the cloth, the barely perceptible checks of the jacket—walked in. He stood at the doorway a moment, observing Pavel, who half-sat, with his neck supported by a cylindrical pillow. Then Yidl came to the bed, sat down in Fela's chair, and took Pavel's hand in his.

Your wife, said Yidl, stroking Pavel's wrists, like a grandmother would do, a grandmother or a mother. Your wife is in labor. Tsipora is with her.

Pavel looked at him, his kind, round face, the eyes hollowed out and bony, the plump cheeks.

God in heaven, Pavel said.

She will survive it, said Yidl. But the tone in Yidl's voice was new to Pavel. Unsure, cautious. He longed to hear an assurance from Yidl, the way he had as a child from his father, from his grandfather. Not to worry, my child. God willing, of course. Pavel wanted to hear and to accept an assurance. But it wasn't to be. Somewhere not far, in a camp hospital, Fela was struggling through labor pains, and a baby was fighting to be born. Before the child even had a form, it had pushed and kicked, troubled Fela with heat and hunger. It had wanted to be free. And yet emerging from the mother's womb—so difficult, so painful for infant and mother—that was the least troubling journey there was.

A twinge rushed through his back and legs, a wish to let her live, even if the child should die. He quieted his head, he let his jaw clamp shut, clear out the terrible thought. He stared at the wall, looked at Yidl, begged for something to read, to look at, though he could not concentrate his eyes or his mind. Yidl did not move from his chair. He rested, he napped, he watched Pavel until the moment Tsipora appeared at the threshhold of the hospital room.

Good evening, she said. And *mazel tov*. You have a son.

PAVEL TOLD HIS NURSE he did not want any more morphine. He would have to live with the pain every day. He should start now. He decided to speak a sentence every hour, even if there was no one in the room to hear him, even if the words came out in unfamiliar chains, phrases from storybooks, songs, prayers. He fed himself the same half-solid food every day, the hot cereals and soups, the fruit compotes. Wire threaded through the joint of his right knee, a deep indentation ran down his right shin, now a full inch shorter than his left one. But with practice, he could almost wink with one eye, on the side of his face where the cheekbone had not been crushed and repaired; he could sit, with help, in a chair; he could walk to the toilet in the corridor on his own if someone lent an arm for balance.

It was a week before Fela left the hospital—it had been a difficult birth—and another two before she came to visit Pavel, no longer sick, no longer afraid to catch an illness from the ward, no longer weak. He did not know she was coming; he awoke and heard her voice.

Pavel, she said. I have something for you.

He looked up at his wife, pale, blood still drained from her face from the birth, carrying her little gift in her hand, sitting by him, stroking his arm.

It is your birthday, she said. And look what I brought.

She opened her palm to show him a photograph of his son. Small, splotched face, a head of dark hair.

He turned his face to Fela, her green eyes, large and tender. Yes, he said. It is my birthday. He looked again at the picture. The little one didn't look so happy to be out in the world. But Pavel would be happy. It was his birthday.

He was two hundred years old.

New Dictionary

1960–1973

Rescue

I N THE SUMMERTIME FELA took her children to the municipal pool in Jackson Heights. When the New York afternoons became painfully hot, she brought them on Saturdays too. Their father did not like them to swim on the Sabbath. But on occasion, in winter, he himself went to work after synagogue. If he could work in December, why, in July, should the children be smothered by the heat? What else was she to do with them?

In the front seat of the Buick, Larry unrolled his window all the way. Fela clucked at him—only a kerchief protected her freshly done hair. Larry gave a loud sigh, rolled the window almost closed again, leaving a sliver of space for air. Helen leaned her head against the warm glass for the short drive. She kicked the back of Larry's seat, and Larry turned around and grabbed her ankle until she squealed.

"Kindlech!" cried Fela.

It made her even more nervous to drive with them making noise.

She slowed down more as they reached Queens Boulevard, with its milk trucks and postal wagons looming, making their own car, so substantial on their home street, seem small and weak.

"Not to fight when I drive!" she said. She used English when she wanted them to be sure to listen. The extra effort should make her children more attentive to her words. "Larry, please. Please."

"She started it!"

"Please, *mein kind*, please."

They fought terribly at home too, cramped in their little bedroom, and there was nothing for Fela to do but to get them outside, give them the opportunity to spend their energy, tire themselves out. And Fela needed an escape too. Pavel and she had fought a silent battle earlier this morning. It made her burn, his stiff face as she took out the bathing suits for the children and packed her straw bag with towels. She seemed to remember him as more flexible when the children were infants, but perhaps that was the result of her shaky memory. No, the change was real: he had become angry at her recently for fixing Friday night dinner late, her customer at the beauty salon having kept her, and she had been stunned, even awed, by his fury. Pavel did not criticize anything she did in the home, not her cooking—even the one or two times she had experimented—and not her housekeeping. The home was her domain. He respected it. But that night he had come home, face aflame from the vodka he had begun drinking at work, and shut the door hard behind him.

He had entered the kitchen with his jaw set. You are still cooking!

His voice was quiet, restrained even, but she had answered, Why do you scream so?

The Sabbath has begun! How will our children learn if their mother lights a fire on the Sabbath?

You light a fire on the Sabbath, Fela murmured, shocked. You smoke, more than I do. Mrs. Fineman was late for her manicure, and then the butcher himself was late with my chicken, what can I tell you?

She turned away from him. Why should she look at his face in this state? She had seen him in his rages before, of course she had—but not so much at her. She did not think the children had noticed. They ate, as usual, and fought, as usual. And what was there to notice? More silence from their father? Nothing so new. He concentrated on his food and on his drink. His anger seemed to have no effect on his appetite: when Helen didn't finish her portion he scraped the remains of her meal onto his plate, Helen watching.

But now they were on their way to swim. At the red light on Thirty-seventh Avenue, Fela looked back at her daughter. Sweat formed on Helen's brow and a tiny drop curled past her ear. Such a hot day! How could Pavel be so stubborn? When he had started going to synagogue on the Sabbath, he had actually driven! But when Fela drove the car, then it was a sin. Such a heat as this none of them had known in childhood. Did God demand that the children be deprived of a little cool water and exercise? Besides, in public places Larry and Helen seemed to behave better with each other. The arguments they had at home, Larry taunting his sister, Helen fighting back with her teeth and fists until Larry grabbed her wrists to keep her still, those fights ceased when Fela took them outside. Outside, at holiday dinners with their aunt and uncle, at school, in the park, Larry was an angel, a ten-year-old protector. It gave Fela a rest to have them there.

No, Pavel had not been so rigid when the children were tiny. She could even say that he had been happy. Happier. Now that he spent his free mornings going so much to synagogue, looking at his books, trying to concentrate on the circles within circles of words, he did not look happy. He was forty-four, and he looked angry. Worse, he looked like he was trying to keep in his anger, pressing himself down, presenting a full and serious front, the way he did when he posed for photographs, as if he were doing hard physical labor, moving the prayers and solemn songs with the bones of his body.

It had not been so with her own father, strict as he had been. There had been a little enjoyment, she thought, in all his observance. But, of course, then everyone had been pious, one didn't think or make choices about how to spend a Friday or a Saturday, and it did not happen that a kosher butcher was late with a chicken. A family had a sense of sameness about the little events of every day. One got up in the morning, washed, dressed, and ate. On the Sabbath one worshipped instead of worked. Or at least the men did. For a woman, Sabbath was just a different form of work from the rest of the week.

Fela turned the car onto Broadway and crossed under the elevated train tracks. It gave her a little shudder to drive under the elevated, so rickety, so easy to have it fall just as one's children were passing under it—but a moment, and it was over.

FELA LOOKED UP FROM her magazine and pushed down her sunglasses so she could see Larry and Helen more clearly. They were in the near corner of the pool, turning somersaults underwater, then coming up to gasp for air.

They had survived their swimming lessons with the lifeguard, lessons Pavel had insisted they take as he watched, fully dressed to cover up his crippled leg. Fela could not watch. But once they knew how to swim, first Larry at age seven, then Helen two years later—Fela allowed her daughter to start younger, at age five—Fela could stretch out on the slatted chair with the *Ladies' Home Journal*, glancing up every two or three minutes as the two of them splashed and tickled, making up games. They had no friends at the pool, though at school, separated, the two of them got on well enough with other children. In the water they preferred to be just with each other.

They played a game she hated: rescue. Helen would dive into the water—Fela had stopped gasping when she saw her daughter's head moving downward, disappearing—and she was good at it, very good at it, the lifeguard had assured her. Look at the shape her five-year-old body took when she curled off the child's diving board! Fela would force herself to watch the dive—she should keep an eye on the dive in order to scream faster if something were to happen. And Helen did dive gracefully. She would stay under, emerge, wave at her brother, then pretend to cough, sink under again, slowly, her arm outstretched, only her wrist above water, then just the upper half of her palm, then her two fingers sticking up in a V. Fela would count the seconds until she saw the two fingers, because at that moment Larry would bound over from wherever he was, pretending not to see, then leap under water, lift his sister out into the air, her body light and thin, her small arms around his neck.

Fela had watched them do it many times and for reasons she could not explain even to herself, had not forbidden the game. Stop, stop! she could hear her own voice whispering inside her mind. Stop, children, stop! But if she said it aloud, then what? Larry would ask why. Helen would imitate him too. Why, Ma, why?

Because I said so, Fela imagined herself answering, the way she had once heard another mother saying at the pool. Because I am the mother. But the words would not come out naturally to her, and Larry would laugh at her falseness—better to remain silent.

Fela looked at her watch. It was almost two o'clock. She wanted to pick up from Stanley the repaired toaster, before Sunday breakfast. One errand every Saturday—a small break from the pool, a moment to herself.

"Children!" she called. "Children!" They wanted her to use English in public. Even on a Saturday, when so many of their friends would not be at the pool. Larry and Helen were far off, silver water pushing off their pale backs.

"Children, please!" Even this word seemed false to her, empty. She had not adapted easily to English. The rules seemed always to be changing. To make a plural, one added an *s*. But to make a plural for a verb, one dropped the *s*. Larry had explained it many times. *Feed* for plural, *feeds* for singular. And then there were the exceptions: *mice* for two mouses, *sheep* for the plural as well as the singular. Well, these words did not matter too much for everyday life. Fela could not imagine why her son bothered to make her memorize them. She supposed it was good to keep hearing the words, in case one day she had to make use of them. But in Queens, sheep? she had joked with Larry. He had looked hurt. He liked his little role as guide in the new world of Jackson Heights. Even Pavel laughed from time to time about it.

"Children!" She was standing above them, on the edge of the pool, letting them know she was going for her toaster, that they were not to dive while she was gone. They stopped and looked up. Children. It had taken her a long time to stop herself from saying "childrens." And even now, when she was nervous, it slipped out wrong. Childrens. The truth was that "children" did not feel right to her without an *s*, as if the word properly spoken in English did not account for everyone.

SHE PULLED THE CAR out of the parking lot and drove down Queens Boulevard to shop. She did it every Saturday, and she did it with the same fear that by turning her eyes away from them in the pool, they would do something dangerous, hurt themselves. It was silly, to believe there was some kind of luck or magic or power in her eyes, but she really believed that if she watched over them, nothing could happen.

She believed it even though she could not swim. If she saw something happen there was nothing she could do to stop it—nothing to do but scream! Was that not worse? No, a scream could help. Still, she had to let them feel alone, feel independence. Everyone did it. Pavel could do it. Pavel could let go, at least a little.

Pavel had taught both children how to ride a bicycle. Larry was more fearless. He went fast. Helen never learned how to go fast. Fela would watch her husband from the window, his hands on the back of Helen's bike rack, dragging his lame leg in a half-gallop after her as she pushed slowly on her training wheels. "I have you," he would call out. "I have you."

But Helen always sensed the moment when her father let go of the rack, and she would stop pedaling and turn around. Larry would speed off, even faster than Pavel had planned, and go veering down the sidewalk. Pavel would have to stop following after a few steps.

It isn't like teaching you to ride, he had said one evening.

Hmm? Fela had answered.

I taught you—don't you remember? How I would run after you, faster than you could pedal the wheels?

Pavel made sure they had what the other children in the neighborhood had, short blue frames for Larry, long wide seats for Helen. He let them ride around the block, on the sidewalk, until Helen ran into the legs of an elderly woman while concentrating on something that had rolled off the curb. After that he took the car and drove them, their bicycles protruding from the trunk, to the park in Fresh Meadows, and occasionally to Central Park, where they cycled in the closed road while he sat on a bench, listening to his pocket radio.

Fela used the time to be alone in the house. Sunday time. She was glad she did not have to observe the small mishaps, falls, flat tires, and stories of pain the children came home recounting. Larry was supposed to ride behind Helen, so that he could keep an eye on her. He would let her get far ahead of him so he could then catch up, pedaling at a sudden, high rate. Once he waited too long. She took a fork in the road, and Larry couldn't find her. He had come back to his father, and they had called the police, who had already picked up a tearful girl and had placed her in between them in the police car, her low pink bicycle protruding from the trunk. They had planned not to tell Fela at all, but even if Helen had not walked through the door and grabbed her mother at the waist, Fela would have guessed something had happened, a near miss, an almost accident. A mother knew! And the children were unable to eat their dinner, because Pavel had bought them ice-cream cones on the way home, something he usually refused to do.

She did not like to leave them alone at the pool. But how could she bring them with her? She could not have them trailing behind if she wandered from Stanley's shop to the grocery or stopped by the beauty parlor to chat with the Hungarian women who took the morning shift on Saturdays. It was summer. They were children. A lifeguard stood watch at the pool.

Besides, Larry was responsible. If Fela asked him not to do something dangerous, he agreed, he complied. He understood something about it, Fela thought, he saw that her worries mattered, they were important, more important perhaps than other rules: go to sleep early, don't fight with your sister, take your clothes off the floor, don't shout so in the house. He was not obedient, but he was sensitive. Certain things he understood.

So when she had told him, "Larry, watch your sister, not to let her to dive into the pool when I'm not here," he had answered, "All right."

And it was all right, it was all right. He was a good boy. The Italians in the hardware store still asked about him. When he was smaller and they were greener he would speak for both her and Pavel. He was their guide, the third parent, the American parent, translating for them when he himself registered for school. Thank God that cheat of a landlord spoke Yiddish. Larry had never had to be an intermediary there.

Or in most things anymore. Now that Pavel and Fela got on by themselves Larry watched over his sister. He watched over Helen; he obeyed his mother. It was all right.

FELA PAUSED BY THE window of a real estate office on Seventy-fourth Street, squinted at the little pink and green papers with black handwriting advertising apartments in Jackson Heights, houses in Corona. She and Pavel were always among the last ones. They had come after the others, stuck in Germany without visas while the others had started their new lives, learning the language of work, taxes, and now real estate after everyone else. She checked the storefront office every week, and every week someone looked up at her through the window. But she did not go in.

Pavel thought they should move. Pavel's cousin was still in an apartment in Brooklyn, but Pavel's sister and brother-in-law had a house in Long Island already. It was true, it would be good to have something larger. But it was difficult to find a home that would be suitable for Pavel's limp. A house with stairs was out of the question, even if they could afford it.

She looked at a drawing of a house two blocks from Queens Boulevard, not too far from the courthouses. Reasonable, but still too much. Kew Gardens, she thought, squinting again at the advertisements in the window. Pavel liked the name Rego Park. It sounds like Riga, he said. It's Jewish. And the Budniks live there.

She stepped away from the window. Perhaps she would stop an extra minute, buy a little sweet thing, some fruit, for the house.

That would be good for them. They shouldn't learn to love so much her baking; it was bad for later. Larry was growing now, of course, and he could eat more steadily even than his father, but they taught him how to eat slow. It was a challenge, with a ten-year-old boy, to teach him to slow down! Fruit was good for eating slow. Pavel was careful about his eating, no matter how trim he was. And she too. They taught their children well. Finish what you eat, but eat slow. It was better for the digestion. Also one didn't gain so much. Not that she prepared so many heavy foods. Cookies and cakes were the only exceptions.

Fela did not love to cook. She loved to bake. Pavel had a nostalgia for stuffed derma, but she could perform only a poor imitation of her mother's recipes, and besides, too much meat limited her baking to cakes without dairy in order to keep the home kosher. She would bring the dairyless cookies with her for holiday dinners at the home of Pavel's sister Hinda, and Hinda would scold her sons for eating too many. Fela and Hinda did not feel a warmth toward each other, even from the first, when Hinda was still a bitter girl without a mother or a sister or even a friend to guide her through womanhood and marriage. Hinda had married before Fela and Pavel, and no doubt Hinda had disapproved of the morals in the house near the DP camp, Fela and Pavel sharing a bed before signing a marriage contract. But that was not all of it. Hinda took herself away from everyone but her husband—to that neighborhood in Long Island, not a single acquaintance from Europe. Hinda did not like reminders, not even of the time in Germany after the war.

Fela was different. She had drawn an internal line and kept herself calmly on the side of the new life. Her mouth and face and hands no longer felt strange to her. For all Hinda's clucking at the cakes, Fela still looked all right, although she felt she could lose two or three kilos. They had come upon her in the last year, without her noticing until summer, when she pulled the slim beige strap of her open-toed mules over her pedicured feet and felt herself teetering at the knees, the extra weight pushing down on her ankles.

As for Pavel, he noticed his own appearance more than hers. Every morning since they came to the United States she would watch him from their bed getting dressed. It fascinated her, the unwrapping of the phylacteries from his arms and forehead, his daily choice of shirt, his struggle to put on his specially made shoes, one stacked higher than the other to balance the limp. She would lie curled, breathing steadily, feigning sleep as he knotted his necktie in the mirror, pulled his jacket onto his narrow chest, and then stopped to stare at himself. Sometimes he would stare thirty seconds, sometimes almost five minutes. She knew what he saw. Scarred body, dented face, worn skin hanging below his thinning black hair. But his clothing was fresh, the shirt pressed but soft, the tie subtly patterned to complement the suit. He drove the children crazy on the way out the door, smacking their winter coats with a lint brush, refusing to acknowledge that once outside for five minutes they would accumulate far more debris than he could scrape off in the few moments before the rush out of the apartment to school.

THERE WAS A COMMOTION at the pool. Fela could see a small group of adults in a half-circle and two boys chasing each other, trying to steal a glimpse of the scandal within. She walked faster, her paper bag of oranges and apples tapping her thighs in an assuring rhythm. Nothing has happened, nothing has happened, she thought to herself, the words coming into her brain slowly, then accelerating. Nothing has happened, nothing has happened, God willing, nothing has happened.

"Mrs. Mandl! Here she is!"

The phrases in Fela's head stopped even as her legs began to run, the inner soles of her mules slapping against the bottoms of her feet, the edges of her toes scraping against the gravel, then the concrete, then the tiles surrounding the pool. She pushed at the women in their half-circle, at the small damp girls crowded by the lounge chairs, she pushed, she didn't know what or where she pushed, but she heard again, this time softer, the American woman's voice that had called her name:

"Now don't worry, Mrs. Mandl, really, don't worry. She's okay."

Blood trailed down Helen's temples.

"*Oy, Gott!*" Fela whispered, her breath cold against her teeth. "*Oy, Gott!*"

Her hair—her child's hair! was dark and matted, thick with blood, more blood.

"*Mein kind!*" she cried. "*Oy, Gott!*"

"Mrs. Mandl!" Another voice, from the direction of Helen. Fela saw suddenly, even as she reached out to grab her daughter's hand, to touch her daughter's pink and swollen skin, that Helen sat in the lap of a large woman whose round face bubbled out from behind large brown sunglasses. Fela looked at the woman with confusion. A man stood over the two of them, wiping the back of Helen's head with a bright white bandage quickly soaking with red, a wave of blood spreading as if through a snowdrift on a narrow cobbled street, but no, there was no snow, there was no snow, Fela turned her head to look past the plump legs of the women to the pool, it was summer, it was New York, there was no snow, but the pool was suddenly filled with dark red water, blood, no, it was blue, it was a pool, the municipal pool of Jackson Heights where she took her children each Saturday in summer, it was summer, and she was looking at the face of her five-year-old daughter, who had stopped her crying and was talking to her in English.

"Don't worry, Ma, don't worry."

"Heads always bleed a lot! Nothing bleeds like a head!" It was the man speaking, his hand lifting and twisting Helen's hair, rubbing his dark bandage on the child's scalp. "She won't even need stitches!"

"Stitches!" cried Fela.

"Mrs. Mandl!" repeated the woman, holding Helen by the waist. "Don't get hysterical. It will only upset her."

But what is it? What happened? My God, dear God, what happened?

The man smiled at her. "No speak English?" he asked. "Doctor." He pointed to his bag, then clapped a hand to his chest. "Doctor."

What has happened? What has happened?

"Does anyone around here speak Jewish?" called the large woman in the sunglasses. "Even a few words?"

"There's no one here today," said someone in the crowd. "It's Saturday."

She looked up for the body attached to the voice, then saw her son was before her, hair damp, shorts dripping, face wet with pool water and tears. She saw her son, and his father's crumpled face in his, and her chest grew hot, her voice was wailing out, she could feel the wail coming out of her, though when it came out she heard it only in a whisper, What did you do? What did you do?

"She just wants to know what happened." Larry's thin voice. "She understands."

A child started talking, a woman cut him off, then another woman interrupted. Diving, the children had been diving, running and diving, the somersaults the little ones liked to compete over, and Helen had made an acrobatic leap and knocked into the wall of the pool, emerging from the water with a line of blood streaming after her. Larry said not a word, and when Fela found it in herself to look at his face, to accuse him, he was looking down at his feet, at Helen's feet, at the cement walk on which the crowd stood.

"Kids get hurt," said the woman holding Helen. "It happens. Now, sit in that chair. Go, sit."

The doctor nodded. "Let Dr. Velasco play hairdresser with your daughter another minute."

Helen giggled.

Fela moved over to a lounge chair, Larry following. The women and children had dispersed, only one woman standing by, a soft smile on her face. Fela smiled back.

"It's okay, everything okay," Fela said. Perhaps the neighbor would turn away. But she stayed. Fela feigned a look of concentration as she watched the doctor's hands, the slim bottle of ointment he twisted open and poured on yet another bandage, then moved her eyes down to his wide feet in brown sandals, to Helen's own feet and legs, her little waist wrapped in damp nylon, the pink and yellow flowers of her bathing suit.

They had no idea, these children. No idea what it took to bring them into the world. If they knew, they could not risk everything in this way, diving against a mother's wishes, running, screaming, hitting, scratching—almost, God forbid, choking each other!—they knew nothing of what it took. If they knew even a half, even a quarter, even a tenth, they would not dare.

No one knew but a mother.

And a mother had to keep quiet, had to stop herself from screaming in fear at every moment. This Fela was good at. When Larry was born in the DP camp hospital Fela herself had kept her words inside her, had kept her groans incomprehensible and controlled, for she had heard the stories, of other women in childbirth crying out, screaming, even three years after the liberation, even four, in the delirium of pain, don't take my baby, don't take my baby, don't take my baby.

Fela closed her eyes.

When Pavel learned of this he would want them to go to synagogue for weeks. No. She would stand firm. It was too hot in the summer for prayer. Job's wife had screamed at her husband, Curse your god and die! And the wife was right. What kind of husband accepted this pain, the damage coming and coming, until the end of the stupid tale when God presented the mourners with the false new family, the lie of peace after all the suffering, the lie that the new family itself would not suffer its own wounds? No one was exempt, no matter how much one had suffered before or how much one prayed now. It was the opposite, yes, the opposite.

Her son was speaking to her. "It's my fault, it's my fault."

"Larry," she answered.

"It's my fault," he repeated. Then he looked up at her. "I'm the worst person in the world."

"Larry," she said again, watched him put his face in his hands.

She should touch him, comfort him, but he was using his own words for comfort. It's my fault, I'm the worst person in the world. Did not this make one feel safer than the random truth, that a mother turning away caused blood to flow, that an inch more forward and Helen would have emerged from the pool laughing, blowing out air, spitting water at her brother?

She should touch his anguished face, but instead her voice was loud again, crying at him in Yiddish: Why? Why? Why did you not listen to me? Why did you disobey me? Do you think you are another mother, another father? You are a child, you obey!

"I'm sorry," said Larry in English, crying. "I'm sorry." He paused for a moment, choked on a word, then gurgled out: "I'm the worst person in the world."

"Yes," she answered him. "You are. The worst person in the world." The words sounded good, hard, powerful, precise. She said it again, this time in Yiddish, with deliberation, the power of her voice startling her, relieving her.

He stopped crying and looked at her, his face wet and small, astonished. The worst in the world: her son. Fela's brother, her youngest brother Lieb after whom her son was named, had been like Larry, so sensitive, so soft. There had been a time in her own youth when the children had run the lives of their parents, smuggling and trading, maneuvering for news and plans. But no more. Inside her swelled a sudden pity, pity for her son, her sweetheart, as they said in English, her little king. They thought they commanded everything. When she was a child she almost did not have permission to speak to an unaccompanied young man in her father's store. But what had all the strictness accomplished? It had driven out her older sister to a kibbutz in Palestine, long before the war, and it had driven Fela herself out to the arms of a young man, her first love, when the Germans crossed into eastern Poland. But she had not done what she did to punish her father, or to make politics. She had left the home and fled to Russia for love. Her beloved had been arrested and disappeared, and their infant had died, but she had lived. Perhaps love had saved her life, as politics had saved her only surviving sister's, taking them out of the town that was destroyed, every person, every baby.

And now, with her errands, with her impatience, with her need for silence and privacy, she had turned away from them and risked everything, stupid, stupid, as if she knew as little as her children about all the blood and torn flesh through which they had passed to enter this world. But she did know. Her son did not. Little man. Always trying to be good, and yet suffering the world's punishments and random accidents, just like his parents.

Her pity made her speak again. She would cover over her cruelty, she would wash it away. Don't worry, she said in Yiddish, don't worry, my child. Helcha is all right.

She caressed her son's head without looking.

Family Business

October 1961

ON THE TABLE BETWEEN them lay a bolt of silk the color of dark wheat. Pavel's old friend Fishl Czarny had delivered the material straight to Pavel, a remnant from a manufacturer going out of business. For the first time in several weeks, perhaps longer, Pavel felt calm, his bad leg stretched out to the side, his hand caressing the cloth, taking in the fineness of the weave. The silk could make a lining for a dozen suit jackets, and with an important contract for a small retailer due in two weeks, the order would be completed with a touch of elegance.

His brother-in-law was speaking to him. "I go down to get a soup," Kuba said. "Should I bring you a coffee?"

Why the pretense of English when they were alone? Pavel thought. It was a battle they fought silently every day, each trying to last as long as possible in the language of his choosing, as if Kuba were afraid of his mother tongue, as if Pavel would be able to teach him otherwise. But Pavel was in a good mood today, and his brother-in-law would not spoil it. He could be generous for a moment, he thought, and reply to Kuba in English. "Beautiful, no?"

Kuba's round face was a mask. He said, "What have we given away for it?"

Pavel sighed. He was not angry, but he might become angry, and it was stupid to enter an argument without full command of one's words. He answered in Yiddish. I don't give away. I make business. Shouldn't he have a suit from us, for all he does?

So he deals in fabric now? Kuba relented halfway, spoke in Polish.

He has a friend, yes, who has occasion to supply—take a look! What it will add to the Steiner order! Pavel spread the silk across his palm and wrist, stretched out his arm toward Kuba.

It's the bartering that I don't like. Like peddlers in a village. We can't account well for it.

What is to account? There is no man I trust more.

Ah. Kuba looked at him, half-cold, half-hurt. Of course.

But Pavel didn't regret his words. Of course! Of course! He was with me in—

Yes, yes, I know, Kuba interrupted.

He's a religious man! More, he is a loyal—he and I—

"I have not yet eaten," Kuba said. "Do you want I should bring you a coffee?"

No, said Pavel. No—I— He was standing, he suddenly realized. "No, thank you," he said, slowly, to make himself calm. "No."

He stood another moment after Kuba had left. Another argument was coming, this time about the space for the shop. Pavel wanted to lease from the landlord the space next door when they expanded. Kuba hated their location, a few blocks north of the garment district, on crowded Forty-sixth Street near the electronic shops and jewelry dealers. But Pavel loved it. He liked being outside the center, apart and distinctive. And in the seven years he had been in New York, seven lean years after the hell of waiting four years after his accident for new visas, he had made for himself a skill not just in cutting but in handling cloth, and had built for the family a network of connections with his friends in the nearby businesses. So what if they were outside the main pole? They made for themselves another small pole, catering to people who made their money on other things, who introduced Pavel to luxuries at a discount, a slim chain for his wife, a good wallet for himself, and the watch for his nephew, his sister's firstborn. Could Kuba have forgotten the watch? Even if Pavel had to push himself up the narrow staircase to his shop and office, grasping the railing with one hand and his cane with the other, even if on occasion the accountant next door complained of the noise made by the steamer and sewing machines, the location was ideal.

But nothing was too good for Kuba. Even if here they were more secure, with cheaper rent and plenty of customers who found them convenient, Kuba wanted something in the center. On occasion they went together to the wholesale dealers and damp workrooms on Seventh Avenue to look at the shops of some of their suppliers, and Pavel could sense Kuba looking at the jobbers' shop floors with a bit of envy. He knew what Kuba longed for, a view every day of workers bent over long rows of wood and metal, a factory setting, where every item that changed hands was exchanged for money, American dollars, not favors or promises of future assistance from a button dealer or a ribbon salesman fallen on hard times.

Kuba made good accounts of the ledger books, and he oversaw Enzo's tailoring with as much authority as was credible for someone with not too much expertise. He claimed to know textiles from his childhood, but the story seemed always to change, always to put Kuba, with each revision of the tale, in a wealthier, happier position before the war. The history was part of Kuba's argument, that it was natural for him to oversee a group of workers. But Pavel did not like that image, everyone in a row at a long table, sweating and squinting, the buzz of machines like a broken orchestra. He did not like it. He preferred the family business small and customized, selling to his friends and his friends' friends, people who knew they would be purchasing an expert suit often altered from someone else's manufacture, once in a while stitched on their own as contract for another company. That was why he managed the relationships with suppliers and redrew the designs from their oral specifications, because they trusted him. Everyone knew him, and he knew everyone. Sometimes people brought in suits purchased elsewhere, because Freddy in the shop knew how to fix it just so, not just with the machine, but by hand. Was there something better? How would their little shop stand out among the bigs on Seventh Avenue?

If we moved there, Kuba would argue, we could be big.

Pavel never knew how to answer him. One did not go from small to big, but from small to less small, to slightly less small, all the way up to not so small. American business, yes, he thought. But Pavel had learned his lesson in Germany after the war. One time, just one time, he had tried to make big money, enough to feel safe to emigrate, and someone greedier, more ambitious—Kuba's childhood friend, that swindler, that thief!—had almost killed him for trying. Pavel's bones were still crooked, his skin still scarred, his body still pained. No more. The best progress was slow.

It had taken enormous effort to make it to their current location. In the early years Kuba had sold clothing from a hand truck while Pavel sent money from his black-market coffee business in Germany. It was only four years since an American cousin of Pavel's lent them the capital to open a tailor shop under a real roof, and the loan was not yet repaid. Of course now it was Kuba who was the sophisticate. Would Kuba even know how to judge a row of inner stitching on a lapel without the skills Pavel had shared, skills acquired basting and sewing pockets for the same cousin? Would Kuba have anything if not for Pavel's determination to make a family business? It was Pavel himself who had managed to win this latest contract, the third of its kind for them, and as a result they had hired the two cutters, each of whom kept a calendar with photographs of nude women at their workstations.

When Kuba returned he sat at Pavel's desk and opened his soup. I think we should talk a little, he began in Yiddish.

Pavel sighed.

About the lease.

Of course about the lease, answered Pavel. Always the lease. Do you have an idea for a better lease somewhere else?

I don't know why you are against a big loan. It is what everyone does here. Since when are you so afraid? You had a bigger business in Europe, in and out of every zone.

Pavel said, Afraid?

Perhaps not afraid, said Kuba. But I don't understand it. All the risks you took there! Hinda talks about it still.

Pavel said nothing.

Why, continued Kuba, should we be more cautious here, where here we have so much more safety?

Here we have children, said Pavel. He gave Kuba what he hoped was a righteous look. Mine will go to college, my daughter too.

Who says no? All I say is—

All you say, said Pavel, is that I am afraid. So!

Kuba's face turned pink. You would think, after all we have done, you could consider how Hinda and I—

All you have done? Pavel said, his voice beginning to scratch. What, letting Fela and me stay in your apartment when we came with the baby? You want the rent back, I give you the rent back. I did not know it was such a favor.

That is not what I am talking about. Kuba made his back even straighter. That is not what I am talking about.

Pavel looked at him. A sound came out, then a sentence. Then what are you talking about, Jakub?

The pink from Kuba's face subsided a little. But he did not answer.

Tell me. Let us not have secrets! We are family. Tell me!

There is no need to shout, Pavel.

Pavel breathed in. He was not shouting. But he would not dignify the accusation. And so what if he raised his voice? He had earned the right. Pavel's cousin had started them in the business. Pavel's friends helped them. But Kuba had friends who had tried to kill Pavel for profit, who could not clean out the stain of the war, who remained violent, criminal, who spread pain at the first opportunity.

What you did for me? Pavel breathed. Your friend, your dear friend Marek, could not even leave me with the coat on my body after he broke me into twenty pieces! Is this what I owe you for?

That is not what he said happened. Kuba looked Pavel straight in the eye and then took a step back, as if to see the impact of his words.

Pavel's tongue moved in his mouth. What he said happened? Pavel's voice came out in a low hum, shocked. What he said? You have spoken to him?

Hinda begged me not to say anything to you.

So, say it! It's already out.

He came to us when you were still in Germany, and said you owed him money.

Pavel stared, uncomprehending. I owed him! he whispered.

He came to us here. He said he would report us as Communists from the past to the immigration authorities.

Communists!

He said you had visited your aunt Ewa in the Russian zone, he said you made deals, he said he could give proof that you, and we, all of us were associated with it, with the Red Army, did business to profit them—

You believed him! You believed him over—

It was not to believe or not to believe, said Kuba. It was a threat. We thought—

What did you pay him?

Kuba told him.

I need to speak to Hinda, said Pavel. I need to speak to Hinda.

Don't upset her, said Kuba. Let me tell her first.

HIS AUNT HAD BEEN a Communist as long as he could remember, fleeing to Russia even before the war started. In Germany, just before Hinda and Kuba left the displaced persons camp for England, Pavel had come across a British captain with whom he did a little trading, before the restrictions made things too complicated. Indeed, the captain had not paid him in full, and Pavel had laughed off the debt in order to keep things smooth. When they ran into each other again, as Pavel was returning from his visit to his aunt in the Russian zone, the captain had driven him to an abandoned storehouse of parachute cloth. Pavel had wrapped his body in layers of artificial silk, covered the silk with his clothes, and returned home to Celle with material, just enough for a dress for Fela and a scarf for Hinda. He had never seen Hinda wear the scarf.

Hinda had always been jealous. When he married Fela she acted as cold and as careful with Fela as she had in childhood with their father's new wife. But Kuba she worshipped. And because Kuba loved Hinda too, Pavel found it in himself to tolerate the occasional pretensions. If Kuba liked to make himself bigger than Pavel, so be it.

But this, this debt out of a crime, this payment to a criminal, worse, this idea that there was another version of the tale to which Kuba and Hinda had listened—that Kuba's childhood friend was anyone but the most treacherous—not just trying to kill, not just stealing from Pavel, but blackmailing Kuba—this did not make Kuba big. It made Pavel small.

He sat in the back office alone, watching the red light of the telephone. Kuba was using the line in the front room, for twenty minutes, a half hour, more. He thought about calling Fela. But she would ask him what the matter was. The quiet background noises of the shop became loud, Grinberg's steamer pressing the suit trousers, the clacketing of the meter-high sewing machine pedaled by Ramos. He unlocked his front desk drawer and opened the small envelope that held the restored photographs of his mother and father, but looked only for a moment before replacing them and locking the drawer again.

At last the red light turned off. Pavel stared at the phone handle, its dark brown plastic, then at the face of the telephone, the wide finger holes in the clear cover for ease of dialing. When it rang, he jumped.

Pavel. It was Hinda, her words thick, as if her mouth had swollen from the crying. I did not want to tell you.

So! Now I know anyway.

He threatened us, Pavel, he—we were afraid.

How can your husband associate with such animals? How? How is it possible?

He was—Marek was a different person in his youth, Kuba was so happy to find him, he did not know, he did not know what happened to him.

But what he did—he tried to—he wanted to—a murderer!—and then he took the coat off my back as I lay dying, because he knew inside the coat I had—

I know, Pavel, I know, you have told us so many times—

So many times is not too much! You believed him when he told you that I—

We did not believe him, Pavel. She was still crying, he knew, but he could hear that she had lit a cigarette. We just—we were afraid.

PAVEL COULD NOT SPEAK all through dinner. It was as if his face was covered in dirt, smudged and sweaty, even in the winter cold. He could feel his children looking at him in curiosity, a little fearful of his quiet as Fela served them their potatoes and chicken.

Pavel, you want more pepper?

Hmm? he said. Yes, *mammele*, yes. He twisted the mill twice over his food.

I talked to Mrs. Benfaremo about the hot water. She says on her side it comes on sooner.

Hmm? said Pavel.

The hot water. You said you wanted me to—

Yes, yes, we should talk to Weisenfeld.

She said the people below us have always had the same thing. It's the boiler for our whole line.

Larry interrupted. "May I please be excused?"

Fela looked at his plate. "You didn't finished."

"I almost finished. Look."

Pavel leaned over his son's plate, scooped off the potato skin and chicken bone and put it onto his plate. Helen passed her plate too.

"Helen! You haven't eaten nothing!"

"Ma, I'm full. Please. Can I go too?"

"Ask right."

"May I please be excused?"

The children grabbed their plates and forks, and from behind him Pavel heard a clanging in the sink.

Not everything from Hinda do I like, said Fela. But I like the phrases she teaches them. I forgot to tell you. Last week the mother of Henry, Larry's friend, told us what a good boy we had. Polite.

Yes, said Pavel.

Fela was silent a moment. So, what happened today?

Nothing, nothing.

Something happened.

What should have happened?

I just ask you, that's all.

Business, said Pavel. It's not so good.

HE AWOKE IN THE night, cold but not remembering his dream. Fela stirred only a bit as he sat up. He stepped out of bed, holding the night table for balance as he pushed his feet into his slippers, then limped through the hallway to the kitchen, his hand touching the walls as he went.

His lighter was in his jacket pocket in the bedroom, but he still had a few cigarettes in the pack he kept in the bill drawer. Sometimes they smelled more delicious than food. He drew one out, placed it unlit in his mouth. Just the taste of the paper made him feel better. He took a large wooden match, what Fela used for the candles on Fridays, and struck it against the wide red strip on the box. The flame gave a light to the kitchen, dark in the hours before sunrise.

Hinda would be sleeping now, resting from the agitation of the afternoon. She rested in daylight also, lying in bed for hours at a time, sometimes crying, perhaps sometimes just thinking, too tired to cry. Once in a while Fela went there to help and to cook, and when they were a little younger Pavel would take the boys out to the park with his own children. Lately Hinda's resting had become more frequent. She went to a psychiatrist. No doubt today's telephone call had not helped.

What a family they were, Pavel awake at night, Hinda in bed during the day. Everything in reverse. What a thing to pass down to the children. It was true what they said, some people could not recover. Even here, in the golden city spoken of in his youth, where everything was to be made new, where even before the catastrophe people had come in to build and to earn. Even here. But Pavel was strong. He did not let it come over him the way Hinda let it. He did not let the questions sicken him the way they sickened Hinda. Why did he survive? Why he and not another? He did not let the questions sicken him. He was strong. And his children were strong and good. His nephews also were good, if a little wild, the elder already smoking cigarettes, the younger disappearing with the car before he had a license, scaring Hinda and Kuba into calling the police. But Pavel's children were not wild. They studied. They earned praise. Hinda doted on Helen like she was her own daughter, presenting her with tiny dolls dressed in the costumes of nationalities all around the world, the names of which Helen rolled around her tongue like an expert importer. Cambodia, Dahomey, Brazil.

His children were good. They would not be affected, he thought, because he and Fela tried, they kept things private, they did not let the children hear of anything they worried about. Hinda too tried. She did not speak of any past, even to Pavel. Perhaps she spoke with Kuba, but Pavel thought not. Kuba cared for her like she was a wounded soldier. He was a good husband—he let her stay quiet. When Pavel decided to go to the first commemoration of the Belsener displaced persons, Pavel asked them to go, and without even looking at each other both gave him the same look of doubt, even disdain. It upset Hinda to think about anything at all, and in Kuba she had an ally.

But sometimes she could not escape. Some things were too public, blared in the news, not just in the Yiddish weeklies she refused to read but also in the American papers and magazines, the capture of a war criminal in Argentina, the beginning of a trial in Israel. She had gone to bed this last time just after the High Holidays, when the trial was already under way some months. Pavel had almost not noticed her disappearance. Instead he had been calling Fishl twice a day, once after reading the morning papers and once after reading the eve-

ning papers. The numbers, the statistical testimony, consumed him
but also gave him some relief. It was true, it was true, it was true. And
if the American papers printed terrible photographs, images he had
to skip over, at least the text of the articles gave counts and countries,
cold figures. Everyone saw it was true.

They already know it is true, said Fela. They knew it was true
long ago. Just no one did anything before.

They did, said Pavel. They did. Even in Hamburg, even in Celle
there were trials.

Ha, said Fela. Ha! Celle! The man had a chicken farm not a mile
from Belsen, even closer to the DP camp than we were! Didn't you
read how the Americans caught him once, then let him go? They
believed lies a child would not believe! He was allowed to leave Germany before we were!

Yes, they were stupid. Sometimes I myself do not believe it was
true.

Maybe you did not believe, but they believed. They knew it was
true before any trials, Pavele. So! Only Jews are willing to put in the
time to search out and punish.

Pavel stubbed out his cigarette in the ashtray, lit another. What
had Hinda said to him once? If you came out of camp, you came out
punished. Kuba had told something like this to her. But Pavel did not
want to have come out punished. He did not think he had. Punished!
She was using it as an excuse for Marek, that thief, no words were
enough to describe him, every time Pavel heard the man's name evidence of another crime came out, attempted murder, thievery, now
blackmail. Could one be punished before one had committed crimes
instead of after? Did Marek commit his crimes to justify the earlier
punishment and suffering? Was that what Hinda was trying to say?

But why have compassion for Marek and not for her own brother?
When Hinda looked at Pavel he knew she saw a broken face and a
crippled body. He wanted to laugh at her—could she not see how

strong he still was, how his children thought he could lift a building? But something in her face when she looked at him—he did not like it. And yet here she was, full of pity for Marek, the man who had made Pavel this way.

Stealing from one's own people—was that not a bigger crime, well, perhaps not bigger, not as big, but still, it was enormous, it was unexplainable—and for Marek to do this next thing to Kuba, the lying, like stealing from a brother! Almost worse than the original injury to Pavel. Imagine Fishl doing this, or Yidl Sheinbaum, who had sent them their largest customer not too long ago. It was impossible. One did not have to cripple another to walk straight oneself. That was American business. One got ahead, yes, but by stealing from others? By blackmail? A young man had gone to see his aunt in the Russian zone, had kissed the last remaining evidence of his mother's bloodline, and another man had accused this pitifully small family reunion, a reunion of two, of being a front for communism. Enough to ruin a family.

If he could make all his own personal trials, Marek Rembishevski would be one of the accused. Not the first, not the priority, that honor would belong not just to the grand leaders who made paper orders but also to the specific soldiers and guards and commandants, who had done what he still did not know to his brothers, his baby sister, his father, even his stepmother, poor woman. His cousins, his aunts, his uncles. His girlfriend—how long since he had thought of her, a curvaceous girl who liked sweets—he could make his own long list of the accused, and if Marek were not at the top of the list, he was not at the bottom either. Even Kresser, that tormentor, that shame upon his people—but Pavel did not even like to think the name. No, Marek was not at the bottom of the list. Pavel felt the smoke from his cigarette burn against his ribs. Could a person really be so confused that he could mistake theft from a fellow Jew after the liberation for the fighting for food and blankets during the war? That was the first question

Pavel would ask at Marek's interrogation. A simple question. Could a person really be so confused? That was what a trial was for, to ask the questions and await the painful answers. Pavel wanted to know how Marek would answer. It would make him feel better to know.

Hinda did not ask questions. She did not feel better from the news of the trial in Israel. She felt sick, just as sick as some of the times before. Fela too did not seem so happy. After the children got up from dinner each evening she watched Pavel read the same news stories over and over, until he could memorize the passages in English, not leaving the room until the table and sink and counter were spotless and he picked up the telephone again to call Fishl.

Perhaps Fela worried he would pass down his thoughts to his children. But even if they kept their pact to keep the children away from the suffering, it was all right for them to know something of history. A public event like a trial—he knew at least Larry talked of it in Hebrew school. If Larry would ask questions, Pavel would answer. This he and Fela had agreed they would do. His nephews asked questions, mentioned Kuba's exploits in the war. They thought their father a hero, a soldier who had fought and resisted while living in plain sight, on Aryan papers. And Kuba had been wounded. It was not so bad to pass down an example to the children. Hinda tried in her own way. She tried to teach her sons polite words and taught Larry and Helen too. She spoke slowly to them, in careful English. Pavel's English was also careful. Better than Fela's, he sometimes thought. It made him proud and ashamed at the same time. It wasn't just the grammar that he mastered better, it was the tone and inflection. His English retained a hint of German underneath the Polish accent, but Fela's had a strong Eastern sound, the consonants exaggerated, the vowels round and mournful. He understood, from the way his American cousins spoke to him and the way they spoke to his wife, that this small difference gave him a kind of prestige. Hinda understood this too, and so her resentment of Fela only grew with time. Why couldn't

Fela turn her words around? It seemed to Pavel that Hinda thought of Fela's accent as a personal affront, an attempt to keep down the whole family.

And of course Pavel's reluctance to move the business, to expand, caused more problems. There had been a period in Pavel's life when any risk, no matter how wild, any successful effort to organize merchandise or food had given him its own reward, a kind of happiness, almost physical, the way he used to feel as an adolescent kicking a soccer ball or even as an adult, hopping off his bicycle at the house in Celle, or in the middle of the night, after lovemaking with Fela. But now he did not feel it. He did not feel anything like it.

His children were provided for now, and to take out a big loan from a bank that could make it all go bad, he could not see the purpose. Pavel's family had a clean, bright apartment. His children wore new clothes and went to Hebrew school. Never had they felt the fear that so many did, that if they became poor, or sick, they could be deported back to Poland. Perhaps Kuba wanted to pass down a big business to his children. But Pavel would pass down something more. His son would be something big, a doctor or a lawyer, and his daughter would be elegant and educated, a teacher perhaps, with beautiful children. He would pass down something more.

PAVEL WOKE UP AGAIN a minute before his alarm clock buzzed, the heat knocking at the radiator. Had he slept more than three hours? He thought so. And then the two before the dream. Not so terrible.

It was still dark. In the kitchen he took a few quick puffs on his cigarette before wrapping himself in his tefillin. After praying and removing the tefillin, he cut six oranges and squeezed the halves over the juice dish. Helen did not like the pulp. He poured half the juice through a sifter into a glass for her and poured the thicker half into a glass for Larry. Then he came back into the bedroom for his shower.

He took off his robe and turned the shower on, waited for it to grow warm. Perhaps it was time to discuss a move. A bank officer would again visit, they would show him the merchandise, explain the ideas for branching into finer textiles and handmade suits, the officer would be young and healthy, would call Kuba Jake and Pavel Paul, full of enthusiasm until they began to discuss in earnest, when the grim looks would appear and everything Pavel and Kuba had worked for would be assessed as trifles, pitiful collateral against possible financial disaster.

Pavel didn't want it. Right now he didn't want it. The excitement was lacking. He did not feel an urgency. Perhaps Kuba did not either, only wanted to, trying to recapture the feeling that every action had a grave importance, meant life or death. Moving the business did not mean life or death. But perhaps a move, or if not a move, at least an expansion, would mean greater savings for college for the children, a bigger apartment, perhaps it meant—he did not know what it meant.

Could Kuba really believe that Pavel owed him something? That he, Pavel, kept the whole family down? It was impossible. The steam seeped into his chest, warming his body. Yes, that was what Kuba thought, that Pavel kept the family down, that Fela kept the family down, that by having this accident and being forced to stay even longer in Europe, by doing all this—all this trading in Europe, even trading that had helped Kuba and Hinda live here when they first came, that this too seemed to make the family illegitimate. Pavel shook in the shower with the outrage of it. His fist made an involuntary movement in the air, into the water, and the shower turned cold.

He cried out in surprise and almost slipped, grasping the faucet with one hand for balance. Shampoo still in his hair. The water was cold as ice! God in heaven, was there no end to his torments on this earth? Was there no end?

Pavel? he heard Fela's voice calling from the bed.

The water! The water again! That swindler! That thief!

I'll call him now.

Don't call him! he shouted through the door, shivering as he rinsed off the soap from his body, wrapped his shoulders in a towel. I want to speak to the thief myself!

Teeth knocking in the cold, he sat on his side of the bed with his robe untied and dialed the number. Nancy answered.

"Nancy," said Pavel. "It's Mr. Mandl. Six-E. I want—"

"He's in the shower."

"Ah, of course. So! Could you tell your father that I wish to speak with him?"

"All right."

"No, Nancy, wait, not to speak with him, to show him something. He should come up to my apartment. Before I go to work. Please."

"All right."

"Please."

Pavel breathed out. He would show Weisenfeld, he would show him, that what Weisenfeld could provide for his own daughter, warm water, Pavel could not provide for his children. The home—what kind of father was he if he did not make his home secure for his children, here in America, of all places? Fela made the apartment beautiful with her cleaning and cooking, and the children made the apartment alive with their games and their studies. Pavel would make sure the home was strong and secure, something the landlord, any landlord, should respect. Pavel would show him, he would be calm, he would explain, he would demand that the problem be fixed. He went into the children's room to wake them up for breakfast.

"What will it be today?"

"A butterfly," said Helen.

Pavel cut a triangle out of an untoasted bagel, then sliced it open to make wings.

"With cream cheese," she added.

"Same for me, please," said Larry. He still liked the game.

"Coming right up." Pavel put two butterflies on the center plate, then cut straight cylinders, giving Larry one, so he could spread the cream cheese on his own.

"How come he gets the drum first?"

"I'm older," said Larry.

"It's true," said Pavel. "But also he knows how to butter. See?" He took his daughter's wrist, moved it along the bagel.

"I like it better when you do it," said Helen.

"So, Helcha, for this Larry gets his first. There's extra wait for the service."

"What is it called when you cream cheese something?"

"What?"

"She means, Dad, you know, is there a word for it—like there is for butter—you know, you put butter on something, you say you are buttering, but you also say it when you put cream—"

"I know what she means. I was just thinking."

"There is no word, Hell-face."

"Larry!"

"Sorry."

"Do you know what a beautiful name her name is? Her name is after my mother, just like yours is after your—"

"I know, Dad, I know. Sorry. I said I was sorry."

"All right."

"I said I was sorry!"

"All right, Liebl, all right."

The doorbell rang. Larry ran to get it. Pavel heard the landlord move his heavy feet through the hall, Larry pattering after him in his socks. Pavel stood as the landlord entered the kitchen, and Larry slid back into his seat, shoved a butter-smeared drum into his mouth.

"Good morning," said Weisenfeld.

"Good morning," Pavel made himself say. "But actually, Mr. Weisenfeld, it is not a good morning." He looked Weisenfeld straight in the eye, the landlord's hair still matted from his shower, his jacket hanging loose around his broad shoulders. "It is not a good morning because I, and my children, are not able to bathe in hot water."

"So, is that what you have to show me at this hour? The same complaint?"

Pavel breathed in. Keep calm. But he felt his words rising inside him. He kept himself speaking in English, so he would be forced to speak slowly and with care. "What I have to show you," he answered, "what I have to show you is this." Pavel stretched his arms above Helen's head and pushed open the window. "It is almost twenty degrees. Fahrenheit."

"Ah, so I am responsible for the weather now?"

"I have never called you responsible," Pavel said.

Weisenfeld turned to leave. "I did not come up here to be insulted. If you have some emergency for me to fix, that is one thing, but to be—"

Don't you go! called Pavel, his voice in Yiddish strong but not loud. I don't have just the air to show you. I have the water. Come!

"Daddy, I'm cold."

Come, Weisenfeld, come! I want to show you what kind of water we have in this apartment, where I have to shiver with cold as if I am in a hovel in Kazakhstan, and where I cannot trust the water enough to bathe my children in the morning!

I've already told you, Weisenfeld answered in his gutter Yiddish, we're having the boiler repaired next week. There is nothing that can be done. There's a few minutes of hot water every morning, you shouldn't waste!

Waste! Waste! How you dare! Do you think I don't know what waste is? Do you think I do not know?

How I dare? How I dare? You call me up here in the early morning, waking my wife and daughter—

I wake you because I cannot sleep! I cannot sleep because I throw money at you for nothing, to have my wife, and my son and my daughter, frozen in the morning, to have my own body like ice! If you want waste, that is waste!

What a tenant I have! No one is like you, no one complains like you, no one rages like you—

Maybe the others are too afraid, but Mr. Weisenfeld, I am not! What do you want? That I should tremble before you? That I should be a refugee in my own house? That my wife should be a refugee? My children, refugees?

Ah, now you blackmail me with your guilt!

Blackmail? Pavel's voice ripped through his throat at the word. Blackmail? I? It is you who blackmail us! You are a thief! The worst kind of thief, who steals heat from women and children!

And you, a rager! You let your children see you—

Don't bring my children into it! Don't bring my children into it! You so much as mention their names, I—I—! You are here because I want to know, Weisenfeld, I want to know, what do we need to do to get hot water from you? Beg? Steal? Scream in the middle of the night?

Already you scream in the middle of the night! Everyone hears you!

Pavel felt the cold wind behind Helen's head push at his cheek. His heart was burning, his face was bitter cold. I will bury you, Weisenfeld. I will have you under the earth. I will bury you, bury you, bury you!

"Stop screaming! Stop!" A noise was filtering through the fog around Pavel's head, it was his son, his mouth open and red, his small arms grasping his sister, holding her head to his chest, a tiny adult with a tinier child clasped to him, protecting her, and shouting his little boy's voice at the landlord. "Please stop screaming!"

Or was Larry shouting at him?

Both men stopped. The room was quiet. Pavel saw that Fela stood in the doorway, her body wrapped in a bathrobe, her face a stone. But he could read the stone. It was wrong to scream in front of the children. You have mercy on everyone, she would say to him, mercy on everyone, how about for your family?

Weisenfeld said, Enough.

So, answered Pavel, his jaw still forward. Enough. And what else?

I will call your wife. He motioned to Fela, who followed him out of the kitchen into the hallway in silence.

The door closed, not loud. Pavel stood at the kitchen counter, watching his son and daughter, Larry's hair combed straight, a napkin hanging over Helen's neck to protect her shirt from stains.

Helen looked at him. "Will he scream at Ma too?"

No, he answered, still in Yiddish. Your mother doesn't scream.

Larry carried his plate to the sink.

"What," Pavel said. "Don't you finish your food?"

"I'm not hungry."

"Me neither." Helen picked up her plate too.

Pavel looked at the two of them, Larry scooping Helen's plate from her hands, the little one pale, only a bite or two eaten. On an ordinary morning, Pavel would have insisted, he would have told them eat, *kindlech*, eat, a person's breath when he doesn't eat is a terrible thing, not even brushing your teeth will cover it, eat, how will you concentrate in the day, eat, you are growing, eat, eat. He thought he saw Larry wait a moment for the speech to begin, but at this moment Pavel didn't have the strength to beg them to put something in their bellies. He turned his back so as not to see his son push the uneaten bread into the garbage.

"We're late for school, Dad."

I can drive you, Larry. You won't be late if I drive.

"Then you'll be late for work. We'll just go now, okay?" Helen took off her napkin, then went to collect her schoolbag.

Pavel looked at his son, now quickly rinsing the plates with a spatter of water.

"Okay, Dad, okay?"

Pavel thought he saw his son's nose turn pink, almost red. Was he about to cry? But Larry was looking away, putting the milk and cream cheese back in the refrigerator.

"Dad, I'm talking to you."

"Okay," Pavel answered. "Everything's okay." He reached out his hand to touch his son's shoulder. Larry shrugged from under his touch, then hurried to the coat closet for his jacket and scarf.

The Suit

BEREL WANTED A SUIT. He mentioned it to his son-in-law one Sunday morning. He mentioned it while standing at the back door of the apartment, watching Chaim polish his shoes. Chaim, who sat on the third step of the building's rear stairway, responded without looking up: A suit. I know a place.

Yes, said Berel, I'd like to buy a suit like the suit you wear. Something like that.

Chaim worked in one of New York's radio stations, where he used his smooth if accented English to fit in easily with the other technicians and engineers, who had bought him a new tie last year for his thirty-third birthday. Chaim wore a different suit every day. He had five. He had ten shirts, all blue or white or pink or yellow, and combined them in different orders with the suits.

Chaim said, Go to the place I go. Only go there. The tailors speak Yiddish. I know the owner from before. I'll tell him you're coming.

The ankle of each shoe Chaim polished glimmered at the seams. They were good shoes, solid black leather with a layered black sole.

Those are good shoes, said Berel.

They are, said Chaim. Nothing like American, no?

No, said Berel. Chaim was right. In the dairy where for seven years Berel had scooped out milk curds from metal barrels and for the next seven had operated the machine that sealed shut the plastic milk bags, he had worn heavy brown boots. They had come apart at the soles from too much contact with the cleaning fluids; in fourteen years he had gone through eight pairs, all produced in a kibbutz factory from which the dairy bought supplies. Chaim was right, but he said that phrase, nothing like American, only American, too often. Berel wasn't emigrating. He had made that clear.

It was August, three months after Berel's wife had died of a typhus relapse in a small hospital in Tel Aviv, two weeks into Berel's grief-trip to America to visit his only daughter. He had been in Tel Aviv or nearby since 1949, sixteen years, longer than he'd lived anywhere since childhood. Yes, his wife had died. His daughter Sima was here. But Berel's home was there, the home he had made, alive on the stove where his wife had boiled soup out of eggs and water and potatoes, alive in the small freezer where he kept his sharp, homemade seltzer. He had less there, but also more. He could do for himself. Besides, he wasn't so alone. He had a surviving brother in Jerusalem, and a sister in Rehovot. They were married, but they were older, and Berel was not yet sixty; what would they do without him?

He wasn't emigrating, yet he wanted a suit. For no reason. The clothes he had, short-sleeved shirts and plain trousers, were enough. But his nephew could replace him at the dairy for up to three months; his wife had saved the German reparations money they had started to receive; perhaps he would stay in New York for the High Holidays; he would need a suit for synagogue in America. Chaim was lanky, with a flexible, loose-jointed sway to his walk; nothing he had would fit Berel's round body. But Chaim wasn't one to ask for reasons. He accepted the stupid occurrences and irrational violences of the world, and he accepted particularly the odd desires of others to sell and to buy. He accepted and he advised. He wrote down the address of the tailor and told Berel to take the number five bus from Riverside Drive.

BEREL WAITED. IT HAD been very humid, and he spent his days with the baby, inside at noon and outside after four, when the air cooled. He walked sometimes a few blocks uptown, to the garden of the church of St. John the Divine. Sometimes he went a kilometer south, to look at the stone memorial to the war, hidden in the bicycle lanes at Riverside Park. The baby was six months old and could crawl on the grass. She could laugh. She pushed the buds of her teeth against stale bagels and rubbed her head at Berel's shoulder. He talked to her in Yiddish and sang to her in Hebrew. No Polish! He didn't want her to hear it. She stared up with purpose and seriousness and made noises to his songs. They hummed at each other in the living room and the street and in Riverside Park, where Berel pushed the perambulator Tuesday to Friday afternoons while Sima rung up postcards and art books and little reproductions of classical sculptures at the cash register of the Met's enormous gift shop. He fed the baby from a bottle, filled with formula, from a grocery; she was weaning.

He went to the tailor's, finally, on a Monday, when Sima had her day off and could stay home the whole day. The directions were complicated: bus, long blocks, short blocks, narrow alley. One had to climb a dank staircase, but once inside the shop, Berel thought the place was wider than the building itself. It wasn't that it was so filled with clothing, although there were several racks on which hung rows of suits in wool and serge and even perhaps cotton. It was the mirrors on the opposite side of the door, mirrors folded in threes and reflecting off each other, that made the place seem large.

"Can I help you?"

"Hmm?" said Berel, startled. But the question was one he understood.

"Can I help you?"

"Yes," Berel said. "I look for Pavel Mandl." It came out quickly, easily, a sound he had used before in a context he no longer remembered. The little bit of paper on which Chaim had written the name lay folded in Berel's pocket.

"He stepped out."

"Excuse me?" said Berel.

"He stepped out. He isn't here." The young man worked his brows together. He said, loudly, "Not here."

"Excuse me," said Berel. "Excuse me," he repeated, gaining time for the sentence he wanted to squeeze from his mouth. "Please, em, Yiddish?"

"No," shouted the young man. "*Nein.*"

Berel's chin began to itch. What was the English word for *Polish*? He had no idea. But that was stupid; if the man knew Polish, he would understand. "*Popolsku?*" Berel tried.

"One minute," yelled the young man. "Just a minute." And disappeared into the back.

Berel stood still at the counter. There was a small fan near the cash register and a large fan near one of the three-way mirrors. The streams of air hitting each other collided at the back of his head and cooled the sweat behind his ears.

A smaller, older man came out. Good. The man put out a pale, wide hand. Pavel isn't here, he said in Yiddish. I am his cousin Mayer.

Berel shook his hand. Berel Makower. My son-in-law sent me here to look for a suit. Chaim Traum.

Wonderful, said Mayer. Yes, Chaim. He's a good customer.

I am here from Israel. On a visit.

Wonderful, repeated Mayer. Wonderful. So! He stood up a little straighter. We now do a little custom work, but of course this takes quite some time. What is your preference?

Oh, said Berel. He managed a polite smile. I can look at what you have ready. I don't know how long I will be here.

Mayer led Berel to a rack of thin gabardines. These are right for any weather. Even the midsummer if you have air-conditioning. Thin, airy, but warm enough for winter. Really, the best material.

He took out a measuring tape from his pocket, then circled Berel's neck. Berel shook a little: it tickled.

Stand still! Mayer muttered, sharply. He roped Berel's waist, then bent to the floor, stretching the tape at the inside of Berel's thigh and up the length of ankle to hip. Let's go, he said. He had written nothing down, but at the rack he shuffled through the almost identical hues of dark colors and handed hanger after hanger to Berel, who waited by him.

Between them they carried ten suits, navy and brown and beige and gray, into an area divided off from the center of the shop. Mayer kept talking as Berel pushed off his shoes and removed his trousers: the business that wasn't so good in New York summer, the heat that wasn't so bad, the Hungarians who had moved into his block in Midwood, the chance he had to move to his own little shop in a few months. Berel gave nods and smiles of encouragement, then put on the first suit: double-breasted, dark blue with thin, faint maroon stripes.

Wonderful, said Mayer.

In his socks Berel slipped over to one of the three-way mirrors. The cuffs of the pants turned over around his ankles; so as not to rip or stain, he lifted the cloth at the thighs as he walked, like a woman in long skirts.

He paused before the center panel of the mirror. Under the wide set of buttons his chest and belly seemed enormous, and his neck emerged like a bent branch, small and fragile. He could see Mayer behind him in the reflection, but Berel turned around to look at the tailor directly. Do you have something simpler?

Of course! Mayer riffled through the remaining nine suits hanging on the hook of the wall. He pulled out something in gray, dark and polished, like the tip of a pencil. It had a row of black buttons up the chest and one button at each wrist.

Berel pulled the pants up, tightened the zipper. The lining of the pants felt cool against his legs. He removed the jacket from its hanger with care. The jacket created a tiny breeze as it lapped against his chest. Mayer leaned over and pulled the shoulders out from each end.

Beautiful, said Mayer.

Berel moved to the mirror. These pants weren't so wide. And the jacket, it fit perfectly. He looked tall and elegant, his metal gray hair floating above the dark collar, his shoulders broad but not heavy, his legs—was it possible?—longer, steadier under the vents at each side of the jacket.

"I'll take it," said Berel, in English: he had heard this in stores.

Mayer laughed. We can alter it for you and have you pick it up, or you can wait and we'll do it now.

Now is good, said Berel. How much will it cost?

Mayer told him.

It was more than a month's salary, but Berel kept his face blank. A good price.

Well, it's actually quite high for us, but the quality makes it worth it. You'll have it for years. Mayer was bent again, pinning the ankles. Do you want cuffs at the ankles? Or just plain?

Plain, said Berel.

He went back to the stool where his own clothes lay folded and began to undress. Mayer took the pants from him and walked away. You take your time, he called to Berel. We'll be at least twenty minutes.

Berel sat on the stool in his trousers and shirt. He felt a bit cold. The buses and taxis outside honked like animals in a zoo. He could hear the people on the street chattering nonsensically, louder and louder. The door to the shop opened and closed, opened and closed.

A bell rang out whenever someone stepped across the doormat. There was chattering inside too.

Pan Berel. Berel looked up. A man who looked bitingly familiar. His head was narrow, his eyes large, his face thin, one cheekbone slightly flatter than the other.

Pavel Mandl, said the man. A good friend of your son-in-law. He told me you were coming, but I did not know when.

Berel lifted himself up and shook hands. Good day.

I see you've picked out something exquisite. You have good taste!

Berel swallowed, and smiled. You have very nice things. He stepped back for a moment. The man's voice.

I'm glad you decided to wait. So I could meet you—

What is to meet? Berel thought.

Mandl was going on and on, almost hoarse. Chaim—I love him like a brother!

Then it came to Berel. I know! he blurted. We have met! In Belsen. And immediately a blush began to come over him. He tried to push up a tear to his eye, make it look like he was overcome with something other than a sudden shame.

Pavel Mandl stood still. Ah! he cried, slapping a hand to his cheek. My God! You—of course—you—you performed the marriage ceremony for my sister! To Jakub! In our house—my God—

Of course, of course. Outside the camp. You were one of the few who lived like a real—it was the first time my wife and I had been in a living room in—

Berel Makower, your name! But Chaim did not tell me—he married so quickly in Israel—I never knew his father-in-law was a rabbi!

Berel smiled, still nervous. He would not be found out, not now. What was it, Pan Mandl, twenty years ago?

What a wonderful coincidence! What a joy!

Berel was always a terrible liar. And if he remembered correctly, this Mandl had some scholarly background. What if he began to converse about some Talmudic problem Berel would not even begin to remember? What a crazy thing he had done, performing a false religious ceremony for a young couple. For what, a bit of money and a visit to a house?

Berel stood up straight, tried to affect a tone of sadness. Yes, well—what I work in now—and I went through a period of, well—I no longer am so—and I hadn't quite finished all my—you know, so many of us lost faith, after—

But Pavel did not hear what Berel tried to say. That Chaim!

Yes, nodded Berel, his face cooling. He did not even warn me that we knew each other.

Pavel bent toward Berel. I think sometimes he forgets his past. Not forgets, exactly—he was always very intelligent—it is just that his mind is somewhere else, he doesn't like to go back—and we love your daughter, from the moment we met her, we said—Chaim was even smarter than we thought!

Pavel's face bore a look of pride, as if Chaim were his own, like an older brother after the father has died, his face worn and misshapen, the face of a man ten or fifteen years older, Berel's age. A camp face. One could tell the difference even years later. Berel's palms began to itch a little. No, he would not confess.

Yes, he is smart, Berel agreed. He tried to think back to the little house and the ceremony, Chaim guiding them to the center of the room, the sound of his own voice above the murmurings of the guests, Dvora weak and feverish but excited, his daughter clinging to his thighs, the bride straight-backed and quiet. But what became of your sister—she is in America?

She is here! And her husband—we are partners still! This—Pavel motioned to the ceiling, then to the back room—this, in a way, is from you.

Oh, no, Berel started. But the young man whom Berel had seen upon first walking in trotted over to the dressing area and shouted, "It's ready—try on?" He pointed at the pants and at Berel's legs.

Berel looked at the pants, worried again. Do you mind if I don't? said Berel. I'm so hot. He laughed a little. I'm sure it fits.

Pavel said, Of course! Just come back if there's a problem. Come back even if there is not a problem! Oh, what a day. What a day! He clasped Berel's arm again, then took the pants and jacket from the American boy.

Berel followed Pavel to the cash register. He felt in his front pocket for his wallet and took it out. He had half the money he had brought to America with him and removed all of it, placing it flat on the glass counter.

What is this? said Pavel Mandl. No, that's far too much. That's really more than twice as much as it costs. That would pay for two suits, maybe three.

Two suits? said Berel. That's not possible. Your cousin said—

Yes, yes, it's a special, said Pavel. It's a special. You see? Look, it's a good quality, but we haven't been selling too much lately, so that one's a special. He smiled, then looked down at his receipt book.

Your cousin said—Berel repeated.

Ah, Mayer. Pavel leaned forward, spoke in a low voice. We brought him in when he lost his position—his experience really is as a cutter—sometimes with prices he makes mistakes.

Berel looked at the ears and the mouth of the tailor; Pavel was gnawing his lip, his face almost angry, trying not to laugh. Berel's palm sweated on his wallet, and suddenly he heard the puffing noises of the street breezing in from the outside, as if a classroom door had opened to the school yard and the real mischief of the students had come to the hearing of the teacher. He had been taken. Behind his back his daughter and son-in-law had arranged to pay. He saw the face of Chaim, solemn, careful, bent to his shoes, insisting that Berel go to this Mandl. As if insisting were necessary. Berel could go nowhere without their instructions. He could just imagine the mouth of this Pavel, pursing up a bit, Chaim smiling, charming, making a joke of Berel's pride that he not take from his daughter, Chaim not even remembering, not even blinking at the idea that another man would be mocking him, or worse, treating him as charity. Berel had been tricked like a boy. He had been tricked. And this Pavel, no doubt a father like himself, in on the joke, not knowing how Berel himself had cheated him all those years ago. Berel was trapped: had Chaim already paid? Or was the plan to have Chaim pay the balance after Berel left with his ridiculously cheap purchase, miraculously chosen over all the other expensive garments?

It's too cheap, Berel finally said, looking at Pavel's long hands, then at his face. And I don't understand why.

Pavel stopped smiling. Look, he said. That's the price. Really.

I don't understand why it's so cheap, Berel repeated.

You married my sister.

I was paid then.

I know, said Pavel. I know. But I think you should buy it. Just buy it. Believe me, you won't be sorry. That's how we do it here. I always give Chaim the best price.

Not so good a price.

Pavel continued. Think how happy it will make your daughter, to see you in something you like so much. Think.

Berel's hands fell to his sides. He did not want to touch the dark gray cloth with his damp fingers. He wanted to go backward in time, to the moment he walked into the shop, to the bus ride downtown, no, before, to the first week he had arrived, when he sat feeding the baby on the entrance steps of the art museum and thought that his daughter worked in the most beautiful place in the world. He wanted to go backward, to the hour before he had decided that he wanted something this unnecessary, something too luxurious for his everyday life, something like a good gray suit.

He looked at Pavel: I don't know.

Pavel said, I've known Chaim a long time. Do you know how I know him?

No, said Berel. I do not. And it does not matter. I cannot accept.

I know Chaim at random. An accident. He recognized Fela—my wife now—in a market in Poland—not recognized, just found her, he knew she was Jewish, incredible—I asked him once how he did it—he did not know—and he smuggled her across into Germany. All by himself. In a policeman's uniform.

Chaim? said Berel and shrugged. It's hard to believe.

Smart, even then. Already smart. You remember—he taught there, yes, of course he told me Sima had been in the school there—but I did not put it all together—

A lot of people are smart, said Berel. That does not mean I take money from them. But already his words came out more slowly; he was beginning to feel embarrassed by his reluctance. He had given something false to Pavel all those years ago, but he knew he would not confess. He had done something shameful, and this Mandl would never know.

To him, Pavel said, his voice deepening, to him I owe my wife. I owe my children. I would have nothing—nothing without him. He moved in with me; we sent him to school in the DP camp at Belsen. He would do anything for me, anything for Fela. Anything for his wife.

I am not his wife, Berel said. I cannot accept. Not from him, not even from you.

Pavel Mandl did not seem to hear him. When someone wants to do anything, it is all right to let him do something. It's like a gift to the giver. Let him have it.

Berel said nothing. I cannot accept, he thought. I cannot accept. But no sound came from his mouth.

He's a good boy, said Pavel. Now this suit. It needs a garment bag. You hang it inside like this.

IT WAS AFTER FIVE but still hot. The air here was thick; people on the street walked slowly, trying to dry their wet faces with their wet hands. No rain, but moisture everywhere. Berel stood directly behind the bright sign, waiting for the bus home, but after twenty minutes and two number fives so crowded he would not have been able even to grab a strap to stand straight, he decided to walk, following the path of the bus, garment bag slung over his arm. What was it, four kilometers, five? He could do it.

In general he did not like to take buses home. He rarely took them after work, preferring to walk through crowded Tel Aviv; only in the mornings, because he was not so good at being early, did he catch the route that passed three blocks from the apartment. One was almost always alone on a bus. Almost always. The night Chaim and Sima had boarded their flight to America, where Chaim would have more opportunity, real work for a young man, as he said, not to mention no army and no children in the army, Berel and Dvora had taken the bus home with Chaim's cousin Rayzl from the airport. Rayzele had been weeping silently, staring out the window of the bus at the blue lights and buildings-in-progress by the highway. Dvora had sat next to her, with her hand covering the cousin's. Berel had sat behind, fuming. Everyone's sorrows were larger than his wife's. The sight of other people's tears stopped her own from flowing. He would cry later without shame, shaking in the kitchen chair before they went to bed. But she would have to wait until he slept; he'd know from her swollen cheeks and stiff eyelids in the morning, when he glimpsed her as she padded into the bathroom after having laid out his coffee and bread.

He would not have thought that his child would be able to leave the country that held her parents. Still, she had. Sima had to do what Sima had to do. She had a husband. Berel had pointed this out in arguments with Dvora. Had not one of Dvora's young brothers left Poland some thirty years before, with a woman not yet his wife, to

settle in Palestine? The turmoil it had caused in the family! But looking back, with no one else but Dvora and another sister surviving, it
seemed to have been very wise.

And now, even now, there was nothing in Israel, especially for
the postwar immigrants from Europe, who stumbled over strings of
Hebrew phrases as if they were reading from an ancient prayerbook.
For the young it was even worse. At seventeen Sima had begged him,
begged him, not to speak Yiddish to her when her friends visited to
collect her for a night out or to loan her a bicycle for a day at the
beach. It was the language of sheep led to slaughter. That was what
people said. But Berel would mock her and ramble incessantly in Yiddish to her and her companions, throwing in a few Hebrew words so
the friends could, with some struggle, understand. Let them struggle.
He did not feel sorry. Now, in New York, Sima loved to speak it.
Something had changed.

"*Tatteh,*" said Sima. I have to confess something.

They were at the table, after dinner. The baby was asleep in Sima
and Chaim's bedroom. Chaim began to peel a green apple with a
short knife. Berel had won the last game of rummy, a game played
with the slippery, laminated green-and-black cards Sima had bought
discount at the museum store and kept in a cushioned brown box, in
a drawer next to the dish towels.

Berel looked at her through his glasses. Her bottom lip shook.
Perhaps he would not need to say anything. She would say she was
sorry, she would say she wanted to do good, and he would say, Don't
worry, my lamb, my heart, don't worry. I just wish you had told me
directly. He would not admit the shame of taking money from them,
from Pavel; for what? He would just remind her, please, not to go behind his back. He wasn't stupid. She knew that.

I have to confess something. Her eyes, like her mother's, were clear and green.

What is it?

Chaim kept peeling.

I feel so terrible.

What can it be? Berel stared at his daughter, trying to seem naive, watching her hands pull at a strand of her dark blond hair. What can it be?

It's been bothering me since she died.

Oh, said Berel. And tilted his head to the side.

From years ago. From when we were in Russia. When you were taken away. She was going to the black market every day, for food for me. She was looking for milk; there was no milk.

I think I know this story, said Berel.

Chaim said: I haven't heard it. He was smiling. He liked war stories, at least the pleasant ones, the ones without blood.

Sima said, I had the most brave mother in the world. The most brave.

Berel nodded.

Do you know how she got that milk? said Sima. I still don't know.

Berel breathed out. Oh, she sold something she had stolen from her job. Something like that. The real adventure was getting it back to you, in an open clay cup she had, no lid, in the snow. And she had to hide it. You remember how she had that coat with the pockets sewn inside?

Yes, yes, I remember, said Sima. It was winter. She hid it in the coat pocket on the inside and walked with her hand behind the sleeve to hold it steady, like she had a broken arm. If she had been caught carrying milk! Because how could she get such a thing?

Berel leaned back in his chair. She was proud of the milk. She told me about it, I don't know how many times, after I came back.

I don't know why she tried so hard—even as a baby, you didn't love milk. But she didn't think like that. Your mother, when she wanted something—

But Sima had tears in her eyes. She was so proud when she gave me the cup!

Chaim coughed softly on his apple.

It's not funny! choked Sima. It's terrible. Still, I couldn't help it, to see that cup, with frozen pieces of curd floating on top, and the coating, broken, sticking to the sides—

Berel didn't look at Chaim. He sat forward again, stared down at his winning game, the cards laid out in rows of three and four. What a little tragedy! His nose made a small noise.

You're laughing too! Sima cried; tears were streaming down her cheeks. I took the cup to the back of the hut, where she couldn't see, and I poured it out into the snow! All at once! Everything was white, so she couldn't discover what I had done! I just poured it out!

Berel was laughing out loud now. Oh my god, my god, he snorted. Oh my god.

"Jesus Christ," said Chaim, in an impressive American accent, and grinned. Sima smacked him on the hand, but lightly. She had begun to giggle herself.

Berel gasped. Inhaled, exhaled. He put his head on the table, his cheeks pressed to the open cards. What a little tragedy. He pushed his glasses up onto his forehead. He heard them quieting down.

Oh Sima, he breathed, mouth still at his elbow. I don't know what to do.

She put her fingers on his wrist.

Chaim said: Didn't you get the suit today? I thought you were going today.

Berel picked up his head and peered at Chaim. Chaim's expression was plain, blank. He let nothing mix up the creamy calm of his face. So? It would drive Sima crazy soon enough.

Yes, Berel answered, I did. You did not tell me that the man—but yes, I got it.

Well, show it to us! Chaim strained his voice.

Not right now.

Please, said Sima. Her cheeks had swollen. Please. Just try it on. Or do they have to alter it?

They did it while I waited.

Please.

Berel got up, pushed his chair to the table. He went into his room, where his suit, still in its garment bag, lay on the bed. He sat on the bed, next to the suit, and looked at the room. A drawing of a boy at a fruit stand hung in a green frame above the yellow dresser. Otherwise the walls were bare, light brown. The room would soon be his granddaughter's. She could play with her own toys and wear new clothes until she outgrew them. Sima had worked from age fourteen until she left, but his granddaughter would go to high school, even university. She could attend class every day and study in her own room every night with the door closed, if she wished. The water from the sink, the toilet paper, the pale cotton sheets one could buy for a reasonable fee, everything here was soft and good. It really was. Already he was used to it. But he didn't think he would miss it.

He fingered the garment bag. So, let them see him in it. He took off his shirt and wiped under his arms with a towel from the dresser. Then put on a white shirt—a gift that hadn't fit, Chaim had said when giving it to him in a pile of items—and the gray suit over it. The hem grazed his heels. He did not have appropriate shoes. He put on his slippers. They would still see how it fell on his body. Should he check in the mirror that leaned in the closet? No. He knew how it looked.

He returned to the table.

Chaim grinned.

"*Tatteh*," said Sima. And then in Hebrew: How beautiful.

Yes, it is a beautiful suit, he answered in Yiddish. He stood himself straight, turned around once, like a model, and then stopped to look at her, stretching his eyes as open as possible, lips pressed against his gums in a grimace she knew, a grimace he used, not always successfully, to keep himself from crying.

It is beautiful, Simale. And you know what? Berel lifted his eyebrows high, almost, it felt, to his hairline. He imagined the skin on his forehead folding and pulling. His lips and his gums were dry. You know what? Simale, you wouldn't believe it, this place your husband sent me, but this beautiful suit, it was so cheap! So cheap.

Sima twisted her lips to the side of her mouth. Her fingers covered an eye: in shame?

He smoothed the lapel to his chest.

The Customer

S LIVOVITZ. SLIVOVITZ. PAVEL HAD to say it twice, three times. He even wrote it out for the liquor store clerk, a young boy, not twenty-five, surely Jewish—how could he not know what Pavel was saying? At last the boy nodded, squinting showily at Pavel's careful, fine capital letters.

"Oh, the clear stuff. Why do you say it with a 'sshh'? There's no *h*."

Pavel maintained his dignity; he refused to answer. He stood at the counter and waited.

The boy pushed brown curls out of his eyes; they bounced back onto his cheeks. "In English the *s* means 'ss,' not 'sshh.'" The words came out loud, slow but tinged with impatience, as if Pavel couldn't possibly decipher them. The boy bent down for a key.

"Do you have it?" said Pavel, his voice smooth. "Or shall I take my business elsewhere?"

"I have it," said the boy.

Pavel had to suppress a smile. I! Who was 'I'? Only the owner was 'I'! And if the owner, no doubt the boy's father, knew how he was speaking! Pavel unbuttoned his raincoat, pushed his hand inside his jacket for the handkerchief, unfolded it, coughed gently, subtly. I!

The boy walked to the back of the store, toward a glass cabinet, and opened it. He took out a bottle and handed it to Pavel.

"What is this?" said Pavel.

"Slivovitz," said the boy, pronouncing it wrong. "What you asked for."

"I did not ask for this." Pavel pointed to the label: MADE IN YUGO-SLAVIA. "Don't you have other kinds? A little higher, you know, quality?" He placed extra emphasis on the word *quality*. Let this child understand! He was a new customer but a real customer, one on whom the store would be able to depend. And, more than a dozen years in this country, not so much of a greenhorn, either.

"Well then, why don't you take a look yourself?"

A note of challenge in the voice. So! In fact that was exactly what Pavel wanted, a look himself. He moved in front of the cabinet. Dust sparkled on the corners of the bottom two shelves, scattered with flasks. Ah—there was something. He pulled out a large bottle: MADE IN CZECHOSLOVAKIA. "This," said Pavel, victorious, tapping the picture of dark plums on the label, "this is slivovitz."

"One hundred and eighty proof," muttered the boy, ringing him up. "Jesus Christ."

"Who?" said Pavel.

"Forget it," said the boy.

ORDINARILY, PAVEL WAS SURE, he would have turned and left, having given a bitter retort, at the first or second sign of the disrespectful behavior of the clerk. There was a phrase Pavel loved, one he learned even before coming to the United States, in English classes organized by the refugee committees in the displaced persons camp: *the customer is always right.* He had said this to himself often in the shop he owned with his brother-in-law, where he frequently dealt with men who liked their suits only one way and not the other, then changed their minds after a good deal of work had been done. The customer is always right. Even now, when the business was adjusting with the times to include more wholesale, textiles and fabrics to be sold to larger companies, he found the phrase useful. It wasn't only the individual trying on for a special occasion who liked to be difficult. A buyer, a retailer, these people were controlled by their superiors; they haggled and bargained, but Pavel would be calm and flexible. One had to be cautious, of course, not too foolish, but even business-to-business, the sentence was a useful one to keep in mind. The customer is always right! It helped quiet the anger that sometimes pulsed up inside him when a man used a high tone, a loud voice, a harsh word.

Didn't the boy know about the customer? And to correct Pavel's language! *Slivovitz* was a word as familiar to Pavel as *orange juice,* or *Coca-Cola,* was to this boy. When Pavel was a child, his father would ferment the plum brandy at home, storing the bottles on the shelves of the kitchen. When it came time to open and taste, every year, without fail, Father would march around the house in fury. The slivovitz was terrible! It was true. His father really did not know how to make it. The cherry *vishniac* he made was good—sweet perhaps, a drink that women liked—but good. As for slivovitz, it was Pavel's mother's side that knew how to make it. Father couldn't compete.

No, for certain, ordinarily Pavel would not have stood for the boy's manner. At the least, he would have promised himself to speak to the owner. But this was a new neighborhood. The houses were each separated by wide lawns, the few apartment complexes, like the one he now lived in, were spread out, low to the ground, not cramped, with several stories piled one on top of the other. It was a good neighborhood, the kind where the liquor stores were not so close together. This one was near the new apartment; it didn't pay to make enemies too quickly.

It was something else too. Lately, the sight of boys in their twenties, younger, made Pavel quiet. Silent. It had been worrisome at the time, but now Pavel thanked God every day and every night that Fela had had difficulty conceiving and carrying. If Larry had been born even two years earlier, he would be of draft age. It had happened to a friend of Pavel's from camp, that his son had been sent to the war in Vietnam. So far, one month of unbearable anguish for the parents, and the boy was still in one piece—a miracle, but just that, a miracle. Pavel preferred not to count on miracles.

Better, he preferred not to deal with luck at all, good or bad. People out of danger did not deal with luck. They did not invite it into their lives, not even for a moment. To antagonize a boy in a liquor store over disrespect—this seemed like a way of asking an evil eye to come into the new apartment and gaze hard at Larry. The war would have to end, people said one year, at most two, but what if? The draft age was eighteen. One could avoid it even longer if one went to college, and Larry was smart, very smart, he would be in college and safe if the war did not end.

The rule was, the boys in college could stay in college. And if they changed the rule? But it was America. Laws were difficult to change, even with so much agitation. Pavel knew this with his head, with the mind that read the paper every day, but still he couldn't get rid of his worry. Pavel's father had served in the First World War, for the Austrian empire, no less. It was just before Pavel was born, and Father had never spoken about it. Never. No one had ever said so, but they all knew it was a forbidden subject. Father was the only one in the family to fight. The rest, on Pavel's mother's side and on his father's, had managed to hide themselves in the small villages of Poland that thrived on the influx of young Jewish men evading the armies. What failure in the family had made his father a soldier? As far as Pavel had heard, in the emperor's troops at that time, the Jews weren't treated so differently from the rest. Officially, everyone's blood was more or less the same. Still! A needless risk, unimaginable if Father's family had moved east sooner. In Poland a good family did not let a child go to the military. No question. War or no war, for a Jew it was a death sentence. One saved for years for the bribes.

THE FEELING OF TRIUMPH over his purchase had returned by the time Pavel arrived home. Fela had finished cleaning up from dinner, and his walk had reinvigorated him, as it did every night.

Fela saw the paper bag in Pavel's hand as he walked into the kitchen, where she sat at the white table, drinking tea.

"Hello," she said in English. A bad sign. But then changed to Yiddish. Did you get what you went for? she asked him, still unsmiling.

I found slivovitz! said Pavel, pressing his lips down so as not to smile too much. I didn't think there would be a store in the neighborhood that sold it! But you see, if you try, you can get everything. And a good quality!

"*Mazel tov,*" said Fela. What about the milk?

She was angry. Pavel slapped his hand to his forehead. Oh. I forgot. Completely forgot.

Fela kept sipping. Why do you ask me what I need if you can't remember it?

I know, I know.

Nine-thirty. It is too late to get some now. There's enough for their breakfast, but you won't have it for your coffee.

Pavel stood at the head of the kitchen table. He had no response.

All right, Pavel. Could you go in to Helen? She won't sleep. She won't listen to me. She wants to read. A book you bought her. She should sleep!

It was true, Pavel thought, Helen did not like to sleep. She asked for permission to finish her chapter before shutting out the lights, then cheated and slipped in another one. Fela claimed it was a function of what the child was reading, suspense novels. Crime novels. If Helen read something else, Fela insisted, she would get tired more easily. Of course she couldn't sleep! Couldn't Pavel buy her something more appropriate for a young girl? A girl did not have to choose everything on her own.

Pavel loved to buy books for his daughter. But he let her pick. How should he decide what she should read? She was eleven, "going on twelve," as she liked to say, a phrase Pavel found very funny. There was a paperback exchange in Jackson Heights that she adored, although Pavel felt some embarrassment walking in there and breathing the odor of old paper, smudged ink. He could afford new books for his children! And if they weren't new, they should be in the library, where it was natural for people to share. Still, the used bookstore had a pleasant atmosphere, with a little couch and pillows in the corners between the bookcases. Pavel and even Fela would sometimes leave Helen there under the supervision of the shopkeeper while they ran a few doors down to the pharmacy or butcher shop. But mostly Pavel would sit on the couch, stretching his leg toward the corner, reading his paper while Helen cocked her head and imitated the adults browsing. Occasionally he would give a little smile to the manager, a lanky man in his thirties, who smiled back without saying anything. He had a certain look in his eyes, something like friendliness, Pavel thought, but not exactly friendliness. He watched Pavel too closely, too—Pavel did not know what it was. It made Pavel uncomfortable. Perhaps the owner was a little strange, he had customers who were not so clean-looking, who got into discussions about politics and stayed late into the evenings, after other stores on the block had closed. Fela had learned the owner's name, but Pavel had forgotten it, and he felt, after a few visits, that it would be impolite to ask him in person. Each time Pavel left the store with his daughter he promised himself to ask Fela the name—it would make it easier, less awkward, Pavel thought, if he could greet the owner by name, as an equal, when he walked in—but each time he returned home his head was full of other thoughts.

Helen had cried on the day of the move from Jackson Heights to Rego Park. It was terrible. For Larry, five years older, a little change was not a problem. He was looking forward to the move, even, and he knew some of the children in the neighborhood from Hebrew school already. That was Larry, always independent. Helen grew attached to things. She loved the small playground she no longer played in, the fraying, unbalanced swings that made Pavel's stomach twist in fear when he watched other children; even as he lectured to Fela that she protected too much, he had never allowed Helen to go on them. She loved the bakery that made a special chocolate cake and, when she was smaller, had handed her a sandwich cookie, dyed green, in the shape of a leaf, every time her mother made a holiday purchase. She loved the bookstore owner. A week or so before the final move, when most of the clothes and things in the apartment were already in boxes, she had peeked into the store—its door was open despite the April rain—and shouted something toward the cash register.

Pavel hadn't quite caught it. "What did you tell him, Helinka?"

"I told him we'd be back, we'd be back," said Helen, gripping his hand, stumbling after him on the wet street.

"Rego Park has a bookstore, too, *shaifele*. It's a good neighborhood. You don't have to go back."

"But I want to!"

"All right, you want to."

"Oh, Daddy, come on." Her voice was shaky.

"All right, all right! If we have time."

"I have time!"

"True," said Pavel.

"I told him we were going to move, and he said, That's too bad. That's too bad, he said, because I'm a very good customer. An excellent customer, in fact." Helen had dropped her father's hand, stopped on the sidewalk. "I told him not to worry, he wouldn't lose our business."

Pavel laughed, teeth bared; he couldn't help it. "All right, *mam-mele*, all right. I promise."

"Swear?"

"What?" said Pavel.

"It's like a real promise."

"Of course it's a real promise. I promise. Have I ever broken a promise?"

"I don't remember," said Helen.

"Have I ever refused you anything you asked for?"

"I don't know," she murmured, looking at her shoes as they scraped along the sidewalk.

"Ah-hah," Pavel had said.

Now, pushed by Fela's annoyance, he went to Helen's little room, opening the door as he knocked. The lamp above Helen's bed was on at its dimmest, as if she would have longer to read the less electricity she used.

Her hands gripped a yellow-edged paperback. She didn't look up. "Helinka," said Pavel.

It was her turn to promise. "Look," she said. She flipped the book to face him. "Just two more pages."

"That's what you said to your mother a few minutes ago."

"It was such a short chapter, it wasn't fair."

"Just to the end of this chapter, you really have to promise now. Okay, *shaifele*? Please?"

He closed the door, then stood outside, hearing the page turning. A minute, he would give her, maybe two. He walked to Larry's room. With Larry he was afraid to go in without knocking, but he didn't want to interrupt. Pavel tried to glimpse in through the light in the doorjamb. Just to see. Through the crack Pavel could see the outline of his son bent over his blue desk, doing his homework. Diligent.

Then, from inside: "Hello?" Sarcastic.

Pavel backed away from the door. Then came back. Shouldn't he be able to say good night to his son? He knocked.

"I know it's you, Dad. Just come in."

Pavel opened the door. "Oh, hi," said Pavel, casual. "You're doing your work. Good, good. I won't disturb."

Larry pushed the strings of black hair out of his eyes. "Why do you do that? Wait outside the door?"

"You want me to knock, so I knock. I didn't wait, I don't wait."

"Fine, Dad. Fine. Sure. Okay."

"Why do you have to get so upset?" Pavel said. "A father shouldn't say good night to his son?"

"You're telling me I'm upset?" Larry's tone began to rise. Then he pushed it down. "Okay, Dad. Sure. Fine."

"I'm not telling you anything," said Pavel. "I'm not telling you anything." And closed the door. He walked the four feet back to Helen's doorway. It was good they had separated them. For this reason alone the move out of the small apartment in Jackson Heights was good. A young man needs his own space, Fela said, but also the fighting—it was something Pavel couldn't tolerate, fights between brother and sister. The screaming, inside the house. He would tell them, tell them again and again, not to fight, but this was perhaps the most difficult instruction for them to follow. Larry, so sharp in school, so well liked by his teachers, why couldn't he do a small thing asked by his father? He was the elder, to set the example.

Pavel didn't remember such fights with his brothers. He told this to his children: he never fought with his brothers and sisters. Never? Helen asked, genuinely surprised, every time Pavel said it. Larry had learned to guffaw at the comment. But it was true; Pavel had not fought too much with them. He was the eldest, and respected among them, and responsible for so many things in the household and the family business, he did not have the time. His own adolescence he had spent in his grandfather's house, after his mother's death, when all the children were scattered among the relatives. Upon Pavel's return to the home, a year or two after his father remarried, he was already separate, above the rest. He developed a closeness with his two youngest brothers and kept them apart from each other when they became mischievous. He didn't fight. He made peace.

The light in his daughter's room was still on. Pavel opened the door.

"*Gei schluffen, maidele,* go to sleep."

"Okay."

"Turn off the light."

"Okay."

"Now." The light went off.

LARRY WAS TELLING A story. His mouth was full of salad as he spoke.

Fela looked attentive, smiling with interest as she cut her baked potato, but Pavel found it difficult to concentrate. There was always some complaint! This one was a teacher Larry didn't respect, had played a joke on, something or other. How Fela could smile at this, Pavel did not understand. How Pavel himself could keep silent, he did not understand that either.

The story came to a dramatic break, Larry flourishing his fork, a piece of lettuce flying off a tine and down to his plate. Pavel emitted a loud sigh.

Pavel, do you need more mustard? said Fela, in Yiddish.

No, no, he said. No. He took a delicate sip from his glass of slivovitz.

Larry's story continued. A trail of heat from the liquor crept down Pavel's chest. He began to catch fragments from the tale. The teacher, something about the teacher had made Larry angry, he and his friend. They had gone to look something up in the library, to prove the man wrong, no, to the bookstore, the used bookstore in Jackson Heights, they had gone to ask the owner something and had come upon a meeting of some kind. Just a few men, but why had they let Larry, and his friend, that boy whose hair was too long and always looked dirty, stay?

"So I brought Hell in the next time, one girl and all these men— don't worry Ma, she was with me the whole time—and he still remembers every book you got from him, didn't he, Hell?"

"Helen," she said.

Something about the story was confusing to Pavel. When could this have taken place? Larry was in Hebrew school in the afternoons, or he played with the sports team, track and field. Would Larry have missed a sports practice for this? No. He would not have. Pavel turned his full attention to this interesting event that had pulled his son out of religious lessons.

Larry said, "Shell shock, you know, that thing after World War One, that's when they named it, shell shock, where the soldiers would come back and hear bombs going off in their heads."

Pavel swallowed another few drops of slivovitz. Larry's voice floated from his mouth. He would ask Larry after dinner, what time this all had occurred, he wouldn't let the whole thing bother Fela— if it would bother her at all, she took Larry's side about the Hebrew school—he would wait. He would be calm. He would talk to his son with respect, with care. If he didn't, Larry would probably try to trick him, to lie, and that would be too painful to witness. After all, had not Pavel performed his share of mischief in his youth? Perhaps, but not with school. Once, when he was already in high school, studying late, forgetting something he was to deliver on credit to a neighbor, his own father had tried to hit him, and he had grabbed his father's hand and stopped it in midair. He had made his father afraid.

"Daddy," Helen suddenly said. "You look so sad."

"I do?" said Pavel, startled out of his thoughts, taken aback. "When?"

"All the time," she said.

He looked at her. His daughter had the ability to shock with three words, four. Larry had to perform a whole dance, to entertain, but Helen, so quiet, could cut him open.

At last he answered: "But I'm not sad. I'm very happy." He felt tears coming to his eyes. "I'm happy, happy."

Then he stopped. What had he done a moment ago, what had he looked like? A child shouldn't see her parents sad. There was time enough for that. On the other hand, could it be helped? Was it not a normal part of life, of everyone's life? He thought suddenly of the people around him at work, at the deli counter where he bought a sandwich or soup for lunch. Were they so different from him? Didn't they look sad on occasion? It never had occurred to him to notice.

"Daddy," she repeated, her voice sounding distant, a false echo of her real voice. "I didn't mean it. I thought that's what he meant. *Depressed*, he said, not *sad*."

Depressed. Now this new word mixed with the old one and rang through him, breaking in his chest a small glass of bitterness.

"Who said?" he rasped. "Who said?" But he already knew.

The bookstore owner—moderately tall, sandy hair, thin face, those narrowing eyes—that was what was in them. Examination, inspection, curiosity. Depressed. That was what he thought. Depressed, like a sick man. Pavel looked at his plate, at the chicken cutlet he had sliced into neat rectangles.

"How can you be so stupid?" said Larry, in the tone of half-awake superiority he used only for his sister.

Helen blinked.

"Sha!" said Pavel, turning to face his son, bitterness transforming itself into rage, rising in a wave. "Who taught you to use such a word?"

But Larry wasn't to be quieted. A word from his father sparked his energy, opened his lungs, made him sing. "You did, Dad. You say it all the time." Larry slapped his forehead, mocking Pavel. "Stupid, stupid. How I could forget something so stupid! How I could be so stupid!" Pavel thought he heard, in the scratch on his son's voice, a faint imitation of his accent.

"How are you talking to your father!" The familiar growl was burning a hole through Pavel's rib cage. His jaw was set forward, his teeth clenched, his eyes focused straight at the eyes of his son, who, instead of returning the look, stared off to the side, transfixed. Pavel looked instinctively to his right; his own arm was lifted at an angle, his palm flat, ready to slap.

Fela said, "Pavel."

Her voice was water, a mother's sound. It was not a reprimand. It was a call back to the table. Pavel dropped his arm, rose up from his seat.

"Excuse me." He coughed. And, dragging his bad leg behind him, he moved out of the kitchen toward the hall. He stopped, some meters from the front door, to listen. The family was silent, waiting to hear what he would do. What would he do? He did not know himself.

He would go out. The apartment was hot; he was hot. Still, he should take a jacket. He opened the closet, pulled his raincoat off the hanger with his right hand, the hand he had raised toward his son, and limped out the door.

THE STREETLAMPS WERE ALREADY burning when Pavel stepped off the bus in Jackson Heights, two blocks from the bookstore. Eight o'clock. Would it be open? Perhaps. He kept strange hours, the bookstore owner. Probably it was open; it was like a gathering place. For young people to discuss, to get angry.

It would rain; he could feel it in the lower part of his right knee. But Pavel moved quickly, his legs in a stiff gallop, the right following the left. Thirty-seventh Avenue—a street he had walked alone after dinner or with the children on a Sunday, so many times—looked strange and abandoned, spotted by a pink haze that clouded the signs above the beauty parlor and the eyeglass shop. It wasn't part of his scenery anymore. He had left it. It had left him too, he was sure.

The bookstore was open; Pavel pulled open the door and marched in, back straight, serious. Everything was as it had been: the beige paint chipping from the bookshelves, the man bent at the register with his hands on a crumbling paperback, the smell of dead cigarettes drifting up from the couch. Pavel stood at the entrance of the store, waiting.

"Hello?" A voice from the register.

Ah, it would start. But what would? Pavel stood still, a little afraid. He was here to confront the owner, but with what? He was here to shout at him, to explain to him—why was he here? Perhaps merely to look at the man in the eye, to let the owner observe in person, for as long as he liked, that Pavel's war-bruised face had already healed into something else, that Pavel was not just eating and breathing, not just walking and working, but living.

Something had to be said. It was silent in the store while the manager waited for him to speak.

"Yes," he said to the man, and looked again.

It wasn't the owner but someone else. A large fellow, a beard, a battered black cap in the style worn by students.

"Yes," he said again, slowly, confused. How to explain? "Yes, I would like to buy a book."

The man looked surprised.

Immediately Pavel understood: it was the wrong thing to say, the mark of a stranger. People who came here, the regulars, his daughter, they took care of themselves. It was the kind of store where you spoke with the man at the register, but not for help, just for chat. You looked yourself at the books; conversation developed naturally, informally, like gossip among friends. *Have you ever read something by so-and-so? What's next on the list? How did you like the French history?* Customers here did not ask certain questions; they had information already. Pavel, with his crippled leg and pained accent, his tie and dark jacket, his unschooled knowledge of wool and hard damask, was the wrong type of customer.

But the man was answering. "Well," he said, in a soft tone, a kind tone, "you came to the right place."

Pavel gazed at the broad face, the scraggle of hair that matted the chin, the too-thick brown mustache that drooped past the lips, the lips upturned in a smile. A polite, youthful, store clerk's smile.

"What sort of book?" the clerk continued. "Or should I recommend something from our elegant collection?"

He opened his young arms to emphasize the joke; they were covered in a shirt of bone white. It seemed to Pavel that the color spread over the crowded shelves behind the register, sending a brief light onto the wall of the store.

Flight 028

March 1973

IF THERE WERE NO delays, if the plane left New York at six in the evening, Sima would arrive in Tel Aviv at noon the next day. It was an eleven-hour flight, but because of the time difference, it would feel as if eighteen hours had passed. It was irrational, but the extra seven hours made her even more nervous. There was not much time left. Her aunt Zosia, waking her up with a predawn call, had made that clear. Her father had been hospitalized again, this time with bacterial pneumonia, his immune system weakened from the chemotherapy, his lungs at half capacity from the surgery.

Chaim put the suitcase down between them as they waited to check in, then moved with her to the center of the terminal, with its large signs announcing arrivals and departures. Flight 028 was departing on time. He will wait for you, Chaim said in Yiddish. Then, in English, as if to reassure her more, "You'll make it. Nothing to be afraid of."

But Sima was afraid. She hated flying anywhere, much less overseas, and the two hours of waiting alone to have her bags inspected gave her time to imagine every terrible scenario: hijacking, bombs, engine malfunction, her body burned, vaporized, drowned, her father dying alone, her daughter motherless. She could have bought a cheaper flight on another airline, but El Al was the safest, and after the disasters on TWA and Swissair she and Chaim had decided that they didn't want to use another airline, even if the frequent trips since her father had become sick became more of a financial burden. She worried about leaving her daughter for an unknown period of time, alone with Chaim's casual views of nutrition, with only the promise of visits from Fela Mandl to keep the household from chaos. She dreaded the nausea she got when the plane began to climb, and she did not want to risk an extra tablet of Dramamine, above and beyond the maximum recommended on the label. She was afraid of her father's face when she arrived, the tubes and oxygen tank her aunt told her he was attached to, his face masked and ashen. She was scared to see his death and she was scared to miss it.

She did not know which outcome would be worse. When she emigrated from Israel it had not occurred to her that she would not be with her parents when they died. But now she realized it had been a fear of theirs. From the fold-out couch on which she spent her teenage years she could hear her parents whispering in the bedroom, and one night she had heard her mother crying, a rare occurrence, the same words over and over again, I hope they were together. They had heard a report from hometown, most of the village shot in the forest behind it, the rest eventually transported to a small camp in the East, one from which no one came out. Her parents did not know where their own parents lay buried, or even whether they were buried. Still for Sima the idea of visiting a grave of a relative seemed abstract, something she read about in books. Until her mother had actually died, Sima had not been convinced it would happen. It was her mother's unspoken wish that Sima be there, and she had been, leaving new-born Lola with Chaim. If she had not been there, holding her father's hand in the hospital, she might not have truly believed it. You'll be here for me too, her father had said at the rabbi's office, making the funeral arrangements. When her father had a wish, he spoke it.

"You'll make it," Chaim said again as they reached the security gate. He might not go, she wanted to say. It's pneumonia. Curable. But she remained quiet, embraced her husband, and continued alone to the waiting area.

SHE HAD NEVER BEEN in this terminal by herself. She had gone with both Chaim and Lola for the Christmas school vacation, during her father's second round of radiation treatments, and with Lola at the start of the summer, for the surgery to remove the cancerous section of his lung. Then she had felt hopeful. It had been a nighttime flight, and Lola had been excited to be awake so late, had talked and laughed about the book she was reading. Now Sima counted the passengers in the waiting area ahead of her, awaiting their individual luggage inspections. Eighteen. Now seventeen.

It seemed impossible to her that she was here, that this had happened, that she should be pulled across the earth, one arm here, one arm thousands of miles away, like a doll made of rubber. She had begged her father to move to New York after he had retired. But he had told her not to consider it. What would he do there, without his sister and brother and cousins, alone among men his age, not knowing the language? To be alone was a terrible thing, he had said during one of their discussions, and she had grimaced in guilt.

He had seen her face and taken advantage. You could move back here.

Chaim's work, she started, looking the other way.

Ha! her father had answered.

It had not come up again, not even three months before, when she had brought Lola. It had been an unusually warm December, and Berel had been happy to see his granddaughter, even if his own daughter displeased him with every move. On a day Lola was at the beach with some cousins, Sima took her father to a nursing home, a reputable one, with green lawns and air-conditioned rooms. Chaim's raise would pay for what Israeli state insurance would not.

Her father had said nothing through the tour until he stepped into the car, newly thin, jittery from not smoking.

If you put me there, he said, we won't have to wait for the doctors to kill me. I'll do it myself.

Sima felt ashamed. You won't go there. It's only if you wish.

I don't wish, he had said.

He had become bitter and depressed, angry at his doctors, angry at her. The summer before, after his surgery, she had stayed with him for a month, making him food without salt. He paced around his tiny apartment in his dark robe, not getting dressed, complaining about her cooking. He wanted cholent. He wanted derma. Sima did not know how to make any of these things. They had rarely been able to afford more than the occasional chicken when Sima was growing up. What her mother had taught her to cook, she had mostly forgotten.

Sima's aunt cooked for him now. Zosia cooked with no salt for her own husband, who suffered from angina. While Zosia bustled around them, serving, clearing, rearranging, the two men would sit sullen at the table, shaking the pepper onto the food to make up for the lost flavor. After, they would play cards. Berel loved cards. When Sima was in the army he could disappear for two days at a time just to play, and when he returned, Sima's mother would be waiting for him, furious, silent. Zosia was more tolerant. Berel would go over to her house to play with Zosia's husband. The summer Lola was there,

Berel took her with him. When her grandfather lost she would cry in loud, hopeless sobs.

AT LAST SIMA WAS ushered into a private curtained area. No matter how often she had done it, each time Sima passed through the orange curtain, an El Al stewardess already unzipping her black valise, she felt a shudder of anxiety that they would find something dangerous, that someone had managed to slip something in while she wasn't looking, and that she would be arrested and prevented from getting on the plane. Ridiculous, childish. She should worry more that the stewardess would judge her packing, but of course even in the rushed few hours after the call from her aunt and the purchase of her ticket, she had managed to arrange her clothes neatly.

The white counter on which her suitcase lay open looked to Sima like an operating table. The stewardess wordlessly removed Sima's bathrobe, blouses, slacks, brassieres, with fingers that were bare of polish but still neat and soft-looking. Sima's own hands looked terrible, her knuckles chapped, a hangnail at her thumb. She should have gotten a manicure last week but had not had the time, and now this week—well. What a thing to think of. Still she put her hands behind her purse so that the stewardess, a pretty girl, thin as an actress, olive skinned, wouldn't look at them in passing. She had once tried to be one of those perfect girls, had managed a pale version of that look while in the army, but she had never felt right. She felt more at home in New York than she ever had as a teenager in Israel, trying terribly to fit in.

The stewardess was speaking. "What is the purpose of your trip?"

Sima felt annoyed at the use of English. It was as if people thought she betrayed Jews everywhere by emigrating to the States. She replied in Hebrew: My father is very sick. She turned her wrist to look at her watch, a stupid gesture, automatic, as if a faster inspection would make her arrive in Tel Aviv sooner. The stewardess motioned to her to zip up her suitcase, her face blank.

"Have a safe flight," she said in English.

"Thank you," Sima answered, defeated.

SIMA BIT DOWN ON her chewing gum as the plane rose into the night, clutched at the skin of her forearms, a nervous habit. She had a window seat, two rows behind the exits at the wing, close enough to escape quickly, but not so close that she would have to figure out how to open the emergency doors. The seat next to her was empty, and an older woman had the aisle.

When Sima was a child her mother had a little folktale she repeated on the High Holidays—the sky opening, a chance to see the home of God and perhaps to make a wish. One was supposed to see three stars, and then the angels would write the stargazer into the book of life. Sima had thought of a big composition book, her own ugly handwriting, and the scratchy pencils provided by the refugee aid organizations, and could not understand her mother's pleasure at the idea. Still, looking into God's house sounded interesting: warm light, meat on the table, enough bread. In Palestine, her mother had said, the oranges are more plentiful than potatoes.

When Lola was smaller Sima had tried to explain the story to her, but she had forgotten its details and had filled in her own. Stars like fruit trees, blazing chariots of angels, all the dead smiling down, covered in silver raiment. Lola thought planes were temporary stars, their green and red lights cutting across the cold night sky without the help of God or a holiday. No, no, Sima had said, but when she called her father to help her fill in the outline of the folktale, he said he did not know what she was talking about.

He had gone along with her mother's pretty stories for most of his life, but now that he was ill himself he had abandoned the practice. It was eight years since her mother's death. She was sentimental, she knew, even a little superstitious, but she thought that her mother would watch over, guard her and her father, make sure she arrived in time. She looked at her watch again. 6:15 P.M., New York. She would not adjust her watch until the very last minute. In no time at all she would be there. She looked at the magazine lying unopen on her lap, thought about opening it, decided to wait. She would sleep for the second half of the flight and afterward find her luggage right away. She would go straight to the hospital from the airport, kiss him, comfort him, then take a quick taxi ride to his apartment to pick up fresh clothes for him. She imagined the apartment, his pajamas folded neatly under his pillow, the odor of his sheets and blankets. Her father would come home, and his bed would be undisturbed, just as he had left it. Or perhaps she would do a washing. He might expect her to. She thought of the wallpaper of her parents' bedroom, the gold flowers skimming green stripes. Her mother had pasted the paper up herself, more than fifteen years ago. Her father kept it just as clean as her mother had. It still looked new.

SHE EXAMINED HER TRAY of hot food. The smell of the meat nauseated her, but she could pick at the roll and the cold margarine that came with it. Chaim would take Lola out for pizza tonight, she thought, and would let her have a soda. Well, once in a while it was not so bad.

I don't think it will rain when we arrive, she heard. She turned— her neighbor on the aisle seat was speaking, her thin lips moving on a face spotted from the sun. They hoped so, of course—the woman added, nodding to Sima. It has been so long. But I don't think it will.

Sima smiled, nodded. The woman might be the age her mother

would have been. I think you are right, Sima said. Not today.

May I look at your magazine?

Oh! Yes, of course. She handed it to her. I'm not paying attention to it. Keep it.

No, no, I just want a look.

A native Israeli, Sima thought. Not from Europe. Not just the accent but the boldness. Her mother never would have asked a stranger for a magazine. How her mother had sheltered her, protected her. Not that those acts were enough to eliminate the constant fear and hunger, of course—but the stories she told her—lies, even—had kept Sima calm, at least in the moments of the telling. In Russia, when Berel had disappeared, sent away to hard labor, and she and her mother had been alone, her mother had spent night after night quieting her with stories, folktales, small events from her hometown before her marriage, the lives of her sisters, her brothers, the dry goods store the family had owned, the small cousins who tore down a shelf of dishes one awful day. Her mother had a superstition for every event, a little tale for every night. Why couldn't Sima remember them? That one about stars and the wish bothered her in particular. She could remember conversing about it, her mother's small round face, but not the tale itself.

If we had a calendar it would be easier, Dvora had said one night. But it is around that time. We can approximate. So get ready for your wish.

What should I wish for?

It's your wish. Only don't wish for something foolish, like bread or meat. That's the kind of thing God doesn't have any control over.

Sima had looked at her mother's face, serious and focused.

And you don't have to wish for your father to come home either, because I've already taken care of that with my wish.

You wish for him to come back?

I wish for all of us to get out of here alive, so your father coming back is included. It's wasteful to have two of the same.

Maybe it's better if two people do it.

Believe me, think of something else, something bigger.

I can't think of anything bigger.

Yes you can, said her mother. Think of something very big, something that takes a long time to come true. You have to give these things time. And you can keep it a secret.

What had Sima wished for? She could not have been more than five, and thirty years had passed. Of course she did not remember. But in the end her father had returned, and they had lived, and they had come to Palestine. Was that what she had wished for? It would have been like her, taking her mother's cue. A country, a real home, no need to run from anywhere. Absolutely, that would have been just like her as a small child, wishing her mother's wish without even knowing it.

And then, of course, it would have been like her to move away anyway, to leave her mother and father, just for the love of a man.

For a time, Chaim could leave her parents' apartment flushed with an enthusiasm for living in the heat, working with his hands even as he studied, safe, almost safe, in control, as Berel would remind him, of his own destiny. But the optimism would leave him. He did not feel in control of his destiny. He had no parents to cling to, and he felt a constant numbing fear. And Sima felt the fear too, of the monthly calls into the reserves, of their Arab neighbors whose poverty and resentment seemed to accuse them of some ongoing crime. Chaim felt it more, he felt it even of his own people in uniform—it scratched at him from inside, so much that he confessed it to her once in a while. He wanted to go.

And at that time she had not felt Israel to be her home. Her father's attachment to a country, her mother's too—perhaps this was what they had in common, this was a dream they had shared, for all their differences in temperament—they had been devoted, accepting, even eager for this new life, where her mother cleaned houses and her father cleaned milk vats and Sima—younger, stronger—cleaned offices. Really, what did it matter to them? Her mother still had vanity of course—she bought a pair of gloves that she used for the sole purpose of putting on her nylon stockings without tearing them, stockings she wore twice a year on the High Holidays—but for Sima, the pain of her job and her ugly hands and her two worn dresses was overwhelming. She had worked hard to look cheerful and pleased for her parents, and to push down the darkness inside her in front of her new friends, and even in front of her oldest friend, a hard girl she had met somewhere in Russia, then found again in Rehovot in the first years. Sima had worked hard to ignore the darkness, to make her outside light.

Her mother had had difficulty with Hebrew—at least her father had his boyhood schooling—but to Sima it was just another job, learning the new language, the experiments with her teeth and tongue to imitate well, to laugh properly, to slide in like a native. A false native. She always felt some anxiety in Hebrew, as if about to be caught, recognized, accused: Sheep! Soap! It had happened to her maybe once or twice when she had arrived, the mockery of schoolmates for being among the weak of the diaspora, the old Jews, the ones who let themselves be slaughtered for fear of fighting. The name-calling had happened only once or twice, maybe three times at most, but it was enough.

By now she spoke English very well. She spoke English to her daughter. She had lived in New York twelve years, longer than in any other place in her life. And soon, she felt, it was inevitable, she would speak it better than the languages she had been born into but did not speak outside her home. It was something to be proud of, her English, and it made her excited, the ability to move things in and out in a new language, the language the world thought of as powerful and important. In her head sometimes she would search for a Hebrew or Yiddish word, once in a while even something in Polish or Russian. Occasionally something indeterminate and jumbled, a private language whose sound she could not name but which was the language inside her, the language of a lost place, would bubble up. But her mouth spoke a careful and lilting English. And even this was something to be proud of, the accent people took to be European, of uncertain origin but sophisticated. Even at the beginning, sleeping on the sofa bed at the Queens home of Fela and Pavel, she had felt herself an object of admiring curiosity. It was more than her youth, she thought, but she had responded by acting young and cheerful, flirting with Larry and painting rouge on Helen's cheeks, Pavel standing at the threshold of the living room, watching in silence, happy.

Chaim had felt it too, she thought. Not just in the Mandls' house, with Fela touching his arm constantly as he washed dishes with her, but everywhere. When they had come to America it had been a pride to be from Israel. All the things she had not felt when she lived in Rehovot, she felt in New York, people impressed with her service in the army, with what they presumed to be her knowledge of the land. Not like now, all the criticism, all the judgment. That's right, feel sorry for the Arabs! Well, she had been poor too, poorer yet, without a home either, without anything! And who had spoken out for her?

SHE GOT UP TO stretch her legs, use the bathroom. Seven hours left. When she came back to her seat she had to tap awake the woman on the aisle. She looked at her watch again. Six hours and fifty minutes left. She had had no communication with anyone in her family for the last six and a half hours.

She sat down, rustled under her blanket. To be alone was a terrible thing. In Russia the people who had their families with them lived; those who came there alone starved, fell ill, took risks that led to arrest again and again. It amazed Sima that her husband could have emerged alive out of Poland alone as he was, without a friend or a brother to accompany him.

It amazed her, and yet she forgot it all the time. Chaim's face had a smooth health, his blue eyes had a flatness that made him seem untouched. Like the sea, her mother had said all those years ago, and Sima had felt a thrill that her boyfriend had looks worthy of comparison to something so grand and enveloping. But in time Sima thought: Not the sea, but the sky. Not something she could dive into, searching and breathing, not something she could cross. Unreachable.

Chaim had opened up to Sima's father. Berel had remembered him from the DP camp in Belsen. When Chaim walked through the door the first time, on one of Sima's weekends home from the army, Berel had given him a sharp look that Sima took to be suspicion. But it was recognition: two questions later, Berel knew for sure that Chaim was the young man who had worked as an aide in Sima's camp classroom. Sima had been surprised—it had changed her view of him. Chaim had taught her when she was a child, he had stopped her from crying, he had held her hand on outings. The excitement she felt when she saw his slim frame now seemed to be part of something deeper, fate or destiny.

In those days Sima had known nothing about him. He was her boyfriend, a swaggerer like all of them, but also kind, quiet in private, gentle. The cocky walk seemed to her an imitation of his fellow soldiers, a public gesture to show he had adapted to the desert. He was from Europe, of course—their shared accent in Hebrew had made them exchange a smile when they first met, at a café one night, among a large group of young people. So few in her group were from Europe—so few of his friends, too. No one talked about such things then; they tried to blend in. But their little cadences, softer than native Hebrew, slower, less confident, made them feel they already knew each other without saying so much; and alone, outside the hearing of native Israelis, they could speak in Yiddish.

They spoke in Yiddish at Sima's home too, and with Chaim Sima did not feel the embarrassment of her mother's shaky Hebrew, her father's pointed ventures into Yiddish, diaspora phrases he uttered just to irritate her native friends. She could see how Chaim felt special, touched to be recognized, moved by the ease with which her parents welcomed him into their tiny home. He became warm, relaxed. Questioned, he told fragments of his history to Sima's mother and father that Sima herself had never heard. And even as she felt driven to hear them, she hated hearing them, hated their light, harsh detail. Her father would be laughing, and her mother too: Chaim in a girl's dress, wobbling on low heels; Chaim managing to be fed and sheltered for a few weeks by a brothel; Chaim wandering through the forest and coming upon an isolated town, convincing a Pole with an enormous dog to take him in. They really were very funny snippets—the only time, before or since, she had heard him say anything longer than a sentence or two about his past—but Sima had begun to cry a little. The other three, caught up in the tales of escape and trickery, did not notice.

SHE AWOKE SUDDENLY AS the plane began to shake, her neck stiff against the window shade. Four hours left. She heard the coffee cart being wheeled down the aisle and dug into her purse for a washed apple she had wrapped in a paper napkin.

She wondered whether his surgeon would make an appearance. Avishai. Probably not. She hadn't even noticed him until lunch one day with Netta, not far from the hospital last summer. Her father had sent her away, telling her he needed to rest. She had been relieved to go, a chance to gossip with a childhood friend.

I think I am the only person I know who does not sleep with men other than her husband, Netta had said.

You are one of two, at least, said Sima.

That's different, you're in America.

There must be others. What about Yael?

You're joking, right? Every time she goes to a convention there's something else. Being a doctor—you can't imagine the opportunity.

Sima giggled a little.

What, don't you think about Avishai? The man's attractive. And the way he dotes on your father—surely—

What, flirt with the doctor while my father is so sick? I walk outside the hospital and am shocked to see people walking, laughing, buying groceries.

I'm shocked you don't notice people looking at you—your clothes—

Netta!

Really, you are so fresh, Sima, and pale—

No, no, no! You're making me feel—I feel like locusts are about to come down on my head.

The sky doesn't open every time someone gets cancer.

I know, said Sima, I know. I have to tell you—it's strange to hear you say the word. In America they whisper it.

You don't think Chaim does it?

What, whisper?

No! Sleep with women!

Netta! It's different there. You just said so yourself.

Oh, yes.

Besides, he's a man who doesn't like anything in his world to be upset or overturned. He likes things calm. And believe me, if I found out something like that, a storm from the sky would not be—it would not be—

They were giggling.

Really, though, said Sima. She thought seriously for a moment. The truth is, I don't think so. I really don't—we—she stopped, then began again. I do wish he would be a little more hysterical. It's lonely to be the only one screaming at Lola.

Well, I don't have that problem, said Netta. Uri is the screamer. I think the children are angry with me for how quiet I am.

They are right. Lola is the same! She tries to see how long he can ignore her.

So it makes Chaim a good cardplayer.

Ha! Good liar, that's what.

You have to lie to keep things peaceful, said Netta. Even if just to keep the car running smoothly.

I'm not so good at it. When Lola used to fall, she would look at me to see how terrible my face looked. That's how she knew how loud to scream. Chaim could cover it up more.

Netta laughed. My kids just screamed no matter what.

Chaim had a habit of closing his face. After twelve years of marriage Sima could occasionally detect that moment when his face was half-open. And just as suddenly it would shut itself. It made her more attentive to his every blink and twitch—it made everyone more attentive to him. But once in a while, once in a while, could he not react? Could he not betray himself even to her? Could he not see how the calm bothered her? He could see through everything else. She still listened for the elevator stopping at their floor around dinnertime, bringing him home.

Walking down the hospital corridor, she had seen Dr. Avishai walking out of her father's room and felt her face grow pink and warm. Ridiculous! A word from Netta and already she was distracted. But he did have a nice chest—not too broad, but fit—she loved that part of a man's body, Chaim's too, Chaim's too.

She had entered her father's hospital room smiling. But Berel's face was stiff. Where were you?

Hmm?

Did you think I had already died? Underneath the sarcasm, Sima could detect something new: a desperation, his voice rough, as if he were trying not to cry.

I—said Sima. But you told me—

What did I tell you? I suppose you think I also told you to move across three oceans, to keep my granddaughter from me—

Sima's shock stopped any tears. Her mouth was open.

You dare to laugh at me?

I wasn't—I'm not—

Yes, you are. Now Berel was weeping openly. You are, and you are right.

Sima sat down, grabbed his hand. Her lips were trembling; her hands were shaking; her father's was calm, a little cool.

Sima, he whispered after a moment. I am empty.

She looked at her father's wet face, skin hanging from his jaw-bones. He had stopped crying, he was still, but he did not bother to wipe his cheeks.

Sima waited another moment, forcing herself to swallow and breathe. If he saw even the beginning of a tear, he would—she did not know what he would do.

Finally she answered: Maybe you want something to eat. I bought some halvah near the café. She reached into her purse. Just a *bissl*, she said.

Hmm, said her father, watching her unwrap her little package. Have you broken a rule for me?

Perhaps.

Ah, he said. He couldn't help smiling. All right. Of all things, this won't kill me. So when I go, you tell the doctor it wasn't the halvah, and even if it was, I absolved you.

Don't tell jokes, please, not about—

Who said it was a joke?

IN THE AIRPLANE LAVATORY, she washed her hands twice to rid her skin of the odor from that terrible beef they served. She hadn't even eaten any, just opened the plastic wrapper and pushed it to the far end of her tray once she smelled it. Her hands looked dry, and the soap smelled like artificial cedar, terrible, but it made her feel better. When she returned to her seat they had already taken the tray away.

When she was a child her mother would become angry if Sima did not finish her food. Her father would help her when her mother wasn't looking, would take what was left on her plate—it was a secret partnership, Berel helping her look like she obeyed, Sima giving him a little more to help him feel satisfied. She and her mother had small, slim-boned bodies, but her father's had been broad, expandable, always ready for more, a hunger they had joked about in Russia.

She thought of her father's lips lapping at the piece of halvah she had cut him that day in the hospital. His head leaned against the hospital wall, and he looked calmer, his eyes less red from the tears a few moments before.

You know, Sima had ventured, your attitude is part of the problem.

He glared at her. I think it is your attitude that is the problem.

She said nothing. Anger, that was good, she thought. Or not so bad. It cut her, it always had, but it was better than his crying. Much better. He had been angry and sharp since she was a child, she remembered it well, his quiet rage at her. There had been one night in Osh, she must already have been five, or six, maybe younger, they had both left her for work and she had wandered outside—how old was she then? She felt that they must have left Russia and gone to Germany soon after, but perhaps—

Where had they been after Osh? She wanted to ask, suddenly— why did she not know where she had been?

No, she could not ask.

But she felt her lips moving, the words slipping out of her mouth. *Tatteh*, where were we after Osh?

He looked at her, a little satisfied smile. She knew what he was thinking—at last, she's admitting it, with a deathbed question.

Hmph, he said, eyes small and alert.

Oh, don't answer it, if you can't remember either.

Of course I remember. Osh was the last place before Uzbekistan, and then from there we went back.

How did we hear to go back to Germany?

We didn't hear anything. We were told to register to get on a train, and we did it. It was the rumors on the train, so many rumors that we knew it was true.

I don't remember the train out of there, she said. Only the train to Russia.

It didn't feel like a train, he said, it didn't feel like a train because it was so slow. They had to keep stopping and hooking and unhooking the cars. And the tracks! Destroyed. It must have taken us more than a month to get to Germany.

I wish I remembered it better.

No you don't, said her father. Her father leaned back into his pillow. His eyes glittered, triumphant.

Forget about it, said Sima.

No, no, I am delighted you ask.

She leaned toward his ear and continued. There is no reason for you to be angry with me. No reason!

He did not answer.

She continued. What is it with you? Acting like a little child who did not get his way. What do you want, to prove to me you can die?

I wish it were a little easier to prove.

Terrible! You have a nerve!

Oh, I see, I have a nerve. I do. His voice came out in a whisper. What a daughter I have!

She stopped, sat in the large chair near the head of the bed, looked away from him. How ridiculous he was. Always so dramatic. He wanted to make her burst into tears! Well, she would not. It was a bad habit she had gotten into with him in the last few years, matching his moods, shout for shout. She never would have dared with her mother. No, her mother had been a mother, scolding her, hitting her—even when she was twenty already, smacking her with a towel when Sima did not come home one night, she was out with a boy from the army again—a real mother, who had died when Sima had only just become a mother herself. But her father—her father had lived long enough to become her friend.

THE PASSENGERS APPLAUDED AS the plane rolled down the runway. The national anthem began playing through the speakers. Lola would be waking up, struggling with her father, begging him in her raspy sleep voice to let her have five more minutes, just five more minutes, then dressing lightly, stealing one of Fela's cookies from the upper cabinet before Chaim saw, ignoring Chaim's shout to go get her galoshes, now, right now, forgetting to grab her wool hat. She smiled at the thought of it, relieved at being here at last, of arriving on time, in time. Her neighbor in the aisle seat smiled back at her. Sima had new photographs to show her father, in a little envelope in her purse, and she touched them as she stood up to exit.

ABOVE THE CUSTOMS HALL she could see the second floor of the terminal, families peering through the glass walls for the arriving passengers below. She looked up absently, out of habit, from when her father used to come and wait for her and Lola to arrive, then shook her head. She saw a face that looked like her aunt Zosia's. Her heart began to pound. Why would Zosia be here? She had told her not to pick her up. But Zosia had not listened to her, of course she had not listened to her, she had not wanted Sima to come alone to the hospital, she was worried that Sima would be tired after her flight, her aunt was like a mother to her. Sima had told her not to, but of course Zosia had come to the airport to pick her up. She looked up again and squinted. Yes, that was Ze'ev with her, no doubt reluctant to let Zosia drive alone. Sima's hands began to sweat. Are you all right? said the customs agent.

Of course, said Sima.

But the agent eyed her carefully and again ran through the list of questions she had just answered, just to make sure. Time was wasting, but Sima answered politely, calm. It was only noon. Nothing could have happened yet. Not even a day had passed. She walked out of the baggage check and looked for her aunt and uncle. There they were, her aunt in a blue cotton shirt and gray skirt, sunglasses on her head, her face straight, expressionless, her unshaven husband grasping her hand, her eyes—that look, thought Sima in a panicked flash, that look, something terrible has—

What has happened? said Sima. What has happened? My God, what has happened?

Your father—her aunt began.

But Sima could not let her finish. *"Oy, Gott,"* she cried, again and again. God, *Oy Gott,* her words and grief were pulsing from her bones, through her skin, in all the languages she knew.

HE HAD BEEN ALONE. She had come here to be his companion, and he had died in his narrow bed alone.

You were with him, said Chaim. It is a blessing.

Her husband's voice, clear, strangely near despite the telephone, was breaking; he was crying. She could hear Fela's voice, faint garbles of concern in the background, and she felt a wave of hate for her husband. Here she was, all alone, abandoning her daughter to her husband's secondhand telling. She was alone here, her daughter was alone there, or almost alone, and her father had died alone, alone, alone.

Sima's shame was great. Yes, she lied, dry-voiced. Yes. I was with him, and he fought it. He fought with me near him. He was not alone.

A blessing, wept Chaim. A blessing. He got his wish.

The Performance

April 1973

SOMEONE AT WORK HAD tickets to a concert. A commentator whose companion was sick. Would Chaim like to come instead?

Yes, he thought. He would. Normally the reporters and announcers did not mix with the technical people—it was a nice gesture, he should not refuse it lightly.

He called Sima at home. She answered on the second ring, her voice compressed, more flat than sad, as if she was lying down.

Go, she said. Go. Don't worry about me.

HE DECIDED TO STAY a bit late at his desk, grab a bite with the commentator. Bob. They sat at a coffee shop two blocks from Avery Fisher Hall, Chaim nibbling on unbuttered toast, Bob swallowing a hamburger.

It was a concert at a small orchestra society, with a soloist whose face, when he opened the program, he thought familiar. And the name—Basia Lara—Basia. He read her biography in the program twice. Yes, it must be her.

Basia Lehrman, now called Lara, Basia Lara. She too had gone from Germany after the war to Israel, but he had not seen her since—since when, perhaps since Europe, when a teacher in the DP camp had taken the musically gifted children to a concert in Hamburg. How old had he been, that concert? No more than fourteen, still living in the house in Celle with Pavel and Fela. He had not seen her since, but he believed he had heard something of her, a picture some years ago in a Tel Aviv newspaper, accounts of a large international prize she had won, the first for an Israeli, let alone a refugee.

Basia had become professional, successful. She lived in Baltimore with her conductor-husband, who taught at the conservatory. But that was all he read of her before she appeared, large and dark haired, skin pale against a gleaming dress, on the stage. She began to sing, love songs in German and Italian, to the accompaniment of a piano. Lieder from Schubert, music he had not heard before and did not melt into, then an aria in Italian that flowed into him, her voice falling in minor notes like dripping water, slow but detached. *Mio ben ricordati*, it began, please remember, remember, my beloved, the awkward English translation almost unnecessary, the small vocabulary he had absorbed in youth budding up inside him, words he could recognize once he heard them but not call up before they came out of her mouth. *Mio ben ricordati*, how my heart loved you, and if ashes can love, from the grave I still will love you. When the song ended, there was a long pause. Chaim saw the singer's face register surprise at the silence, then a broad smile as the clapping began.

He told Bob he would take a walk before going home, but instead waited in the receiving room adjacent to the recital hall. She entered from a door Chaim had not noticed until she walked through it, her pianist at her side. Even at a distance he could see a silver swath of makeup extending from her eyelids, reflecting against her white skin and rouged cheekbones.

Chaim waited until the number of concertgoers flanking her had dwindled to four. He thought he saw her looking at him with some concentration as he approached. As he came near he put on a slight smile, then murmured, "I was with you when you attended your first concert, more than twenty-five years ago."

She took in a breath, let it out in a laugh. Of course she remembered him, her fellow refugee, along with every detail of the concert hall, what their teachers wore, the exact music played. That night was one of the most beautiful nights of her life. The others around her moved away.

Do you like my dress? she said, in Yiddish. It was floor length, the color of lilac, entirely sequined. The neck scooped down, leaving the plump white skin around her collarbones bare.

Yes, said Chaim.

You'll never believe how I got it. One of my first recitals here, I sang in a church. Through the music school. I had nothing! I wore something I thought was very elegant, borrowed from a teacher who had worn it years before. A man came to see me afterward, backstage.

Chaim shifted.

An elderly man. He said—Basia moved into English, "Miss Lara, you sing beautifully, you dress terribly. I want to buy you a gown." Basia laughed.

Chaim said, He was Jewish.

Of course! But I couldn't understand. And when he wrote me the check—it seemed a shameful thing to do. I said, No, no. Finally he started to speak in German, and I answered. My German, perhaps you remember my German—but it has improved with the schooling.

I can sing it, if not speak it. So! He was here tonight, I wore the dress he helped me buy, one dozen years ago. Let me tell you, it was hard to get in it. I hope I get out.

Chaim laughed a little, stole a glance at the waistline of the dress. It did seem a bit tight. It turned out he knew the man too, an acquaintance of an acquaintance, a professor who had come from Germany in the 1930s, before the war.

I am so glad we saw each other, Chaim. It was fate, wasn't it, to meet again at a concert?

Maybe fate, said Chaim. Maybe luck.

I perform again tomorrow, and I go out of town in a few weeks. Why don't we have lunch before I go?

Wonderful, said Chaim. He took down her number.

I MET SOMEONE FROM Germany tonight, said Chaim, his hands calm on the kitchen table.

Yes? said Sima, half-smiling.

Basia Lehrman—a classmate from Belsen. She was the soloist—

Basia. Basia Lara? I know her.

You know her? How? The words came out louder, more shocked than he anticipated.

Not from camp. She's much older than me, you know.

What, a year, two?

Maybe four. Sima's lips went straight. Maybe five. She lies about her age, of course. I was in the army with her. She'd subtracted some years to postpone service. No birth certificate, no documents, impossible to prove. But still, hard to do, given that figure. She was developed like a thirty-year-old when she was eighteen, at least, when she said she was eighteen. Men always after her.

She was singing.

Ah, you heard her. She was in the acting troupe of the army. I heard her a few times. Beautiful voice.

Yes, Chaim agreed. She had a pretty voice.

Sima's careful hands were cutting a pear; the juice spilled onto her polished pink fingernails. It was night. Lola was asleep. Chaim felt his hand push itself across the round table to cover his wife's. She didn't stop cutting.

Do you want a piece? she said. It's so good.

No, said Chaim, withdrawing his hand. No.

Sima had started for Lola one collection after another, the most extravagant and least successful being an intricate dollhouse. Lola was not delicate; she broke things, and miniatures made her nervous. She was quite tall for her age, lithe and loud. The dollhouse was kept in Lola's room, but Lola rarely touched it. Sima dusted the insides, bought tiny furniture, small rugs, even little dishes. Sima had not had a girlhood, Chaim thought. She had not had a girlhood and so still was a girl. She had been poor and deprived but sheltered in youth, protected and watched. Now, suddenly learning to be without parents, she was learning what it was not to be young.

Basia was old.

SIMA GOT UP AND washed her plate. Chaim stayed in the kitchen, then went to the living room, turned on the hi-fi. He put on Rachmaninoff's Third, a new Lazar Berman recording he had brought home from the station. He played it low and sat on the sofa, waiting for Sima to come out from the bedroom and ask him to join her.

They had lied to Lola until Sima had come back. He had lied, because Sima had wanted him to. She wanted to tell her daughter about Berel's death in person. He would sit in the living room with the record player on, waiting for the telephone to ring while Fela made dinner for him and his daughter in the kitchen, Lola convincing her to put chocolate in her apple cake, Pavel smiling wider than Chaim remembered ever seeing, Lola looking happy and ignorant.

Every night the same thing. Chaim would tell a funny story about Lola. But Sima's laughs would come out unnatural and short, barked over the international phone lines.

Chaim, she said. How will I tell her?

I can tell her, he offered again.

I want to. Please, let it wait.

But it made him nervous to wait, to watch his daughter's mouth opening like a bird's: "How is Sabah? What does he say? When is he coming out of the hospital?"

He would turn away and say, "Not good, not good." Then, as if to make himself feel more truthful: "Very bad."

He thought their daughter was stronger than Sima believed. Lola was healthy and exuberant, more trouble than her school could handle: good trouble, the trouble of a strong child. She was mischievous. She laughed uncontrollably at jokes made by schoolmates, whispered during emergency drills when the rule was silence. Chaim went to the meetings with Sima, nodded solemnly over their daughter's failings, flirted gently with the teachers. Lola would burst into tears afterward and quickly recover. She knew that people died; if he told her the truth she would not collapse. Grief was grief, it did not matter who bore the message or in what form the message was given. It was not good to give their daughter the luxury of believing that when death came, it came gently, accompanied by a mother's comfort.

HE COULD NOT REMEMBER what he had felt when he had learned of his father's death, when he had seen his brother—and even if he could remember he preferred to blot it out. Chaim remembered only flashes of shock and horror—the sadness had come later, when the world he once knew seemed a forgotten story, something in films, grief forming in a fog, surrounding him, but refusing to fill him the way he saw that his wife was filled.

Upon her return Sima had become silent and inward, even with Lola. He wanted to talk to her, to tell her that he too wept for her father, the man who had given him a new family, but he felt that crying in front of her would seem intrusive, presumptuous. Berel had mocked him at their first meeting. That was how Chaim remembered it—Sima's father's sarcasm at his painfully new Hebrew surname: Halom. Chaim had changed it, cleverly, he had thought, to the translation of his own name, his father's name, Traum, dream. He wanted to feel new in his new country, new and native, his names rolling off the Hebrew tongue with thoughtless ease. He fooled almost no one, of course: his accent, though mild compared with that of the other Europeans, and perhaps more his face, its telltale fatigue and suspicion, gave him away as a boy from the diaspora, a meek goat who had escaped the slaughterhouse by accident, by intervention from forces stronger than himself. But the change of name signified at least a willingness to adapt and to fight. He would use the word for *dream* as it occurred in the Bible, not as it had been handed down to him in a murderous Europe.

Your father's name was not good enough for you? Berel had asked.

Sima's mother had scolded. Berele! Let the boy eat.

I'm finished eating, Chaim had said. He smiled, keeping his face free of trembling. I feel I kept my father's name. It is not as if I chose something completely different, like the others: spring or zion or song. I do not reject my father's name. The meaning is the same.

Ah, said Berel. The meaning.

Sima protested. I had thought about it myself.

So, Simale, why did you not do it? And do not try to convince your boyfriend that it was out of respect for your poor father and mother. We all know—perhaps Chaim knows too—that you always do as you please.

I like our name, said Sima. That is all.

Well, reasoned Chaim, the meaning would not have made a difference in Hebrew—Makow, what, a little town?

A big town! answered Berel. With no Jews now. That is why we keep it. Even if—he shot a sly look out of his eye—even if our daughter is the last to carry our name, until she marries, of course.

Sima flushed. But Chaim was relieved. The old man did not hate him—in fact perhaps liked him a bit. He continued his logic. If you can translate the name into Hebrew, you don't lose the meaning. If it can't be translated, it can't be translated. So, of course, it is different to try to change Makower—he nodded at Sima's mother—than to change Traum.

Dvora broke in. I was Zambrowska, she said. Before I was anything to do with Makower. And now, look, after I married: no more of the sisters Zambrowska. No brothers Zambrowski. Nothing.

Hmph, said Berel. You see? Are there so many *Traumen* left in the world that you felt you could make it one less? Berel chuckled a little at his own pun. One misses the sound too, not just the meaning. Some things cannot be translated. Now, where was your family from?

Chaim had let himself be drawn out. A small town, north of Warsaw. Dvora had smiled—she had had family not far from there. But Chaim did not want to dwell on his origins—the facts of his family, scholarly, somewhat secular, poor, he could mention, but the details—the sisters and brothers—he did not want to spill it. He told instead scenes from his life after the ghetto—scenes of escape with the five boys, then the three, then just Tsalek, the last friend he had lost, the traveling from small town to town, the hiding in the forest, trapped in a group of incompetent gentile partisans, then in an abandoned shed in the city. To his surprise he had delighted Berel and Dvora with his tales—they chuckled and laughed, poured him tea, asked him for more. Adventure stories: preferable to the tale of his name.

Yet when he applied for the visas to America he had put himself and his wife down as Traum. What did *Halom* mean in English? It would mean nothing. And once he moved he did like the sound of his father's surname, in the open American voice used by his new employers or in the lilting Yiddish of Fela's kitchen. Pavel, overjoyed to be reunited, had introduced him to friend after friend by his full name, and the sound stirred in him relief, nostalgia, as for a tune he had heard in his childhood but had difficulty singing himself. It was easier to say the word *Traum* in English than in Hebrew—here the gaze at the Europeans was less accusatory. Here he had less to prove or to show. And for a man his age there was no army requirement in New York, and all the protests the students did over the war in Vietnam did not pain him the way he thought it should. Here he did not face his own death or the deaths of others—people he himself might harm—as he had in Israel, each time he was called for reserve duty, each time he heard of activity on the border. In Europe it had not occurred to him that a life in Palestine would mean the constant fighting and fear of fighting. Before the war even the most idealistic youths—his brothers had been among them, his cousin Rayzele and her brothers too—had thought of Palestine as a place to work and live in a peaceful collective, no neighbors to battle or expel or kill. And after the liberation, what little he had understood of the battles between Arab and Jew had not included the thought that he would join an army to move others out. He had left the house in Celle, Fela crying, Pavel, half-furious, grasping his shoulders again and again, with the idea that he would be on his way to a real home, that the fear he felt every day in Germany would dissipate and his comfort with Rayzele and her friends would grow.

He had been thrown in with the rest, inexperienced European boys near the border with Syria; with his small understanding of rifles and stealth, he had stood out as less nervous, more poised, able to lead a group of five, assisting the lieutenant with his halting Yiddish. He was a new man, he wanted to be a new man, but even as his body looked calm, stiff, in control, his mind shrank from the idea of violence, and the patrols to which he was assigned were a slow torture.

He could wear a strong face with his peers in the three years of straight military service, but once he was married it became terrible, a mask he dreaded putting on. He developed stabbing pains, giant knives in his gut that woke him up in the night, thinking of his future, the prospect of reserve work: his strong years spent dreading the month of patrolling, his old age spent watching his children—would he have children?—it seemed so much to take on, another life—go to battle against their neighbors. But he had found himself unable to confess to the army doctors, for fear of arousing their disdain at his diaspora cowardice. Each time he was called to the reserves he was pulled out of his peaceful life with his wife, her terrible cooking of which he made fun, his work as a technician at one of the radio stations. He did not want to fight. After all his troubles in Europe—once he had time to think, he became afraid, then angry. His life had been struggle enough. Jewish natives of Israel thought him a traitor, even his wife felt reluctance and guilt, but he knew he couldn't protect himself there. He needed a life without battle.

Here the pain was much less frequent; it did not distract him: that was America. A phone ringing in the evening did not signify a military emergency but simply a request to visit a friend of Pavel and Fela's, to install the new hi-fi just so. A police car speeding by, siren wailing, was on its way to someone else's tragedy. An argument with his wife did not result in him doubling over and her giving up on the discussion, horrified by his suffering; he could buy pills over the counter that quieted him down, sometimes for a week. He had his morning ritual of choosing a shirt, he had the coffee shop where he picked up his coffee with milk, no sugar—on doctor's advice he could drink moderate amounts—he had even the little office disputes, the routine he had devised for organizing his morning tapings, the frenzied after-noon shouts of his supervisor, whose endless ability to misunderstand the new equipment could on occasion seem endearing, sweet, naive. Once Lola arrived, and with her the increased company of Fela and Pavel, substitute grandparents, he had almost no episodes at all; it was as if the intense, almost disturbing love he had for his child had mitigated his ability to feel pain.

Sima felt pain. At times he could gather up envy at his wife's grief, parents to care for as they died. He envied even the solitude of her burden, the fact that she shared nothing with a brother or sister, that she alone was responsible, full. He was empty.

HE WENT TO BED after the recording ended and fell asleep quickly. But then he awoke in the night, no pain, no dream. Restless. He looked over at Sima, lying in the bed beside him, shoulders hunched, breasts hidden, the grief in her face apparent even in her sleep. A good woman, a good mother. On drives she would paint her lips, blot with a tissue, then draw with the lipstick a face above the lip print to give to Lola in the backseat. He was a lucky man. Lucky. But he wanted to be more than lucky. He did not want his happiness to come in bursts. He wanted the explosions of his life to be over. He wanted to have the sound of happiness moving softly within him, beside him as he walked, following him and guiding him, like an accompanist at the piano.

HE MET HER IN a café near her Midtown hotel at two, just after the lunch rush. Basia was waiting for him in a booth; he was surprised, expecting her to be later than him. She was dressed simply, in a caramel-colored blouse and skirt, a wedding ring her only jewelry, but still she seemed to glitter.

Chaim, she said.

Hello, he answered in Hebrew.

But she continued in Yiddish. You grew up. I meant to say it to you yesterday, but I was so shocked—so taken back in time, you know.

He nodded.

So I say it now, she continued. You grew up.

He gave a nervous laugh. Yes. As did you.

Yes, she said. I have two daughters.

I have one.

Don't tell me her name. I'm sure she is beautiful.

Not beautiful, said Chaim. Not exactly. But a charmer. Very smart.

Of course, said Basia. How could it be otherwise?

He ordered a soup and half a sandwich, but when it came he found it hard to swallow more than a spoonful or take more than a small bite.

Such a delicate eater, said Basia. But she herself had a full salad in front of her, almost untouched.

Sometimes my digestion is unpredictable, said Chaim.

He waited for the pains to flicker inside him at the reminder, but he felt nothing. Calm.

She began to hum. "*Vedrai carino, se sei buonino, che bel rimedio ti voglio dar.*"

That is something you sang last night, yes?

Basia smiled. From *Don Giovanni*. She is trying to heal her lover, trying to comfort him.

What does it mean?

"*Sentilo battere, toccami qua,*" Basia sang. "It means: feel it beating. And *toccami qua*: touch me here. Touch me here, touch me here."

She is almost ridiculous, Chaim thought. But he did not laugh.

She repeats it, said Basia in Hebrew, until he does it. He knows he will be healed.

When she excused herself to go to the ladies' room he called for the check, breathing slowly, blinking away the image of her chest struggling against its sequins as she sang the night before.

Do you have the afternoon? Basia said, returning. Let us walk.

He had told his supervisor Russell that he was sick, and Russell had waved him off—it occurred to Chaim that he had not taken a sick day since eight years ago, when Sima had given birth, and he felt more troubled by his deception to Russell now than by his betrayal of his wife.

Was it a betrayal? No, no, it wasn't to do with her but with him. It wasn't expected that he should be a man in hiding while she grieved. He had remained steady to her, in love with her, truly attached to her all the years of their marriage.

He had been with other women in Tel Aviv, of course, though not in the first two years they were married, and only on the reserve weekends. Since Lola's birth he had been with someone else only once, a young woman he had met one morning when the church down the street had burst into flames, an electrical fire, they said, the same church in which a deaf black boy had been killed by police because he had not heard them shout at him to turn around. But this was different from the girl at the church fire, this was a real wind in him. At the lobby of Basia's hotel, when they stopped, he did not wait for her to ask him upstairs. He clasped his arm around her full waist. She did not try to escape.

BASIA DECIDED TO STAY an extra day and made some excuse to her husband and daughters. Chaim had two days of her, one afternoon and another full day—he was sick, he told Russell, working late, he told Sima—spent in her hotel bed and walking in Central Park, and he felt himself to be in a French movie. When she left he felt a half-pleasant sensation of pull and loss, an easy loss. He carried her bags for her the morning she left, and on the train platform she gave him a modest kiss on the cheek that he imagined he could smell and feel throughout his day at work, cutting tape at the radio station for a public service announcement, adjusting the volume in the recording room for the announcers.

What was it that Basia had sung that night? He wanted to call up the tune in his head, but he couldn't remember it completely, only a note or two, the shadow of the melody. He thought of her plump white chest in the hotel bed beside him, then in the sequined dress. Her voice the opposite of her body: thin, unembellished, pure. Her body as full of music as his own was empty.

Why had she left Israel? Her career had called her. Her husband, a Hungarian pianist, had left Hungary for the same reason.

Really?

Well, when the Communists came, it was more difficult.

He must speak Yiddish.

Of course, but now I speak a little Hungarian. I speak everything! She laughed. I am a citizen of all countries. It is crazy, but we com-municate most in English now. I don't know why. His Hebrew is all right, anyway.

But he did not want to move there.

You know what they say about us, Chaim. I felt that people looked at me like I had committed some crime, or else I would not be alive. Didn't your friends say such things to you?

I didn't talk to my friends, said Chaim. They did not want to hear it.

But on the subway home he thought it was not quite true. Berel had wanted to hear it, and Dvora, and even Sima. Yet Sima knew almost nothing. Her willingness to listen had softened his need to talk, had relieved him of the burden of having to say anything, as if the only reason to tell her was to make sure she would believe it. But if she already believed, he was absolved of the obligation to speak. Almost a healing silence, as if she knew with medical precision where not to cut.

On the subway he felt thinner, cleaner, a new man. But Sima did not look up when he came home. He went into their bathroom, washed his hands, rubbed them hard with his wife's embroidered towels. While brushing his teeth he hummed to himself an American song, words he half remembered from a tape Basia had put on in her room. *And I seem to find the happiness I seek.* The rhymes so clean and easy. *When we're out together dancing, cheek to cheek.*

AFTER DINNER HE STAYED in the kitchen, reading a Yiddish weekly that Pavel had left for him and sipping tea. He slipped a spoonful of jam into his mouth, rolled it around under his tongue.

I need some things, said Sima, her voice sharp. She had appeared at the doorway of the kitchen without his noticing her arrival, her dark robe tied loosely around her waist, her hair pulled back. On Ninety-third Street the drugstore is still open. We need Q-tips.

Chaim's lips parted. There was a question in his mouth, but no sound came out.

And soap, Sima continued. Dial soap. The kind of soap we use is Dial.

I know what kind of soap we use, Chaim said, then regretted it instantly. He had showered at Basia's hotel.

Sima looked at him, a kind of puzzled expression on her face. Please go, she said.

It was eleven o'clock at night. He wanted to ask, What, now? But as he thought the words he stopped them, and his face flushed with relief at having held himself back from what would have been a terrible stupidity, possibly something worse than what he had already done.

Words moved into his head, bubbled inside his chest. Please—I don't know what you are talking about—let us think about it—you don't know—I did not—my love, I have missed you so much, I only—it was about the music, it was something from my past—how can I—

He said: All right.

His mind turned blank as soon as he got outside, marched uphill to Broadway in the chill. Dial soap, Dial soap, he thought, the words bouncing in his head in an even rhythm, Dial soap, Q-tips, Dial soap, Q-tips. When he came back he sat in the kitchen for an hour, the pharmacy bag on the table in front of him, staring at the red and yellow lettering. He had a feeling he should be scared, but he was not. At last he got up to walk to the bedroom but stopped at his daughter's door and pushed it open. Sima was lying in Lola's bed, her arm thrown over their daughter's waist.

LOLA HAD A RECORD that told the story of Mozart's life, interrupting the narrative with music. A child who played his first chord at age three, who, under the tutelage of his father, had written his first compositions for piano at age seven, his first symphony at thirteen or fourteen—out of his body and hands had come these pieces that now flowed through the mouth and body of a singer, a pianist.

They gave their daughter piano lessons, though she struggled with them and would cut short her required half hour of practicing a day. She wasn't a musical child, not a performer. She preferred stories, records, lying around listening to her mother tell tales of Siberia, tugging at Pavel's arm for some story of escape, begging Chaim to describe what his mother had looked like. She did not understand what she was asking. When Berel was last in New York, after the first surgery, he had gone into a rage at Lola one night when she refused to finish what was on her plate. He had snapped at her in the middle of his own meal, and then, confronted with the child's stunned face, shouted at Sima and at Chaim. Then he had gotten up and gone to the room he shared with Lola and closed the door.

It makes him suffer, unfinished food. Sima, tears in her eyes, had tried to soothe their daughter. And now his medication, it bothers him. He is sorry, Laiush, he is sorry.

Lola was forgiving.

ON SUNDAY CHAIM SAT on a park bench watching Lola roller-skate around the little median in Riverside Park.

After a few rounds she came and sat down. Next to him on the bench was his radio, turned off, and a magazine, unopened.

"Daddy," she said.

He felt a little sweat come out on his forehead. Sima had spoken maybe twenty words to him in the last four days, and he had a sudden thought that Sima had told Lola that she was asking Chaim to move out, that Sima had told their daughter before telling him. Irrational, crazy, but the images of what might happen hurtled through his mind like a movie, Lola would ask him where he was going, when he was coming back, what could she do to make him and Sima live again in one bed—all things he knew from his workmates that children asked when their parents separated. What did one say? Everything would be all right, it was not Lola's fault, whatever her mother told her she should listen.

"Yes, Laiusha."

"Don't worry so much."

"Do I worry?"

"I don't know."

"Your mother and I are—we—" But he stopped. Perhaps Lola did not notice anything amiss. Sometimes when the air-conditioning in their bedroom broke down, Sima slept in their daughter's bed too.

"Uh-huh."

"So, everything will be—" He stopped again. His words sounded unfeeling, almost false but not quite. He did not feel the remorse or pain Sima thought he should feel—what, should he not live, after all he had lost, should he not live?—no, he felt instead the slightly sick feeling of having taken a risk that had failed, that twinge of fear right after being caught but before the punishment and suffering to come.

"Dad, okay. Don't worry about me."

He looked at her face, pink from exertion, her rough hair in a tight ponytail, only a few strands falling out. *Dad.* Had she used that word before? She must have. But he was used to Daddy. Come Daddy me a little, he would say when she was younger, even sometimes recently. I love it when you Daddy me.

"I don't worry, Laiush."

"Dad," she said. "You are an orphan, and now Ma"—he saw her eyes water—"Ma is an orphan. I'm not an orphan."

"Of course not."

She stood up and teetered forward, motioned for his shoulder, then grabbed the back of the bench instead. "I'm going around another time."

She wheeled off. He watched her waving her arms for balance, elbows straight, hands relaxed. "Lola!" he called.

"What?" Her voice pushed through a small breeze. *And the cares that hung around me through the week.*

You are my life, he wanted to say. "Be careful," he called.

She kept skating, as if she had not heard him, her arms out at her sides for balance. *Seem to vanish like a gambler's lucky streak.*

He called out again. "Lola, do you hear me?"

She turned and waved, then skated farther away.

"Be careful," Chaim shouted. "Be careful."

Stones

1989–2000

The Curtain

November 1989–February 1990

FELA DID NOT LIKE it, but she let her husband go. It was easier, now that the Iron Curtain was down, for him to visit Poland, and he had two projects: to visit his mother's grave, and to visit his mother's youngest sister, still living, at eighty.

Fela had sworn not to set foot in Poland again. And Pavel's aunt, even if she was the baby of the family, had survived Russia by working as a professional Communist. That Pavel could choose to ignore this was a mystery. The Communist youth of her childhood were hard ones, impulsive, though frequently intelligent. They had been smart to hate Poland as it was. But to come back after the war! She had gotten a job, this aunt, she and her Communist husband, good jobs in the new Polish government, jobs they had lost in the purges of Jews in the 1960s. When it came to Poland, a Jew was still a Jew, Communist or no. Well, she was an aunt. A remnant. It was important for Pavel to see her and the husband and the son, a professor who, with his Catholic wife, had come to New York once. Pavel had sent money for years; now, at the age of seventy-three, he and his cousin Mayer should go.

Three weeks, he said. Three weeks to do everything.

Why now? Why don't you wait until you finish with selling the business?

I don't know when I finish. How long can it take, with Kuba deciding this way and that? Better I go now, and when I return, then I feel relaxed to do it. Then I feel unafraid.

But November, she had tried. Why a winter in Poland? Why not wait until spring?

November is when Larry can take his vacation, said Pavel. And Larry wants to go.

Larry did want to go; it surprised Fela, but she kept it inside. Good for the men of the family to share something, she supposed. Though she didn't know how their son would get along there, with no Polish, the Yiddish he knew useless, the German he had spoken in childhood almost completely forgotten. Larry couldn't stand to depend on his father. He'd bought a phrase book and tried out his accent on her: Black coffee, please, he would say. No sugar. No milk. Toothpaste. Eardrops. Shoe shine. Gauze. Where is the bookstore? The bathroom? The phone? She hoped he would not come back speaking Polish. It wasn't a language she wanted her children to speak.

FELA COULD APPRECIATE THE time by herself. She liked once in a while to be alone in her home, to organize, to wash and rehang the curtains so the home looked clean from the outside in. The outside came first; then one could do work on the inside. She had cloth Pavel had brought from the shop, and she planned to sew a new bedspread; she had evenings free to bake a few things to freeze for Pavel and Larry to take to work upon their return. Helen didn't like to eat too many sweets. Fattening, she said, though she was always quite thin. Too thin, even now. Fela took Helen's refusals to take home the cookies and cakes and raspberry strudels like a door in the face. Who didn't eat food prepared by one's mother?

Fela's friends planned to invite her over, for coffee, for tea, for lunch, for dinner. No one believed a wife could survive without a man, though from what Fela had seen, it was the man who had troubles when he tried to do without the wife. It seemed the phone was ringing constantly. Pavel and Larry called very often; Helen called very often; her friends called all the time. Who knew she was so popular? she joked to Vladka Budnik. Pavel would have to be on guard for her admirers when he returned.

But Fela was happy for company, and happy to bring the dessert, her specialty. An excellent cook she wasn't, but as a baker she was gifted. Everyone said so—she could start her own business, make a killing by selling to the orthodox bakeries in Kew Gardens. But business she didn't want. Work was all right, work in the home, work was for love; but business, that was something else entirely. Fela saw the troubles her husband had with his brother-in-law in making a business. It pressured the heart. Besides, the kosher bakeries liked only cakes made parve, no dairy. Fela did not like to substitute margarine or oil or the white packaged shortening that looked like shaving cream for butter. Fela liked butter. Butter and Coca-Cola: sometimes she thought these were her favorite foods.

Fela's sister had liked butter too. They all did, the whole family in Poland, though of course then those desserts came only with meals made from fish. It never happened, never, that they ate their mother's cream-filled desserts when there was meat for dinner. The home of Fela's mother had been pristine, perfectly kosher, perfectly clean. Plates for dairy, plates for meat. And two additional sets just for Passover, hidden away for the rest of the year so as not to expose them to risen bread. If her mother could see the way Fela was living now, with the milk in her tea after dinner, the seafood she tried in cafés with her son, she would simply collapse. And the Passover plates! Now that the children lived on their own, Fela had abandoned the system. Separate dishes were for company; otherwise, she used the gold trim for meat, the flowers for dairy. And even these she allowed on occasion to be mixed.

Her sister had been even worse. Fela had inherited at least a fraction of their mother's neatness. All the household rules had been less of a priority for Bluma, who had her own ideas. She had left before anyone else had thought to try. An idealist, a Zionist, and—though the family hadn't been sure, they suspected—a passionate person. She had a lover she followed to Palestine in 1935; only Fela and another sister had been taken into confidence about Bluma's secret plans. It had seemed desperate, unimaginably wild at the time—they were a good family!—but Bluma had survived, the only one but Fela among the children of their mother and father.

Fela's sister hadn't cooked; on the kibbutz she had eaten in communal kitchens. But at home she still baked. The same recipes, the same timing, the same ingredients, the same restraint with sugar and generosity with butter, but a slightly different tang to her cookies, something softer in her cakes. At home before the war, a similar phenomenon had occurred at the tables of the older sisters who had already married. A stranger wouldn't have noticed, but inside the family one could tell the difference, one could identify each baker's mark even on a plate where everyone's pastries were mixed together. Each cake came with a sister's own flavoring. The unmarried sisters worked at the store, selling linens and hardware; they baked for pleasure. And because of the pleasure, the family excelled. Now that Bluma had died, leaving only sons, it was up to Fela to take care of the family creations, the buttery progeny Helen refused to acknowledge.

Well, so what! Fela could bake by herself. It was a lot of work, but good work. Though now it was quite a bit, what with all the invitations. She felt people expected her to bring, because she always brought. So when Sima Traum called to invite her to coffee, Fela thought it best to say no.

My calendar is crowded, answered Fela. I have something tonight, and something next week—Mina, you know, is having a dinner—you don't have to worry for me—

That's not so busy, said Sima. I can come out there—

No, no, no, said Fela. But now that she spoke with Sima, she felt a desire for her company. Actually, since you mention it, I had a plan to go to B. Altman's on Saturday. They have a special on a perfume I like. When you buy a small bottle, they give you a lotion, and some other little things.

See? said Sima. That's a wonderful time. Saturday's very convenient. And Fela, I am providing. Everything. Please.

I take the bus straight to you after I shop; I won't have much to carry.

Good, said Sima. Good. See you then. But please, Fela, bring nothing. I will be insulted if you do.

IT WAS NOTHING TO carry, Fela said, no longer out of breath. Just a box of cookies and a few blueberry pastries wrapped in paper. She was sitting in Sima's kitchen, her back to the window overlooking Riverside Drive. What Fela preferred was the view of Sima's kitchen, the white-and-blue wallpaper, the copper containers for coffee and sugar arranged, in order of size, on high wooden shelves. They were in private.

I told you not to bring them, but of course I am glad. So delicious.

My sister's were even more delicious. She really—but no, we were all good.

Who could be better than you?

I don't like to compare, Simale, but really, she was excellent, when she put the time to it. Ah, Sima. It is said that the tie between sisters is the closest in the world, closer than mother and daughter. The tie between sister and brother, also close.

I don't know, said Sima. But of course often I thought, perhaps it would be less—I would have company. I think, now, especially, since my father died, that to share would have—and of course Chaim has almost no one—

I feel like you are my niece or my sister, said Fela. Like Chaim is my brother. Pavel feels this too. Not just about you, about the Belsener people, the people from after the war.

I was just a child there, said Sima.

Still, said Fela. That is why you and Chaim are so close.

Sima looked at her, then got up. Had Fela said too much?

I'm just bringing some lemon and honey, Sima called. Is it hard for you without Pavel? said Sima, reentering the room.

Hard? said Fela. It's a rest!

Sima laughed. She placed a soft lemon on a board on the table and quartered it.

No, said Fela. Of course, I miss him. I worry. But—it's not for so long. And it's not the same when—

Sima interrupted. When you're older? Please.

No, no, said Fela, sensing the beginning of a blush at her neck. No, I wasn't going to say that.

Forgive me, said Sima.

No, no, said Fela. I was going to say—was Chaim your first, your first love?

Sima paused.

I don't ask for you to tell me your life before him, Simale. Israel, who knows what they do there?

Sima laughed. It's true. The army, no one escapes intact, you understand.

Fela understood. They both giggled, uneasily. Then silence. Sima looked like she was thinking, the folds at her mouth deepening.

Yes, said Sima. He was my first love. The words came out soft, almost strangled.

Fela felt a sudden remorse for having asked. She should apologize, she thought, for having tried to dig. But she didn't. Instead she said, I had a husband. A husband before the war.

Sima said nothing, and Fela felt a small hot circle underneath her ribs, like a match had been struck and lit in the darkness of her chest.

He was my husband, but we didn't have a wedding. You understand? I was sixteen.

Sima nodded, her mouth slightly open.

We ran to Russia before the Germans invaded the town. We had heard. Before they came in, we were gone. My parents, they must have gone crazy with shame. But it was only I, and another sister who left to Palestine, before, who lived.

What happened? said Sima.

He died, said Fela. He was taken by the Russians into the army and he died. I heard, and I was—I was pregnant, I was pregnant and I lost the baby. A miscarriage.

The match had taken the air in her chest and gone out. It was a lie Fela was telling Sima, for the baby had been born, had lived, and had wailed before dying, but it was enough for Sima to make out the picture. The lie was easier to say than the real fact, the fact that no one on earth knew, now that her sister had died. No one on earth, not Pavel, not the children.

No one knows, said Fela. Pavel knows about him, my first husband—but not about the baby, the pregnancy. My children know nothing.

Will you tell them?

Never. Never, as long as I live. She looked suddenly at Sima. And you shouldn't either!

Fela! cried Sima. Your secret is mine.

But Fela felt tears trailing down her white cheeks. I'm sorry, she said. I'm sorry, I'm sorry. It's only—I feel afraid to speak his name. I never say it.

You didn't say it now.

Moshe Lev, said Fela. Moshe. Our town was Mlawa. Did you hear of it?

No, said Sima.

Small, said Fela. Small. Almost every person in our town died; now no one in the world says his name. No one to say his name, no one to say Kaddish. Just I do, once a year, in the night, when nobody hears. Really a man is supposed to do it, a son. What I do is close to nothing, and when I go, it will be nothing at all.

You are not going, said Sima. Where would you be going?

No, no, said Fela, impatient, shaking the tears off her face. I meant only, in the future, not now. Don't be so serious. She took the paper napkin, refolded it so the clean part was on the outside, then moved it carefully under her eyes. There! It was better.

Sima said, Did you ever hear how—

No, said Fela. No, no. In Russia you just heard it happened. No explaining. It made it hard for me to believe it. In fact—Fela hesitated. Perhaps she was pouring out too many secrets. But this wasn't facts, it was thoughts; it was all right to unburden. Sima wasn't upset by it.

In fact, after I came back, after I met Pavel, in Germany, I thought I saw him, Moshe, walking down the street.

Where?

Once in the DP camp, once in another town. Here, there. There was one time I was so sure—I saw the man, he saw me, and we both kept walking. After I crossed the street I understood it couldn't be him. But it happened many times, sometimes alone, sometimes with Pavel, once when I was walking with Larry, just a baby—each time I would see him and pass him, ignore him. Afraid. Each time I would think my heart would fly out of me. And each time I would realize it just was not him. But still, I would think—isn't it possible? What would happen if I said hello? And the man I would look at, sometimes I would see the same thought in his mind.

Sima said, If it had been him, Feluchna, you would have stopped.

Yes, said Fela. I think so.

WAS CHAIM HER FIRST love? Sima was more than fifty years old and had never put the question to herself in that way. She had been infatuated, crazy, before him, with a colonel above her in the army, and with a native Israeli boy who played soccer in the fields near the high school she had attended one year. But first love—yes, Chaim was her first love. Even silent, spoken only in her head, the phrase pained her. First love was clean, excited, empty of fear, spilling over with self-satisfaction. None of these things remained between her and her husband any longer. Something spilled between them, but not smugness, not pride or triumph. Relief, resignation.

At one time Sima had fantasized about divorce. They had had terrible problems after her father had died, at a time when all of Lola's schoolfriends seemed to be traveling from one parent's home to the other during the week. She had suspected him of having an affair but never confronted him. Instead she swiveled wildly between hatred and love, finding him irritating one minute, then wishing him near her the next; she had lied to him about stupid things, the cost of Lola's clothing or a discussion with a teacher, then felt anger at him for not divining the reality. More than a decade had passed, but a period still active in her memory—easy to go back to, revisiting each scene. Sima had gone so far as to call a lawyer, one whose number she had memorized from a late-night television commercial, but then she had not appeared for the appointment, and the lawyer's secretary hadn't even called to ask what had happened.

At home during the day she had paced the apartment, looking for changes to make. In the evening, ordinarily, Sima and Chaim would have read or played cards together while Lola did her homework. Sima's desire to talk to him pulled at her after dinner was done, the dishes washed and dried. But when she articulated this wish to herself Sima would suddenly feel a rush of fury and strength rising in her. She was a small woman, light-boned, but there were evenings she could easily picture herself pulling the sink out from the bathroom wall, tearing it away from its thick steel pipes. She could imagine the water gushing from under the ceramic, flowing into the bedroom she shared with her husband, drowning the bed. She imagined Lola screaming, afraid. It's all right, my *neshumeleh*, *nechmada*, Sima would say, it's all right. We're washing it clean. She imagined a call to the plumber, a pale, lanky man in a big, gray sweater, a man whose face was innocent and blank but whose body was Chaim's. She imagined the plumber in a bent position, kneeling down at the sink to fix it.

At the new bath store on Broadway she had purchased a cheap wooden cabinet, do-it-yourself. She built a box around the pipes, screwed hinges on the miniature doors, painted it white, glued on two knobs. Lola wanted to paint the knobs red; Sima let her, and the clumps of paint, dried unevenly on the white cabinet, gave her a pained satisfaction when Chaim first saw them, so out of place among the pastel tiles. You see? she had wanted to say. You see what we have become? Her bathroom might be ridiculous, but her daughter's room would be beautiful. She bought expensive shades, pale green shades that kept out the glare but not the light for Lola's books.

Chaim did not say no to anything she wanted. It made her sure that he had betrayed her, as if he was agreeing with every whim out of guilt. A conversation she had overheard in the building lobby between two neighbors, one of them in the middle of a divorce, stuck with her for weeks afterward. Think of this as Jewish Christmas, she had heard the woman say to her friend, as they'd waited for the elevator, you're not celebrating, but you might as well take advantage of the paid vacation; it won't last long. The words had echoed in her mind, sickening her. That's right, buy, buy, buy, she thought. Before her father became ill Sima had worked in the museum shop, become a manager. But now such a job seemed offensive, stupid, hateful, selling reproduction Greek sculpture paperweights and Impressionist-print scarves. Sima needed real protection. She could help people, make her life something meaningful and important. She studied for her high school equivalency and enrolled in summer classes for her bachelor's degree in social work at Hunter.

Going to school changed things. She talked about her program with Lola, and Chaim asked her questions, which she answered politely, then with more interest. She thought about asking him to see a marriage counselor with her but instead took a course in marriage counseling, the tenets of which seemed helpful, important, but then suddenly useless. She no longer wanted to force Chaim to talk; if she was right about what she suspected, she did not want to be told. She dropped the class after two weeks, substituting a course in geriatric care at the last minute, and found to her surprise that she loved it. She took an advanced course in art therapy for the elderly; she took an internship with a group that specialized in postwar refugees. When it was done she was offered a part-time job, before she had built up even half the credits she needed to graduate.

The less dependent she became on Chaim, the more he seemed to stick to their home. She continued her classes at night, and he would cook dinner for Lola and wait for Sima in the kitchen until she came home. He would talk to her about the class or her work, or occasionally his, and then they would go to bed. They did not touch each other, and perhaps three years, maybe four, passed this way.

Funny, she now did not remember what had made things thaw. Her graduation from the program? He had bought her a huge vase of white lilacs. No, it was later than that, when Lola began to go out at night in high school, and they were alone in the apartment early on a Saturday night, worrying together in front of the television.

ALL OVER THE NEWS, people were reuniting. At card games, at work, over sandwiches at the local luncheonette, everyone worried. How long could a people remain so excited about a wall? It had fallen more than a month ago. Cousins who had not seen cousins in years crossed over to greet their families in the West, to be tourists, to find jobs. The governments insisted there would be no major change, no reunification of East and West. It shouldn't happen in our lifetimes, Vladka Budnik had once said at a dinner—and Sima remembered that all had agreed—it shouldn't happen that Germans should be so happy in our lifetimes. Let them wait for our deaths! Then let them be happy.

At Sima's workplace, the immigrant center, the number of Russians coming for help had grown in the last two years. Now it seemed all of Eastern Europe would start coming too. The center didn't have so many languages, though Sima could be relied upon for those who spoke Yiddish and Polish and Russian. But how many Jews had remained in Eastern Europe? Almost all the Jews coming emigrated from the Soviet Union.

On the Monday after her coffee with Fela, Sima arrived at work to find several files on her desk. She gathered them up, went to the desk of the receptionist, a twenty-year-old college student they had hired the month before.

"Gloria is sick," said Carmen, not looking up from her novel. "She called in and said to give her interviews to you."

"But I have my own! My job is not to do hers," said Sima. "It is Monday—I don't think she really is sick."

"That's what she told me," said Carmen. "Am I supposed to question her?" The phone rang, and she picked up, switched to Spanish. No, she sighed to the phone. You need the legal office. This is counseling, not immigration.

Sima peeked out from behind Carmen's station. Already the waiting room was beginning to fill up.

By eleven, Sima was almost done with her list as well as Gloria's. She was in need of another coffee. She looked at the list of clients. Two more, then a break; she'd be only a half hour behind.

A small man, jowled and plump, with a full head of white hair, waddled into her office.

What language is most comfortable for you? she said in Russian. Yiddish or Russian?

Russian, said the man. I prefer Russian.

But Sima heard the tight sound at the vowels; it wasn't, she thought, his mother tongue. From another part of the Soviet Union? Elsewhere? She liked to be friendly before giving the little speech about housing and food stamps, welfare and jobs.

Where are you from?

Where do you think? said the man, abruptly. I last lived in Kiev.

No, said Sima. Before Kiev. Before Russia.

From Poland, said the man. Poland, before the war.

Poland, said Sima. I was born there too.

Yes, said the man.

But they continued speaking in Russian. Sima gave him a list of applications for elderly housing. He looked at the pages while she examined the copies of his application for refugee assistance.

When she looked up, he was staring at her, almost angry. I don't know where any of these places are.

She returned the sharp look. We'll give you directions to find them, after they process your applications.

He snorted.

All these people complaining! thought Sima. As if they came from a country of luxury. Gloria's clients were always rude. Sima suspected Gloria didn't treat them so well at the intake. But it hurt Sima to be blamed, and so she continued in a cold tone. You waited in Russia to emigrate here, when you could have left before. Why not Israel?

The man shrugged. My daughter was here. I wanted to be here.

Sima glanced again through the top pages in the file. Something struck her on one form. Place of Birth: Mlawa, Poland.

I know someone from Mlawa.

No, said the man, I doubt it.

Yes, I do, said Sima. Fela Mandl—her family name was Berlinka.

Ah! The man's face changed. The mouth that was straight, moved up, showing gray teeth in what Sima wanted to believe was a smile. The sisters Berlinka. Of course I remember them. And now that I think of it, you know, I heard that one or two had survived. I had a friend in Israel, went to a reunion of the Mlawer, those who had left before the war, and he met one of them. We all knew them, of course. Prosperous family: a dry goods store.

It's a coincidence, said Sima. She's a friend of mine. Should I say hello?

Yes, said the man. Tell her hello. Hello from Baruch Sosnower. My father worked at the lumberyard.

SIMA TOOK A SPECIAL interest in the fate of Baruch Sosnower. Normally the interns did the follow-up from the office, with the clients coming in to report on their adjustment after a month, then, if they remembered, after two. But neither of the interns Sima currently supervised was particularly reliable, and Sima thought she could expend a little more effort. She sensed that Baruch had little help from his daughter, who was married with her own children, and Sima worried that it was too late for a man like him to acquire a new set of habits appropriate to New York. She drove him herself to his food stamp interviews and made special calls to several women who ran the lists at senior housing developments in Brighton Beach, in Jackson Heights, places where Baruch could get by all day speaking Russian. She exaggerated the situation to Gloria, told her the man was an emergency case. Gloria could not be relied on for everything, but she knew how to pull a string in an emergency.

She did not feel comfortable telling Fela of the discovery just yet. Pavel was back—a new man, Fela said, he had fixed his mother's gravestone—and it seemed wrong to Sima to bring up the topic of Fela's life before him. And Baruch was still at odd ends, unsettled, a public charge—it would diminish his dignity for Sima to talk about him while he remained in low straits, while he was still so clearly a man in need, unromantic, unburnished. She wished almost that he was someone else entirely, someone who could dissolve the older woman's pain. It was a child's wish, the kind of dream Lola had about her own parents' separation. But Lola's dream had come true. Wouldn't it be something, if the man from Mlawa were really the Moshe of legend, if the first love were alive to remind Fela of first life? Sima began to spin a story in her head, how it would have happened. Fela, alone, not yet discovering herself pregnant, working two miles from home on the Siberian steppe, hiding flour in her shoes to bake in secret at night, just as Sima's father had done. Waiting for word of her lover, who had been drafted away from his home, with poor Fela watching.

When Sima was a child, her parents had been separated. Her father had been caught for dealing on the black market, sent to hard labor, an open field on the steppe. Her mother had taken over the work that her father had done, a nightwatch in the hospital. But Sima was alone, five years old in their cold hut, and Sima's mother would steal away from the job to watch over her daughter. One night her mother was seen leaving her post. Sima had woken up early that morning, alone in the hut, no sign, no smell, no sound of her mother. She had gone outside to wait for her: nothing, no horses, no people, no one passed their isolated road. And so she had tripped a mile to the hospital steps; perhaps her mother had fallen asleep. But no one was there. It was daylight; the hospital buzzed with loud adult movement.

It had been terrifying, those hours alone. Sitting with her case files, remembering, Sima thought she could imitate to herself what Fela had experienced: the uncertainty and constant fear of being without the last loved one left in the world. But it was hard for Sima to glimpse even her own past life now. Her adult griefs were fresh; her infant ones were not. She tried to think of her memories as animals hiding inside a small hut on the steppe, a hut made of mud and stone but hung with the stiff muslin curtains her mother had found on the black market.

A miracle had happened to Sima's mother, a miracle that no doubt saved Sima's life. Her mother had been taken to jail and had fallen to the floor, begging the guard to release her. She had a child at home and a husband, she had lied, at the front. The little girl would starve, would freeze, would not live without her mother.

The guard had watched blankly, in what seemed to Sima's mother a strict, controlled rage. Stop crying! he had ordered. Get up, stand up! He had pointed to a door. Go inside that room and wait, without making a sound!

Sima's mother had scrambled up and opened the door. It was a dark room, but cold: she saw immediately that a large window was open. The words of the guard: without making a sound. Shoes off, she had crept out the window into the steppe and run home to find her daughter.

It seemed impossible that this could have occurred, that what Sima had wished could come true. She had sat alone on the hospital steps, making promises to herself: When two women with gray kerchiefs pass by, the third woman will be my mother. When the door of the entryway slams seven times, the eighth noise will be my mother. At her social work program, Sima had learned the English words for these wishes: magical thinking. But the magic had happened, not precisely according to the numbers Sima had calculated, the thirteen old men, the three pregnant women, but magic nonetheless, if a magic of errors. Her mother had stumbled to the hospital after finding Sima gone, had wrapped her in a blanket before wrapping her in her arms, and had carried her red-faced, five-year-old body home.

No one believed stories like this anymore, but these were the stories of anyone who lived. In Europe, on the steppe, to look at the world practically, realistically, with a cold, knowing eye, was to read only death sentences. It was when magical thinking came true that one lived. An open window here, an abandoned work camp there. Her father had escaped from hard labor; he too had come home.

Baruch was not a dazzling figure, and it was hard to imagine how even in youth he could have wrapped himself around the heart of a girl from a good family in a small town. He murmured gruff thank-yous for all Sima's favors and calls, but did not seem to like her particularly well. He never asked for her personal advice, only for technical assistance with his housing and welfare and job applications. Once he missed an appointment with Sima and forgot to call; he had been accepted as a salad man in a moderate-priced restaurant not too far from downtown. It frustrated Sima, though everything in her training had taught her not to let it hurt her. Usually she succeeded.

She adjusted the tale to accommodate her irritation. The new story unfolded in a less dramatic series of scenes: Baruch was not the lover but the friend of the lover, the confidant of Moshe himself, told of the plans to flee Mlawa, perhaps inspired to flee himself because of the lovers. In Russia, Baruch would have encountered Moshe again in the Russian army, would have heard a message from Moshe before he died, would have tried to bring the message to Fela despite the obstacles and chaos of cold and hunger and battle. In another version,

Baruch knew Moshe as a living being, a man who had lived side by side with Baruch in postwar Europe, just as Fela had imagined: married, attached, but alive, still longing for news of his first love. They would go together to a reunion—yes, a reunion of their *landsmanner*, the remnants of their broken hometown, and they would see her. No, better, the reunion would be in Israel, without Baruch. Moshe, along with the other new émigrés from Russia, would attend, not daring to be hopeful. Alone, without the interference of assistance bureaucracies or immigration authorities, he would see Fela's sister Bluma, only partly disguised by age and fatigue, and Bluma would respond to a tap on the shoulder.

Excuse me, he would say, is your name Berlinka?

Yes, the sister of Fela would say. Yes. And you?

I, he would say, I am Moshe Lev.

In the shock that would follow, Bluma would reveal that Fela was alive. She would ask what had become of him; had he seen her, those days in Germany, after the war?

No, he would answer, no.

Then sudden anger. Bluma would turn cold. Why didn't you look for her after the war? How she suffered. How she suffered.

And who says I didn't look? Moshe would exclaim. I was in prison. There was nowhere to look. I wrote to the Red Cross, to the Joint— but nothing, no word. It wasn't so easy, at that time, if you stayed in the East. No committees for the refugees, no communications in the Russian zone. What do you think—I would not look if I could?

She's married, said Bluma. With children.

Yes, Moshe would say. And I am too.

The drama would close with an anguished silence beween Bluma and Moshe, the two closest figures of Fela's first life: To let it alone or to tell her? The truth, or peace?

In Brooklyn Baruch would receive the letter from his friend. He would think on it and think on it. He would divulge the tale to Sima.

And then? How would Sima and Baruch contrive to put the two back together? Each could know a version of the tale, but it was up to the romantic pair themselves, separated by continents, to reveal their identities.

AN EFFICIENCY STUDIO HAD opened in the Brighton Beach project for seniors, and the administrators had squeezed Baruch to the top of the list by the start of February. Sima paid a follow-up visit on Friday morning, in the middle of the month. It was a long way out; she took the agency car.

The day was uncommonly warm and sunny for the time of year, a taste of spring before the snowstorm predicted for the weekend.

She lied to Baruch. I wanted to tell you a hello, said Sima. Hello from Fela Mandl.

Who? said Baruch.

Excuse me, said Sima. Fela Berlinka.

Berlinka, said Baruch. Berlinka, Berlinka. The word chimed out of his mouth in a singsong.

The sisters from Mlawa? Sima finally said.

Yes, said Baruch. Oh yes, a very good family. Yes, she said hello? He seemed gratified, but only slightly. What else do I have to do? he said to Sima. Will you still keep visiting?

Only if you want me to, said Sima.

I'm all right on my own, said Baruch. Do you know how much a private phone costs here? It's very expensive. How can anyone do it? I have to use the common one downstairs, and there's always a wait.

Sima pushed her fingers into her purse for a business card. Here, she said, placing it on the table near the window. Just in case you need something. She closed the door behind her, then stepped toward the elevator. She pressed the button to call it. Through the porthole of the elevator door Sima could see the compartment lowering itself down.

But then she turned back and knocked on Baruch's door.

Did you forget something? His face was softer than it had been a moment ago.

He likes to think that sometimes I too can be weak, Sima thought. She returned the soft look. Yes, Mr. Sosnower. I forgot to ask you—

She paused. He looked at her, waiting. Should she go through with it? Could she really alter a woman's history with a question? Then Sima pressed down the thought, forced herself to continue. Did you ever know a Moshe Lev? From your town, from Mlawa?

Moshe Lev—Baruch said, his soft look vanishing. Of course! Yes, he too was from Mlawa. How funny that you ask—how do you—

I remember hearing his name from my friend. She wondered what had become of him.

Really? Hmm, well, I did not know him so well in Poland. But I suppose—Baruch's face remained blank, still surprised but not excited—I suppose everyone wonders, still, after so many years. It was a funny thing, running into him in Kiev when I did, after so many years living in the same neighborhood, and not seeing him since we were schoolboys. Of course he was a bit older than I, but a brother of mine would have gone to school with him—a fine man. We were on a line together to buy something, maybe milk? Yes, that was it. He recognized me, actually. He said he did not forget faces from his hometown. But that was so long ago.

Sima's breath was steady in her chest. How long ago?

Oh, long before he died. Maybe 1975 or so? We met from time to time. But his wife and mine were not so friendly. She was a quiet one, his wife, had to be to keep up with him—very sociable. You bring back things, Mrs. Traum. Moshe Lev! I had not thought of him for years.

❧

SIMA LET HERSELF INTO the agency car, parked on the street outside Baruch's building. She was dressed too heavily for the day and pulled off her scarf.

Now Sima too had a secret. There was nothing she could say to Fela. The story would be the same, whether Moshe Lev had survived and reappeared, or whether he had died, victim to hunger or a bullet. Another life to which no one could return or even imagine without pain. How could Sima have flirted with such a story?

She turned her face toward the row of small terraces on the west wall of the building, searched for the one belonging to Baruch. But he wasn't looking out. In the February warmth he had opened a window, and his blue cotton curtain beat softly at the glass.

The Lecture

May 1990

PAVEL STRAIGHTENED HIS PROGRAM on his lap. Perhaps a dozen people waited in the chairs of the auditorium, watching the student arrange the microphones on the podium. Others would come. Pavel liked to arrive with plenty of time to spare. He had a seat on the aisle to stretch out his leg, and he placed a scarf on the seat next to him for Fela. The four of them would all be together.

He tapped at the name tag on his lapel and looked over at the white sticker on Chaim's jacket, the solid blue letters. Chaim took after him in attitude, intelligent and quiet. Still with a full head of hair, even if it was pure silver, cut close to his head. He was very distinguished, with his bright eyes and straight posture. Pavel liked to be sitting next to him, this boy he had cared for as a brother. Their wives powdered their noses and chatted outside.

It is good we are early, Pavel nodded to Chaim.

Very early, said Chaim.

I don't like to go when people are fighting for seats. It can be a terrible chaos, sometimes. The ceremony—you used to have to arrive at least an hour and a half in advance. But it is better now. Since they moved it out from the synagogue—when was it?—five years ago, now we have space. That theater—you know, at Madison Square Garden. But no, you didn't go this year.

Chaim smiled. You know I did not go.

Pavel put Chaim on all the mailing lists that he himself was on. Still, after so many years of suggestion—not pressure, not pressure, for Chaim was almost as stubborn about these matters as Hinda, she never came to anything like this either, not even the events with senators, with luminaries—Chaim had finally given in for this. Why this one—Art and Culture in the Warsaw Ghetto? Pavel did not know. But it was not for him to question. He was glad to have the company, and sophisticated company too, someone with whom he could do a little criticizing, perhaps hear something a little different from what he heard from his friends and his cousin. Chaim was younger than everyone, and he had an energy that the others did not have. It was good to sit with him. Chaim remembered Pavel when he was strong and fit, when he could watch over a household and feed any number of guests and travelers. Chaim remembered.

CHAIM READ THE LYRICS to "The Song of the Partisans" at the bottom of his flyer.

> *Never say that there is only death for you*
> *Though leaden skies may be concealing days of blue!*

The words looked alien and awkward in English. Strange. He had not remembered the song sounding in Yiddish, so stiff, almost—he felt ashamed even to think the thought—almost silly. He tried to re-translate it. Never say that you travel on your last journey. Not good, not elegant, but at least not so blunt as the English. And "days of blue!" It was out of a Broadway musical. Americans needed a rhyme. Chaim had noticed a piano on the stage. Would the audience have to sing? That was the new thing: an interactive lecture. It wasn't just the English translation of the song that was printed alongside the Yiddish letters, it was also the phonetic English. Yes, it was very possible there would be singing.

Chaim breathed. It would not be so terrible. Theme song or no, a professor would introduce, and another professor would speak. The hall would fill, he would see people he did not always see. A good reason to come. And it made Pavel happy for him to be here.

Tell me, Chaim, you know this man?

Who?

The professor who wrote the book.

No, of course not. How would I know him? I was just interested in the topic.

I don't say no, I just thought—you know, since you don't go to the commemoration—

I can't go to the commemoration, Pavel. I feel like a pretender. So I don't like to go.

What pretender? said Pavel. What have I to do with the Warsaw Ghetto? Nothing. Less than you! You think the Brooklyn borough president has something to do with the Warsaw Ghetto? It's a big event, so he comes.

I went with you to a film two years ago, no, before. The documentary.

A film! It's not the same. It was a long time ago—and anyway, I left in the middle! But you know, I think I knew this one, the professor's father, very slightly, not well, of course, he's from Romania, but—

Chaim looked at the flyer again. Why had he agreed to come?

Fela had asked him to, that was why. He always felt a pull in his abdomen when he refused Pavel, but it was a discomfort he could overcome. Fela's requests were a different story.

She had caught him on the phone a week before. There was a lecture at the New School, a new book, she thought it would be very interesting for Chaim and Sima, they would be in their element, since it would be full with professors—

I'm not a professor, Chaim had said. I'm an adjunct. And it's technical, not intellectual. Radio engineering. You know, Fela, I—

Chaim, she interrupted. I know you don't go to these things. I know you don't. I don't like it so much myself. I go because—I go, I don't know why I go.

Fela, with the songs and the speeches, it is something I can't—

This is not one with speeches. I made sure.

I will ask Sima, he tried.

I already spoke to Sima. She said to speak to you.

Ah.

Fela's voice became quiet. Chaim. I want from you a favor. I need you to talk to him. He does not listen to me. Maybe he listens to you.

Could he not have talked to Pavel at another time? But no, Fela had wanted it to be casual, she had not wanted Pavel to know that she had called and pleaded with Chaim to reason with Pavel about the business, to reason with him about Kuba.

Pavel tapped at his shoulder, held out a half-finished packet of mints in his palm.

Do you want?

Chaim shook his head. He felt like a fraud simply sitting here, deciphering lyrics to a resistance song, even though he himself had once taught them to the younger children in the DP camp classes, long after the resistance fighters had been crushed. He had never heard the song during the war, the few months his family had been crammed into the ghetto housing, shipped from their small town to the North. There had been a time he had claimed otherwise. If asked, he would say he was from Warsaw originally, he would date his flight through the sewers of the ghetto as happening after the battle, not a full year before, he would add a few exploits to the short time in the forest with the gentile partisans, he would ascribe his ignorance about weapons to the ancient technology accessible to the forest fighters. Sometimes when speaking he had not been sure what was true and what was not, for the stories he told came out in pieces, not in order of time or place.

And he had been caught once, during his second or third year in the military. Now he could not remember the particular lie, but when he thought of the Tel Aviv café on an autumn evening, sitting with a few friends from his company, his stomach still folded in shame. Two women had been at their table. What had he said? He did not want to remember. But after he had said it, one of the women—she must have been European, even Polish—had given him a quick look in which he saw first warmth, then puzzlement, then—accusation. She wore glasses but was pretty, a slim brunette, long legs that folded under her seat as they drank, perhaps a bit older than he. Her head had given a half-shake, not perceptible to his companions but clear to Chaim. She did not believe him. He had felt himself blush and quickly had stood up to use the bathroom. Suddenly the shame of the lie had seemed greater than the shame of what it covered, that he had not borne arms, that he had roamed through the city just after his escape with a friend, then from village to village looking for work as a field hand, that his time with the partisans had come so late, after he had found himself all alone, that it had seemed more a shelter than a battleground. He had lost his brothers and the last friend he had escaped with, and he felt himself a traitor just for being alive.

⁓

PAVEL SPOTTED SOMEONE HE knew. A man on the arm of his wife waved and walked past, then took a seat a few rows ahead of them. Glick. Pavel turned to Chaim.

I know him from the business. A prominent man. Manufactures the linings for the biggest designers. Pavel threw another smile in the man's direction, then nodded to Chaim again. He is interested in buying when we sell, but Kuba wants to wait for something bigger.

Hmm? Chaim seemed surprised. So you sell already.

Not yet, not yet, no evil eye, it is just—well, you know, my son is not in the business, of course, that was never his interest, and for me to hold on—

What does Kuba say?

Well, you know. Pavel sighed. Kuba still wants Michael to draw a salary from there, he is our finance manager, you see, very good with numbers, excellent—and, of course, we want to sell so that we still work for the new owners, just without the risk—I am not ready to retire, you know, I have something in me still!

It's a good time, isn't it? All these big companies buying.

I think so, said Pavel, his hands and cheeks growing warmer. How long since he had discussed business with Chaim! Yes, Chaim was coming closer to everyone, finally, after all these years. He was coming closer.

I think so, Pavel repeated. For a long time I didn't think it was, now I do. Now I do. He turned his face from Chaim's. I used to make business, didn't I, Chaim? You remember. I was afraid of nothing.

Chaim looked at him for a moment. It's different, Pavel. A completely different time now.

I think it's the right time, Pavel said. I do. And Kuba also thinks so.

Kuba had seemed cheerful that week, more than usual. Pavel had begun to agree with him more. It made Pavel nervous to give in, but he did not have the energy for the arguments anymore. He was more than seventy years old. His son and his daughter would not go into the business. They were doing something better. Larry was a doctor—Columbia Medical School!—and Helen had a master's degree. It was too early for Pavel to retire, of course, too early for Kuba too, but now they could sell at a good price, maintain good salaries as employees to the new owner, even hold on to a job for Michael, who wanted to make changes, work for a more modern company, not be stuck in the old style of his father and uncle.

Still the plans made Pavel nervous. Every idea he had for a sale, to an acquaintance or business colleague, Kuba did not like. With you it is only to friends, only among friends, Kuba would complain. This is business, American business! We can do better! All right. If Kuba thought a better deal was in the making, let Kuba find it. Pavel would not lose anything by letting Kuba have his way. And as yet Kuba had not found anything. So! There was time. Pavel still had strength, he could hold on while Kuba looked for the perfect purchaser. He could hold on.

He did not speak to Fela about the details. He did not speak to Fela about any of it at all. And for the most part she kept silent. Except in the last few days. He had mentioned, casually, accidentally—really, he was beginning to forget what to tell her and what to leave out—that Kuba was meeting with a prospective buyer in the coming week. Someone big. But then Pavel revealed he had agreed with Kuba that this was something for Kuba to handle on his own. Kuba knew Pavel's wishes.

For the first time since he knew her, his wife had opened her mouth about his business.

Pavel, Fela had said. I want you to go to the negotiations with Kuba.

Why? I trust him. I have so much work—

You are being—you have no—you are being a fool, just giving him everything over you without asking a single question. He probably goes with Michael and not with you.

Pavel had refused to answer. So what if Kuba went with his son?

Fela read his look. Pavel! Are you crazy? Do you think I don't have anything to do with your decisions? All right, you don't care about yourself, but what about your wife? He thinks he knows more than you, but he is wrong! You think he knows more than you, he and this little brat of his son!

Fela!

It is true!

I know whom to trust!

You! You know whom to trust! You, of all people!

Her face had made Pavel worry. But he did not know how to interpret her worries. It was a fact, Fela and Hinda were not the closest of friends, and it was also a fact that Kuba was not the easiest man in the world. But this did not mean that one attributed to him the possibility of a double cross, of betrayal—

Chaim, Pavel said. What did you think of Kuba when we met the first time?

Nothing, said Chaim. I don't remember. I never liked his friend, of course. From the beginning he was—Chaim paused, then switched to English, "a phony."

Of course. That's a nice way to put it.

Of course I couldn't guess what he would do in the end—Pavel looked at him, shook his head, and Chaim left the topic—but Kuba! I don't remember thinking too much one way or the other. I was so young.

You're not in love with him, this I know.

So! I'm in love with other people.

What? Are you—

Pavel, please, I'm just joking. I thought we talked of your business.

Your family is my business too! Pavel grinned again. But Chaim seemed to do all right without his interference. Pavel and Fela had liked Sima from the beginning. Chaim had made a good choice, Pavel reflected. Even as a boy Chaim had not taken to Marek Rembishevski. Chaim had a sense about people, for bad and for good too. He had attached himself to Fela the moment he saw her in a Polish market. He had a sense.

BUT I DO THINK, Chaim continued, keeping his face calm, I do think that Kuba—he thinks he knows more than he does. He was always a little too sure.

Kuba. Well, he always thought of himself as smart. I don't say he isn't, of course.

Of course. Chaim smiled.

I just say that a more intelligent man than himself, he doesn't happen to know.

I think it is all right to keep an eye on his plans, if it doesn't insult him. Chaim gave Pavel a sideward glance. With Pavel's face in profile, Chaim could see the crushed bones of Pavel's cheek in the space between his glasses and his eyes. I think it is all right for you to watch.

Pavel looked at him. Has Fela been talking to you?

Chaim blushed. No, no! Of course not. I just say—

She says the same thing. She wants me to watch.

Why do you think she says it?

Pavel stiffened. I think she spoke to you, Chaml.

Chaim turned around to face the back of the auditorium. What a mistake this had been, mixing into Pavel's work. How had he let himself be talked into it? The auditorium doors were open, and he could see into the hallway. Sima and Fela were not coming.

So she spoke to me! So what?

She doesn't trust my brother-in-law! She doesn't trust my own sister!

It's not a matter of trust, it's just a natural—

I said I wanted nothing to do with it, that's all. The truth is that this kind of negotiation is not my most—it is not where I—but then I decided I wanted to participate, but he already had set up the meetings, I don't feel—if I interfere now, what will he think?

Perhaps he will think, Good! Pavel wants to be involved.

No, Chaim. Pavel sighed. Kuba will not think this. He will think I worry he will not do right by the business. He will think I try to control him. Perhaps he even will think I don't trust him to—to do right by me!

Pavel's jaw was jutting forward, his teeth clenched. Chaim put his hand on his shoulder. I'm sorry I mixed in.

My sister! Pavel breathed. My own sister!

But it's your business too.

We have separate roles! How do you think I survived all these years with him? He does his part, I do mine. If I don't trust him, almost my own blood, I cannot—I cannot trust anyone!

It's not my affair, I just—

Chaim, they are coming. Look, they are coming! Not a word!

All right, Pavel.

Here. Take another mint. Then they won't wonder why we don't talk.

PAVEL STOOD UP WHEN Fela and Sima came to their row. He could not look at Fela. Instead he took Sima by the shoulders and gave her another kiss on the cheek. I'm so glad you are here! Your husband and I are catching up on old times.

Give me your coat check, Pavel. Let me hold it in my purse before you lose it.

Since when do I lose anything? He pushed his hand into his front jacket pocket. No, it was in the inside pocket, for safety. He stretched his hand toward Fela, still without looking at her. If it makes you happy, here it is.

She had been very unhappy with him, this week and the last. But one had to be optimistic. One could not give in to one's worst beliefs. To give in was to say that nothing meant anything, that one could throw away one's own family as easily as one sent an old suit to charity, that a human was nothing more than an animal, alone.

A sister was the only thing that held him to the past. There were people who came out with no one, not a bone left to say Kaddish for the whole tribe, only these gatherings and memorials filled with strangers who prayed to sanctify the dead. Look at Chaim! Chaim had nothing, only a cousin in Israel, now mooning over her grandchildren. But Pavel was one of the lucky ones. He had his sister. He had Mayer, his cousin on his mother's side. He had friends who were not his blood but were like blood, more than blood. He had, he had.

So why, why was everything so difficult with Kuba? They had different ideas, that was all. But now they had the same idea. Pavel felt an excitement over it, gladness that Kuba had finally stopped disagreeing, that Kuba and he saw the same way for the first time since they had moved their operations to the center of the garment district fifteen years ago, when the economy was terrible and rents were cheaper than cheap. Pavel had been right in his way, delaying until the time was right, and Kuba had been right in his way too, because the business had grown since the move to the center. And now Pavel felt the same sense of agreement. It was good to have a partner. Others were alone—Fishl, but he had done very well—and others had worked for bigger men their whole lives. Perla's husband Tulek had never left the box factory he had first worked in when he came to America. But it was good to have a partner to share the burden with, even if relations were not always so smooth, even if there had been times they did not speak to each other for days at a time. To make a family business, to be solid into one's retirement, that was something that showed they had survived. Perhaps this young professor, who thought he knew the secrets of the Warsaw Ghetto uprising, might not agree, but making a new business, a new life in a new language, this too was resistance.

Not that it was more important than other things. Having a grand-child, that was the great resistance. It would be nice, very nice, if Larry and Helen would understand that, too. Helen was almost thirty-five! Did she not know how old he was? What was the delay? And Larry, his wife a doctor too—she did not seem to have the time.

That was something Hinda and Kuba had already, with Michael and Joel already fathers. And if Pavel criticized Hinda for not joining a little more in the community, he could also privately sympathize. It had not been the same since—well, really, since Yidl had gone. Tsipora still came, even now she was so sick, but the younger ones who had taken over for Yidl did not give the ceremonies the same feeling of importance.

Pavel went, he listened, he gave. But these acts did not give him the same comfort. Yidl made it all seem like a way of saving the world again, even for all his faults, not just the gambling, not just the speculation that had allowed Yidl to live as he did. He had died without warning. And suddenly everything had become coarse, the way friends had dropped Tsipora completely, dropped her except to come by the apartment and pick up a painting in return for money Yidl owed.

Pavel had become very close with Tsipora, speaking with her twice a week, coming by her home almost as often, bringing her flowers, a luxury she used to take for granted. Now she put the tulips in the re-frigerator for the night to make them live longer. She had nothing. Not even life insurance from Yidl. She moved to a small apartment where her lawyer son paid her rent. Pavel himself put her on the payroll of the business so she could have health insurance.

Incredible, that it should come to this, these people who had cared for everyone suddenly dependent. If something like this happened to him—but it couldn't. He had a business that made things, and unlike Yidl he had been cautious when he came to the United States, he had shed the habit of risk that had allowed him to survive and, after the war, almost thrive. Now his goals were more modest. All he wanted was a good price for the business and the ability to work for the new company a few more years. If Fela thought he acted stupidly in giving his trust to Kuba, to his sister, even—his sister, his last connection to his parents—well, then—Fela was wrong.

SIMA HELD A COPY of the professor's book. Already they were selling it out front. Fela had bought one too. She passed it to Chaim. An orange cover, the faint outline in black of a bonfire.

"It looks very interesting, no?" Fela said. "I'm sure Lola will be interested too."

"Perhaps."

"Pavel, did I ever tell you?" Sima smiled broadly. "You won't believe it. I was telling Fela in the ladies' room. She once took a class on the history of genocide! Can you imagine?"

Pavel looked at her. What? At Yale?

At Yale!

I imagine they explain, Pavel said.

Explain! said Fela. What is to explain? I always hope, whenever I go somewhere, that they will explain. But every time—

So why did you want to come to this? Chaim saw Pavel glare at her, jaw stiff. It was your idea.

Pavel, I thought it would be interesting. For Chaim and Sima. They like it when it's professors. Chaim did not see even a blink of nervousness on her face. She was used to keeping calm with Pavel. Perhaps she lied often.

Sima continued speaking, Lola's past studies, Lola's old successes. Now that Lola was out of school, still casting about, working with homeless people, singing in a band, refusing to go to graduate school, Sima found a little less to brag about and a little more to criticize, Lola's activities, her long-haired boyfriend—not Jewish, Chaim too had felt the panic, had forced himself not to say anything—but still, Sima could weave around the problems and present to Pavel and Fela a fact that would make them happy. Lola had studied genocide at Yale University, years ago. What Chaim would not discuss at home, she discussed in class, read in books, wrote in papers. Sometimes, when she was home for vacation, he would steal a look at them.

Sima was more open. She liked that Lola looked for a theory, that Lola investigated on her own. We should be happy she is interested! We should be happy some *goyische* boyfriend is interested! My father always said—

The truth was, he was not sure he wanted his daughter to have a theory. There was no theory to cover everything, to explain. Fela was right. Nothing could be explained, and trying to explain caused even more pain. He had a daughter who graduated from the Ivy League, Pavel had a son who was a doctor, but others had children who had terrible drug addictions, friends who betrayed and stole, who threw money away for fancy commemorations and extravagant dinners only to make themselves feel big. Some people made good, some people did not. Some people came out so close they were almost one body, some people came out with a passion to push themselves forward, never mind the suffering it caused to someone else. Look at Pavel, his body broken by another survivor, sitting in the aisle seat next to Fela. Once Sima had stood on a chair in the kitchen to put away a dish, and had fallen and broken her shinbone. She had been in a cast and on crutches almost eight weeks. How long, she had asked Pavel, how long does it take for the pain to go away, completely? And Pavel had looked at her, genuinely surprised, and said, But it doesn't. You just get used to it.

He opened his program, looked at the description of Sima's book. *Resistance in Everyday Acts: Cultural Life in the Warsaw Ghetto.* The author must be Israeli, he thought, where one had to resist to be worthy of survival, or pity, or memory. In the back of the book the professor looked solemnly out at him, his black hair wavy and dashing. The same photograph—no doubt ten years old, if not more—graced the program.

Oh, God. He snorted.

Sima turned from Fela. You don't have to pay attention, she said softly. I'll pay attention. If there's something worth hearing I'll wake you up.

He lifted up the program and pointed to the song. This idiot was going to make them sing as a group. I told you! He wanted to say.

She answered in English, as if he had said the words aloud. "Not everything has to be a philosophical dilemma, Chaim. Just sing it, that's all." He looked at her to see if she was angry. But she was smiling.

THE VICE PRESIDENT OF the memorial committee come toward the front, passing by their little row. Pavel nodded as he passed, but the man did not stop. Not even a hello. What suddenly made him so important? He shook his head at Fela, forgetting for a moment his fury at her.

Yidl remembered everyone, he said.

Even if Yidl did not remember, said Fela, he pretended.

The auditorium grew more full. It was not a large crowd, but certainly a respectable showing, and there would be opportunity to talk of the lecture at the next card game.

Pavel stood up for a moment to stretch his leg. A man brushed against him. Pavel turned to see who it was, and the olive-skinned face, the sunken eyes, gave Pavel a chill of familiarity. The man returned Pavel's glance but without recognition. Pavel pressed his glasses farther up his nose and squinted to look at the name tag.

Then he stood up, his heart thick in his chest. It could not be. Rembishevski, he said.

The man looked startled, almost afraid. Yes! Do I know you? He had asked in Yiddish.

Pavel breathed out. Pavel, he said. Pavel Mandl.

But the man did not blink. Saul Rembishevski, he said.

Pavel's hands, so warm a moment before, had cooled. He had waited for this—he had waited for the sight of a Rembishevski. In 1980 Pavel had gone to the world gathering of survivors, the first one in Israel, with Fela. She had not seen her sister in ten years, he had not seen his mother's cousin in more than that. It had been a beautiful trip. They had toured the sights, and they had filled their days wandering from seminar to speech to meal, Fela on her sister's arm and Pavel walking beside them. Pavel had had hope—hope of something, some kind of miracle, a miracle he did not even dare name to himself—but in the end all he found were acquaintances he had lost touch with since the war, and one neighbor from childhood whom he had not immediately recognized. He had found nothing. But he had sat and talked and prayed with his friends, who had come to Jerusalem all together, who played cards together in the evening when there were no events, who stayed late into the night at the memorial ceremonies. And behind Pavel's hope had been his dark wishes to see him, Marek Rembishevski, to show that he, Pavel Mandl, was alive and in possession of a beautiful family, or perhaps only to look the thief in the eye and say nothing. Pavel had even looked him up in the registry when he had a moment away from Fela. But Rembishevski had not shown his face.

Now, looking at the man in the lecture hall, Pavel said, his voice very quiet, I knew a Rembishevski, just after the war.

Oh, tell me—I had only one brother who I knew came out from the war, only one from all my—just Marek, and now that he has gone—

Gone?

Terrible! A cancer of the throat, how he suffered. To tell you, but I don't need to tell you—Pavel recognized the man's patterns of speech—I don't need to tell you, but to die as he did, alone, with no wife even, no sons to say Kaddish—he lived in Los Angeles—but you—you say you knew a Rembishevski—perhaps another—do you? There were tears in the man's eyes. I hope always to find someone who knew something about my family, I hope to find.

Pavel was silent, and he felt the silence all around him, the other three a small circle of quiet amid the noise of the auditorium. It was so quiet he thought he could hear his own blood moving through his veins. But he was not hot, he was not trembling. He was steady. There were no words in his head. He bent forward and pretended to squint again at the man's name tag.

I'm sorry, Pavel said, the words flowing from his mouth. I—I knew a Retishevsky. I—I saw your name and was confused.

The man's face changed—disappointment? Or was it—yes, it was relief. Pavel could see it. Relief that Pavel had not added to the rumors.

You did not know a Rembishevski?

I—I am sorry, said Pavel.

He sat down. Fela's hand went to his knee. Now he was trembling. But he did not turn his face. He breathed.

A small man came onto the podium. A microphone whistled, and Pavel put his fingers to his ear to block out the noise and to stop his hand from shaking. The other three looked at him with grave faces. He wanted them to pass over it. Perhaps they wanted him to relieve them. He felt all right. He felt good. One had to believe in a brother, even the memory of a terrible brother, one had to believe that it was not all blood and dirt and shit and bone. One had to believe.

Everyone here, I trust, Pavel said. It is family.

A half-smile spread on Chaim's face, and Pavel felt himself filled again with the heat in his chest, like what he felt for his son, but different, almost closer.

Chaml, Pavel said.

Chaim nodded at him, perhaps about to answer. But the microphone stopped screeching, and a man's voice pushed through the mutters and rustles. Then the auditorium fell quiet. The professor would begin.

Oral Histories

WITH HIS EAR FOR a tune and facility with languages, Chaim should have excelled at eavesdropping, but he did not. Something went wrong in the step between deciphering and understanding, a failure to move inside the conversation and string all the fragmented phrases together. Sima was more skilled. Through their daughter's adolescence, she had made daily collections and nightly summaries of small grimaces, soft mutterings, detritus from book bags and coat pockets, little scraps of nothing that maternal interpretation transformed into overwhelming evidence of boyfriends, drugs, minor transgressions. Lola was already thirty, no longer a teenager, but the information Chaim gleaned from listening to her on the phone was no greater than when she had lived with them, making secret plans.

"Okay, okay. Right. Cool!"

It was her vacation from work, but Lola missed her home in San Francisco, her exciting neighbors, the coworkers at the homeless shelter moonlighting as musicians. Lola wrote notes as she spoke, and though her pen moved quickly and the pages turned with a flurry, her conversation was limited to a few words: That's really cool. No. No. Ohmigod, no. Exactly.

Lola had gotten the idea to make a children's book with the title of *Stinky.* Lola's mother had twisted her nose at the word. "That's exactly the reaction we want!" Lola had said, between quick sips of coffee. The story of Stinky would be written by Lola and illustrated by the California neighbor, who worked as some kind of social worker, art therapist, with disadvantaged children. The tale was of a homeless child, Lola had told them, who was mocked in school, called names because he often was unwashed. Lola and the neighbor weren't yet sure whether the child and his mother would move out of the shelter by the end of the story; some part of them thought that ending too optimistic, even for a children's tale.

"We just don't want that to be the focus," said Lola. "We want it to be about his friendships, how he adjusts or doesn't in school. You want kids to be aware, not too many illusions, you know? If we have to move him out, I guess we will, but we don't want that to be the focus."

"Why?" Sima responded. "Let him have a home at the end. Does it have to be so depressing for everybody?"

"Reality, Ma," Lola said. "You should see how difficult it is for these guys to find a place. It's the fucking Bay Area. Biggest rent-to-income gap in the country. Worse than New York!"

Sima straightened her back. "Well, Laiush," she said, "I don't care what anyone says about rent-to-income. I know about children. Children do not want to hear something so dark and terrible before they go to sleep. And by the way, why does everything have to be fucking, fucking, fucking?"

Lola did not respond. There were ten days left on her vacation, and she owed a mother-daughter trip to the museum. Lola would want to go quickly through a short exhibit, and Sima would be hurt;

they didn't have enough time together, what with Lola going on and on with her political discussions with Chaim, things Sima did not feel invited to participate in. How can you say that? Chaim had asked his wife in the privacy of their bedroom, Sima tearful and sullen. But in truth he liked his talks with Lola to be private, even if they disagreed. Sima took offense if he said something she could not agree with, and she hated his cool speeches about politics or religion. Must you talk on so? she would say. I don't need to be lectured.

Lola did not feel lectured; Lola argued back. She asked questions. She was rude, yes, she wore lipstick too dark for her mouth and it made everything come out more harsh, especially with her mother. But it was not malice so much as heat. She was socially conscious. He didn't want to discourage her. It was good to be conscious. Once upon a time he had been someone she would have been conscious about. But Sima felt personally betrayed by Lola's opinions. Palestinians! Sima would cry. What does she know? And why should the family argue during the brief time Lola spent at home? No, Chaim tried to encourage his daughter to speak; it was good for her to speak, even if she was experimenting with her thoughts. If he silenced her the way Sima silenced her, she would not learn to speak.

CHAIM AND SIMA DROVE to their monthly card game at the Elbaums in Forest Hills. Tonight they arrived a little late. The others were already deep in conversation about the oral history project from Hollywood. Steven Spielberg. Chaim listened with interest. He was the youngest of the men by more than ten years, and among the few in the room who had the stomach to sit through *Schindler's List*. Still the rest read of the director's every move with pride and thrill, every article strengthening their bond with the genius that had brought their miserable history to life.

Lily was trying to convince the group to join. "We should not be the only ones out," said Lily, in English. "The Glicks do it. The Treppmans do it."

"Birds do it, bees do it," sang Charlie. "Even da-da-da-da fleas do it."

"We did it," Pavel announced. Fela took a small cluster of grapes from the central bowl, put them on her plate, and brought one to her mouth.

What? exclaimed Lily, in Polish, excited, almost angry. With the Spielberg people?

Why not? answered Pavel, in Yiddish. They came to the house.

To the house? What, with the camera, everything?

A whole crew, answered Pavel. And very professional, no, Fela?

Oh yes, said Fela.

You know, said Pavel, Helen wanted me to do it. A few years ago, there were some people from Yale. She tried to get me to do it. To go there, they have a whole center for it in New Haven.

So? What happened?

He wasn't ready! You have to be ready! cried Abek.

I was ready! protested Pavel. But I didn't like them. I wanted her to go with me on the train, and they had said yes, of course, but she can't be in the room.

So what? said Dovid. Why should she be in the room?

I didn't want her in the room either! It was the way they said it. Why should they decide where I put my family? So I didn't return their calls. Let them find some other idiot, who lets them order the family around.

Fela looked at Sima. See? she said.

But Spielberg, Pavel continued, the Spielberg project, they come to one's home. That is different. A different story.

Did you do it too, Fela? asked Lily. Chaim could hear the envy pressing down on her voice.

I wasn't feeling so well that day, said Fela, folding her napkin into her lap. I was tired. But I told them they were invited to my house anytime.

It's important to do it, someone said. To save for posterity.

Should we be the only ones without something on television?

What do you mean, without something? Spielberg isn't enough? All over the world people see it. He's a millionaire from that movie.

He's a millionaire already!

We don't have anything big. We have that crazy museum, it made me crazy to go there.

No, no, not a museum. You have to go all the way to Washington for that. I mean on television. The black people have it. You know, there was—what was it?—*Roots*!

Roots was many years ago! *Roots* was twenty years ago! How can you mention that to prove anything?

Plus, they deserve it, after all they went through!

I'm not saying anything against them. No, no. *Roots* was a good program.

I learned something, said Sima, I didn't understand what it was all about until that program. My aunt was here from Israel when it was on; she was very impressed by it, by what went on here.

You see? We should have a big program like that!

There was the miniseries with Meryl Streep, that one, with Tovah Feldshuh, remember?

Please! That was garbage, pure garbage!

Shouldn't we too have a *Roots*, something for everyone to understand? Is it more important, slavery, than what we went through? Now they want a museum too, so why shouldn't we have a television program, but a good television program? Should they have everything?

I don't think we need to compare, said Charlie. I don't think we need to compare. Slavery was bad too.

Sima smiled, sincere, approving.

Chaim saw something interesting last week, didn't you?

Hmm? said Chaim, startled.

"On Channel Thirteen," Sima said in English. "The civil rights? You couldn't take your eyes off."

"Oh, yes," said Chaim. "Very interesting." He paused but could think of nothing in particular to mention. His daughter had recommended that he watch it, a repeat on public television of a long documentary. He had watched the first portion. He liked to have something to talk about with his daughter, something to agree upon but also debate, without too many hurt feelings on either side.

I have a joke, a good joke, said Lily. You know, Dovid, what I told you in the car.

Too dirty, said Dovid, shaking his head. Too dirty.

Chaim sat back in the chair, his belly expanding with milky tea. In the documentary, a young black boy had come to visit his relatives in the South and made a flirtatious remark to a white girl. White men had come to his uncle's house in the night and demanded that the uncle give up the boy. The son of the uncle had told the tale for the film cameras, and he had skipped the most terrible portion, the portion where the uncle, faced with the guns and the threat that every person in the house would be killed, had gone up to retrieve the child, sleeping, at peace in his soft bed. The boy had been taken and killed, and the case had become something large. The trial had been famous, newspapers had declaimed, politicians had made speeches, but that small moment, the moment where the uncle was forced to deliver a child of his family, that was erased. Too terrible to speak it, the uncle's moment of obeying the murderers.

Chaim couldn't fault it. A story was supposed to end in triumph. And facts? Sometimes it seemed pointless, all this documentation. What did it serve? The world did not change.

Still he had been impressed with the mother of the murdered boy in the documentary. In an act of great innocence, the innocence of thinking that anyone cared, she had given to the newspapers the photograph of her mutilated son. Anyone who knew anything knew the photograph would do nothing. And yet, in this one case, something happened. Men were arrested and tried. The killers went free, of course they went free; but they went free with the whole country watching their escape, the whole country implicated in their freedom. To want to have justice, one had to be unrealistic. One had to make a fantasy out of one's observations and pursue the fantasy as if it were real, as real as a piece of bread or a warm home.

IN THE CAR, WITH Chaim driving home, Sima put her hand on his lap. What do you think about it?

Hmm? said Chaim. Soon after the Germans came to the small town he was born in, they ordered each family to bring one young male to the square to be hanged. The head of each family had to choose, and all the members of the family had to watch. Chaim had been ten years old. The lot had fallen to his eighteen-year-old brother, no longer a boy, but not yet married and responsible for a wife and children. It was the only decision that made sense. Sense. That was what the soldiers did: they made the victims into killers, into perversions of their own stories, five hundred Abrahams leading their sons to the sacrifice. Chaim did not look at the face of his brother, who had had to wait more than half the day for his turn. He looked at the boy next to his brother, a neighbor he did not know well, whose red curls, blowing lightly in the fall wind, flopped and waved over his ears. The crowd had been oddly quiet—or perhaps that was just the way he remembered it—and Chaim had wondered if the redheaded boy had been able to hear his mother's weeping while he waited.

I said, What do you think about it?

He knew what Sima meant, but still he asked: About what?

Chaimke, you know.

I don't think I can do it.

Think of Lola—something to give to her. To her children.

They were at a red light. Chaim looked at Sima. She was taking the earrings out of her ears, and in the reflection from the streetlights he could see that they were red, sore from the pressure.

To tell you the truth, Sima continued, I had called them before. Fela gave me the number. She turned to face him.

Fela didn't even do it herself!

So? Pavel did. I made an appointment for next Saturday. After Lola leaves, when we have time.

He looked at the road.

Of course we can cancel it, she murmured. She dropped the earrings into her purse, ran her hand over her hair. Hmm, Chaim? Ten years from now we'll be glad we did it.

THE SPIELBERG PEOPLE WERE to arrive at the house at 10 A.M. Sima had cleaned until nine in the night on the Friday, in honor of the apartment's capture on film. Then she had stayed up three more hours, writing notes for herself, to make sure she touched on certain points for the video. Sima would go first, then Chaim after lunch. She sent Chaim out for fresh food soon after the men came in, set up the umbrellas they used to control light, arranged Sima in the center of the dark red couch.

Chaim had his paper on the bus, but he couldn't read it; he looked out the window instead, at the women in T-shirts and long skirts wheeling their toddlers in heavy blue strollers, at the broad young men bouncing home from a morning at the gym. The neighborhood had changed. A kosher butcher's was now a real estate office. A bookstore was now a pharmacy. The specialty food store, a fixture for immigrants and striving middle-class families as long as Chaim had lived in the United States, had expanded to cover almost the whole block.

On Saturdays it was filled with young professionals packing up ready-made foods for their after-work dinners. He went first to the fish counter. Sam, Sam, the smoked-fish man, Lola would sing as a girl. Sam was old already, bent at the neck, his once-round face now thin and spotted, but he still called out to Chaim, casually, to let him skip in front of the others on line. When Lola was a child Sam would give her slices of pickle, when the store was small and the fish counter was the centerpiece. Sima would take fish cut only by him; Sam reminded her of her father, and in any case he was the only man who really cared to make the slices so thin they could dissolve in the mouth. Chaim had once asked Sam for a cut of Scottish salmon that had been on sale. Sam had refused: he cut only American fish. The smell of the salmon through the wax paper mixed with the odor of meats at the deli counter, absorbed into the saliva in his mouth, trickled down his chest. A throb of fear fluttered through his abdomen.

There had been a fight with Lola, just before she left for California, about the Spielberg film. Sima had gotten upset.

"So even *Schindler's List* is not good enough for you?"

"I didn't say that, Ma. I said there were problems. Why does everything have to be so extreme? I mean, let me have an opinion for chrissake!"

"I see. Now we have Jesus Christ involved."

"You know what I mean."

"No, I don't know what you mean. What do you think, that Germans understand already? You may think so, you may have friends, what do I care. But they do not understand."

"All I'm saying is—it's cheesy. Cheesy! Why do they have to make the guy such a hero, with the Jews all little mice? And that ending, with them singing a Zionist song. It was like it was all worth it to create the state of Israel, practically! It grossed me out. I heard in Israel they cut that part out—the propaganda was too naked for them. People can understand subtler things, Ma. They can." Lola's voice was beginning to shake, losing its authority—almost plaintive.

"So tell me, Lola, how should people understand? Only on Lola-time? Only with Lola-language?"

Lola stood up from the kitchen table. "It's a beautiful day, I'm going out."

Sima turned to Chaim, silently sipping his tea. "Just like her father, marching out in the middle of an argument!"

Why do you look at me? Chaim answered in Yiddish. I didn't say anything!

Exactly. You did not say a thing.

I do not say anything because there is no reason to fight over something like this. A movie!

But how she answers me!

Yes, yes, but you provoke her, Sima.

I provoke her? I provoke her? You hear what she says to me, Chaim. Sima was pale, her eyes bright. But no tears were in her eyes. "Yes, Ma, you care about homelessness here, but what about Arabs being evicted in East Jerusalem? Yes, Ma, you say this. Yes, Ma, you say that." But let me ask you, Chaimke, do you think she feels superior only to me, not to you too?

Sima. You're being terrible.

Now I am the terrible one. I don't know why I do anything for you anymore, or for her. She's on vacation, I bring her all her favorite foods, she won't eat them, this one is bad for her, that one has too much dairy. Why do I do it? I should forget it. I should forget everything.

Chaim sipped. He wanted to get up to add more hot water to his mug, but to get up, even to move to the stove with his back to her, would be to prove her right, that he fled rather than fight.

"I'll say something," he said in English. "I'll talk to her."

He waited until the next morning to approach. He found his daughter in the kitchen, scooping large amounts of coffee grains into the filter.

"Maybe you can put it a little less harshly when you speak to your mother," he began.

"I don't think it's a good idea to discuss it."

"I wasn't going to discuss anything," Chaim said. "I just wanted to say it."

They poured their coffee in silence.

"Your mother has arranged for us to make a little film." The words came out of his mouth before he realized he was raising the subject.

"I heard," she said.

"You did? What did you hear?"

"Ma just said—you know, she was doing it, she hoped you would do it—" Lola sat at the table, began cutting at an apple, the same neat gesture her mother used.

"But you don't think I should do it. I think you're right, the Spielberg project makes me a little uncomfortable too."

"I didn't say that. That's not what I meant yesterday. Anyway, the movie has nothing to do with us. With real people."

"But you think I shouldn't do it."

"Just the opposite, Dad. I think it would be—I mean, but only if you wanted to."

"When did your mother talk to you about it?" So they talked about him. That was new.

"Couple of days ago." She looked up at his face for a moment, then away again. "She said you can still cancel." Something in her voice was hesitant. Her mother must have said something to her much earlier, long before yesterday's argument. Did Lola realize then that he would be afraid? Coward, she might be thinking now. Shirker.

Her face was turned to her plate, concentrating on the apple. She cut what remained of it into thin slices, saying nothing, his strong-willed daughter, of whom he was asking advice, genuine advice, for perhaps the first time.

"Sorry, Dad," she finally offered. "I really don't have an opinion."

HE HAD A BURDEN of shopping bags to drag home. He supposed he should take the bus, make sure he arrived home with enough time to lay out the food, make everything comfortable for Sima, who surely would be tired from the talking and remembering.

But he wanted to walk. The cool April air would clear his mind, and the mile on a busy Saturday street would do him good. A man needed exercise. He looked at his watch: it was almost eleven. He still had plenty of time to come home, prepare the table and plan what to say. In fact, the walk would save him time. He could think as he walked, pacing his points to the beat of the warm bagels and cheeses tapping his legs, even and steady.

He passed the movie theater. Years ago they had all gone to see a new documentary, many hours long, that profiled old men who had worked in the crematoria of the camps. There was a special screening for survivors in New York, and Pavel had gotten Chaim a ticket, because Fela hadn't wanted to go. Survivors would be able to sit through it, or so it was advertised; the film had no blood and no hunger, only old men, now more or less healthy, living in Israel, speaking. But Pavel had lasted ten minutes. Chaim had been able to watch the whole way through.

There had been a scene in the film where a man had stopped speaking. The man had been describing something terrible, not ashes and flesh, but something personal, a conversation he had overheard between two people, one on the way to her death. He didn't want to tell what he had heard. But the filmmaker and his translators had told him: You must tell it, you must. You know that you must. *You must, you must*, spoken in the film in French and in Yiddish, written on the film in English subtitles. The scene hurt Chaim for reasons he couldn't explain to himself. But the man had been witnessing for hours of film. Already the testimony caused him much pain. He was testifying to all the crimes he had seen in his youth. But he himself was not on trial. Why was he forced to add this small piece? Was the piece worth more than the man's wish to rest his memory, to keep a woman's death face private, to sleep without that particular dream disturbing the night? Why must he? thought Chaim. Why the word *must*?

HE TURNED THE CORNER on Broadway, walked slowly toward the river. It was close to eleven. A father and two children were walking their bicycles toward Riverside Park. Lola had jogged there in the mornings during her visit, even when it rained. She had become very fit.

With Lola gone, their life had regained its peace and emptiness. Chaim and Sima returned to their own schedules, no center to gravitate toward, each separate from the other, working, sometimes reading alone, sometimes a movie together. No competition, just peace. And affection—Sima was still, after so many years, an affectionate woman. She touched and caressed. After thirty years of marriage she no longer walked around with no clothes, teasing him into bed, but still they had their nights of intimacy, once a week, much more, he knew, than others far younger than he.

There were nights he could talk for hours to Sima. But when pushed for something to say, he became trapped, afraid of hearing how he sounded, afraid of being corrected. To plan to say something, one had to be careful, eloquent, poetic. That was what speaking was for. In his day-to-day life he was successful at sounding quite refined, he thought, even at rambling too much to his friends and coworkers. But to speak of his childhood—he didn't know how to make it come out clear. It wasn't so clear in his own head, and he believed he preferred it that way. Besides, did these cameramen really care what he

had to say? He had been on the run for most of the war, and sometimes Americans lost interest if one did not say the words *concentration camp*. As if what gave the experience its importance was the form
of torture one had endured, rather than the loss of everything, mother,
father, family, culture, language. They preferred violence—the gory
details, as Lola would say—to grief. Or perhaps people simply liked
tales that matched with the pictures they had already seen.

Chaim fiddled with the lock in the door. What would he do? It
was so easy for his wife. She was quiet and careful in public, but
when telling stories she became a comedian, making fine and elabo-
rate tales about everyday business, a drive to the airport, a trip to the
shoe store. Her stories from forty years ago came out like folktales,
varnished and distant, colored and shaded, not photographs but paint-
ings. He already knew what story she would recount over lunch, the
one with her father making his favorite joke to her mother, in Siberia:
*You know, Dvora, one day, you'll come to the table and say, Berel, would
you like more bread? And I'll say, No, my dear, no thank you.* Sima
would let a second go by, a pause. And then the punch line: *No thank
you, I am full.* The way Sima told it, it still sounded funny.

The bags suddenly felt heavy. He lifted them into the kitchen, tried
to unpack them as quietly as possible, so as not to disturb the filming.
Perhaps they would be tired after all the morning work. Perhaps he
could speak better if he went to them alone, to their offices. Perhaps he
did not have to do the Spielberg at all; he could call up the Yale people,
the ones who did not like family involved. Surely the cameramen in
his home would be relieved to have one less interview today. It was
one thing for them to hear the dramas of Sima's childhood; she knew
how to keep her listeners rapt and pleased. He was a different story. It
couldn't be so interesting for them, just to see a man suffer.

He began to wash the grapes, let them sit in a colander to drain.
Then he set out the plates, turned on the coffee percolator Sima liked
to use for guests. She would be disappointed that he would not join

his story to hers on tape. But here he had made something else, a small but elegant meal, laid out on a clean cloth, for the two of them to share with strangers. The table was ready. For this Sima would be glad. She would acknowledge his efforts with few words, not history words, not memory words, but the same words she gave him every day. *It looks nice. Thank you. Did you put out enough sugar?*

He stepped out of the kitchen to breathe. The door to the living room was closed, and a white line of light emanated from the crack at the threshold. Inside, his wife was making her testimony. Chaim pressed his ear to the door. If he stayed quiet, he knew he would hear her bright voice.

Garment

T HEY HAD BRUISED HIS throat and vocal cords when they ripped out the breathing tube, so on the day Pavel met his sister for the first time in seven years, he could announce with sincerity that he could not speak. He could not speak! It was true. He made the statement in a pained rasp that was only slightly more exaggerated than the day-to-day mutterings he gargled to his wife. He was thirty pounds thinner than he had been before the by-pass surgery, and he had been a trim man to begin with; worse, his lung capacity was down, perhaps forever, from the effects of fifty-six years of smoking. He was weak. Anyone could see that.

But not so weak. He had agreed to the reunion only if Hinda and his cousin Mayer would come to the small club at which the fine-textile traders on Seventh Avenue did business, where he had a membership and they did not. He had a tab in the dining room and would pay for lunch. Neither could get in without him, although he brought

Mayer often. He was proud of the membership, even if he used it only to play chess or cards with the retirees. He hadn't had it when they'd had the business together, and even now Hinda's husband couldn't get one. Pavel knew someone on the committee, and that someone was loyal to Pavel. Everyone knew what had happened.

Mayer had found a parking space right at the corner, and Pavel had sat in the passenger seat, looking straight ahead through the windshield. It was too cold and windy for him to be standing, waiting. But Hinda came more or less on time. Mayer saw her from across the street, ankles wobbling despite the low heels. Tiny, tinier than before—Fela had heard that she had put on weight, but this was not the case—and whiter, her hair unconvincingly red near her pale forehead. When they got out of the car, Pavel shook her hand. She let her hand go limp and turned her eyes away from his, past his ear, as if she was hoping for someone else to come down the street and rescue her. He didn't want to kiss her, and she looked like she did not want to kiss him. That was fine. He could not speak; he told her and coughed.

Hinda said, "All right."

They went up the three entryway stairs, Pavel ahead, holding on to the railing with one hand, onto the lapel of his serge coat with the other. He put two feet on each step before lifting to the next. No need to rush. Inside, Mayer and Hinda waited before the security man while Pavel dug into his wallet and flipped through the cards for his membership identification. He went slow, and why not? What did the other two have to do with themselves?

Mayer couldn't bear the silence. In Yiddish, he said, Do you have it, do you have it?

Pavel gave him a glare and exhaled heavily. The moment he got sick, it was as if Pavel could do nothing. Who was the eldest, after all? He had the card, of course he had the card; he signed them in with his own pen.

Mayer pointed out to Hinda where they were going at each step, as if the place belonged to him. Here's the conference room, he said, and here the lounge, and here the dining room. This is where we eat. Pavel thought he could hear her joints stiffening; perhaps she did not want Mayer to speak Polish so publicly. But better than Yiddish, no? An ugly language, she had frequently said, and Pavel had felt fear, at all those holiday dinners and Thanksgiving lunches, that his children would believe her. Sha! he would say to her, his jaw jutting forward. And she would mutter something bitter under her breath. Her husband, that thief, that swindler, was no better, but he had the excuse, linked as it was to his cosmopolitan pretensions, of speaking Yiddish like an ox. In Pavel's family they had learned how to speak it, and what's more, how to write it. It was a pride, not a shame.

Mayer drew out a chair for Hinda in the dining room. Hinda took off her own coat; she wore a pleated wool skirt and an olive sweater, what looked to be silk knit. Pavel hung his coat on the coatrack, tipped his hat onto the coat's collar. The room was bright: wood tables, no cloths, plain menus. They were next to the window facing out on the street. The waiter was not familiar, but Pavel didn't care. They got ice water. Hinda ordered coffee.

Pavel looked at the center of the room. There was a friend sitting there, someone from years ago, from camp. Hersh waved a hand. Pavel lifted his in a half-salute. They had morning coffee together once in a while, more now since Pavel was out of the business. Hersh dealt in damask, and Pavel had had occasion to buy in small supply at prices advantageous to Hersh. Pavel had not minded mixing business with pleasure. Business was pleasure, or at the very least, loyalty. Business was loyalty. To work among materials like silks and chintzes and wools, soft objects that would become intimate coverings, blankets, curtains, upholstery for the home, garments for the body, one had to take seriously the idea of trust and loyalty. Family.

Pavel turned to his own table. His sister, ordering tuna fish salad like a teenager, rubbed at her napkin as she talked to the waiter. Skinny hands, skinny fingers. And nervous, so nervous. Her wrists seemed to shake. Mayer still attended to the menu. Always difficult for him to choose. Pavel ordered the same thing every time, a fresh turkey sandwich on rye, with onions, no tomatoes. He asked for extra mustard on the side. Now more than ever he needed the taste of something sharp. Otherwise it was simply impossible to stimulate his stomach to digest, to keep the food down. And he had to keep it down. The thought of vomiting scared him. His throat could not take the trauma.

They began to talk, only in Polish, gossip, children, acquaintances, funerals, with a few words tossed in English. "Needs a vacation," nodded Mayer, talking of his son; "nervous breakdown," said Hinda, in reference to her daughter-in-law. She almost seemed pleased to say it, thought Pavel. Imagine! But maybe it was true. Pavel thought he had heard it from someone else. There were grandchildren. Hinda's were younger than Mayer's. She just got a new one, it seemed. How was Hinda with an infant? He couldn't remember from the early years of his nephews. They had been difficult teenagers, hippies almost, at least the older one, but as infants, he could not remember them or their parents. He lived with them then, when he first came to this country and they had been resettled three years, maybe four. He lived with them, but he could not remember how she was with infants.

The food came. Pavel looked around for his extra mustard. He motioned for Hinda and Mayer to start without him, but the waiter brought it and added coffee for Hinda.

You look very thin, Pavel, said Hinda. Like you've lost too much weight.

He was so sick, said Mayer. So sick, it was terrible. A short operation, a long recovery.

Pavel glared, but Mayer wasn't looking. It wasn't her business!

She was still speaking in Polish, and looked at him, her lips turned downward: Don't you smoke anymore? You always said you would never stop.

He didn't want to speak. He could not speak!

"No more!" he croaked, in English, pushing his hand through the air, as if to swat at a fly. It was over, the cigarettes. Since the first heart attack. He saw Hinda fidgeting. She was dying for one. Dying. It made her more nervous. But what could she do? If she left to smoke outside, she couldn't come back in. Not without him.

Pavel bent to his coleslaw. Swallowing was not such a pleasure either, thanks to the damage done by the respirator, but he had to gain weight, add muscle. It was necessary. His daughter had given a start when she saw him standing the day he left the hospital, wearing his own clothes, his dark pants ballooning around his waist and legs. He had looked different, pretty good even, in the step-down unit, at least next to the others. But in the apartment things had worsened; he had lost another two pounds upon first arriving home, like a baby in the first days after birth.

Kuba was very sick, said Hinda. Has an ulcer that started seven years ago.

Pavel kept eating. Was he supposed to sympathize?

All the stress gave him an ulcer. He bled from his stomach.

In English, Mayer said, "Hinda, please."

It was difficult for everyone, said Hinda. Not just you, Pavel. Her hands were shaking.

Pavel looked at her straight in the eye. He couldn't have spoken even if he'd wanted to, even if his voice was a young man's. Was she crazy? She must be crazy. He'd lost his business! To his partner, his brother-in-law, who had pushed him out when it came time to sell, who had taken more than his rightful half, plus a salary too, from the company that bought, who had told Pavel that the new owners did not want old blood! Who, to make Pavel go along, threatened to report some mistakes Pavel had made years ago, taxes on wholesale or retail, it hurt Pavel even to remember exactly. Yes, Hinda must be crazy. Married to a blackmailer and traitor, someone who lived to rip things apart, and pretending it was all just a little argument.

Mayer went to Yiddish. Hinda, this is not how to talk about it.

"What I'm trying to say is, I still love you." She forked her tuna fish.

Love! thought Pavel. Love! He needed a new dictionary to find out what she meant by that word. There she was, trembling like a drunk into her salad, not even hoping that God would forgive her. There was nothing to forgive! She was just covering all points, just to make sure. Just in case she one day stopped sleeping so well.

Mayer said, That's it. That's better.

Pavel stared at his cousin. Mayer raised his eyebrows toward him. This was all that Mayer had expected. A statement of love. No apology, no admission.

Mayer went again to English. "I heard Sally Klein had a baby. At her age! And it was healthy."

"Yes," said Hinda. "She did. She was in bed rest, but it was fine. I went to the party."

Mayer chattered on. Pavel sat back in his chair. His belly seemed to him to be growing toward the table, swelling like a starving person's. It was clear, wasn't it, that nothing more would be said. He wished suddenly that he had something to tear, that he had torn something that month seven years ago, when he had come back from repairing his mother's grave and suddenly realized what was happening, realized but did nothing to stop it, sure that it wasn't, sure that she would speak for him, order her husband to negotiate a deal that would keep Pavel in the business they had built together, keep the family intact. He knew that she knew. He had smashed eggs in the sink out of rage. He should have torn something then, a piece of good clothing, a new scarf, a favorite shirt, and worn the scrap pinned to his jacket like in the week of mourning after a loved one's death. He should have, but he didn't. He looked at her napkin, white cotton stained with pink lipstick. What if he grabbed it and ripped it to shreds right this second?

He made an involuntary noise with his lips. His mouth was dry, but he did not want to take in a drop of water. He was full. Anything else would spill out of him.

The waiter came over with the bill. Pavel signed without checking to see if it was right, and took out ten dollars as a tip. Mayer looked at the cash but said only, Are you ready?

"Yes," said Pavel. "I have something to do."

They stood up. Pavel twisted into his coat while Mayer brought over Hinda's. Mayer had no hat. Pavel looked over at the center of the room. No one he knew. Hersh was gone. Pavel pushed his legs forward, letting Hinda go in front of him, not for politeness, but so she wouldn't see if he had to stop and rest.

Outside, Mayer told Pavel to wait while he got the car from the corner.

"No," said Pavel. "I'll go."

Hinda turned to walk in the opposite direction. My best, she said in Yiddish.

But Pavel's face was already sideways, his hands in his pockets. He followed Mayer, who rushed to the meter. Who cared if Hinda saw him so slow? He doubted she even was watching.

FELA WAS NOT HOME; he could tell as he turned the key that it was locked from the outside. His magazine lay on the hallway table, with unopened bills from the hospital. The insurance was not paying the doctors on time; day after day Fela complained on the phone; he did not have the patience.

When she came home after five, carrying two bags from the grocery, Fela found him sitting in the kitchen, light not yet turned on, watching the news. She had bought potatoes and would warm up her good barley soup. A piece of chicken if he felt like it.

That was good, Pavel said. Everything she made was good.

So? she said.

So, he answered, so nothing.

How can it be nothing? said Fela. She poked around: Hinda's clothes, her face, her sliver-thin lips. She must have said terrible things about someone, no? Pavel tried to comply with her questions, but there was nothing to say. Empty. He fished around the soup bowl, waiting for words to come out.

Fela moved the bowl away, angry. You still won't eat anything. Maybe Helen will have something. I don't know why I make so much food.

His daughter was visiting after their dinner, on her way home from work. They saw her quite often now, every two or three days. Not a big talker, Helen, not a shouter and laugher like her brother, but a good girl. A good girl, a professional, a public-health worker, doing what, exactly, he had difficulty remembering, but with a satisfactory husband, if only one child. Well, maybe more children would still come. He was not supposed to say anything about it to her, Fela said. It just got her upset.

But Helen did not appear to be in a sensitive mood as she tripped into the kitchen, dropping her satchel in the hallway as Fela cleared off the table and brought out the tea. She took off her jacket and pulled out the white chair between him and Fela. A kiss on his forehead. All right.

"You must want something to eat," said Fela. "I have extra soup. He didn't finish anything."

"No, no, no. We're going somewhere for dinner. Jonathan is meeting the sitter. I'm going straight from here."

"Did you change your hair? It looks a little red." Fela stretched her hand to touch her daughter's head.

"I got highlights. And, you know, a trim."

"Guess who he saw today."

"Who?"

Helen looked at Pavel. There had been a big discussion, not four weeks ago, when he lay flat in the bed, barely able to make it to the window seat to eat the egg and toast Fela brought him. Mayer, the big peacemaker, had wanted to bring Hinda to the house. Hinda wanted to see Pavel, claimed Mayer, it was Hinda's idea, he insisted, she asked about him all the time, desperate. Fela had refused to be home for it; she had seen enough of Hinda to last several lifetimes, thank you very much. If Pavel wanted to see her, she was his sister, and who was Fela to stop him? Fela did not have a sister living, and so she could not judge. She could not judge, but she did not have to be in the apartment to officiate, to give the idea that this person called a sister was being invited like a piece of royalty into her home. Larry had called from a conference in Chicago, furious. She just wants to see you lying down, that's all! She wants to feel good about herself before someone dies! This had shaken Pavel. The words were harsh. But perhaps Larry was right.

Fela had left to talk to Larry from the kitchen. Helen had stayed. She had sat on the bed and asked what he wanted. I don't know, he had said. I don't know what I want. I can't make a decision. Helen thought he might be too tired to make a decision; why didn't he decide when he felt a little better? It wouldn't be long. He had whispered, Everyone wants for me to decide. And Helen had answered, hands folded in her lap, There's plenty of time to decide. Plenty of time. No need to rush.

"He saw Hinda. With Mayer."

"That's news."

"Nothing new," said Pavel. "All the same."

"What happened?" Helen was looking at Fela, but Fela said nothing. She almost was smiling, making fun, perhaps, but trying to hide it.

Pavel tapped his mug with his fingers. "I took them to the club."

A pause. "Did you wear that shirt? It looks very good on you." It was cornflower blue, casual, and he had worn a dark gray tie.

"I told you, Pavel! It's beautiful!" said Fela. "I bought it for him, Helen. It's maybe five years old."

"How did it go?"

"Fine."

"I mean, how do you feel about it?"

"Okay." He turned his eyebrows up, lifted his hand to the side.

"Okay?"

"Okay, like nothing." Pavel smiled. His throat was beginning to hurt again, even after the soup. But what could he do? It was worth it to give some little conversation when his daughter was here.

"What do you mean, nothing?"

Fela interjected. "That's just what I said. I came home from the store and he was sitting, just in his chair. Nothing, nothing. Like now." She went on. " 'So how did she look?' I said. And he said, 'Like a shriveled-up old woman.' "

"She did," rasped Pavel. "Like a shriveled-up old woman."

Helen turned from one to the other. "I guess it's been a while."

Fela slanted her eyes. "He saw her on the street once, in Midtown, not so long ago. But from a distance." Then said, almost sharply, "Do you want some fruit? I have grapes."

She got up from the table. Pavel watched her back, wide and regal, swathed in a violet cardigan. She banged around the kitchen counter, clapping the plates and bowls together. But nothing would break. She took care with dishes. He sniffed his light tea. He knew he was better, that when they went for his checkups the doctor now told him the same things he told her, that there were no terrible whispers about his health, the way there had been before the surgery, when his lungs would fill up with water in the middle of the night and Fela would hear him gulping and expelling air like a locomotive. He wasn't eggshells anymore. She snapped at him and he snapped back. He wasn't glass.

He was a tough strip of twill. More, he was human, he was Joseph, the slave and prisoner pricked with bad luck and good, and smart enough to keep quiet, at least after he had learned a few lessons. The brother sold down the river, robbed of his beautiful coat. Everyone wanted Joseph dead and Joseph had held out. But Joseph died in the end, as Pavel supposed he himself might too. But not yet. He had something in him still, he was sure. Something in him still.

"I have a big box of letters she sent me when I was in Germany after the war, waiting for the visa. What she said in those letters! I was to her like a king, a prince!" He stopped, his throat aching, and took a sip of tea.

"So what, Pavel?" called Fela, from the counter. "You think she remembers?"

"One day," he croaked, "one day I'll take out that box and send her those letters. In one package. Just to remind her."

"Ha," said Fela. "And what will she do with them?" She came back to the table and moved into her chair.

"Why would you do that, Dad?"

"I don't know," said Pavel, looking at Helen's lowered chin, at Fela's tight mouth. "Just to see. Just to see."

"I think you should keep them." Helen pulled at a grape.

"You think?"

So maybe he would keep them. Maybe Hinda felt no guilt. Maybe he felt nothing either, no grief, no sorrow, not even, after seven years, humiliation. Maybe no one felt anything. It was all just people, the members of a family, streams of wool thread, separate, hooked into the same loom by coincidence, touching and twisting only when the design required. Maybe no one felt anything for anyone but the missing. Wouldn't that be a joke! Surviving in order to argue and hate.

His daughter was staring. "You're laughing," she said. "Why are you laughing?"

Was he laughing? He supposed that he was. Pavel looked straight at Helen, trying to stop.

"I'm laughing," he rasped, beginning to grin, his gums dry and exposed. "Why am I laughing? I don't really know."

But really he did. He patted her hand. He laughed, he thought, because it was funny.

Eulogies

THE FUNERAL OF TSIPORA Sheinbaum, once married to the leader of the Belsen refugees, was to begin at nine o'clock in the morning, promptly. Rush hour. But Fela was not nervous. Now that Pavel had been forbidden by the doctors to drive, they would get a ride from Rego Park to the memorial chapel in Manhattan. They would arrive on time, relaxed, their stomachs calm. Pavel would sit in the front to stretch out his bad leg, and she would sit in the back, staring out the window, her lower back resting against a cushion, with time for herself, not worrying. No responsibilities except to sit. Serene.

Pavel's oldest friend, Fishl, picked them up in front of the house. He was three years older than Pavel, but he drove more stably, and without the twenty-mile-an-hour caution, not to mention the bravery against motorcycles and sports cars, that had made Pavel's driving notorious among his friends. Fishl drove an Oldsmobile, the kind with the long fronts that protected people in case of accident. With such a big vehicle, parking would be a problem in Manhattan, but it was worth it. Fela liked Fishl's car, its unused lighters in the backseat, the windows that came down at the push of a button. The front had room for Pavel to stretch out his bad leg. She knew he was relieved not to drive, despite his protests to the contrary.

They would see everyone; with Dincja so sick, Fishl was excited to be out. These were not his close friends, although he knew one or two of them as long as Pavel had, and he wondered aloud, all across the Triborough Bridge and through Central Park, who would be there, who would be missing. There had been a feud between Tsipora and Gershom, now a prominent donor to charity, a feud that had started five years ago, about this project or that museum, some board that one or another was on, a big to-do. Pavel had trouble keeping up with this kind of detail—he never liked the politics, and they didn't have the money to participate anyway—but he knew, from his head to his feet, that Tsipora was in the right. And even if she wasn't, Gershom was in the wrong. They had been somewhere recently, Pavel and Fela, and Gershom had come up to them and greeted them warmly, all the while ignoring Tsipora, who stood next to Fela. It was a terrible humiliation for Tsipora, one that implicated Fela and that made her feel ashamed to this day. So what if he was prominent! Did that mean they all had to bow down to him? To the point of abandoning a friend?

Tsipora was the last link that bound them all together. No nickname, although there must have been something as a girl. Fela could not imagine it. She was a very grand lady. To Fela and to everyone else living she was always Tsipora, and the name, three syllables, biblical yet modern, elegant and large, evoked exactly the story it came from: Tsipora, wife of Moses, traveling with him, a partner. Yet the Moses of Tsipora's life, her husband Yehuda, Yidl, was long dead. Twenty-five years now. And what had happened to the first Tsipora, the one from the Torah? No one knew. Not worth mentioning, the life of the wife. Ha. So, times had not changed too much.

Tsipora had deteriorated. Yidl had passed away when his natural force was still unabated. But Tsipora, a strong woman for at least two decades after his sudden departure, had not made it whole to her death. It had been a relief for her friends, it tempered the sadness, that the suffering of her last days was over. Even at the last she had struggled to attend the card game, sitting in the backseat of the car of the Budniks or the Krakowskis, traveling through Queens and inner Long Island and even, twice, to the Upper West Side of Manhattan, where Chaim and Sima had unfolded their pretty mahogany card tables and fed them all with smoked fish from the local shops. The women played separately from the men, and Sima, toward the end, was the only one who would take Tsipora as a partner. Much younger than the rest, Sima, and so less angry about the money. When Vladka Budnik lost! It was a scandal, the way Vladka screamed. Her husband was afraid of her, afraid of losing among the men, which he did often. But Tsipora, that was the tragic thing. Couldn't remember what happened from one hand to the next, and started in on a terrible speech in the middle of everything. This was one of Fela's oldest friends in all the world, a friend to whom she and the others owed plenty. But in the last few years, women moved to the side of the room, bent toward the dried fruit when they weren't hungry, began talking loudly of something important, anything, to avoid being Tsipora's partner. And really, did Fela have the right to judge? She herself liked to win.

Fishl let Fela and Pavel off in front of the memorial chapel and went to park the car in the garage himself, waving Pavel off. They would save Fishl a place. A crowd was gathering outside already, though they were maybe twenty minutes ahead of schedule. Sima and Chaim stood on the line to sign the book of the mourners. Pavel became nervous when he saw a line, but someone would let him cut in front. Fela watched him pull himself over to Sima and Chaim, eager to chat.

Pavele, Pavele. Fela! Where are you? Come here. Sima gave Pavel a hug and a kiss, then rubbed Fela's shoulder. *Mazel tov, mazel tov.* Fela told us last week! When is Helen due?

Fela blocked the sound out. She turned this way and that, looking for the family. There was a separate room the funeral home had, a room where one spoke to the family in private. A guard watched the room, so mere acquaintances, strangers, couldn't push their way through. Should she try to go in? She decided against it. From behind the guard she thought she could see Tsipora's son and daughter, even the grandchildren, tall and grim, the girls in short black suits.

The people on the line to sign the book filed into the chapel. Someone had told them to. Fela and Pavel took seats in the third row. The first row, of course they couldn't; but any farther back, it almost would have disrespected the friendship. Sima and Chaim sat just behind them. Very appropriate. Fela looked around. She didn't see Gershom. She shouldn't be surprised, but still. A young woman, perhaps forty, in a bright yellow dress—like a traffic light!—trotted past. Fela squinted. Her glasses were not for public use, even at a funeral, where one needed to look only dignified, not beautiful. Yes, the Kalmans' daughter. A professor of some kind, still unmarried. Even she was here. Fela nudged at her husband with an elbow, then shook her head in the direction of the yellow dress. Pavel nodded. Fela faced toward the front again. Tsipora had a big following. It was nice that people's children came. Still, to dress so flashy. Little kings and little queens, they had all raised their children to be. To do what they wanted. Little kings and little queens. The Kalmans were not the worst in spoiling, either. Even her own children, and no doubt their children after them, if Larry ever remarried—but Fela stopped the thought in its tracks. Wasn't this what everyone wanted, children so carefree?

It was one of Tsipora's qualities, a quality that Fela envied, that she truly did not begrudge anyone a bit of cheer and joy. They had been wealthy, splashy, for some years after the war. An enormous apartment on the Upper East Side of Manhattan, with artworks and sculpture, expensive furniture. Parties not to be believed. The food enough for a banquet, and two dozen or more people, some refugees, some Americans, everyone mixed together, important and not important, rich people and people with nothing. Beautiful, and very giving, both Tsipora and Yidl had been. Against everything, they believed in their own happiness. That was what made the parties strange, the terrible effort they and everyone, all the guests, even the ones who knew better, exerted to make it joyful. It was strange, two people, each of whom had lost a child during the war, before they knew each other, making a new world, a golden calf, even, out of money made—well, who knew where.

Fela and Pavel had been at a party maybe two years after their arrival in the United States; Tsipora and Yidl had already been here some seven years. A Passover seder, but one that bore no resemblance to the noisy but orderly routines that Fela had been used to in her childhood home of nine brothers and sisters and many more cousins, nephews, nieces. The flowers in the apartment! Huge arrangements, that was what Fela had noticed first. Arrangements like sculptures themselves. Tsipora and Yidl's possessions had not yet attained the heights that they would in the decade to come, before Yidl died and everything, all the money owed here and borrowed there, had come crashing into Tsipora's well-kept home. Not the heights, but nonetheless impressive.

In that time they all were still very careful about the rituals; they couldn't begin eating until the opening blessings and ceremonies were done. Time was passing, because a guest was late. Tsipora had invited an orphan to the seder. A woman who had grown up in the DP camp, gone to the schools Tsipora and Yidl had helped build, and moved to Israel on a children's convoy Tsipora and Yidl had helped organize. Then she had come here, on a scholarship, to study opera. Opera! She knew two names in all of New York, and those names were Tsipora and Yehuda Sheinbaum. Tsipora had taken her under her wing.

But the girl had not arrived. How long would they have to wait? The guests were hungry. Fela had managed; she knew how to keep her hunger to herself; she prided herself on her ability to stand it. Pavel, too, he was very controlled. It made them a good pair. But some of the others! One wondered how they could have made it through all the deprivation, the way they peered anxiously at the parsley and shank bone on the seder plate, the way they sniffed in the air for the boiled chicken.

Tsipora had begun to worry. Where could this girl be? She told the story of their meeting not once but twice, how the girl had made a call from the public telephone of her music school, then met Tsipora for a coffee near Carnegie Hall. The girl had never been to Tsipora and Yidl's home; she was in for a jolt. But a half hour passed, an hour, and more, and still she wasn't here. Yidl opened a bottle of wine. They could start on that, just with the first blessings, he told his wife. Don't worry, he had said. She's fine. There's an explanation. But he had looked concerned too. She lived in a dangerous neighborhood— perhaps—

It couldn't be stopped. Tsipora had given in and started serving soup and fish. Perhaps with a little in their stomachs, the guests could wait on the main course; they'd do the Passover readings in between. Pavel clucked but kept silent. He liked things in their rightful order. And the fish was difficult, for all the guests, really, because to eat it in a home, one longed for one's mother's recipe. This was good, of course it was. But one liked what one had in one's home, if one still could remember it.

It was maybe two hours from the arrival of the first guests that the room filled with a ringing. Tsipora had stood up and strolled to the little nook where the telephone stood. It was the orphan girl. Was she all right? Was she sick? Was she injured? What? From the dining table Fela had seen Tsipora's wide face, plump even then, taking in the story over the telephone. Tsipora's lips were set together, covering her teeth, and her eyes narrowed downward in concentration. After what must have been a pause in the confession on the other end, Tsipora heaved her shoulders in a shrug and sighed. Then she closed her eyes and opened them again.

Well, my dear, she said into the mouthpiece, switching from Polish to Yiddish, her voice in a lullaby. Did you enjoy yourself?

Tsipora returned to the head of the table, settled herself at her chair, and said to the audience, You will never believe it.

Yidl was shaking his head.

You'll never believe it. She went to a film. This afternoon. *The Life of Liszt.* She cried, she said, it was so terribly sad. And when it was over, she stayed for the next showing. She couldn't get up. And when the second one was over, she stayed for the third. She walked all the way home before she remembered us.

What did she say? asked an outraged guest. What did she say?

I told you already, Tsipora said calmly. She went to the movies. It was a very tragic film.

But I don't understand! The guest couldn't calm down; the memory of the hunger he had felt made him angry. What did she say?

She said, said Tsipora, that the movie was beautiful. And I think it must have been. Yidl, you know, perhaps we should see it. I told her she makes good recommendations.

Fela remembered this as a lovely gesture, the gesture of a woman elegant inside as well as out. Fela's own daughter had once done something very embarrassing, years later, after Yidl had died and Tsipora had lost all the luxuries to his debts. They had been at the small apartment to which she had been forced to move. It was a Sunday visit, just Fela and Helen, and Helen had been touching everything there was to touch: ashtrays, doilies, embroidered pillows. These were things that were still valuable in their own way, although not, of course, to be compared with the crystals and textiles of the old apartment. It was all right to touch. Helen was careful, anyway. Fela's son—she wouldn't have let him near anything, even a book. But it was Helen who had gone toward the books. Fela and Tsipora had gone on talking, in Polish and Yiddish, back and forth without thinking, laughing a little. Fela had been totally absorbed, who knew in what. Important at the time. But Tsipora had seen, out of the corner of her eye, what Helen was doing at the bookshelves. She was touching a miniature set of Shakespeare's plays, tiny, like for a doll, but readable still. Helen had dared, even, to remove one of them from its little white case to squint through the pages. During a pause in the women's conversation, Tsipora had turned around and said to Helen, "Helinka, what are you reading?"

"Nothing," Helen had said. She was at the beginning of high school, shy and explosive. She placed the little book back in the case.

"Nothing?" said Tsipora.

"We're reading *Romeo and Juliet* for school."

Fela had stood. It's time to go, perhaps, Tsipora?

Tsipora had hoisted herself up from her armchair and gone to the shelf, patted Helen on the head. Helen bent away from under her hand and went to the closet to get the coats. Tsipora fingered the gilt lettering on the little Shakespeare set herself, gently but unsentimentally. I don't even know who gave these to me, she said, in Yiddish, to Fela.

No, Tsipora, Fela had answered. She was just playing.

But Helen was back already, and Tsipora had the white case in her palm. "Helen," she said. "Why don't you take them? I really don't have room."

"No, Helen," said Fela, harshly. Helen had dropped her arms to her side and stood still, awaiting the decision.

But Tsipora was not used to being refused. People did what she said, here in America. That was what she was like! You complimented her on a brooch she was wearing, she moved to take it off her dress to give it to you! And to refuse was to imply her weakness; that could not be done, particularly in her widowhood. It made one afraid to speak, to say anything, for fear of provoking that tyrannical generosity. Still. A lady to the last. Tsipora had pushed the set into Helen's coat pocket, and Helen had displayed it in front of her English paperback mysteries until she went to college. Now Fela had them herself.

TSIPORA'S LAST YEARS HAD been very difficult. The death of Yidl and the loss of position had meant an exiling from the main activities of her group, the gathering and the speaking. Slowly Gershom, others with money, rabbis and writers, had taken over her legacy. But now! Who had not remembered Tsipora in her impoverished years following Yidl's death, now could not be quiet about her great exploits. Who had not defended her, even recently, in the dispute with Gershom—and it was certain that he would not appear, people were gossiping about it already—now called her a heroine, a word Fela personally hated. A heroine was not a person, but a character from stories. A heroine to do what? Help build a war memorial in Manhattan? That was a job for an architect and for construction workers, not for heroines. Not for heroes either, no matter what Gershom thought of himself. This was the big project that Yidl had not lived to see?

Times had changed quite a bit. No one had cared then, no one had cared even twenty years after, but now, all of a sudden, what had happened in Europe was very fashionable to talk about. There were movies, there were books. Everyone wanted to be associated with it. Even Tsipora's children, weeping through their eulogies, could not stop talking about the history, the history. This rabbi, that rabbi, everyone built his own importance out of a pile of dead bodies. Who talked about Tsipora? Not a one. One of the younger rabbis, tanned and plump, spoke of reading stories in the Jewish weeklies of Tsipora's husband, organizing the refugees into a government within the displaced persons camp. Yes, it had been a very big accomplishment. Yidl, for all his flaws—leaving his family in such terrible straits at his death!—knew how to draw people around him to believe.

But what was this rabbi saying, his voice rising in excitement, then falling on its own weight? He had been a little boy in that period. "But even as a child in Brooklyn, I was interested in such things." Well, so what? He was a rabbi! They were supposed to be interested in such things! The rustle of Fela's scarf made Pavel look at her. She had been shaking her head.

The rabbi who read newspapers as a boy was replaced by a little man who spoke like an American. But it seemed that he was born in Poland, so he said; he had come to the Bronx in the 1930s, with his parents, no less. Still, he pointed out, he had left his whole family, his cousins, his aunts, his uncles, his grandparents, his great-aunts, his great-uncles, not to mention neighbors and friends who probably were related to him too, from way back when people lost track, everyone, everyone, in Poland. Everyone dead; it had been a small town just across the German border, one of the ones, like Fela's, where almost everyone had been killed. And, in absentia, this little man was saying, he was a victim too. Fela felt her scarf rustling again. So what, so what? They would have the opportunity to hear about all this at his own funeral. Why should they waste time over it at Tsipora's?

It was making her hot, her anger. And because it was September, there was no air-conditioning in the chapel. It was practically a heat wave outside, and all these elderly people here. Vladka Budnik, perhaps eighty years old, how could she take it, if even Fela, some five years younger, was suffering? A fan, at least, the staff could have provided. No one thought about these things. And who was she to complain? But she needed a rest, a breath, a sip of water, something. Her hands began to shake. She stood.

"I!" cried the old man, the little rabbi, American but not American. "I am not a normal person!"

Fela hesitated a moment before Pavel's leg, which stuck out, twisted, from the aisle; she lifted one foot and then the other, slowly, over him, balancing herself on the pew in front of her. She was in the aisle; she thought she saw a sign for an exit.

"So imagine," continued the speaker. "Imagine what Tsipora was, with a child, a child who was murdered!" The lament hit the inside of Fela's head, bounced against an ear. She came toward the sign, walking down the side, careful not to look into the rows of people, then squinted: EMERGENCY EXIT. No, no, that was wrong. It would set off an alarm. There must be something else, the door, the regular door. And yes, there was a soft red light calling EXIT, EXIT against the climbing wail of the little rabbi. Fela managed to push herself outside the door of the chapel and began shuffling along the wall, her hand skimming the molding for support, until she reached the elevator and stumbled in. It closed in on her; she felt her face break out in a sweat, a drip, mixed with face powder, falling toward her brows. When the elevator opened again, on the ground floor, she moved three steps into the carpeted lobby, felt her feet pressing heavily, her fingers turning to ice, her stomach lurching with fear, then stopping, then moving again, side to side, side to side—

She was on her knees, her torso bent forward, contorted, her hips straining to keep herself upright; someone's hand was behind her head.

"Ma'am," said a voice, a man's voice. "You're sick."

"No, no," she lied. "It's fine, it's my ankle, just." She moved her head away, turned, shaking, still on her knees, to look at him. A heavyset man, brown face, perhaps Puerto Rican, older, gray hair curling out of his ears. Uniform. A security guard.

"Do you have family here? Somebody I can get for you?"

"No, my husband, but no, he will be disturbed, and it's nothing."

She felt the carpet burning through her panty hose; she had landed on the soft part of her leg, just below the joint. Lucky. There was pain, but the pain of a bruise; nothing was broken. And her heart was beating fast, but normally; that, at least, was something.

"You don't look too good." He had helped her up; she was grasping at his jacket sleeve for steadiness. Her feet were solid; she could feel the floor. But at her hips there was still the strain, the weight of the upper body resting on her thin bones. "I'll just call up and ask them to bring him down."

"Yes, I'm sorry," said Fela, quickly, "but no. It's my ankle, always it bothers me, and also, it was hot. Air, just, I needed." The guard led her to a bench outside. "Look," she continued, sitting down carefully, navy skirt smoothed under her. "See? It's better." Her heart was light, floating. She rested her back against the granite wall of the funeral home.

He peered at her a moment. "There's water inside. Would you like some?"

"Oh, yes, thank you," she said. "Yes, thank you, sir," she repeated when he returned, blue plastic cup in his hand. "It's much better now. Thank you."

She sipped and stared at the exercise club across the street, young people in bright pants moving their thighs on stair machines, treadmills, stationary bicycles. So busy, the club, in the middle of a workday. Strange. All watching a show on the television that hung above them. Commercials, mostly, she would guess, though she couldn't see at that distance. Well, something to entertain. Everyone needed it. She tried to concentrate on the colors in the window.

"Difficult service, was it?" murmured the guard.

"Oh?" said Fela. "Oh, yes. I mean, not so much. But maybe a little long."

"I knew it would be long when I saw them starting so early," said the guard. "Usually they give it another half hour, even an hour or so before starting. It can be difficult, especially when—was she a good friend of yours?"

"A good friend?" Fela was startled by the question, the word *good*. "Yes, well—" She paused, then whispered, "The best. The best."

"Yes, that's very tiring. A friend that passes away, especially at our age—it's like family, better than that sometimes."

He looked to be at least a decade younger than her, but the mistake flattered her. "Yes," said Fela. "I have to agree."

"And when a lot of different people speak about it, it can do more harm to the mourners than good, if you ask me. Sometimes you have your own memories of the person, ones you don't want to have mixed up with those of the others."

"You know," said Fela. "I have to agree with this also."

FELA WAS FEELING SOMEWHAT better by the time the congregants filed outside. Still, she was glad for the extra moments to sit, waiting, the burn in her knees subsiding, while they all said their good-byes before stepping into the limousines for the cemetery. Pavel found her first.

What happened? he said. A reproach: she had left him.

Nothing, nothing, I just couldn't stand it, she said, under her breath. He looked at her, suddenly suspicious, worried. All right now to be concerned! He would be in a bad situation if she died first, wouldn't he? But she pushed a weak smile: It's all right, Pavel, I'm fine.

Some of her friends stopped by to talk to her. What was she doing here? Was she all right? Of course she was, of course she was. Just a little hot inside, that was all. She leaned her neck upward to kiss Tsipora's tearful grandchildren while her husband talked to the men. No less than six rabbis had spoken. *Six.* And what did they say, after all? She was surprised Pavel had sat through the whole thing, barely fidgeting. For rabbis he sat still, no matter how stupid.

She saw Fishl pausing at the limousines. Should he take his Oldsmobile out of the garage and follow the coffin to New Jersey, or jump into the limousines with one or another important personage? He was shifting from one foot to the other, deciding.

Pavel was more sure. He wanted to drive with Fishl, in the front. Fela watched her husband debating with his friend. She didn't care, though she thought she would prefer the limousine. From the bench she watched the Budniks step into one.

Fela! called Vladka Budnik, her peach-colored hair stiff as a balloon. Fela! Take Pavel and come with us! It's more comfortable, it's more cool!

Pavel wants to go with Fishl! answered Fela.

Let him! grumbled Vladka's husband.

Yes, let him, concurred Vladka. Just come with us yourself!

Fela shook her head. What if he doesn't feel good?

But Pavel looked good, arguing vigorously, coughing once or twice. Vladka shut the limousine door. Pavel looked over at Fela, motioning with his chin. He thought she could read his mind, that's what. Well, she could. But for once, she did not have to let him know. Let him ask her what she wanted to do. Let him acknowledge what was what. She had fainted, almost! A wife should be respected too.

Not that she had so much trouble from him. She was lucky, she really was. Vladka for years had complained about her husband, how stingy he was with her, how he expressed rage over the grocery bills and counted out change for her clothing. Once Vladka had even asked Pavel for money! Pavel was a generous man, thank God. No arguments on that front. Never. By now, after the disaster with the business and after his heart attack, it was Fela running the finances, as he could no longer concentrate at all, and his impatience got the better of him when he tried to decipher a bill. Fela knew how to do with the bills, and if Pavel felt put out, pushed aside, he did not complain too much, because, after all, what if she stopped?

A tall girl, long hair, came over to her bench. Tsipora's oldest granddaughter, her eyes small from crying.

"Oh, Fela," she said. "You're not coming to the cemetery?"

"Of course I am, sweetheart, *neshumele*, of course I am!" Fela was surprised. "I was just sitting, waiting, you know, for Pavel to arrange our ride."

"Why don't you come with us? We have room for the two of you. It's just my mother and sister."

Fela looked over at Pavel, pacing with Fishl. Why couldn't she go alone? He could drive as he wanted, and she could go in comfort. Why not?

"Sweetheart, have you checked with your mother? Maybe she doesn't want someone outside the family."

"She sent me over. You're not outside."

"Well," said Fela, neck straightening. "Well, maybe I will." She pushed herself up with her hand on the wall of the building, leaned on the granddaughter's arm. "Pavel!" she called. "Pavel! I go with Stacy! Okay?"

"What?" Pavel turned too quickly, wobbling on his good leg. He began calling something in Yiddish. But Fela wouldn't hear it.

"I see you there!" She moved her legs toward the limousine that held the family, then twisted her neck around, seeing Pavel unmoving, stunned. In a moment he would start to fume. Fela would pay later, with his silences and stomping. But at this moment he looked lonely, standing with no one while Fishl shuffled across the street to the garage and the cars began their journey across the river to New Jersey.

Sad, thought Fela. But he wouldn't be left here, forsaken while everyone traveled to the burial. He would arrive; they would be there together. He was her partner, at least for this life. They wouldn't abandon each other for long.

They couldn't. She waved. Pavel waved back. She waved again. Then—and why not?—she blew him a kiss.

The Unveiling

October 2000

PAVEL AND FELA ARRIVED home from the unveiling in time for their Sunday family meal. Larry had driven them in the rain to the ceremony at the new gravestone, the gravestone belonging to Henry Budnik, who, just before his death the year before at the age of eighty-three, had made Pavel promise to watch over the stonecutting. Budnik's wife had died just before him, and he didn't trust his children.

Pavel was forced to lean halfway on his wife and halfway on Larry, who helped him—a little too rough, Pavel thought—move his stiff leg out of the car. But once at the door of the apartment, Pavel pulled himself away. He could walk easier inside.

Helen was there already, waiting for them in the kitchen. She was alone, and she had brought rye bread, and a bit of smoked fish, and bagels for Larry, and dietetic cookies for Fela, who had developed high sugar. Everything was prepared.

Helen was sipping coffee at the table, reading the paper. "Hi, guys," she said.

"Oh, Helen," said Pavel. He grabbed her around the shoulders, pressed her head to his. "But where is my littlest *yingele*?"

"Jonathan took him to a birthday party. His first one! And Nathan is at a playdate."

"So thank God you are here. At least you are here." He pressed his arms around her shoulders again.

"Dad," said Helen. "Don't be so shocked. Wasn't I here on Thursday?" Fela pushed out a big sigh, but Pavel didn't care. He was lucky to be able to see his daughter, that was what. He was lucky to have his family together, all in one place.

"All in one place," he announced. "See how good it is?" He looked at Larry significantly, but Larry had turned, on his way to put the umbrellas in the bathtub to dry.

"Is everything all right?" Helen looked at Fela.

"He didn't sleep last night." Fela sighed. "And because he didn't, I didn't. I heard him from the next room!" Pavel could see her eyeing the white table, making sure there were no smudges from Helen's newspaper. "Maybe I get a sponge," said Fela.

"Ma," said Larry, coming back in, "sit. Just sit. Sit."

"Why didn't you sleep, Dad?"

"He had a nightmare," said Fela, to Larry and to Helen. "He was mumbling, moaning."

"Not a nightmare," muttered Pavel. "A bad dream." He gave his wife a glare. Why should the children worry? He had dreamed about the gravestone for Budnik, and then about the gravestone for his own mother, which wasn't in the right place at all. It bothered him, the place of the gravestone for his mother. He rubbed his lips with a cube of sugar; he didn't like it mixed with his coffee.

"It was my mother," said Pavel. In the dream, the gravestone of his mother was in the wrong place. But how could it be? They had made sure, Pavel and his cousin Mayer, and with Larry as a witness, that the thing was in the right place. There had been a map and there had been a guide when they went back to Poland, just before the fall of the Berlin Wall, to visit the graveyard where Pavel's mother had been buried several years before the start of the war. She had died in childbirth for their youngest brother, a premature death but a normal death, a death that had come with a funeral, and prayers, and a stone to be unveiled a year after the burial.

"It was my mother," Pavel repeated, but how could he explain? He couldn't, not to his son, who had observed the restoration of the gravestone with his doctor's detachment, and not to his wife, that was too painful for both of them, and not even to his daughter, who usually knew how to listen. She understood, Pavel thought, what he was saying—he believed that she did—though sometimes he doubted even this. She never said too much, just asked a question or two. But could she understand? No one could. And part of him did not want her to understand. They had made a pact, Fela and he, when the children were born, not to let them be affected by the whole thing, all the suffering, and possibly they had done a satisfactory job of it! One had to be careful with one's children, not to let it affect them. But it was true, Pavel was lonely sometimes to talk.

"Was it the gravestone?" Helen asked. "Because, you know, I read an article. Those maps they use in the old graveyards are restored from the originals. They're very accurate."

How did she know what worried him? Had he mentioned it before? But surely this was the first time he had dreamed it. Wasn't it? Perhaps not. She tried to reassure him, his daughter, in the same way he always had tried with her: by lying. An article here, a television report there. But it was real, his fear.

"No, no," said Pavel, unable to hide the swell of hurt in his voice. "It was my mother. It wasn't the stone, it was the graveyard itself."

Fela gave a big sigh, again.

"What?" said Pavel. "What did I do?"

"Larry saw the graveyard himself," said Fela. "Tell him, Larry. Wasn't everything right?"

"It was hard to tell," Larry said, his eyes focused on the chair straight between Pavel and Fela.

"Aha," said Pavel, looking pointedly at his wife. Even his son agreed with him, and that was so rare an occurrence that Fela would have to take notice.

But Larry continued. "It was hard to tell, Dad. It really was. But remember? The men gave us a map. They showed it to us. They researched it very carefully. They wouldn't want to make anything up. It's their graveyard too."

Pavel said nothing.

"It was a beautiful stone," Larry went on. "The new one, I mean. The one you got. Now it's easy to find." His son spoke quickly, a rush, always in a rush. But it was true, the stone was beautiful. Plain and perfectly rounded and white. It had stood out from the others in the graveyard, crushed gray stones bent onto one another, stones that had been vandalized by the Germans and the Poles. The remnants of Pavel's mother's stone were still there. Others had been taken recently by the Krakow heritage society to make a memorial wall. Pavel hadn't liked that. A friend of Pavel's came from a town where soon after the invasion the Jews had been forced to remove the stones from the cemetery with their own hands, then pave them into the road to be stepped on by soldiers and townspeople. Was it so different, fifty years later, to make a broken graveyard into a wall for the memory of it? Of course it was different. Memorials were important. But still, the wall had made Pavel's stomach shrink and fold over when he saw it. He was glad his mother's original stone, even in its broken and dilapidated condition, had remained on the earth behind the abandoned synagogue. A synagogue that was now a museum, for people to look, not to gather or pray. Not a real synagogue any longer, but still a real graveyard. A graveyard of graves.

The placement of the new stone bothered him more every year.

At the time of the redesign of the stone, Pavel had worried a small bit about the stone's location. He wasn't too familiar with the graveyard; Mother had died visiting relatives in Krakow, some hours away from home, and had had to be buried near her death place, so as not to lose time. It would have been risky, taking the body back to Katowice. They might have gone over the limit of one day's lapse between death and funeral. But if his father had tried hard enough, couldn't it have been done? Perhaps not with a newborn child to handle. Still, it was a source of resentment, terrible resentment, all the years that Pavel grew up. Why did his mother's grave have to be so difficult to visit?

"Pavel," said Fela. "Do you want the milk?"

"No," said Pavel.

"Then pass it to me." He moved his arm toward the carton. Larry took the milk from him, shook it, poured for himself before passing to Fela. Ladies first, ladies first, Pavel wanted to say, but he stopped himself. It would upset Fela. Well, Larry tried. And he was smart, after all. Maybe not the most dutiful son in the world, maybe not the most respectful, but he was smart, and he could observe and remember what his father and Mayer had been doing. He wouldn't know what was right or not, not for graveyards, but his presence, strangely, had given the task a certain legitimacy. Pavel had been glad that Larry had gone with them. It was Larry's vacation, and instead of Florida or California or someplace that young people liked to go, he had gone with his father and uncle to Poland, in November. It was good when Larry tried.

"You were a witness," Pavel said to his son. "We tried very hard to make sure it was all set in order, her new stone where the old stone would have been. I think we did it right, didn't we?"

"I'm sure you did," said Larry. "Positive."

Pavel looked at the calm smile on his son's face. His son, a grown man, who took care of others, who saw pain and sickness every day, but who still remained naive, innocent. A wind rose in Pavel's chest.

"Then why do I feel this worry?" he suddenly cried, hand slamming the table. Larry's cup rattled against the plate.

"Pavel," said Fela, face softened. "Pavel."

Helen's hand had flown over his, had stopped it from jumping up again. "Dad," she said. "Dad, it's fine. It's a normal thing to worry about. But it's in the right place. You saw, Mayer saw, the graveyard men saw, Larry saw. How could all of you be wrong?"

"The dream was terrible," said Pavel, shaking his head, quieter now. Helen had spooned a serving of herring onto his plate; she never remembered he did not like the cream. But he did not want to waste. He picked up a piece of fish with his fork, brought it to his mouth, then put it down again without eating it. His throat was beginning to hurt from all the speaking, and when he got nervous, excited, it hurt worse. But the words were fighting him to get out. "The stone, the new stone," he rasped. "It was in the wrong place. It was standing in the plot of a complete stranger, a stranger who wanted his own gravestone. He wanted it the same way. He wanted it restored and returned."

Pavel's children listened to him, Larry's face blank, Helen's attentive. Pavel turned from one to the other, then looked straight at Fela. "He was screaming, in pain! With no air to breathe, because our new stone was blocking him. And my mother, all I could hear was her voice, lost somewhere else in the cemetery, looking for us."

Pavel took in a breath, pushed the breath out.

"Really?" said Fela, swallowing a corner of her bread. "The way I heard you in the middle of the night, your mother was calling out to you, saying that you too much focus on her gravestone in the first place." She squinted her eyes. "There's only so much one person can do, Pavel. If she's upset, probably it's because she's stuck still in Poland. Most Jews prefer hell."

☙

PAVEL RINSED HIS MOUTH with mouthwash, patted his lips with a small white towel. It was after nine o'clock, and no one was home. The children had taken their mother to a movie; Pavel hadn't wanted to go. No attention for it, no patience. But now he wondered what kept them so late. They had left at seven. How long was a movie? They could stop afterward for coffee, but why, with him waiting alone?

It was hot, and Pavel hated the air-conditioning that Fela had insisted on using when they still shared the bed, before she took over the old room of their son. If he turned on the air, he would be cold; but now he was warm, sweating. He went to the chest of drawers under his night table and opened the bottom drawer. He had short-sleeved pajamas and long-sleeved pajamas, everything in different shades of blue, except for the newer plaid ones, in red and black, that Fela had bought him two years ago from the Gap. They were the only American kind he liked. He looked at the short sleeves of his pale cotton pajamas, the shorts that folded under them. He took them out, laid them flat on the bed, fingered the white piping that slanted into a V at the collar.

He had not worn summer pajamas since the bypass operation. Ashamed of the new scars on his leg. Stupid. Who looked at an old man's legs? And anyway, he had worn shorts in the summertime, even outside, with the injuries on his right leg, the injuries from the accident, visible for all the world to see, when he was young. But these, the surgery scars, where they had cut open and taken out the veins to attach to his heart, these marked up the good leg. And they came not from accidents, not from outside force, but from sickness and age. All his life he had been a strong man, not big but strong, tough. Nothing could break him. Everyone said so, all his friends. And now, this sickness, this smoke-covered heart, had broken him. He was ashamed, and he could feel his friends' shame for him.

Fela thought this crazy. They're sick too! she would say to him, impatient. We go to a funeral every month! I'm not so healthy either!

Do you see me blaming myself? We're old, Pavel, we're old. Then she would laugh at him, touch his arm.

He would shake her off. In good moments he could laugh at his vanity, but he didn't think it so funny when she said it aloud, only when he thought it himself in his head. He was old. He never thought he would become so old. When he was twenty-five, starving, the idea that he would live to thirty seemed stupid and sentimental, a dark joke. But once he was liberated, he became invincible. Pavel had lived past the deaths of most of his best friends, and he had lived past the deaths of all his worst enemies. He had gone to the funeral of his brother-in-law, the man who had betrayed him for money, and he had cared for the cousin whose dead husband had helped him come finally to America. He had suffered through his son's divorce, and he had woken up one night three years before to the telephone call with the news that his daughter had given birth to a second son. He had lived a long time.

He never thought he would become so old, not so much in numbers as in energy. It wasn't just broken limbs and empty flesh that slowed Pavel now. It was his own soul betraying him, loosening the bones from the inside, shrinking him so he almost was smaller than his daughter. His children shouted at him sometimes; they thought he didn't hear well. When he looked at bills he had to cover the right eye, because it clouded over and distracted him. There was a thick white surgery line that drove down his chest, splitting it in two. His cardiologist gave him pills not just for his hardened arteries and erratic blood pressure but also for his feelings, to make him less depressed, to help him get up in the morning. Pills for his mind, another bottle in the collection of bottles he brought to each meal.

He walked to the hallway and looked through the window that faced the street. Rego Park was quiet on Sunday nights. A few cars rolled down the avenue, but none stopped. He could wait for Fela in the armchair by the coat closet, sitting, looking at a magazine, still dressed. He sat down in the chair, glanced at the framed pictures of his mother and father, the photographs Fela had restored and enlarged years ago. Then he pulled himself up again. Why do you wait here? Fela would cry when she came in. You're making me feel guilty! We asked you to come, didn't we?

Pavel limped into the kitchen to make sure he had turned off the lights, to make sure there was no wetness anywhere around the sink. He looked at the time on the clock above the oven. It was an hour behind; they hadn't changed from daylight savings time almost a year ago. Fela had been gone almost two and a half hours.

He went back to the bedroom. So what if he wanted to wear the short pajamas, feel young again? Who would see his body, who would make him feel embarrassed? When Fela came home, Pavel would put on a bathrobe, that was what. He straightened his back, unbuttoned his shirt, pulled off his undershirt. Then quickly put the pajama top over his head, so as to cover the chest. Certain parts of himself he did not like to see.

Already, sitting on the bed, in the short-sleeved pajama top and the pants he had worn in the day, Pavel felt better. His arms still had muscle; they were thick above his wrists. He rubbed at the skin on the inner part of his left forearm. The numbers had blurred; it was hard to make them out. Outside the blue tattoo his skin was white as an onion, even in summer, when the top of his head became a little red from the sun.

He didn't like to expose his arms, and did it only rarely: too much attention. He had been walking on the boardwalk near Coney Island many years ago. Without the children, just he and Fela, with Sima and Chaim, new arrivals to New York. The women had strolled ahead, talking tentatively; they had never met. Chaim and Pavel chattered quickly behind them, Pavel planning business connections for Chaim, Chaim murmuring polite refusals. Chaim had been tall and joyful, his marriage still young; he had looked away from Pavel's face every few seconds to glance at the slim, swaying figure of his wife. It had inspired

Pavel to look at Fela every few seconds too, her short amber hair and easy walk, her soft hands grasping the purse in front of her.

A night out in summer, a warm night. Pavel was excited; they had eaten a full meal. And he was among friends, an old friend, a boy he loved. Chaim, used to the casual dress of Tel Aviv, was already in shirtsleeves. Pavel decided to take off his jacket. They were on the beach, after all; where else could one wear short sleeves without feeling too self-conscious? A light summer cap protected his sparsely covered head.

A man had walked slowly toward the four of them, passed by the ladies and nodded. Pavel had smiled at the stranger: a Jewish face, sandy haired, not too handsome. But the man did not smile back. He was close to Pavel, nearing him, and peering at something strange on Pavel, below Pavel's eyes. Pavel looked down. Did he have a stain somewhere? Then the man stopped.

"Listen," he said, looking at Pavel, then at Chaim, then at Pavel again. "Why the hell don't you have that removed?" The man's accent was American.

Pavel stared. The man gestured at Pavel's tattoo. "There's surgery that can do it, without too much pain."

Pavel's jaw jutted forward. "What?" he said, very quietly. Then louder, "What?"

The man stepped back. "Listen, I didn't—"

Pavel's rage threw itself out of his mouth. "Should I be ashamed? Should I be ashamed?"

The man's lips were parted. No response.

"Tell me, sir, you who know so much, should I be ashamed?"

The man was several paces away. "Listen, no hard feelings, okay? Just forget it."

"Forget it," Pavel called after him. "Yes, just forget it." He was frozen, his feet unable to lift themselves from the wooden planks of the boardwalk.

Chaim tapped him on the shoulder. Pavel turned toward Chaim's calm, frowning face, then toward the women. Fela's hands shook; the lines in her forehead looked deeper, more numerous. Sima, with no English, stood still, uncomprehending.

But Chaim understood. He's forgotten it, Chaim said in Yiddish, he's forgotten it. The rest of us should be so lucky.

Pavel had breathed out. Relief. His wife had tears in her eyes, and her tears made him suddenly protective. Oy, Fela, he had said. Don't be upset. I told him, didn't I?

But after that night on the boardwalk, Pavel tried to keep to long sleeves. He rolled them up in the workshop, where the cutters and pressers were used to men and women with numbers, or at home, where his children did not seem to notice. Outside his arms were covered. Inside, in his office, in the kitchen, in bed, he wore whatever he pleased.

It was wrong to judge everyone from this one stupid man, but Pavel knew others who had had similar encounters: a word here, a peculiar glance there. Mina Elbaum, a woman Pavel had known and liked for years, actually had had hers removed in the 1980s, when the procedure was no longer experimental. For some people, even looking at it themselves made them upset.

No one would dare criticize Pavel for his tattoo, or his accent, or almost anything now. People today thought more highly of a person who had been through the war. But Pavel kept on his long sleeves. It was an improvement, he supposed, to receive the opposite reaction, something that came like a compliment, it was better than a criticism, but still it was no good. A number made no one a hero. Plenty who suffered worse were not numbered. The dead were not numbered. His children's friends, adults, when they happened to meet him, bore an expression of awe. Sometimes that awe made Pavel feel worse.

What made him feel better was stones. Not just stones, but stones in their rightful place. It was not a hobby of his, the stones. It was the contribution Pavel made. He had friends who made speeches and friends who wrote books, friends who organized the remnants of their town to make a memorial book. He had friends who had made quite a bit of money and gave it to good causes, causes everyone believed in, monuments, museums. What Pavel did was smaller. But just as important. It was said that he who saves one life saves the whole world. Everyone who was alive was alive in part because someone had helped him to be saved. But what about the dead? Their place in heaven could not be stolen. But their place on earth—that was always in doubt. Pavel helped to mark their place.

Early on, some years after the liberation, the French had come to the site of the former concentration camp with an ugly project. They wanted to exhume the mass graves and extricate the Frenchmen, bring them back to France for a real burial. Pavel had been on the Jewish Committee of the displaced persons camp just after the war, and the ones left in New York had called an emergency meeting. It was one of the proudest things he had done, speak out, halting, angry but sincere, that the dead could not be exhumed. It was Jewish law, and Jewish law superseded French desires to have their soldiers and resistance fighters and even their children returned to them. Each mass grave was long sealed, closed with a large stone, inscribed with the approximate number of buried bodies. The committee agreed with Pavel, brought their resolution to the international administration of the camp. The bodies stayed put.

He who saves one life saves the whole world. And he who saves one marker for the dead? It couldn't be the same. But people trusted Pavel to do his one task, his one project. That was why Henry Budnik insisted on Pavel's oversight of his own stone. That was why it was important for things to be in their rightful place. If Pavel made a mistake, who would correct it? If Pavel were not there, who would watch over it?

The one thing he had wanted to do before he died, more than to make an oral history of himself, more than to organize the photo album of his relatives, even more than to see Larry remarry and give him a new grandchild, was to fix the stone of his mother. He had done this almost a decade ago, but now again he was unsure. Was there never to be peace?

And what of his own—but he could not think of that. He could not. If he did, he would not sleep. Fela had suggested he should think instead of the living.

Pavel dreaded sleep, and he dreaded sleeping alone. He liked to have Fela in the house in case something happened, in case he stopped breathing. He liked to have someone there, even in the next room. In the early years of their marriage she would talk to him when he woke up from his violent dreams, comforting him, holding him. Now she did the work of a nurse, giving him a pill in an emergency, judging whether to call 911. He liked to have her in the house when he rested.

Fela would be pleasantly surprised, relieved, to find him asleep in his bed, not waiting for her, letting her relax and have a good time. Pavel raised his legs with his right hand, pushed aside the bedsheets with the left. The remote control was by his bedside. He would watch the news, think of something alive and bright.

But it was a murder they were reporting, a murder and a fire, and Pavel worried that with the noise of the television he would not be aware of Larry dropping Fela off, Larry chatting with his mother before letting her go inside. Pavel put the television on mute. If something important came on he would increase the volume. But nothing important seemed to be happening.

Pavel closed his eyes to help himself hear. Think of the living. He tried to concentrate. He almost heard the door clicking open, the lock turning shut. He almost saw Fela placing her purse on the table by the coat closet. He almost dreamed Fela's body gliding through the hallway, moving toward the bedroom to wish him good night.

I am grateful to my agent, Lisa Bankoff, and my editor, Jennifer Brehl, for their advocacy and insight; to Molly Magid Hoagland, Cathy Park Hong, Emily Krump, Aaron Kuhn, Elizabeth Perrella, Tirzah Schwarz, Kevin Young, and the MacDowell Colony for their crucial support; and to Maurie Samuels and Malena Watrous for their perceptive advice, encouragement, and generosity.

About the author

About the book

Read on

Insights,
Interviews
& More . . .

Meet Ghita Schwarz

Diana Pappas

GHITA SCHWARZ is a civil rights litigator specializing in immigrants' rights. Her fiction and nonfiction have appeared in *Ploughshares*, *The Believer*, and the *San Francisco Bay Guardian*. ∿

Displaced Persons: The Story Behind the Book

I WROTE *DISPLACED PERSONS* because I wanted to read a story about the aftereffects of the Holocaust on ordinary, imperfect men and women, and I could not find what I was looking for in the bookstore or library. In a time when stories of the trauma of the war years are increasingly documented in films, news articles, memoirs, and video histories, it's hard to remember that in the 1950s and 1960s, few survivors talked publicly about their wartime experiences, instead choosing to adapt to American or Israeli culture and embark on new lives with new families. It's harder still to imagine the forgotten, displaced persons era, when a chaotic, polyglot society developed in the refugee camps of a defeated Germany as survivors struggled to find relatives and create new families.

Raised in the 1970s and 1980s by a father who was a camp survivor and a mother who spent her early childhood in flight from Poland to Russia and Uzbekistan, I read Anne Frank's *The Diary of a Young Girl* and *Night*; I watched the docudrama *Holocaust*; I heard and saw wartime adventure stories, in which the hero survives the trauma and emerges battered but triumphant, alive at the end of the war. But I couldn't find portrayals of what I observed every day as a child in New York City: a father in a muted state of permanent grief, a mother afraid to let ▶

her children cross the street, family friends who flew into rages in the middle of a card game.

The Holocaust has a strong pull on generations of American Jewish writers, many of whom heard dramatic stories from their neighbors or relatives but who did not live every day with survivors. In recent years the literary trend has been toward the fantastic: novels filled with miracles and golems, Gabriel García Márquez blended with I. B. Singer, what I think of as magical shtetlism. I admire many of these books, but I longed to read—and therefore write—an American book that avoids portraying survivors as mythological figures.

My characters are not magical, and they have long left the shtetl. They think in a Yiddish inflection, but they are not cracking Catskills jokes, making their American interlocutors laugh; instead, the people to whom they reveal confidences, fears, and funny stories are just like them, residents of a close-knit community of survivors. Nor do my characters experience themselves as protagonists in a wartime plot-twisting dramatic film of escape. *Displaced Persons* is about their interior lives, their grief and anger, their ordinary joys and stupid arguments, their strained relations with their children. It tries to show a community of survivors as particular rather than

mythological, common rather
than noble, alive to their current
circumstances rather than numb
to their new surroundings.

To me this is a political as well as
stylistic choice. Even today, exposed
to so many films and books about the
war, many Americans see Holocaust
survivors as larger than life, either
heroic, mystical sufferers or corrupt
finaglers, their survival proof of an
unseemly willingness to do anything
to live. These perceptions, both
positive and negative, erase the thick,
anthropological reality, much the
way current sound bites about
immigrants deny the mundane,
but often overwhelming, struggles
of contemporary newcomers to the
United States. When I was growing
up, it bothered me to hear assumptions
about my father based on a summary
of his biography. I wanted to portray
my characters without endowing them
with a post-traumatic aura.

It was important to me not just to
examine a survivor community with
a realist eye but also to place my
characters' identities as "survivors"
in historical context. My book follows
a group of Polish Jews who meet in the
Bergen-Belsen displaced persons camp
in 1945 and eventually immigrate to
New York City, ending during their old
age at the close of the twentieth century.
The book as a whole attempts to show
how views of survivors changed in the ▶

Displaced Persons: The Story Behind the Book *(continued)*

fifty years following the liberation of the camps, and each of the three time periods corresponds to a different historical approach to trauma and memory. ～

Questions for Discussion

MOVING FROM THE ALLIED ZONES of
postwar Germany to New York City,
Displaced Persons by Ghita Schwarz
is a novel of grief and anger, memory
and survival witnessed through the
experiences of "displaced persons"
struggling to remake their lives in
the decades after World War II.

In *Displaced Persons*, Ghita Schwarz
reveals the interior despairs and joys of
immigrants shaped by war—ordinary
men and women who have lived through
cataclysmic times—and illuminates
changing cultural understandings of
trauma and remembrance.

1. Put yourself in the place of Pavel,
   Fela, Chaim, and Sima. When the
   world you know is destroyed, how do
   you begin again? How did the war
   brand them? What allowed some
   survivors to carry on and rebuild a
   life after the war when others could
   not? How does a person transform
   him- or herself from a victim into a
   master of his or her own destiny?

2. Talk about each of the characters.
   What kind of people are they? Did
   you like one more than another?
   What of their old lives, the time
   before, did they retain? What were
   their lives like before the war?
   Did they truly love one another,
   or were their bonds the result of
   their tragedy? ▶

Questions for Discussion *(continued)*

3. When Fela first meets Pavel she asks him his name, and the young man pauses before he answers. "It was an intimate thing to be asked one's name. Already he was used to writing his name again in solid lettering, but to say it aloud still made him cautious. One did not say one's name—those who knew it used it, those who didn't received a false answer. He had been name after name." Why is Pavel reluctant to tell Fela the truth? Why does he choose to be honest?

4. Pavel uses bribery and lies to have the German woman who took him in removed from her house. Was he morally justified in doing this?

5. When survivors were finally reunited with other members of their families, the reunion was not always joyful, and the postwar relationship not always smooth. "Maybe no one felt anything for anyone but the missing," Pavel thought. "Wouldn't that be a joke! Surviving in order to argue and hate." Think about the characters and their relationships. Why does a person who is lucky to be alive give in to petty, selfish behaviors and emotions?

6. What was life like for them in the displaced persons' camp? Why did

Pavel and Fela want to go to America rather than Britain or Palestine? Was the long wait worth it?

7. When Pavel, Fela, Chaim, and Sima finally immigrate to New York, how does the reality of their lives compare to what they'd imagined? How do they adjust to their new lives as Americans?

8. Talk about Pavel and Fela's relationship with their children. What kind of parents are they? How does their past color their outlook for their children? How do they communicate their history to their children, both directly and indirectly? Should Pavel and Fela have tried to be more open with Larry and Helen in the 1950s and 1960s? What about Chaim and Sima, raising their daughter Lola a decade later?

9. Should we keep events like the Holocaust a living memory? How is this beneficial—and how might it be destructive? How do Pavel, Fela, Chaim, and Sima try to have a hand in representing their history to the outside world? How do the characters' approaches to their own histories change over time? How do they contrast with public expectations of how the Holocaust should be memorialized? ▶

10. All of the characters keep secrets
    from their spouses, their siblings,
    their children, their friends. They
    also sometimes lie. Why?

11. When the characters speak in
    English, they speak with quotation
    marks around their words. When
    they think, or when they speak in
    their native languages—for example,
    Yiddish or Polish—they speak
    without quotation marks.
    Why? 〜

Have You Read?

THE FOLLOWING BOOKS were in my thoughts while I wrote *Displaced Persons*.

1. *A Scrap of Time and Other Stories* by Ida Fink, translated from the Polish by Francine Prose and Madeline Levine (Northwestern University Press, 1995): I came across this book years ago in a used bookstore, and was amazed. It should be much better known in this country than it is. Ida Fink writes in such an understated style that the painful moments are that much more moving, and her focus is on experiences of Jews from small cities and towns in Poland. Her stories avoid sensationalism and even violence, instead illuminating on the hidden moments that don't get portrayed in documentaries or histories: the waiting, the hiding, the planning, and the aftermath.

2. *Found Treasures: Stories by Yiddish Women Writers*, edited by Frieda Forman, Ethel Raicus, Sarah Silberstein Swartz, and Margie Wolfe (Second Story Press, 1994): This anthology contains powerful tales by women writing about migration, survival, family, and war, told in a language that has almost disappeared as a literary tool. One standout story is Chava Rosenfarb's "Edgia's Revenge," about a group of Holocaust survivors in Canada, ▶

narrated by a woman who was a brutal Jewish *kapo* in camp. Like so much great survivor literature, it dispenses almost entirely with Nazis, and focuses instead on the moral choices among survivors who are neither good nor bad but instead vain, kind, timid, manipulative, generous.

3. *Maus I* and *Maus II* by Art Spiegelman (Pantheon Books, 1986, 1992): *Maus* transformed both the comic book genre and the post-Holocaust memoir. Spiegelman's graphic biography of his father's wartime experiences openly addressed the act of representation, using the author's fears of not getting the story right to cast a critical and compassionate eye on survivors. The principal characters are drawn as mice, but they are fully human.

4. *The Reawakening*, by Primo Levi, translated from the Italian by Stuart Woolf (Touchstone, 1995): This follow-up to *Survival in Auschwitz* begins with Levi's liberation by the Russians and tracks his circuitous journey through a destroyed Europe back to his family in Italy. More than a portrait of the chaotic postwar landscape or even of a polyglot collection of fellow travelers, the memoir shows us Levi's internal transformation from prisoner to free man.

5. *America and the Survivors of the Holocaust* by Leonard Dinnerstein (Columbia University Press, 1982): Among the many books I read to research the displaced persons era, this one was the most invaluable. It contained both vivid renderings of life in the refugee camps and detailed portrayals of the political controversies in Europe and the United States.

6. *Poems of Paul Celan*, translated from the German by Michael Hamburger (Persea Books, 2002): Celan was a Romanian Jew orphaned by the war who chose to write in German, the language of his oppressors. The poem I chose for the epigraph of my book is one that feels both hopeful and bitter. And I love Hamburger's translations. They make the poems sound as if they were written in English, with a rhythm that makes sense even if the meaning is hidden and twisted.

7. *The Selected Poetry of Dan Pagis*, translated from the Hebrew by Stephen Mitchell (University of California Press, 1996): Like Celan, Dan Pagis was a Romanian Jew, but he wrote in Hebrew, the language he adopted after emigrating to Palestine in 1946. The language of his poetry is simple and direct, often using biblical stories and myth to grapple with his ▶

experiences. The characters in
Displaced Persons often contemplate
the religious tales they studied or
heard in their youth, and Pagis's
poems showed me one way of using
ancient myth and religion to explore
modern grief. 〜

Don't miss the next
book by your favorite
author. Sign up now for
AuthorTracker by visiting
www.AuthorTracker.com.